PRECIOUS GEMS

A STEELE OPS NOVEL

ERIN MOIRA O'HARA

*This book is dedicated to five women who are very special to me.
They are my mother, Moira, my sisters, Louise and Maureen,
my daughter Caroline and my niece Hannah.*

Books by Erin Moira O'Hara

The Knight of Castle Kildare

Conspiracy in Emilia Romagna

Beat of the Jungle

Steele Ops Series

The Kalista Diamond

Precious Gems

Jewel of the Kimberley

The Amethyst Code

Bindarra Creek

Tempting Fate

Date with Destiny

A Twist of Fate

He's a trained commando who has been enticed by a pair of emerald eyes.

Former SAS Captain James Talarico (Talos) is on a mission to locate a ring of people traffickers before they succeed in killing the person who can identify them. Talos saved the life of this beautiful young woman and delivered her baby on a previous mission. Unable to stop thinking about Jane, Talos tracks her down and ends up saving her life again. Now he won't trust anyone else to keep her safe. Nor can he ignore his growing attraction to her. Yet the perfect solution will place her and the baby in much greater danger.

She's never met a man like him.

Jane Rossini didn't know she was married to a mobster's son until she walked out of her short-lived marriage and ended up as a hostage in the middle of a gun battle. She owes her life to a handsome giant who makes her heart race wildly. Yet she refuses to commit to another man unless she can be sure he truly loves her. Under the constant threat of death and with the police insisting she be relocated and given a new identity, Jane decides to take control. She demands Talos and his Special Ops friends take her with them to Vietnam, so she can identify the ring members before they succeed in killing her. Little does she know what awaits them.

ACKNOWLEDGMENTS

Thank you to my wonderful beta reader Michelle Stefani and my superb critique partners, Susanne Bellamy and S.E. Gilchrist.

My thanks to Deadra Krieger for her brilliant editing skills. My talented cover designer Fiona, of Fiona Jayde Media. And my excellent formatting team from Author E.M.S.

Particular thanks goes to my friends at the Hunter Romance Writers, for their friendship, advice and encouragement. And of course my family for their steadfast support and love.

CHAPTER ONE

James Talarico stared out through open sliders at the spectacular vista of Sydney Harbour. Diverse marine craft listed on their moorings, the iconic bridge, a centerpiece to the iridescent blue sky. This state of the art home belonged to his boss, Jarred Steele, and was now headquarters to Steele Intelligence & Personal Protection Services.

Talos beat a rapid tattoo against his thigh as he studied the serious expressions on each of his mates' faces. These five men he trusted above all others, having trained and served with them in the Australian Special Forces.

Ajax, the team's German shepherd, nuzzled Talos's hand and whined. Talos gave him a pat then rubbed his own bristly chin and wondered how he could be trained in advance weapons, surveillance, reconnaissance, and combat skills, yet feel completely adrift over a woman with green eyes and a teasing smile.

He thought back to their first encounter when Jane attacked him with an umbrella, mistaking him for an underworld thug. The reckless woman had been eight months pregnant. He'd delivered her premature baby under a barrage of gunfire, then got them both to safety. *Does she ever think about me, because I sure as hell can't stop thinking about her?*

"Captain Talarico, would you care to join us or do you have something more important on your mind that you'd like to share?"

Shifting in his chair, Talos met his chief's grey-eyed stare. At thirty-three, Jarred was one of the youngest Colonels to have ever work in the SASR Special Ops Command Center. Six months ago, he'd left to start his security firm, persuading each of them to join him.

"I'm having trouble letting go of our last mission," said Talos.

Sam Locke, Talos's best mate chuckled. "Wasn't the payout enough for you? Or is there something else you miss? The floods, the flies, the dust."

"Smartarse. You're only grinning because you got the girl."

"True, and right now she's planning the wedding and setting up her horse stud."

Talos frowned. "Surely you didn't leave Kallie up the coast on her own?"

"No, she's doing a few laps in Jarred's pool. If you'd come in the back door you would have seen her."

Nick Flanagan, their chopper pilot who'd taken a bullet on their last job, stood and rubbed his shoulder. "How's Kallie doing? Marzetti's identity must have been a shock?"

"She's fine but worried about Jane." Sam looked to Talos. "Have you heard where the AFP are keeping her and the baby?"

"I've spoken to Jane's mother, Liz. She told me Jane's in a safe house within sight of the city, but she doesn't know the address. Inspector Gibbs allows Jane one phone call to her mother every second day."

Jarred sighed. "The Feds have got to keep Jane safe until the trial is over. She's a valuable witness and I've been told she could potentially identify Marzetti's inner circle. It's a wonder Gibbs didn't stick Kallie in witness protection too."

Nick laughed. "I think Gibbs realized he'd have a fight on his hands if he attempted to separate Sam and Kallie." He glanced at Talos. "What's got you so riled, mate? You don't have a thing for Jane Rossini, do you? Christ, she's the wife of a criminal and gave birth to his kid six weeks ago."

Pushing his chair back, Talos stood and glowered. "Fuck off, Nick. Jane didn't know she was married to the son of an underworld criminal and her marriage was already over."

Nick raised his hands in surrender. "Take it easy, Talos. You're too involved. We caught Marzetti, end of case. Jane is no longer our problem."

Placing his hands on his hips, Talos glared around the table. "I disagree. We know Marzetti and his son were planning to eliminate Jane, and we know they had at least one informer inside the police. It stands to reason that they will do everything in their power to stop her testifying. It's our moral duty to protect her and the baby."

Jarred turned to Simon Hawke, the team's communication and intelligence specialist. "Can you find out where Gibbs is keeping Jane Rossini?"

"I can hack into her phone carrier and get the area she's in. And if she can give me a couple of car registrations in the street, I can hack into the Roads and Maritime Services computer system. We might get lucky."

"You'll have to work on the registrations. The AFP wouldn't allow her to keep her own phone." Jarred glanced at Talos. "Marzetti's trafficking network is the reason I called the meeting today. The whole time he was hiding out in Willaroi, Marzetti had his people coercing Vietnamese girls into coming to Australia as seamstresses and manicurists. They were then forced into sweatshops or prostitution."

"What has that to do with us?" asked Nick. "Shouldn't the Immigration Department and Federal Police be handling it?"

Rubbing his hands together slowly, Jarred nodded. "They *are,* but I have been approached by certain parties who would appreciate our assistance in identifying Marzetti's accomplices and bringing their trafficking to an end."

Ryan shifted on his chair. "Why don't the Feds just interrogate Marzetti?"

"Marzetti isn't talking. His son however is ready to spill the beans in return for a deal."

"You can't be serious." Talos slammed his fist on the table. Rage swirled in his gut that the AFP could even contemplate such a deal.

"Sit down, Talos. You might be six-foot-five and as strong as a grizzly, but I'm still in charge and you can hear me out."

Leaning back, Talos crossed his arms. "I don't fucking believe this."

Jarred picked up a file and slid it across the table. "Gibbs has no evidence Andrew Rossini actually killed anyone with his own hands, but Rossini does have intimate knowledge of Marzetti's network, his partners, and the location of two missing bodies."

Talos opened the file. "What exactly does Gibbs need from us?"

"Yesterday I met with Gibbs, officials from both the Australian and Vietnamese Government, and representatives from two charities who rescue and rehabilitate trafficking victims. Apparently young girls are marketed for marriage, cheap labour, and sex work by increasingly organized networks in a number of Asian countries. The girls are lured with the promise of well-paid jobs or an arranged marriage, but many are forced into domestic slavery, sweatshops, or brothels. It's estimated over eighty-percent of trafficking victims end up in the sex industry and either can't or won't escape."

"How can these girls be used as slave labour?" Simon spread his hands. "Surely in this day and age it's no longer an acceptable practice?"

"Garment factories and nail salons have become one way of exploiting cheap labour. The girls can be as young as twelve or thirteen and usually have no English."

"Fuck. What's the penalty for child trafficking in Australia?" demanded Talos.

Jarred grimaced. "It varies, but the maximum is twenty-five years."

"You're kidding," muttered Sam. "They should get fucking life."

"If we take this job, who's paying our fees?" asked Simon.

"We have a client who is prepared to foot the bill and pay us handsomely." A smile spread over Jarred's face. "As the twenty million dollars we recovered on the last job is considered tainted money, it will go to the Crime Commission, but I believe we're receiving a finder's reward of two hundred thousand, plus one million in reward money for catching Marzetti."

Talos whistled. "Nice. That's two hundred thousand each. It'll help pay off my mortgage. What's next on the agenda?"

"All those in favor of taking this new job?"

Everyone raised a hand.

"Good, I'll let our client know. In the meantime, it's New Year's Eve. I've got cold beers in the fridge and a stack of meat waiting to be barbecued." He looked across at Talos. "Do you know when Jane Rossini is due to ring her mother again?"

"Around seventeen hundred this evening."

Jarred checked his watch. "Ring Liz Macey. When her daughter calls, she is to ask her for the registration plates of any vehicle within sight then call us back. Once Simon locates the street, you and Sam can figure out Jane Rossini's exact location."

Glancing at Sam, Talos paused at the bemused smile on his friend's face. He followed the direction of Sam's focus to find Kallie, Sam's fiancée, strolling across the terrace. She wore a much too large robe and Talos felt his lips curve. Kallie was a real stunner with her dark eyes, golden skin, and curvy figure. She'd also brought life into Sam's eyes, for which Talos would always be grateful.

His mind returned to Jane, another stunner. Not as slim as Kallie, but then she'd been eight months pregnant and married; hence none of the boys had paid close attention. *But I noticed her delicate beauty. I witnessed her strength and courage under fire, and I as sure as hell felt an attraction I've never experienced with any other woman.*

Entering the conference room, Kallie smiled radiantly. Talos's heart lurched at how close Sam had come to losing her.

When Kallie glanced his way, Talos winked. She padded over and hugged him.

"Talos! Have you heard from Jane?"

"No, but we're working on tracking her down now."

"Good. I don't understand why Inspector Gibbs took her and the baby in the first place. They should have been allowed spend Christmas with family and friends. They would have been safe with us, and I know Jane was hoping to speak to you."

"Oh?"

"She wanted to thank you again for saving her and Eloise." Kallie turned to the rest of the team. "So, what's happening? Are we talking tactics or planning our operation?"

Jarred's lips twitched. "As usual, Miss McNeil, it's none of your business."

"Oh, come on, Jarred, don't be like that. I can help, especially if it's to do with Jane. She's my best friend and Eloise is my goddaughter. Deal me in."

"Miss McNeil."

Kallie gave Jarred a quick peck on the check then twirled around and sat on Sam's lap. Talos hid his grin as she fluttered her eyelashes at their boss.

"Who got the locals in Willaroi to accept you? *Me.* And who helped you catch Dominic Marzetti? *Me.* You may all be macho ex-SAS, but you have to admit, I did help you."

"You may have made a small contribution, Miss McNeil, but you also caused my team a great deal of trouble and anxiety. One of *your* horses killed a major felon before he could be interrogated. *You* nearly lost your life on several occasions, and to top it off, you enticed one of my men to go and fall in love with you."

Talos grinned as Sam wrapped his arms around Kallie. She cuddled closer and sent Jarred a conceited smile. "That's true, but one of these days you'll all be as *enticed* as Sam."

Laughing, Sam slid his arms under Kallie and lifted her as he stood. "Come on, Cupid. Let's get the salad out of the cooler before the boys decide to run for their lives."

"But I'm serious," she cried. "I've got big plans for these guys.

As Sam carried Kallie out of the room, Talos noted the solemn expressions on the rest of the team's faces. None of them appeared ready to run. Talos stood. *We've been on our own too long, but for some of us, old habits are hard to break.*

CHAPTER TWO

Rocking her precious daughter in her arms, Jane stared out the window onto the wet street below. Vehicles lined the opposite curb. Several houses lay in darkness, while others were lit up like a Christmas tree, the residents celebrating New Year's Eve. Her gaze fell on a street lamp, casting a soft glow on the cars below and illuminating the drizzling rain. All was quiet, nothing moved.

She'd thought the first two weeks horrid, stuck in a Sydney hospital under protective custody. If it hadn't been for Talos's company, she would have gone mad. Then Inspector Gibbs had moved her and the baby to this inner city house with its small backyard and stark furnishings. Her only outlet had been kickboxing sessions with Sharon, her daytime minder. It had been the loneliest Christmas she'd ever experienced.

Jane's attention returned to her baby daughter's sweet face and the thick lashes framing her beautiful eyes. "At least we're alive, my little angel, and that is due to Talos and his team."

Ella's tiny fingers gripped Jane's locket as if she knew it held something secret. Jane's gaze lifted to the hazy lights of the city skyscrapers in the distance. It still hurt to know Andrew only married her to get close to Kallie and her exquisite diamond. *What a fool I was to fall for him. I would rather stay single than suffer the humiliation and rejection of another man who didn't love and desire me.* Her thoughts went to Talos, a giant of a man with a sexy smile, eyes the color of cognac and big broad shoulders. She longed to hear his deep, calming voice and experience that zing of excitement whenever he was near. Jane heaved a deep sigh. *Who am I fooling? I am the last woman Talos would be interested in.*

A movement on the street caught Jane's eye. Pulling the curtain aside, she leaned against the cold glass and squinted. Was there someone down there? Her pulse quickened, along with her breathing. *Stop it. The police officers downstairs are vigilant and armed. They won't let anyone in and no one knows we're here.*

A figure ran from behind a white sedan, and then ducked behind a silver station wagon. Another figure sprinted across the road and for a brief moment he was caught in the light of the street lamp. Jane swallowed. The second man held a gun.

"Shit." Jane dropped the curtain and picked up the baby sling, pulling it over her head. *I may be jumping to conclusions, but better safe than sorry.* She wrapped Ella in a bunny rug and placed her in the sling, then ran from the bedroom, along the hall, and down the stairs.

Her two minders were sitting at the kitchen bench playing cards. They both glanced up as Jane ran through the doorway.

"What is it?" asked Brian, coming to his feet.

"I just saw two men outside and one has a gun."

"Get upstairs," ordered Steve, leaping off his stool. He turned to Brian. "I'll ring Gibbs then check the rear of the house, you keep an eye on the front." He glared at Jane. "Move!"

"I'm going."

The two officers drew their guns and disappeared in separate directions. Jane eyed the portable phone lying on the bench. She swiped it up and dashed out of the kitchen, cushioning Ella as she raced up the stairs. Once in her room, Jane opened her locket and pulled out the scrap of paper with a mobile number scrawled across it. She keyed it into the phone then closed her eyes and drew a shaky breath. "Please be there." On the third ring a deep familiar voice answered.

"Talarico here."

"Talos. It's Jane. I'm sorry to ring so late, but I think I'm in trouble."

"Jane! What's wrong?"

"I saw two men ducking behind cars and one has a gun. I told the police officers and they're checking it out but I'm scared. No one is supposed to know where I am."

"Can you describe the men?"

"Um, one was short and Asian looking. I didn't get a good look at the other one."

"All right, we're not far away. Take the baby and go up to the attic."

Jane ran toward the door. "Wait, how do you know there's an attic?"

"We traced the registration plates you gave your mum, then Sam and I did a little reconnaissance. You're in a rendered terrace with a closed in veranda, right?"

"Yes." Jane stepped into the hall as glass shattered downstairs. "Talos, someone just smashed a window and I can hear people coughing."

"Fuck, they're using tear gas. Hurry."

Jane looked up. "I see the trapdoor but..." She stretched up. "I can't reach it."

"Get a chair or a thick book or anything, quick." His breathing sounded heavy as if he was running. "Come on Sam, Jane's in trouble."

With her heart in her mouth, Jane pushed the nearest door open. Beads of sweat broke out on her forehead as she scanned the bathroom. "There's a stool."

"Good, use it, but make sure you take it with you into the attic, otherwise they'll know where you are. We'll be there as fast as we can."

Through the phone, she heard an engine start. Placing the stool under the trapdoor, Jane climbed onto it and reached for a metal ring. "Got it." She pulled and a long door lowered revealing a sliding ladder. Stepping off the stool, she pulled it aside and slid the ladder down. Her hands clammy with moisture.

Another window smashed. "Talos, I'm afraid. Who are they?"

"Don't panic. I believe in you, Jane. Get up the ladder then pull the trap door shut."

Squealing wheels sounded in her ear. "Are you okay?"

"Christ, that was close." She heard him exhale. "Don't worry about me, just hurry."

Tucking the phone in the sling, Jane picked up the stool, grabbed the rail with her spare hand and scrambled up the rungs. Ella kept bumping against her chest, but mercifully she remained asleep.

Gunshots sounded downstairs. *They're inside.*

She set the stool down, wiped her sweaty hands on the sling and hauled on the pulley cord. The ladder retracted, bringing the door up with it. Jane let out a shaky breath and snatched up the phone. "I'm in the attic and the door's shut, but I heard gun shots."

"It's all right. Now hang up and find somewhere to hide. I'll alert the rest of the team and we'll be there as fast as we can."

"Okay." She hit the end call button and turned around. Her gaze skimmed the large attic and her heart plummeted. The streetlight outside cast a long beam through the small window illuminating every inch of the completely empty room. "Oh no."

Gurgling came from within the sling. Jane moved the blanket to find Ella's eyes wide open. She cooed when she saw Jane.

"Oh my darling, we need to stay really quiet."

Running feet and doors crashing against walls sounded below. *They're searching for us.* Jane's gaze fell on the attic window. *It's that or let them shoot me.* She picked up the stool and tiptoed across to the window, relieved to discover it wasn't nailed shut. Unlatching it, Jane leaned back as the window swung in, bringing a cold breeze and the drizzling rain with it. Ignoring the stinging bite, she squirmed through and placed her bare feet on the coarse wet roof-tiles.

They creaked.

Holding Ella tightly, Jane gingerly put one foot in front of the other, edging along the slippery roof. She shivered as a fine mist of rain coated her skin. Lights came on in the house opposite and voices sounded on the street below, but from her position she didn't dare call out. Attracting attention was the last thing she wanted. A dark shape rose from the roof further along. *A chimney.*

Below someone shouted then a couple of gunshots rang out and people began screaming. Jane glanced down on the street and stubbed her toe. She gasped, hobbled onto a loose tile and her feet shot from under her sending her crashing onto her backside and knocking the breath out of her. *Bloody hell, that hurt.* Little sobs came from within the folds of the sling. "Shush, honey, it's okay. Mummy just lost her balance. I've got you." Jane patted Ella soothingly. "Please don't cry, sweetie."

Clanging sounded from inside the roof. *They're coming up the ladder.*

Jane scrambled to her knees and crawled toward the chimney, ignoring her sore butt and the rough tiles on her bare skin.

Ella quieted with just the occasional hiccup. Another gunshot rang out and the ridge capping on the peak of the roof exploded. Jane sent a desperate glance down and her lungs seized. A man stood in the middle of the road pointing a gun up at her.

"Oh God." She crouched lower and crawled faster. Another bullet hit a tile and it shattered, showering her in stinging fragments of concrete. "Talos, hurry."

A vehicle skidded around the bend at the end of the street, its engine revving hard.

Jane continued crawling, keeping her body between the man and Ella. Another two shots rang out as she reached the safety of the chimney. Jane peeked down on the street. A black four-wheel drive screeched to a stop beneath. The man with the gun leapt out of the way and tore off down the street. A car door slammed and Jane sighted a tall man in black, giving chase.

"Thank God." She wriggled behind the high side of the chimney out of sight of the attic window and street. The breeze plastered her chemise to her body, chilling her to the bone.

Sirens sounded in the distance and Jane prayed they'd make it in time. She shivered as a cloud passed in front of the moon and the light drizzle intensified, soaking her hair and chemise in seconds. Jane huddled over Ella and prayed for Talos to hurry. *I know he won't let us down.* Talos was a man of honour and integrity. She bit her lip as she recalled the SAS motto. "*Who Dares, Wins.*" Kallie had dared and she won Sam.

A tear ran down Jane's cheek. *Kallie wasn't married to a criminal or the mother of his child, and Sam couldn't help but fall in love with Kallie.* A ferocious roar had Jane peeking around the chimney toward the attic window. She heard a couple of heavy thuds then a man leapt out of the window, hit the tiles hard, and rolled head over turkey down the roof and over the edge. A woman below began screaming.

Police vehicles with sirens blaring sped into the street. Lights came on in the rest of the houses and people came out onto their front porches. With her heart in her throat, Jane kept her gaze on the attic window and waited. After several beats a balaclava-clad head and big pair of shoulders appeared. He glanced left then right.

"Jane!"

"Talos." A sob escaped Jane as her pent up emotions bubbled over and the tears she'd been fighting cascaded down her face.

He heaved his body out of the frame then folded the balaclava up above his eyes and smiled. "I guess you want me to come over there and get you?"

Her heart tripped and Jane cracked a smile. "Yes, please."

CHAPTER THREE

Almost light headed with relief, Talos pulled his balaclava over his face, stooped, and scuttled across the tiles toward the chimney, thankful for the cover of darkness. He found Jane huddled over her knees, shivering uncontrollably. She had some sort of scarf bunched over one shoulder. The other shone naked and wet except for a tiny strap connected to a flimsy bit of material. A wet plait hung down the center of her back. She gazed up at him with glistening tear-filled green eyes and his breath caught. She was as beautiful as he remembered. He crouched beside her, his gaze skimming her long bare legs.

"Struth, what are you wearing?"

"It's a chemise. The dryer's broken and with all the rain, you're lucky I'm not naked."

He considered her appreciatively. *You might as well not be.* Maneuvering behind her, Talos lifted Jane across his lap, opened his jacket, and pulled it around her shoulders, sheltering her from the steady drizzle. She shivered then leaned against his chest. His gaze dropped to her full luscious lips and his senses exploded. He caught the scent of jasmine. *Christ, why does this happen whenever I hold her.* He stamped on his reaction. "Please tell me you're hiding a baby somewhere in there?"

"Yes. You didn't think I'd leave her behind, did you?"

"Show me."

Jane pulled the red scarf thing apart, revealing a tightly wrapped pink bundle, cocooned against a very inviting cleavage. *Lord, give me strength.* Talos lowered the blanket slightly with his finger and found a little pixie with two big eyes gazing at him. Her long eyelashes fluttered shut as if she knew all was right in the world. "She's lovely."

He cleared his throat and blinked away the moisture gathering in his eyes. *Christ, one minute I want to ravish the woman and the next minute I'm tearing up like a girl.* "Let's get out of here." He reached inside his pocket, pulled out his phone, and hit Sam's number.

He kept his voice low. "I've got them."

"Where are you?" Sam sounded breathless.

"We're behind the chimney to the right, but I'm going to need help getting Jane and the baby down without being seen. Where are you?"

"Further down the street. I chased the shooter but he's vanished. The police have the guy who fell off the roof and an ambulance is on its way for an officer who took a bullet."

"What about Jarred?"

"He's just arrived but all hell's broken loose down here."

Peering around the chimney, Talos studied the lively street. Every house along the opposite side of the road had people gathered out the front. Some held up phones videoing the action, others stood around in their pajamas gossiping. Ambulance sirens sounded in the distance and uniformed officers were running about, keeping the neighbours back and questioning everyone. All the commotion was at least diverting their attention from the roof.

"Christ, Sam. I'd like to know how we're going to get away without being seen. Where's my vehicle?"

"I've got it. Jarred's spoken to Jane's other guard and is waiting to speak to Inspector Gibbs. In the meantime we're to get out of here. Get ready for a swift exodus."

"Will do." Talos ended the call and shoved the phone into his pocket. His gaze locked with Jane's. "We'll get you out of here soon."

"How? We're stuck on a roof."

"Have faith, sweetheart. You should know by now, we are the best of the best." He winked and moved her slightly to get more comfortable.

"Ow," cried Jane, flinching.

"What is it? Are you hurt?"

"I slipped on the roof and landed on my backside."

"Remind me to check it out later."

"Talos, I'm not letting you look at my bottom."

"Sweetheart, I delivered your baby. I've seen a lot more than your backside."

Jane opened her mouth then closed it and scowled at him. "That's different, I didn't have a lot of choice." She huffed. "It's probably just bruised."

"I'll be the judge of that," muttered Talos, pulling his jacket firmly around her.

The attic window of the terrace to their right swung open and Simon leaned out. "Hoy, Talos, you want to make your way over here?"

"Yeah, mate, but I'm going to need a blanket to wrap around Jane. She's barely covered and her body is glowing like a beacon."

Jane drew back and glared at him. "It is not."

"Believe me, sweetheart, it is." He pointedly looked down at her long slim legs.

Simon ducked back inside and reappeared with a dark blanket. He leaned out and hurled it across the roof.

"Thanks, mate." Talos wrapped the blanket around Jane, covering her from head to foot. "Now hopefully I can get you inside without anyone noticing." He stood, balancing her carefully in his arms.

She stiffened. "I'm quite capable of walking."

"This will be quicker." Keeping his back toward the street, Talos gingerly stepped across the tiles, placing his feet warily, conscious of the slippery surface. On reaching the attic window, he fed Jane feet first through to Simon.

"I've got her." Simon lifted Jane to the floor. "Where's the baby?"

"She's here." Jane opened the sling thing to show Simon and the blanket fell off her shoulders. Simon's gaze raked Jane then lifted to Talos. His eyebrows shot up and he mouthed the word, "*Wow.*"

Squeezing through the window, Talos swiped up the blanket, replaced it around Jane's shoulders and glowered at Simon. "Stop gawking and tell me the plan."

Grinning, Simon opened the door. "The plan, my friend, is to take Jane out the back door and over the rear fence. Sam's bringing your vehicle around to the street behind and Ryan is riding shotgun. Jarred's out the front dealing with Gibbs and the local cops."

"Where are the residents of this house?"

"In the front lounge. I told them we're undercover and need their attic to keep an eye on what's happening next door."

"Okay, make sure no one's looking." Talos waited until Simon disappeared down the stairs then took Jane's hand and led her out of the room and along a narrow hall.

As they descended Talos heard voices behind a closed door on the left. He turned right and directed Jane toward the back of the house, through a compact red and white kitchen and out onto a small porch. A scruffy grey dog on a chain barked and wagged his tail.

Talos paused and surveyed the small yard. It was soggy from the recent rain and littered with dog shit.

Jane was grimacing as at the ground. "Why do people get dogs when they have such tiny yards?"

"They don't think it through."

A rustle sounded beyond Jane. Talos yanked her into his body as a dark shape exploded from a bush welding a long-bladed knife. Ice filled Talos's veins as Jane shrank against him, turning her body to protect Ella.

"Shit." Talos wrenched her off her feet and hurled her backwards out of the way. He glimpsed her landing on an outdoor lounge as he turned to face a small wiry man covered from head to foot in black.

The attacker lunged. The lethal looking blade flashed within centimeters of Talos's chest. He darted left, almost losing his balance as he slid in mud.

The man leaped after him.

Talos dodged another slash as he observed Simon pull Jane to her feet and urge her along the veranda to what looked like a laundry. As soon as Jane was inside with Simon standing guard, Talos kicked hard, connecting with his attacker's wrist. The knife flew wide and Talos leapt forward, slamming hard into his attacker. They hit the sodden ground awkwardly and aquaplaned several meters. Talos clambered to his feet, hauled the man off the ground by his sinewy arms then head-butted him.

The man made a strangled sound and dropped to his knees.

Still running on adrenaline, Talos brought both fists down hard across the man's shoulders, sending him face first into mud. He didn't get up.

"Enough, Talos." Simon sprang off the veranda, rolled the man onto his back and ripped off the balaclava. He was Asian.

"You look after Jane, I'll see that Gibbs gets this piece of garbage," muttered Simon.

Nodding, Talos dragged in air, unclenched his fists and forced his rage back under its shaky lid. The laundry door cracked open and Talos locked gazes with the woman responsible for a never-experienced fear that scared the shit out of him. He'd faced much worse than a scrawny little guy with a knife, yet when it involved her, he lost his head and pure emotion took over. *Not good.*

"Are you all right, Talos? He didn't cut you, did he?" Her voice shook and the concern in her eyes humbled him as she came to the edge of the veranda, Ella held tightly in her arms.

"I'm fine, but we need get out of here now." He strode over and scooped them into his arms, the contact a soothing balm to his rattled wits.

"What are you doing?" Jane's voice hitched.

"The ground is covered in dog shit, mud, and scum." Talos strode to the back fence, reaching it as Sam and Ryan appeared on the other side.

"What took you so long?" asked Sam.

Talos stepped closer. "I needed to deal with a cockroach." He looked down at Jane. "Pass Ella to Sam before any more vermin appear."

Jane opened the sling, eased the little pink bundle out, and handed her up to Sam. "Make sure you support her head."

Talos watched Sam cradle the baby for a moment then carefully passed her down to Ryan." He turned back to Talos. "Okay, next."

Placing his foot on a small retainer wall, Talos sprang up then placed Jane into his best friend's arms. "The last time we did this, it was you *throwing* Kallie into *my* arms."

Sam laughed. "And as I recall, you *threw* her back pretty quick." He swung Jane away and stepped off whatever he'd been standing on.

Gripping the fence, Talos hauled himself over and landed beside Sam, narrowly missing an upturned wheelbarrow. "Thanks, I'll take her now." He adjusted the blanket and lifted Jane out of his friend's arms.

Sam's eyes locked with his. "I hope you know what you're doing, mate."

"What's wrong?" Jane looked from one to the other.

"Nothing." Talos turned to Ryan who carefully laid the tiny pink bundle back in Jane's arms. Then Sam led the small troupe through the dark garden and down the side of the house. With all the sirens and commotion, the house was either vacant or the residents were out celebrating New Year's Eve.

At the front gate, Sam checked either way then marched to Talos's four-wheel drive and opened the back door. "Are you going to drive or do you want me to?"

"You can drive." Talos placed Jane on the rear seat and turned to Ryan. "Now what?"

"Jarred wants us to take Jane to his place until he squares things with Inspector Gibbs."

"What happened to Simon?" called Jane as she eased across the seat.

Ryan opened the front passenger door. "Jarred wants him to pick up your mum and stepfather in case their house is under surveillance. They are to be transported to Sam's place in the Yarramalong Valley and hopefully you can join them later today or tomorrow."

"Good thinking." Talos swung into the CX and closed his door. He glanced across to see Jane drop a kiss on the baby's head. Then she wriggled out of the wet sling and fumbled one-handed to get the seat belt on. His gaze dropped to her full round breasts, barely concealed by the damp fabric of her skimpy nightie. Lust roared through his body sending all his blood south. He swallowed hard and leaned across. "Here, let me help you." Tucking the rug firmly around her and the baby, he buckled them in.

Jane shivered violently and bit her quivering lip.

Silently cursing, Talos moved closer. "Are you cold?" He shrugged off his jacket and covered her long legs, then pulled her closer and rubbed her arm.

"No, no, I'm okay." She drew in a deep breath and gave him a hesitant smile. "Where's Kallie? I thought she was supposed to be with Sam in the Yarramalong Valley."

"She was." Sam pulled out from the curb. "But we came to Sydney for a meeting and New Year's Eve party. Then Talos decided he wanted to check on you, so we left her at Jarred's house with Nick and Ajax. At least bringing you back might get me into her good books again."

A smile touched Jane's lips. "Kallie adores you, Sam. It might have been Marzetti that brought your team to Willaroi, but I'm glad you came." She glanced at Talos. "Kallie and I wouldn't be alive if it weren't for you guys." She touched his arm. "Thank you."

"You're welcome." Talos fought the urge to cover her hand with his."

Twisting in his seat, Ryan grinned at Jane. "In appreciation for our brave deeds, might I request you keep Jarred tied up all morning so we can take his speedboat out for a spin?"

"No, you may not," interjected Talos. "After Jane's had some sleep and breakfast, I'm taking her to Yarramalong. The sooner she's out of Sydney the better." The thought of Jane locked up all day with Jarred worried him, which was ridiculous.

Jane lightly tapped him. "Talos. Don't be mean." She turned to Ryan and smiled. "I'll try to answer any questions Jarred has, but I've already told Inspector Gibbs everything I know and it's not much. I had no idea Andrew was mixed up in people trafficking."

"Did you ever meet his close friends?" asked Talos.

She turned back to him. "No. He told me he grew up in foster homes in Melbourne, so I didn't think it odd that he had no friends in Sydney."

"What about work colleagues? Did you ever meet them?"

"Once. I'm a teacher and a couple of months ago I came home from school early with a headache. Andrew was entertaining four men and a woman, but he didn't introduce us."

Talos considered this. "Did anything stand out? The way they spoke or dressed."

"Two men and the woman were Asian, the other two men were white but had accents, one was clearly British and the other had a heavy, thick inflection. I think he was Russian."

"Ages?"

Her nose screwed up. "The men were around forty to sixty and the woman in her late twenties and very attractive. I remember feeling awkward, like I was in the way and she kept throwing dagger looks at me, so I excused myself and went into the kitchen."

Her gaze dropped to the baby. "For some reason Andrew was

annoyed and told me I should ring if I was coming home early. I think he and the woman were..."

Talos's jaw clenched. "He's a fool, Jane, and you are far better off without him."

Leaning her head against his shoulder, Jane sighed. "I knew that within a month of marrying him, but it was too late. I was already pregnant."

Giving into temptation, Talos placed his hand over hers and lightly squeezed. "My dad always says, things happen for a reason. You've got a beautiful baby and Rossini's going away for a long time. We're going to make sure of that."

Glancing up, Talos caught Ryan and Sam exchange a look of concern. Hell, he was concerned. Being this close to Jane was intoxicating. There was no way this was just a passing fancy. *I've got it bad, but what the hell am I going to do about it?*

CHAPTER FOUR

Closing her eyes, Jane cuddled Ella and rested against Talos, absorbing his warmth. The men's conversation flowed around her as she contemplated her dilemma. Talos seemed determined to take on the role of protector, but was it because they'd been thrown together in such dire circumstances that he now felt responsible for her? Or, was it because of the sexual energy that bounced between them whenever they touched? Jane recalled the awareness in his eyes when she'd pulled the sling off and how his gaze raked over her, but then he'd covered her up pretty quick. Was that lust or embarrassment? Never again would she let a man into her heart unless she could be sure he wanted, loved, and desired her above all else. Never again would she allow a man to use her or degrade her.

She hadn't realized she was crying until Talos gently wiped her tears away with his thumb. She sniffed and turned her face into his shoulder so no one else would notice.

"We have company," announced Sam. "And it looks like they mean business."

Glancing up Jane noticed Talos and Ryan pull out guns and look behind. She swivelled round. "Who are they?"

"Got to be Marzetti's people," muttered Talos. He pulled the chest strap of the seatbelt off Jane, grabbed her shoulder, and pushed her across his lap. "Hold the baby and stay down."

"What are you doing?"

"Saving your life." Sam accelerated and took a sharp right. Talos clamped an arm around her waist. The tires squealed, so did the tires of the vehicle behind. Several shots rang out and the rear window shattered. Jane flinched and clutched Talos round his thigh, cushioning Ella against her chest. *Will this nightmare ever end?*

Ella began whimpering. "Shush, sweetie, I've got you."

"They're gaining on us," called Ryan. "You're going to have to take them out, Talos."

"Yeah, before they put any more fucking holes in my new car."

Jane felt Talos twist. Three rapid whizzing sounds resonated within the car followed by a loud boom, squealing tires, and then an almighty crash. A car alarm began blaring.

"That'll teach the fuckwits to come after a woman and baby," muttered Ryan.

"Cool the language, boys," called Sam. "Everyone okay in the back?" He took another sharp turn and Ella began crying in earnest.

Jane squeezed her eyes shut as her heart thundered and she began to shake violently.

"She's in shock." Talos unclipped the seatbelt and lifted Jane onto his lap, drawing her and Ella against his chest. His powerful arms closed around them. "It's not far now."

"I'm okay." Jane licked her dry lips.

He rubbed her back softly. "You're safe now, relax."

Jane tried, but being this close to Talos was anything but relaxing. She'd never felt so on edge, and Ella's bawling was growing in pitch. She attempted soothing Ella by rocking and patting, but it wasn't working. There was only one way to settle her now.

Hot with embarrassment, Jane turned into Talos's chest, pulled her nightie down and eased a nipple into Ella's mouth. After a couple of hiccups she calmed and began suckling. Jane became aware Talos had stilled. She glanced up to find him watching. He had a look of sheer wonder on his face and Jane's embarrassment melted away as did her heart. He would make a wonderful father and husband to some lucky woman. Leaning her head against his shoulder, Jane closed her eyes. She heard Ryan speaking on the phone to Jarred about the men who had shot at them and extra security measures. She felt Talos's strong steady heartbeat under her ear and then she began to drift.

The vehicle slowed to a stop and Jane opened her eyes to see two high, black gates sliding apart. Ella had fallen asleep so Jane quickly adjusted her nightie and glanced at Talos.

"Are we there?"

"Yes. We took a little detour just in case. This is Jarred's home. Look to the right and you'll see the Harbour Bridge."

Jane craned her neck to get a better look. "Jarred lives here?"

"Yep." Ryan's face split into a wide grin. "Wait until you see inside."

Sam drove down a short curved slope and into an underground garage. It was too dark to make out much of the house, but Jane gaped at the sheer size of the garage. On her right were three vehicles and a high-powered speedboat. On her left were Sam's black Hilux, a large white van with heavily tinted windows, and a sleek wine-red Jaguar. There was also a caged area straight ahead with large crates covered in tarps.

Sam swung into an empty space and Jane's gaze collided with Talos'.

"What is this place?"

"Jarred's home, and our Special Ops Headquarters. Welcome to Steele Intelligence and Personal Protection Services."

Easing herself onto the seat, Jane picked up Talos's jacket and handed it to him. She adjusted Ella and the blanket then opened her door and stepped onto polished green concrete. Not an ounce of oil or dirt anywhere. "How many of you live here?"

Joining her, Talos's lips twitched. "A gardener, slash caretaker lives in the back of the boathouse, but Jarred's the only one living in the house."

"Then who owns all these vehicles?"

"We do." He nodded toward the van. "That's our mobile Operations unit. Jarred owns the Jag and boat. The rest belong to us. We like our powerful toys."

"I can see that. If the garage is this large, the house must be enormous. I assume Jarred is married with a family?"

"Nope. Not married, and that's not likely to change. He's just not interested in settling down to domestic bliss with one woman for the rest of his life."

"None of us are," called Ryan coming round the rear of the vehicle. "Except for Sam. Poor guy is the odd one out now."

Sam closed his door and winked at Jane. "I consider myself the lucky one. These fellas don't know what they're missing."

Glancing up, Jane caught Talos watching her. He shifted from foot to foot. "Come on, we'd best get you upstairs." He led the way to a steel door. On the wall beside it was a keypad and red button. He hit the button and a massive panel lift door began descending, blocking out the steady rain and locking them inside the garage. Jane's attention returned to Talos as he punched in six numbers and the steel door opened. She raised an eyebrow. "You people really take your security seriously, don't you?"

"Of course." He grinned and held the door open for her.

Jane's heart flipped. *God, he has a sexy smile.* She stepped into a foyer. To the right she glimpsed stairs leading up, straight ahead was a lift, and to the left a fully equipped gym. The lift doors opened to reveal Nick, another well-built, handsome man with charisma dripping off him. She'd come across him in Willaroi when she'd been taken hostage. Nick had been shot trying to protect her. His lips curved and his blue-eyes crinkled. Here was a man that flirted his way through life. Beside him stood Ajax, a large German shepherd. He bounded forward, tail wagging excitedly as he sniffed everyone. On reaching Jane his attention riveted to the bundle in her arms and he reared up on his hind legs.

"No, Ajax." Jane recoiled, twisting away from the dog and colliding with Talos. Her blanket fell to the floor as numerous male voices told Ajax to sit.

Powerful big arms closed around her, holding her protectively. "It's okay," soothed Talos. "Ajax is just curious. He won't hurt you or the baby."

Jane melted as a desperate craving blossomed deep within her soul. She hadn't felt this safe or secure since childhood when her dad had been alive.

"Holy cow," exclaimed a voice behind her. "Now I understand what's eating Talos."

Jane looked over her shoulder to see Ryan and Nick staring at her. Overcome with embarrassment, she reached behind and tugged at her nightie. "My blanket."

"I've got it." Sam picked up the blanket and placed it round her shoulders. "Kallie is upstairs. Us fellas will wait in the billiard room for Jarred."

"Thank you, Sam." Resting her forehead against Talos's chest, Jane listened to the other three men ascend the stairs. Ajax's claws clicked on the tiles as he followed them. *Can my life get any more humiliating?*

Ella made a tiny whimper and Talos's hands closed round Jane's shoulders easing her back. "Let's get you upstairs. You'll feel a hundred-percent once you've had a warm shower and changed into dry clothes."

Jane gripped the edges of the blanket and stepped into the lift. Twenty seconds later the doors opened and there in front of Jane stood Kallie, her best friend and closest confidante since the age of five.

"Kallie!" Jane stepped into Kallie's outstretched arms. "I've missed you so much."

"I missed you too." Kallie gently hugged her. "No one would tell us where you were."

"They wouldn't let me call you, but I knew Sam was looking after you."

"You must have been so lonely. Is Eloise okay? Are you coming home with us?"

"Yes, to everything, but I haven't got any clothes. They're all back at the safe house."

"I haven't got much here either. We hadn't intended on staying the night, but don't worry, I'm sure I can find something else in Jarred's wardrobe."

Jane stepped back and observed the blue silk shirt Kallie was wearing. It looked expensive. "Are you sure Jarred won't mind?"

Waving her hand nonchalantly, Kallie laughed. "Don't worry about Jarred. He and Sam are in big trouble for going after you without me."

Talos chuckled. "They did it for your own protection." He turned to Jane. "Get Kallie to take a look at your backside."

"Why?" Kallie's gaze flicked from Jane to Talos.

"Jane fell on the roof and hurt herself. Let me know if it's serious."

"The roof?" Kallie's eyes widened. "What were you doing on a roof?"

"Being chased by men with guns."

"Oh my God." Kallie glanced back to Talos. "You saved her life *again*, didn't you?"

"No, she pretty much did that herself." He winked at Jane. "Have a shower and get into something warm. The boys and I will be in the billiard room."

"Thank you for coming for me, Talos."

"You're welcome." He strode down the wide hall and entered a room at the end.

Jane turned to find Kallie watching her with a silly grin on her face. "What?"

"You like him, don't you?"

"What's not to like? He's a very nice man."

"That's not what I meant and you know it." Kallie leaned over and pulled the bunny rug away from Ella's face. "She's so sweet. Can I hold my goddaughter?"

"Of course."

Kallie cradled Ella gently. "Come on, let's raid Jarred's wardrobe. I saw a new pair of leery pajamas on one of the shelves."

"I can't take his new pajamas, Kallie."

"Hey, a guy like Jarred doesn't wear pajamas. He won't even miss them." She ignored the lift and, patting Ella, slowly climbed the stairs. "Bedrooms are up here. I'll give you a proper tour in the morning after we've all had some sleep."

"I'm so jittery, I don't think I'll be able to sleep. What if we were followed?"

"Not a chance, these guys are really thorough. Did you know Simon's taken your mum and Ken up to Yarramalong?" She stepped onto the landing and turned right.

"Yes, I heard."

"As long as Inspector Gibbs agrees, we'll join them tomorrow." Kallie opened double doors and led the way into a massive room with a king sized bed in the center. A bedside lamp cast a soft glow over the elegantly decorated room.

Jane stared. "How does an ex-SAS Colonel afford a place like this? Have you seen the fabulous vehicles in the garage?"

Chuckling, Kallie steered Jane into an enormous walk-in-robe. "Sam said they get paid very well and they received a huge reward for catching Marzetti.

"They must, to have houses like this and those cars in the garage."

Kallie picked up a pair of brightly spotted pajamas. "Here you go."

Jane spied the engagement ring on Kallie's finger and grabbed her friend's hand. "Oh my God, Kallie, your ring is lovely." She frowned. "I thought you'd use the Kalista Diamond?"

"I did. This is about a tenth of it. The rest I sold to a gem dealer."

Jane frowned. "But it's purple. Isn't the Kalista Diamond pink?"

"When it comes to diamonds there are many shades of pink apparently. I wanted to sell the whole thing so I could establish the horse stud, but Sam wouldn't let me. He insisted I keep a piece of it in remembrance of my grandfather. Come on." She grabbed a dark cashmere jumper and led the way back into the hall.

"Sam and I are in the room next door. This is your room." She held the door open. "The bathroom is there and I've cut towels up for nappies. Show me where you're hurt."

"I'm sure it's just bruised. Talos is a worry wart." Jane lifted her chemise and twisted to have a look. "It's too low for me to see, can you?"

A gasp sounded behind her. "Far out, Jane. That looks really sore and it's not just bruised, there's a nasty graze."

"That explains why it hurts to sit. I'll take care of it after I have a shower." Jane kissed Kallie on the cheek. "You look tired. Go to bed and we'll talk in the morning."

"Okay." Kallie lay Ella in the middle of the bed between two pillows and covered her with the cashmere jumper. "Happy new year. I'll see you later this morning."

CHAPTER FIVE

Lining up the cue ball, Talos hit it hard and sent the pink ball rocketing into the corner pocket. "You've had it, ladies."

"Hmm." Ryan crossed his arms and leaned against the wall. "Your luck can only hold out so long, big man. We'll win our money back."

Chuckling, Talos strolled to the other end, chalked his cue, and lined up the black ball. "It's like taking candy from a baby." He took the shot and sank the black in the middle pocket. "I believe that's another fifty bucks you owe me."

The door behind them opened and Kallie stuck her head round. "Are you guys going to stay up all night?"

"No," answered Sam. "We were waiting for Jarred, but I think I'll call it a night and catch up on some beauty sleep."

"You need it." Nick racked up the balls again.

"Yeah, yeah. You're just jealous that you don't have a gorgeous body to cuddle up to like I do, mate."

Talos followed Sam over to Kallie. "How's Jane?"

"A bit shaky. She's having a shower now but I've checked that bruise. It's pretty nasty. I think she needs antiseptic on it."

"I'll take some up. Thanks."

"Hey." Ryan leaned against the wall. "Don't run away yet. The least you can do is give us the chance to win some of our money back."

Sam laughed. "Not me, I'm out of here."

"Goodnight." Kallie took Sam's hand and pulled him through the doorway.

"What about you, big fella?" asked Nick. "Care to double the stakes. Winner takes all?"

"It's your money." Talos chalked his cue and strolled back to the table. "One more game then if Jarred's not back, I'm calling it quits."

"Deal."

Twenty minutes later, Talos left the billiard room one hundred bucks lighter. *My mind was obviously somewhere else.* He had one foot on the bottom stair when he heard gurgling noises. Frowning he changed direction and went in search of the source. A lamp in the corner cast a soft glow over the entire living room. His gaze fell on Jane sleeping soundly in a two-seater couch with the footrest raised. She was dressed in the loudest pair of pajamas he'd ever seen. Large red, blue, and green dots covered her from neck to foot. The cuffs had been folded multiple times at both her wrists and ankles. Talos grinned. *Add a yellow fuzzy wig and red nose and she could be mistaken for a circus clown.*

He ambled closer. Her shining hair fell about her shoulders in soft ringlets. His footsteps faltered as he noticed her partly open shirt and the exposed curve of her left breast. Every inch of his body tightened. *Bloody hell, not again.* At least in the car, the effect of her divine breasts had been tempered by the fact she was feeding her baby.

A sound impinged on his dazed brain. Walking closer, he noticed Ella deep in the crook of her mother's arms sucking her tiny fingers. *What the hell is Jane doing down here?* He drew her shirt closed, careful not to touch her naked skin, then he gently shook her.

"Wake up, Jane. You need to go upstairs to bed."

"Huh?" Her eyes cracked open then closed again. "I feel safe here."

"You'll be safe upstairs and more comfortable. Do you want me to carry you up?"

Her eyes stayed closed as she moved her head moved from side to side. "I can't go to bed, I might need to make a quick escape and I don't want to be up there on my own."

"What if I stay with you? I can throw a bedroll down on the floor."

She shook her head again. "No, that's not fair on you. Please let me stay here."

Inhaling deeply, Talos rubbed his bristly chin. *I should just pick her up and take her to bed.* He smiled. The idea had a lot of merit, but then neither of them would get any sleep and they only had a few more hours before daylight. "All right, we'll do it your way, this time."

He left the living room and strode into the kitchen, retrieved some antiseptic from the medical kit, then ducked upstairs and grabbed a light blanket out of the linen cupboard.

Coming back into the lounge, he found Jane asleep again and Ella further down between her mother's arm and the chair. *That won't do.* He lay the blanket over Jane then gently scooped Ella up in his hands. She was swaddled tightly in an incredibly soft jumper and making big eyes at him. He grinned and stroked her soft cheek. *What am I going to do with you, little one?* He eyed the other couch. *No, Jane will have a fit if she wakes and Ella's gone.*

Holding the baby in one arm he unlaced his boots, kicked them off and lowered his body into the two-seater beside Jane. Then he pressed the control, taking them to a comfortable reclined position.

He lay in a relaxed state and slowly began to unwind, then Jane wriggled onto her side, pressed her glorious body against his and wrapped an arm around his torso. Any thought of sleep went straight out the window as his body went on high alert. *Holy shit, why does Jane have such an effect on me?*

His torture wasn't over. She snuggled closer and murmured his name, which he guessed was better than mumbling her shit of a husband's name. Pulling his arm free, he wrapped it around her shoulders, cushioning her head against his chest. Something deep inside his soul ignited and flared into life.

Agitated by the night's events, he began to think about his life up until now. Over the last few years in the SAS, he often wondered if that was his true purpose in life or was there something more. He'd looked forward to his daily visits to the hospital to see Jane and Ella, then they'd disappeared one night into witness protection and he'd felt cheated. Now it hit him like a sledgehammer. *I will make sure Jane and her baby have a safe home and that they never want for anything.* The idea made him feel like a man with something to strive for, but how to sell the idea to Jane?

A smooth foot rubbed against his shin, sending a riot of sensations throughout his body, then Jane's hand moved to his chest.

"This is nice." Her voice sounded fuzzy with sleep. Fanning her fingers, she caressed his chest in a wide sensual sweeping motion then her palm skated over his hard nipple. A wave of lust surged through his body. Her hand stilled. Her eyelids fluttered open and she raised herself on an elbow and blinked at him.

"Talos?" Her sleepy eyes focused on his lips and her shirt fell open.

His lungs seized. *God almighty.* "You're dreaming, honey. Go back to sleep."

She blinked several times. "If this is a dream then the last thing I want to do is sleep." She leaned forward and touched her lips to his in the most delicate kiss he'd ever received then she drew back. "You're a very desirable man, Talos." Her full lush lips quirked.

Aware he had a fragile baby sleeping in his other arm, Talos fought to keep his body under control. "This is not a good idea."

She gave him a coy smile. "This is my dream." She kissed him again, more gamely.

Talos's senses began to reel. A raw need surged through his body like molten lava. He reached around her with his free arm and drew her closer, deepening the kiss until they were both breathing heavily.

Ella whimpered softly and Talos silently cursed as Jane jerked back.

"Oh God, Talos, I'm so sorry. I really thought I was..." She blushed.

"Don't be. I'm not."

"You must think I'm desperate." She gasped. "Oh, no, I didn't mean that the way it sounded. You're a wonderful man and any woman would be mad not to want to kiss you."

She groaned and covered her eyes. "This is coming out all wrong."

Chuckling, Talos drew her back against his side. "It's all right. You're tired and confused. Forget it."

Jane scrambled into a sitting position, leaned across and gently took her baby. The loss of the tiny infant unsettled him. Both of these females had worked their way into his soul without even trying.

Talos eased the two-seater into the upright position then stood. "I'll put some ointment on that bruise of yours."

Jane's eyes widened. "It's okay, you don't have to." She hurriedly did up her buttons.

"Yes, I do. We can argue all night or you can give in gracefully and let me take a look."

Chewing on her bottom lip she nodded. "It really is sore." She twisted on her side, leaned back and modestly eased the spotty pajamas down over the right globe of her bottom.

The sight of her smooth, sexy arse had Talos clenching his jaw. He cleared his throat and fumbled to get the lid off the tube of antiseptic cream. "I'll to be gentle." He gripped the elastic of her trousers and pulled it lower, gritting his teeth when his fingers brushed her skin.

She flinched.

"Sorry."

"No, I'm fine." Her voice sounded husky.

Maybe she's as affected as me. That would make his proposition easier. He inhaled and focused on the underside of her bottom where she had a large graze.

"Kallie was right. This does look nasty." He gently layered a thick coating of antiseptic over the bruise then eased her pajamas up. "I'll check it out again later."

She croaked then cleared her throat. "Thank you."

Turning away to hide his grin, Talos screwed the lid on the tube and placed it on the coffee table, then eased back into the chair beside Jane. "Go ahead and feed Ella, there's something important I want to ask you."

Jane discreetly lifted her shirt and drew Ella underneath. Once the baby was feeding she looked up, a soft smile on her lips. "Ask away."

"You and Ella need somewhere safe to live. I'm thirty years old and on my own, so I was wondering if you'd like to move in to my place with me?"

Her eyes widened. "You want us to live with you?"

"Yeah. I own the land next door to Sam in the Yarramalong Valley and I've built a nice place there. You'd be safe and Kallie would be right next door."

"Talos, that's a very generous offer, but what's in it for you?"

He smiled. "I would have thought that was obvious."

Her eyes widened. "You want a physical relationship with me?"

"Of course, but I don't want to pressure you into anything you don't want. I care about you and Ella, and I'd like us to get to know each other, one step at a time, if you're agreeable."

She gulped. "So, I would be your girlfriend?"

"Yeah, I guess you would."

"For how long?"

He frowned. "For how ever long we want."

"I see." Her eyelids lowered and she turned back to the baby.

Talos felt invisible shutters descending, locking him out. He'd handled that badly. "I can protect you, Jane. No one will ever hurt you or Ella."

She glanced up with watery eyes. "No one except you."

"Pardon." *What is that supposed to mean?*

"Thank you for the offer, Talos, but if I ever accept another man into my life, it will be because he loves me and wants me forever, not until something better comes along."

"That's not what I meant." He sighed. "Look, I admit I'm not a kid person, but I will take care of you, and Ella will have plenty of room to run wild."

Jane stiffened. "I'm very capable of taking care of Ella. I have my teaching that I can go back to when I'm ready and my mum will help me with Ella."

"We have a mutual attraction, Jane. The rest we can work on."

She gave him a sad smile. "It doesn't work that way." She stretched up and kissed his cheek. "I know you mean well, Talos, but I've had one relationship fail miserably because a man didn't want me for the right reasons. I won't make that mistake again." She turned away. "I think it would be better if I stayed with Kallie and Sam until the trial is over."

A dead weight settled on Talos. *That didn't go well.* He brushed her long hair away from her face. "You've got me all wrong, Jane. I'd never take advantage of you or hurt you."

"Not physically, Talos, but you have the power to destroy me emotionally." She leaned against his shoulder. "Go to sleep. You're tired and people say things they don't mean when they're not thinking straight."

"I know exactly what I'm saying." He put his arm around her, drew her closer, and took the chair back into its reclined position. "Happy new year, Jane."

"Happy new year, Talos."

CHAPTER SIX

Ella cooed and Jane opened her eyes with a start. Disorientated, it took her a moment to take in her surroundings. Ella lay atop the cashmere jumper, her tiny fists clenched as she kicked and flailed her legs and arms. A man's large finger lowered and Ella grasped it in her tiny hand and drew it straight to her mouth. A deep chuckle vibrated under Jane's ear.

Talos.

Her world righted then crashed as disappointment washed over her. *He's not ours.*

Raising her eyes, she scanned his massive chest where her hand rested, then she raised her eyes to his strong square jaw covered in dark bristles. Her gaze locked with his sexy cognac eyes and time stood still. Their exhilarating kiss from last night came to mind and her heart unfurled like the petals of a rose reaching for the morning sun. *I'm in love with him.*

Somebody cleared his throat.

Jane glanced over her shoulder to see Jarred standing in the doorway, concern etched in his cool grey eyes. He wore a sleeveless singlet, shorts, and trainers. An uncomfortable silence hung in the air and Jane felt her face heat. She pulled away and picked up Ella.

"Thanks for the company, Talos. I'd better change Ella." She shuffled off the chair and padded across to Jarred who unhurriedly moved aside, his hard eyes riveted on Talos.

Uh-oh. Hesitating at the foot of the stairs, Jane observed Jarred enter the living room. Curiosity getting the better of her, she tiptoed back to the door's edge.

"Jane Rossini has enough on her plate." Jarred's deep voice held a truckload of warning. "She's bewildered and vulnerable. I don't want you getting involved then letting her down when you move on."

Exactly what I told him. Poor Talos. Jane leaned against the wall.

"That's not going to happen." Annoyance laced Talos's voice and Jane wondered if he meant they weren't getting involved or he wouldn't move on. "Marzetti's men failed to kill Jane last night, but they got damn close three times and I'm not prepared to let that happen again. If you have a problem with that then tough shit."

"For fuck's sake, Talos, think! The woman already worships you for saving her life and delivering her baby safely. Now you've saved them again."

"So?"

A heavy sigh sounded. "There are things you don't know. Inspector Gibbs informed me that Jane's prick of a husband tried to pressure her into an abortion. When she refused, he physically and emotionally rejected her. He never wanted kids."

Talos made a sound of disgust. "I should have wrung the mongrel's neck when I had the chance. Why the hell did he marry her in the first place?"

Cringing, Jane lowered her head in shame. *Please don't tell him.*

"Rossini claims the plan was to marry Kallie McNeil and get the Kalista diamond but she rejected him, so he went with second best, Jane. Those are Rossini's words, not Gibb's. Rossini intended on ditching Jane as soon as she told him the diamond's location."

"So the fuckwit hasn't touched Jane since she told him she was pregnant with *his* kid?"

"So he says, which would have been a month after their honeymoon. Rossini also admitted to having a girlfriend on the side."

With a heavy heart Jane turned away. She'd been suspicious Andrew was having an affair, but to hear it aired publicly made it so much worse and now Talos knew. *Shit, shit, shit. I shouldn't have stayed. No good comes from eavesdropping.* She took a step as Talos spoke.

"I wish I'd known all this earlier. I've made the biggest arse of myself."

"Why? What have you done?"

"I told Jane I'm not a kid person and asked her to move in with me. She's probably put me in the same basket as the mongrel she was married to."

Jane shuddered. *No, I haven't Talos. I knew you meant well.*

"Christ, Talos, why on earth would you do that?" Jarred's voice rumbled.

"Because I'm attracted to the bloody woman, that's why."

Jane placed Ella against her shoulder and climbed the stairs. *And that's why I can't accept your offer, my gallant knight. I love you and that gives you the power to destroy me.*

Jane reached her room as Kallie's door opened. She came out wearing jeans, court shoes, and a pretty floral top. She'd twisted her long hair into a clip and her dark eyes shone with happiness.

"Good morning, Jane, how did you sleep?"

"Okay. How about you?"

"Fantastic. How about we make ourselves some breakfast then I'll see about getting you some clothes to wear?"

"Sure, I'll just change Ella."

"The kitchen is on the next floor down at this end of the house. I'll see you there." Kallie descended the stairs, calling out good mornings to Jarred and Talos.

Drawing in a deep breath, Jane walked into the room she was supposed to have slept in. It wasn't that she begrudged Kallie her happiness. God knows she deserved it after what she'd been through, but wouldn't it be nice to know you were the center of someone's universe.

After sponging Ella with a warm soapy washer, Jane redressed her. "We are really going to have to get some clothes, aren't we, sweetie?"

Ella blew bubbles, her pretty eyes riveted on Jane.

"I wonder if you'll end up with my green eyes or blue like your beastly father?" Jane swaddled Ella in the cashmere jumper and picked her up. "Let's go downstairs, sweetie. Mummy needs some breakfast."

Jane entered the kitchen and came to an abrupt halt. In front of her was a wall-length window framing a magnificent panorama of Sydney Harbour. The surface of the water sparkled like diamonds in the morning sun. The iconic Harbour Bridge had a steady flow of traffic crossing, and further afield, yachts raced on seriously precarious angles, their sails billowing in the breeze. "Wow."

"It's fantastic, isn't it?" Talos stood behind a massive black granite bench. He held a glass of orange juice in his hand and wore a sleeveless singlet displaying his broad shoulders and chest to perfection.

Jane swallowed. "Yes, fantastic." The view forgotten, her gaze locked with his.

"So, what would you like for breakfast," called Kallie from behind the fridge door. "We've got the choice of avocado on toast, eggs and bacon, or left over pizza?"

Tearing her gaze from Talos, Jane studied the stylish kitchen. The wood-turned cupboards and drawers were finished in a cream sheen. Polished floorboards bore the glass-topped table beside a window overlooking an oblong pool and manicured lawns.

Kallie popped her head out of the fridge and scrunched up her nose. "I was joking about the pizza. We're not eating that." She grinned at Jane. "Oh, I forgot, you haven't seen this place. It's incredible, isn't it?"

"Yes." Jane hitched up one pajama leg and padded across the room. "I'll help."

"No, no. I've got this." Kallie dumped an armful of ingredients on the bench and began searching through drawers. "Sam, Nick, and Ryan are down in the gym and Jarred and Talos are about to go for a run, so it's just us for breakfast."

As Jane slid onto a chair, Talos came around the bench. Her gaze dropped to his muscular legs, black shorts, and runners. He crossed the room, crouched down on his haunches and stroked Ella's cheek. His gaze rose to Jane's.

"When I said I'm not a kid person, I didn't mean I don't like them. I meant I've never had much to do with them."

Jane frowned. "Are you saying that because of what Jarred said this morning?"

He drew a sharp breath. "You heard?"

"I knew something was going on so I decided to eavesdrop."

"No, I'm not just saying that. I really do want to help you."

"Good." Jane held out a baggy sleeve. "Would you please fold this up for me?"

His lips curved. "That's not what I meant."

Strolling in from the terrace, Jarred halted and starred at Jane. "What are you wearing?"

"Your pajamas."

He raised an eyebrow. "I had no idea I owned anything so garish."

Grinning, Jane held up the jumper. "This is yours as well."

Jarred scratched his chin. "Keep it, I never wear it."

"It's cashmere." Jane gaped at him. "Horrendously expensive."

"It's not really my color."

"And the pajamas."

"I assume they were a present from my mother. You can keep them as well."

Kallie placed an orange juice in front of Jane and fluttered her eyes at Jarred. "Can I keep the lovely silk shirt I borrowed last night?"

"If it means that much to you." His eyebrow rose. "Is there anything else you'd like to help yourself to or is the rest of my wardrobe safe?"

Kallie grinned. "No, it's safe, but I did cut up some of your towels as nappies for Ella."

"Really." Jarred glanced at Talos. "This house is a female free zone for a reason. Remind me to change the locks as soon as these two leave. Come on, let's hit the pavement."

Standing, Talos looked down on Jane. "I have my mobile if you need me."

"We'll be fine. Enjoy your run."

Talos hesitated. "I'm expecting a glass company this morning, to replace the rear window of my car. And Inspector Gibbs is bringing your belongings from the safe house, but we should be back before either arrives."

Jarred paused at the glass doors. "The gates are electronically operated and can be opened by pushing the red button on the security panel." He pointed to a small monitor on the wall beside him. "Under no circumstances are you to open the gates unless there's a fire."

"Understood, Captain." Jane saluted.

"I was a Colonel, actually." He strode out onto the terrace.

Talos winked at Jane. "I was the captain." He jogged after Jarred.

Placing the plates of sliced avocado on toast on the table, Kallie sat opposite and sighed. "Thank goodness. Now we can have breakfast in peace. All that testosterone in one place gets a bit much sometimes. The run will do them good." She sat opposite Jane.

"I wish we could go out. Ella is six weeks old and she's never been for a decent walk."

"You need a stroller." Kallie crunched on her toast.

"Why? I can't go anywhere."

"We'll see about that. You also need a proper crib and baby stuff. Maybe Sam and Talos could take us shopping today and then to a park."

"That would be nice."

"Let's make a list." Kallie jumped up, padded to the granite bench and brought back a notepad and pen. Then they spent the next half hour listing everything Ella needed.

Jane was feeling much more relaxed when a buzzer sounded from the security monitor. Kallie ran over to the screen. "It's a hot looking guy in sunglasses?"

"Ask him what he wants," Jane's heart sped up.

Kallie pressed a button. "Hello, can I help you?"

"Hi, I'm Inspector Gibbs of the AFP. Jarred Steele is expecting me."

Releasing the button, Kallie gaped at Jane. "*That's* Inspector Gibbs?"

"Show me." Cradling Ella, Jane stood and padded over to the monitor. A man with an olive complexion, dark hair, and sunglass sat drumming his long fingers on the steering wheel of a sleek silver car.

"That's him. Get him to come around the back then lock the gate."

Kallie turned back to the monitor. "Please come around the back, Inspector."

"Sure, thanks."

Jane strolled back to the table. "Let's take Ella and our breakfast out to the terrace." She picked up her plate and led the way. They sat at a table by the pool and Jane put Ella to her breast, pulling her pajama shirt over the baby to discreetly cover her breast, then she picked up a piece of avocado toast and took a bite.

A car door slammed then Inspector Gibbs strode round the corner of the house and ran up the terrace steps. He wore a stylishly cut grey suit, pale blue shirt, and patterned tie. He'd taken his sunglasses off and looked tanned, handsome, and very much the professional.

Jane's gaze rose to the Inspector's dark eyes. "Hello, Inspector, it's nice to see you again. This is my friend, Kallie, who I believe you never actually got to meet."

Inspector Gibb's eyes widened marginally as he skimmed Jane's pajamas. "No, I haven't had the pleasure." He lowered Jane's suitcase, reached out and shook Kallie's hand, then looked around expectantly. "Where's Jarred Steele?"

"He went for a run but should be back soon." Jane pointed to the chair opposite. "Please have a seat, Inspector. Would you like a cup of tea or coffee while you wait?"

"Thanks, I'd love a coffee, just a dash of milk and no sugar."

"I'll get it." Kallie stood and walked inside.

Jane smiled at the inspector. "How's the case? Are we getting closer to a court date?"

"That's why I'm here. I want you to look at photos of known associates to Marzetti. You may recognize someone who knew your husband, and I need to ask you a favor."

"Okay, and what's the favor?"

He clasped his hands and leaned his elbows on the table. "I need you to accompany me to the Correctional Center."

"What?" She stared at the inspector in disbelief. A shiver ran down her spine. "Why?"

"In return for his testimony, your husband has requested a meeting with you."

Jane stiffened. "Are you for real? I'm not going anywhere near him."

Inspector Gibbs sighed. "I understand how you feel, but we need to know the names of the other members in Marzetti's ring and their method of operation. Andrew's testimony is the only way we'll get it, and for that he wants to talk to you."

"It's a trick. I'm sorry, the answer is no."

"Jane, if we don't get Marzetti's partners, they won't give up until they kill you."

"Didn't Andrew agree to tell you everything for a lighter sentence?"

"Yes, that was the original deal but now he's requested a meeting with you instead."

"Why, what's changed?"

The inspector's jaw clenched. "Even though we've moved him into solitary confinement, your husband is convinced Marzetti will get to him and he says he's got information he needs to give to you personally. If you agree to meet with him, you won't be alone. I'll be there, plus a prison guard and if you wish, a person of your choosing."

Jane rubbed Ella's back, seething that the inspector would make such a request.

Kallie stepped onto the terrace carrying a tray. "Here you are." She removed three cups of coffee, a plate of muffins, a knife and butter.

Pounding feet alerted Jane to Talos and Jarred's return. They appeared around the side of the house, both covered in sweat and breathing hard. Talos took the steps three at a time, his attention went from the inspector to Jane. "What's happened?"

Jane drew a shaky breath. "Inspector Gibbs wants me to speak to Andrew at the prison."

Talos turned on the inspector. "You can't be serious."

"What's going on, Gibbs?" Jarred joined Talos in staring down at the inspector, who calmly picked up his coffee.

"As I was just telling Mrs. Rossini—"

"I prefer Jane Hughes," interrupted Jane, pushing the muffins closer to the inspector. "It's my maiden name and what I will be using from now on."

Gibb's took a muffin and nodded his thanks. "Andrew Rossini has agreed to give us the names of his father's partners and tell us all he knows in return for a meeting with Jane."

Jane passed the butter plate and knife across. "Can't he tell you whatever it is?"

"I asked but he refused." Inspector Gibbs tore his muffin in half and lathered it in butter. "Without those names and the locations of their meetings, we won't stand a chance of breaking up their ring." He took a bite of the muffin.

Jarred drew out a chair and sat. "Why not let the army's interrogators have a go at him."

"We don't have time. Marzetti's partners are due to meet in the next week or so."

Talos moved to stand behind Jane, placing his hands on the chair behind her back. The warmth of his touch infused her with a sense of safety and confidence. She inhaled. "If I do this then I want something in return."

"No." Talos moved his hands to her shoulders. "You're not going anywhere near him."

The inspector's eyes moved from Talos to Jane then narrowed. "As I told Jane, I will be there, plus a prison guard and any person she wishes to bring along. Andrew Rossini will be handcuffed and he won't get within striking distance of Jane."

Talos's hands tightened. "Jane's been hurt enough by that bastard. You're asking too much of her. Give me five minutes with him and I'll get the information you need."

Inspector Gibbs shook his head. "You know that's out of the question."

Jane placed her hand over Talos's. "I have no desire to ever see Andrew again and I can't think of any reason why he'd want to speak to me."

The inspector leaned on the table. "I wouldn't ask this of you if there were any other way of getting those names and the meeting locations."

Jane considered the inspector. "I have two requests of my own, Inspector. I want to go shopping for a stroller and a car safety-seat for my baby. Ella needs to be properly restrained. And, I want to take her for a decent walk in a real park before we both go stir-crazy. If you agree, I'll speak to Andrew, but I want Talos to come with me."

She felt Talos's hand stiffen under hers. Inspector Gibbs gave her a dubious look then shook his head. Jane inhaled deeply. "Fine. I refuse your request, but thank you for bringing my clothes." She picked up her coffee and calmly took a sip.

The inspector rubbed his forehead. "I'll agree to the shopping and walk as long as you have adequate protection." His gaze lifted above her head. "I assume you're Talos."

"I am."

"Are you also the man who delivered Jane's baby and broke Andrew Rossini's nose?

"I delivered the baby. As to the rest, I don't recall."

Jarred drummed his fingers on the table. "We can provide protection for Jane while she buys whatever it is she needs, and we'll find somewhere safe to take the baby for a walk. However, if Talos accompanies Jane to the prison, then I insist no one use his name.

Our continued anonymity is essential for our undercover work and our personal safety.

Gibbs drained his coffee. "Deal." He stared at Talos. "I don't know what your relationship is with Jane, but if you touch Rossini, I'll arrest you."

Talos said nothing and the two men's gazes locked in silent battle.

Jane squirmed uncomfortably. "Talos is my friend, Inspector. He has saved my life twice and delivered my baby. I trust him more than any other man alive."

"Fair enough. If you'll have a look at these photos, I'll be on my way." He passed a manila folder across the table.

Taking the folder, Jane opened it and studied each face carefully. They were all strangers to her. "No, I've never seen any of these people."

Grimacing, Gibbs took the folder. "It was a long shot. Thanks anyway. I'll be back at ten thirty to escort you to the prison."

"No need, we can get her there safely," announced Jarred.

Inspector Gibbs nodded. "As you wish. Let's say eleven at the main gate." He gave a nod and strode from the terrace.

Kallie made a face at Jane. "That man needs to unwind a little."

Chapter Seven

Dressed in her own clothes, with her best friend by her side and a wall of muscle behind them, Jane stepped through the doors of the baby store and heaved a sigh of relief.

With her marriage all but over, she hadn't bothered setting up a nursery. Jane shook her head at the turn her life had taken in the last six weeks. She'd been kidnapped, gone into early labour, discovered her husband was involved in organized crime, and ended up in witness protection. She'd have dismissed it as fiction if it had been anyone else.

Kallie giggled and nudged her. "The sales staff won't know what to think when they see our entourage."

Glancing over one shoulder, Jane smiled. Just inside the entrance, Talos stood cradling Ella in his arms, Sam, Ryan, and Nick positioned strategically about him. All four scanned the store, looking as comfortable as gazelles on the open plains of Africa. A tiny baby and four exceedingly handsome well-built men drew not one but two sales assistants.

Kallie huffed. "Those women didn't even see us. I suppose I can't blame them."

"Neither can I." Jane scanned the well-stocked floor. "Since Ella's birth I've been longing for the day I could fit her out in soft pastels and take her walking in a stroller, and now I can't decide where to start."

They strolled down the center aisle perusing the abundance of baby equipment, accessories, toys, and clothing.

"Car seats." Jane led Kallie to an area full of baby safety seats of all sizes and shapes. The men with both sales assistants in tow joined them.

"There's so many," murmured Kallie.

One of the ladies picked up a seat by the handle. "This is one of our more popular brands. It's light weight, and easy to install and remove from the car."

Talos stepped forward. "It doesn't look very big. How long does the baby stay in it?"

"Up to three or four months then you move on to one of those." She pointed at a range of high backed safety seats. "They will hold a child up to four or five years, then we have booster seats for older children. Or you can pay a bit more and get an all in one that takes a newborn up to an eight year old child."

Ryan crossed his arms. "Sounds more like it. Let's have a look at those."

Jane glanced at Kallie who raised an eyebrow in return and shrugged.

The saleswoman looked up at the high shelf. "The only ones I have left are up there."

Sam moved forward and began lifting seats down to Ryan and Nick. "If we're going to do this, we might as well do it properly."

All four men wore T-shirts displaying their muscles and broad shoulders to perfection. Jane bit her lip to stop laughing as both sales ladies ogled the men's bodies.

Talos handed Ella to Jane, then crouched down to read one of the labels. "This one has a five point safety harness and reclining backrest."

"This one has a six point safety harness and nine reclining positions," called Nick.

Ryan picked up one and weighed it in his hands. "Here's a better one. It's got a sun shade and side pockets for snacks and drink bottles."

"Check this out," announced Sam. "It's got nine reclining positions, a lining that's easily removed for cleaning and a lumbar support."

Kallie giggled and glanced at Jane. "This could be very entertaining."

Jane grinned back. "Hmm."

Talos lifted another seat down and read the tag. "Nope. This is the one. Ten reclining positions, removable sunshade, side impact protection, six point safety harness, lumbar support, removable lining for cleaning and five shoulder strap slots."

Jane checked the price tag. "It's also the most expensive."

Talos stood. "Only the best for little Ella. What's next?"

She wasn't made of money but in this, Talos was right. Ella's safety was paramount. "I need a bassinette and a change table."

Jane noticed Talos and Sam's attention snap towards the front of the store. She glanced that way and saw a man and very pregnant woman enter and look around expectantly.

"This way." One of the sales ladies headed towards the back of the store. The other one looked regretfully at the four large men as they put the rejected seats back on the shelf, then she sighed and went to serve the couple.

Jane and Kallie followed the saleswoman to the bassinettes. She had started to explain its advantages when Sam called out. "Look at this. It's a crib with adjustable mattress heights."

Kallie strolled over. "Saves buying a bassinette."

"This is better," called Ryan. "It's got casters and the side rails come off."

Talos went to inspect it. He pulled the sides off and adjusted the mattress.

Enthralled, Jane watched in fascination. *They're all so into this. Who'd have thought?"*

"Hey fellas, check this out," called Nick. "It's smaller and turns into a bed."

"Here we go again." Jane laughed then seeing a recliner, she sat and nursed Ella as the four men and Kallie examined a pretty little white crib.

The sales lady turned to Jane. "Is there anything else I can help you with?"

"I'm almost afraid to ask." She glanced at Talos, bent over the crib, checking the underneath support structure. "I need a change table, baby bath, stroller, and clothing."

"The clothing is in the right hand corner. It might be best if I help your husband and friends with the change tables and strollers." She hesitated. "Unless you need me."

Jane grinned. "No, I'll be fine. You go help the men."

"Right." The sales assistant hurried off and Jane's gaze fell on Talos. He looked up and winked at her. *Sorry, Talos, I like pretending you're mine.* She smiled back and pointed towards the strollers. He nodded and weaved his way towards her.

"We've got the crib sorted. What type of stroller did you have in mind?"

"I'm looking for one that's reversible and can handle all terrain. It also needs to hold a newborn to four-year old." She stood and shifted Ella to the other arm. "I'm just going to look at clothes for Ella."

"Stay where I can see you." He stroked Ella's head then tracked a course to the strollers.

Kallie caught up with Jane and took charge of Ella. While the stroller analysis took place, the girls found a bath, padded carrier that doubled as a portable bassinette, bedding, and clothing. Then Kallie picked up a couple of hand puppets. Ella cooed and smiled.

"Oh my God." Barely able to see over the items in her arms, Jane placed the lot on a counter and spun round. "Talos."

Talos leapt to his feet and skimmed the shop quickly. "What's up?"

"Ella's smiling."

He strode over and observed as Jane took the orange and brown lion and danced it in front of Ella. Her bright eyes widened, a big smile appeared and she gripped the puppet in her tiny fingers. Her eyes moved to Talos, standing behind Jane's shoulder and she scrunched up her tiny nose and smiled at him, the lion forgotten.

Jane swallowed. "Oh, Talos, she recognizes you."

"So it would seem." He put his arm around Jane's waist as he brushed Ella's cheek.

Ella's gaze switched to Jane and she gurgled and scrunched up her nose again. Kallie sniffed and placed Ella in Jane's arms. "I need a tissue." She turned away and began rifling through her bag. "I know I've got one here somewhere."

Chuckling, Talos pointed across the shop. "We've found five strollers that meet your criteria. After collapsing, reassembling and examining each of them for strength, durability and safety, we've narrowed it down to a choice of two." He indicated a red stroller and a pretty dark plum stroller. "Don't worry about the price, just pick the one you like best."

"Talos." Jane wiped her own eyes and frowned at him. "How much are they?"

The saleswoman smiled. "Your husband told me he wants the best for your daughter."

Heat warmed Jane's cheeks. She glanced at Talos.

His lips twitched and he gave her that sexy wink of his. "Only the best."

She flipped over the price tag on the plum stroller. "Oh my God, Talos."

"I can afford it and Ella deserves the best. So do you."

"Talos. I can't let you—"

He put a finger against her lips. "I want to."

Coming to stand beside Jane, Kallie pointed to the white crib. "And this is going to be my present to my goddaughter, plus the mattress."

Jane gasped. "They're too expensive."

Marching to the counter, Kallie handed the girl her card then smiled at Jane. "Since selling the farm and that other item, I have a healthy bank balance. I want to do this for you."

Talos picked up a canary-yellow bear. "And as I intend spending a lot of time pushing Ella's stroller, I insist." He passed the bear and his card to the sales assistant.

Swallowing the lump in her throat, Jane pulled out her own card and directed her attention at the young woman. "I'll pay for the rest on this. Thank you for your help and tolerance. You've been very understanding."

"It's been my pleasure. If you and your husband require anything else, please don't hesitate to ring. We also deliver." She began ringing up the items.

Jane glanced over to see Sam, Ryan, and Nick staring at Talos. He either didn't notice or chose to ignore them as he pulled out a penknife and slit a large cardboard box open. "You don't mind if we leave you with the box, do you?"

The sales assistant shook her head. "Not at all."

Pulling the car seat out, Talos ripped off the tags and plastic. "I'm going to fit this in the CX so we can be on our way." He turned to Ryan. "Can you and Nick take care of the rest of this stuff? We'll take the stroller with us."

Ryan picked up the boxed change table. "Sure, but we'll follow you to the meeting and wait, then come to the park. I take it Sam and Kallie are minding the baby while you're meeting with Rossini?"

"Yes. Tell Jarred we won't be staying for dinner. I'm taking Jane back to Yarramalong, so we'll only drop in to pick up her stuff."

Nick raised an eyebrow and moved closer. "Gibbs may not like that."

"Jarred can fix it with him." Talos pinned in his code, took his card, and then strode out of the store, the car seat under his arm.

Jane put aside nappies, a container of wipes, and a change bag. "I'll take these too."

The men carried everything else to the van and stowed it, then as soon as Talos had the seat installed, Jane lay Ella in it, strapped her in and tucked the yellow bear in beside her.

"Now you can travel safely, my darling."

Nick and Ryan lingered until the stroller had been stored, then they climbed into the white van and followed Talos as he drove across the city.

The trip to the correctional center was subdued. Jane figured they were each caught up in their own thoughts. She certainly was. The idea of visiting Andrew made her sick, but she was determined to see justice done and if this was the only way to put those criminals behind bars then so be it. She would have Talos and Inspector Gibbs there to protect her. And she knew Ella would be safe with Kallie, Sam, Ryan, and Nick. Reaching into her bag, Jane pulled out an envelope and handed it to Kallie.

"What's this?" A frown crinkled Kallie's brow.

"If something happens to me, I want you and Sam to raise Ella. That's my will. I'm leaving everything in trust for Ella. You and my mum are trustees."

Kallie's eyes filled with tears. "Nothing's going to happen to you. I won't let it."

Jane tried to speak but a lump had formed in her throat. She glanced up to see Talos watching her in the rear view mirror.

"I'll protect you, if you'll let me." He returned his attention to the road and Jane went back to staring out her window, unseeing as she brooded and battled with her heart.

જ્જ

Turning the ignition off, Talos turned to Sam. "Once we've been to the gardens I'm taking Jane to my place where I can keep her and Ella safe."

Sam frowned. "I don't think that's wise. Simon's installed sensors and cameras on all my perimeter gates and fences. Fergie, Roy, and Ken are doing regular patrols, and Nick, Ryan, and I will be in the house. Your place in not secure."

Nobody will protect Jane as well as I can. Temper simmering, Talos got out of the car and opened Jane's door. Across the parking lot Gibbs stood with a plain-clothes officer. Jane slid a trembling hand into his and Talos realized his muscles were locked tight with tension. *What must Jane be feeling?* He squeezed her hand.

The check-in procedure through numerous locked doors and gates was slow and tedious. They were scanned with metal detectors then asked to empty their pockets as several prison guards stood watch. It didn't intimidate Talos but he felt for Jane. She wouldn't make eye contact with anyone. He leaned in close.

"You have nothing to be ashamed of Jane. Hold your head high."

She lifted her head. Distress showed in her eyes. "I know. It's just that it's so ghastly here and I hate the way the guards are staring at me."

They were ushered into another room that contained a solid table with one chair on one side and three chairs on the other. A prison guard followed them in and stood by the door.

Inspector Gibbs indicated Jane should sit in the middle, so Talos took the seat to her right. The inspector took the left and put his folder on the table before turning to Jane.

"They will bring Andrew in through the door at the end. His wrists and ankles will be shackled with cuffs and chains so his movement will be heavily restricted. You have nothing to fear. Talos and I will stay by your sides."

"I'm okay."

Noting her trembling hands, Talos clenched his jaw and concentrated on the door. It opened and another prison guard entered, followed by Andrew Rossini wearing dark green pants and shirt.

His gaze fastened on Jane then flicked to Talos and his eyes widened. "You're the guy who broke my nose?"

"I insisted he come," replied Jane shakily. "He has done more for me in the last six weeks than you did in the whole time I've know you." She lifted her chin. "Why did you want to see me?"

Talos studied Andrew Rossini as he hobbled to the chair and sat. He'd lost weight since being arrested, his nose appeared slightly warped from where Talos had smashed him, and the goatee was gone. Also missing was the cocky smartarse attitude.

Talos didn't envy him being locked away in the police informer's unit, but on the whole it was better than some of the places Talos had been sent. During his time in the SAS he spent days without a shower, barely enough to eat, and the fear that at any moment they could be discovered, shot, or blown up.

Andrew Rossini leaned towards the table and the two prison guards sprang forward, pushing him back in the seat. He sighed. "What am I going to do, seriously?"

Inspector Gibbs opened his folder and pulled a pen out of his suit jacket. "I've held up my part of the bargain and brought Jane to see you. Now you need to uphold your side and give me the names of your father's partners."

"I don't think of him as my father, just Marzetti. I was raised in foster homes until he decided he had a use for his son."

Talos shot a quick glance at Jane. Her hands were clenched tightly in her lap but otherwise she appeared calm, perhaps too calm. The sooner he got her away, the better.

She leveled her gaze at Rossini. "Why did you want to see me?"

"To tell you that everything I did was to protect you."

Talos came to his feet. "You lying piece of shit."

Gibbs stood as well and glared at Talos. "We have an agreement. Sit down."

Jane grabbed Talos's hand. "Tal..." She clamped her other hand over her mouth. "Sorry."

Gritting his teeth, Talos closed his fingers around her small hand. "It's okay." He sat, slammed into the backrest and glared at Andrew Rossini. "I should have finished you when I had the chance." He didn't release Jane's hand.

Rossini noticed then shrugged and returned his attention to Jane. "It's true."

She threw him an incredulous look. "That is rich coming from you."

"They were planning to kill you and I was trying to save you."

"Why on earth would I believe anything you have to say?"

Rossini shuffled on his seat. "I admit in the beginning it was just about getting the diamond, but then I got to know you and I got to like you."

"You're a liar." Jane looked away.

"No, it's true. But then you got pregnant and ruined everything."

"What difference would my pregnancy make?"

He swallowed. "The plan was for me to ditch you as soon as I had the diamond, but you didn't know where it was, so we had to wait. We figured Kallie McNeil would tell you eventually. Getting pregnant almost cost you your life."

Releasing Jane's hand, Talos pushed his fists between his knees, fighting the urge to leap over the table and smash Rossini until he was unconscious or, better still, dead. Jane placed her hand on his knee and squeezed. For some reason it calmed him.

Rossini drew in a deep breath, keeping his eyes on Jane. "You refused to get rid of the kid so I had to distance myself from you."

"Why?"

"I'm in a relationship with the daughter of one of Marzetti's partners. When she discovered you were pregnant, she wanted you eliminated. I told her you and I were no longer sleeping together and that I wanted the kid. It was all I could think of to keep you alive."

Talos clenched his jaw, fighting the urge to throw a punch. He glanced at Jane. She'd paled and her hand shook on his knee.

"Your girlfriend wanted me eliminated? What sort of woman is she?"

Rossini stared at his hands. "She's been jealous ever since I married you, but seeing you at our apartment upset her. The four men with her are Marzetti's partners."

Jane gasped. "You brought your girlfriend and human traffickers' into my home?"

Talos's control snapped. He shoved the table at Rossini, reached across, and hauled him off the chair. "What about after the baby was born, arsehole? How were you going to protect Jane then? Or did you think she'd just hand over her baby and go away without a fuss?"

Gibbs grabbed Talos from behind, locking his elbow around Talos's arm sockets and hauling back. The two guards attempted to prize Talos's hands off Rossini.

Fat chance. He could flatten all three of them without raising a sweat, but he had no gripe with them. He shook Rossini hard. "Answer me?"

"I thought I had time." Rossini voice shook. "I'm the one who leaked information about the warehouse deal and that Marzetti was alive and living in Willaroi. And, I tipped off Victor Vassello hoping he'd come after Marzetti. Then Jane wanted to go back to Willaroi for Kallie's birthday, so I figured I could leave her with her mother and get rid of Marzetti myself. But it all went to hell."

Gibbs yanked Talos. "He's not worth it, mate. Release him or I'll arrest you."

Jane grabbed Talos's arm. "Please, let him go. I don't want you arrested."

Afraid Jane would get hurt, he released Rossini, shook off Gibbs, and pulled Jane away from the table.

The guards sat Rossini back on the chair and glared at Talos. He ignored them and focused on Rossini. "Why didn't you just go to the police?"

"Because I was in too deep." He turned to Jane. "I'm sorry."

Jane stared back unblinking. "Have you any idea of the pain you put me through?" She looked down at her hands. "If that's all you've got to say, I'd like to leave now."

Rossini's gaze turned to Talos. "You have to believe me. I wasn't expecting Marzetti's partners to come to our apartment that day. It was a surprise visit, then Jane came home early and saw each of their faces. That's something they won't forget."

Jane reached for Talos's hand as she stared at her husband. "What are you saying?"

Rossini's gaze flicked to their joined hands then he focused on Jane. "You have two choices. You can go on the run, change your identity, and always be looking over your shoulder or..." He looked to Talos. "Hire someone who will find and terminate them."

Talos narrowed his eyes. "I don't terminate people."

"That's the only way you'll stop them. The ring members each meet with an agent in cities around Vietnam over the period of nine days. I can't tell you the agent's identity, but the first meeting is on Friday in Ho Chi Min City."

"Wait." Talos narrowed his eyes. "If Marzetti's been hiding out in

Willaroi for the past ten or so years, when did he have time to fly to Vietnam?"

"Twice a year he pretended to go to Brisbane for medical checkups and therapy."

Gibbs pushed a pad and biro across to Rossini. "I want Marzetti's partner's names and descriptions. I also want the dates, times, and locations of the meetings."

"I only know their code names. Kazan, Ripon, Lhasa, and Rong."

Jane stood, pushed her chair back and marched to the door. "I want to leave now."

One of the guards unlocked the door and Jane walked through without a backward glance. The guard followed then closed the door again.

Talos placed both hands on the table and glared at Rossini. "What are the chances they'll leave her alone?"

Rossini shook his head. "If you care about her, and I think you do, then you only have one choice. You must get them before they get her." He began scribbling.

Gibbs also stood. "Why do you care, Rossini? What's in it for you?"

He shrugged. "They won't let me live long enough to formally identify anyone, so I want you to take them out before they get to me." He tapped the pad. "If I were to die, you'll need Jane to identify these people, which means she's on their hit list too."

Talos stepped closer but Gibbs put out a restraining hand and directed his attention back to Rossini. "So bringing Jane here today was just a ploy to save your own skin."

Rossini stared at Talos. "I told you once before, you have no idea who you're fucking with or what they're capable of doing to a person."

Leaning across the table, Talos lowered his voice to just above a whisper. "The same can be said of me." He straightened. "If I was Marzetti, I'd change the meeting dates and times in case you gave that information to the Feds."

"Marzetti doesn't know I have this information and as he's in solitary confinement he can't contact his partners. Any one of them can give the order to kill me or Jane."

"I'll protect her."

Rossini sneered. "You're wasting your energy. She's an ice queen.

It took me five months to get a date, then another six and an engagement ring before she'd open her legs."

Rage ripped through Talos. He snarled, shoved the table sideways, and sprang forward. Rossini's eyes widened. He shrank back and raised his cuffed hands but he wasn't fast enough. Talos ploughed his fist into Rossini's face, his full weight behind the impact. Bone snapped, something popped, and Rossini's nose flattened.

The guards hovered either side of Rossini, seemingly unsure of what they should do.

Choking and spluttering, Rossini covered his smashed nose with his hands. Blood spewed through his fingers and down his face. "He broke my fucking nose again."

Having sprung to his feet, Gibbs stared down at Rossini. "You're lucky that's all he broke." He turned to Talos and glared. "Get the fuck out of here."

Gritting his teeth, Talos strode to the door, his temper at boiling point.

He was directed to an office where he found Jane standing by a window with her arms crossed. She turned and swallowed, despair clear in her eyes.

"Talos, I can't involve you any further. It would be better if you stayed away from me."

"That's not going to happen, Jane."

"You heard him. I have to disappear." A tear ran down her cheek. "Mum and Ken will probably insist on coming with me, but I can never see you or Kallie again, and I can't go back to teaching." She bit her lip. "It's so unfair."

"There's another possibility." Talos crossed the room and drew her into his arms. "The team has been hired to break up Marzetti's ring. We *will* find each of them and they'll be handed over to the Vietnamese Police who will deal with them properly."

Jane rested her cheek against his chest. "I wish I'd met you under different circumstances then maybe Ella would be yours. Andrew didn't even ask about her."

"Hey, just because Ella doesn't have my DNA doesn't mean I can't take care of her."

Pulling back, Jane stretched up and kissed his lips. "You're one in a million, Talos, but I can't take you away from your friends and family." She stepped away as the door opened.

Gibbs stuck his head into the room. "Ready to go?"

Jane's shoulders slumped. "Yes."

Talos clenched his fists, looking for something to hit. *I finally meet a woman I want to have a proper relationship with and everyone is conspiring to keep us apart. Well it's not going to happen.*

He stewed all the way to the Botanical Gardens. Each time he glanced at Jane she was staring out her window. Talos's gut twisted and churned. Jane wasn't the sort of person to put anyone in danger, which meant she would distance herself from him and her loved ones. *All thanks to that fucking scumbag. Rossini's not concerned about Jane. He just wants revenge on Marzetti and the other partners.*

Chapter Eight

Wearing a baseball cap and sunglasses, Jane strolled beside Kallie, who had control of the stroller. Sam and Talos were close behind, deep in conversation, although each time Jane glanced over her shoulder she observed them continually scanning. Nick and Ryan were also in the gardens, somewhere.

They ambled along a pathway until they came to a rose garden where they stopped. Jane leaned down to smell a fragrant pink bloom. Its scent reminded her of spring and the soft petals were like velvet.

"It's so calm and peaceful, isn't it?" Kallie swept her hand across the lush green lawns. "I had no idea it was so big an area."

"Neither did I," agreed Jane. "Let's head down that path and see where it takes us." She checked over her shoulder again and met Talos's gaze. He smiled and her heart somersaulted. *Maybe there is hope for us. It happened for Kallie and Sam.* Looking ahead again she made a silent vow to find out everything she could about Talos and his life.

They descended to another path and a giant lily pond, café, and restaurant. Talos bought drinks and hamburgers for everyone, then they crossed to a giant paper bark tree to sit, eat their lunch, and chat in easy camaraderie.

Ella woke and after feeding her, Jane changed her nappy then lay her on the bunny rug, free to kick and gurgle in the fresh air, without a worry in the world.

"I wish we could stay here all day." Jane leaned back on her elbows and absorbed the scene before her. The gentle sloping grass led down to a large pond with several fountains in its center. Beyond the pond and parkland of trees, the Harbour Bridge and Opera House could be seen. Ducks paddled to the edge of the pond where an Asian family was throwing bits of bread to them. Two elderly ladies sat on a park bench chatting and a jogger ran along pushing a stroller ahead of her. *Lucky things.*

Talos moved closer. "What's up?"

"Nothing. I was just enjoying the view."

"When we have more time, I'll take you out to Mrs. Macquarie's Chair and around Farm Cove to the Opera House. You need several hours to see the gardens properly."

She smiled at him. "You promise?"

"Yes." He brushed an insect off Ella then leaned back on his elbows and looked around. "We'll come in September. There's more flowers then."

Jane closed her eyes and inhaled his cologne. "I'd like that." *I'd like that very much.*

"We're just going down to the pond," announced Kallie.

Opening her eyes, Jane watched Kallie and Sam stroll away hand in hand. She smiled when Sam pulled Kallie closer and kissed her lightly. Jane glanced at Talos; he was observing two teenage boys sitting on the grass several meters away. Ella lay sleeping, tucked snugly by his side. Jane shuffled round and lay down, resting her head on Talos's stomach.

Closing her eyes, she let her mind drift to the kiss she'd shared with him and the feelings it had awakened. Not once had she experienced that kind of connection with Andrew. *If only I could be sure Talos's feelings are genuine and not as a result of feeling responsible for me. I'm so afraid to give him my heart and then have him reject me.*

As she began to drift off something tickled her cheek, she flicked it away then it tickled her nose. Jane opened her eyes to see a piece of grass suspended above her nose.

"Talos, I was nearly asleep."

He chuckled. "If you fall asleep now, you won't sleep tonight."

"I haven't slept well for months. I need my catnaps."

He scooped Ella up and lay her in the stroller. "I know a sure way to make you sleep." He smiled slow and sexy then slid his arms under Jane and lifted her onto his lap. "I guarantee it."

Jane's pulse leapt. To spend her nights in his arms would be heaven on earth and then hell when he left her. She raised a finger and touched his lips. "As tempting as that sounds, Talos, it's not going to happen."

"Want a bet?" He kissed her nose. "I'll still be here when you change your mind."

"Talos."

He placed her back on the grass, surged to his feet and held out his hand. "Come on, we'd better get moving if we intend getting home before dark."

Home. Jane gave him her hand. The sun seemed to lose its heat at the mention of the word home. *Damn Andrew.* She picked up Ella's rug and tucked it round her. Talos pushed the stroller and they rambled across the grass towards Kallie and Sam, standing by the pond.

"Wait." Talos put the brake on and crossed to an ice-cream vendor. He came back with two cones and presented one to Jane, wrapped in a serviette. "A walk in the gardens is not complete without an ice cream."

"Thank you, Talos." Biting into the creamy confection, Jane's gaze fell on the two elderly ladies, sitting on a park bench beaming at her. She smiled back then one of the ladies waved at her to come over.

Talos glanced around then nodded and pushed the stroller closer. "Hello, ladies, it's a lovely afternoon, isn't it?"

"Yes," replied one peeping into the stroller. "Oh, what a sweet little baby."

The other lady touched Jane's hand. "My sister and I were just commenting on what a lovely couple you and your husband make."

Jane's heart constricted. *If only that were true.*

A large hand slid around Jane's waist. "I couldn't agree more." Talos smiled at the two ladies then handed Jane his ice cream and pulled out his phone. "Would one of you ladies mind taking a photo for us?"

"I'd be delighted," crowed one. "Just show me what to press."

Jane elbowed Talos as discreetly as she could and whispered, "What are you doing?"

"Getting a memento." He showed the elderly lady what to press, then pulled Jane closer and locked his arm around her. "Smile."

Jane donged him on the nose with his ice cream.

His eyes widened then he laughed and took a bite out of it before grabbing her wrist and donging her on the nose with her ice cream. Jane laughed so hard tears ran down her face. She gave Talos his ice cream and used her serviette to wipe her eyes and nose.

"Thank you, Talos. This *has* been a lovely day." She dabbed the ice cream off his nose, stretched up, and kissed his cheek. "And you're a lovely man."

"Oh what a nice thing to say," cooed one of the ladies.

Jane begrudgingly dragged her gaze away from Talos to see the elderly lady holding out the phone. Talos was still staring at Jane intently. She pulled out of his arm and took the phone. "Thank you, I hope you enjoy the rest of your day."

Both ladies smiled then went back to their conversation.

Maneuvering the stroller around, Jane handed Talos his phone and they continued on the path to Kallie and Sam, then all four took a path leading uphill towards a tall pine. The others went to walk on by, but for some reason Jane felt it pulling her.

"Wait, I want to read the plaque." She ran across to the pine. "It's a wishing tree."

"Really." Talos raised his eyebrow in what could only be described as skepticism.

Kallie jogged round to join Jane. "It *is* a wishing tree. It says here that back in 1816, Mrs. Macquarie, wife of Governor Macquarie, decided she wanted a Norfolk Island Pine planted in the Botanical Gardens. People would come to make wishes because they believed ancient trees contained spirits. If you walked around it three times forward then three times backward, your wish will come true. This is where the saying touch wood originated. Wow, I never knew that."

"That tree is not two hundred years old," stated Sam.

Kallie rolled her eyes. "No. It says the original tree decayed and was removed in 1945. This is the first Wollemi Pine to ever be planted." She grinned at Jane. "Let's make a wish."

Jane glanced at Talos rocking the stroller back and forth as he stood beside Sam. If only she'd met Talos before Andrew. Their two families would have been so close.

They could still be.

"Okay." Squeezing her eyes shut, Jane tried to decide what she wanted most then decided to cheat as she combined the most important things. *I wish for Talos to truly love and desire me as we raise Ella together without the threat of Marzetti or his partners hurting us.* She opened her eyes, grinned at Kallie and walked around the tree three times. Then did it backwards and repeated the wish, just in case.

Kallie did it as well and then they both hugged each other and joined the two men who had captured their hearts.

Several hours later, Jane followed her mother through Sam's house and decided Kallie was a very lucky girl. Sam had built the house out of stone with cedar windows and polished timber floors. Kallie's touch was everywhere. Colorful cushions, framed photos', a plate of fruit and several decorative pots with striking floral arrangements. Jane's heart swelled with the knowledge her friend would be happy here with Sam and her precious horses.

Jane's mother stopped at the bottom of the stairs. "I'm so glad you and Eloise are here." She rocked Ella in her arms. "It's been terrible not knowing where you were and having a granddaughter I couldn't see or hold."

"I know." Jane forced a smile. Her mother would flip when she discovered they were to be separated again for who knew how long.

Liz led the way upstairs. "Kallie's put you in the room at the top of the stairs. Did you know James Talarico lives next door? His father, Costa, has been bringing me fresh vegetables. He has three daughters as well and divides his time between all of them."

Jane hesitated, guilt washing over her. "I didn't know Talos had three sisters." *Another reason I can't get involved with him.* The idea of taking him away from his family and into witness protection was impossible. "Where do they live?"

"Adelaide, Melbourne, and Newcastle. Costa has a caravan, which makes things easier. The two eldest girls are married with children and the youngest one is still single."

"It sounds like you've spent a bit of time with Costa."

"Not as much as Ken, but now that your stepfather's reputation has been cleared, he's very sociable. Dominic Marzetti has a lot to answer for."

"Yes." *If you only knew.*

"Jarred was afraid Marzetti might have someone watching our house or listening in on our phone calls so he suggested we come here. I must say, it's very generous of Sam to open up his home to us." Liz shuffled Ella and opened a door. "Here we are. This is your room."

Jane walked into a pretty bedroom decorated in autumn colors. The window looked across green fields to a large timber home on the property next door.

"Is that where Talos lives?"

"Yes. Costa told us his son built the house practically all on his own. Apparently James is very good with his hands."

I can only imagine. Jane stared at the house in the distance. It had a Swiss chalet look about it. "Have you met Costa's wife?"

"She's no longer alive. Costa said she died when the youngest girl was five."

A shiver ran down Jane's spine. So caught up in her own problems she'd never thought to ask Talos about his family. Yet he knew so much about her. "Is Costa here at the moment?"

"No, he had to race off this morning and check on his youngest daughter. Apparently she lives in a ground floor unit and someone's been knocking on her door late at night."

"Does Talos know?"

"Costa didn't want to bother James while he's on a job, so he went to check on his daughter himself, but now that you're here, I'm sure James would want to know."

"Yes, so am I." Jane sat on the edge of the queen-sized bed and watched as her mother lay Ella in the padded carrier and fussed over her.

The door flew open and Kallie rushed in. "Isn't this house incredible? Sam and Talos built it from scratch, then Sam helped Talos with his house." She sat on the bed.

"It's lovely, Kallie, and it suits the two of you perfectly. How are your horses?"

"Fine. Aramis has completely recovered from his ordeal and is busy flirting with the mares. I was so scared the police would shoot him after he trampled that jerk to death."

"No way. Aramis is a hero. What else have you done since coming here?"

"We've built a stable block and lunging ring. Oh, and Roy is having a cottage built. He and Bunny are getting married and coming to live here."

Liz huffed. "And it's about time too. Since the plane crash Roy has put his own life on hold to raise Kallie. Now he and Bunny can finally have a life together."

Glancing at Kallie, Jane rolled her eyes. Would her mother ever think before speaking? The plane crash that had killed Jane's father and both Kallie's parents and grandparents had left a hole in all their hearts. Kallie hadn't been put into foster care thanks to Roy, an Aboriginal stockman who had thankfully been made her legal guardian.

Jane's mother smiled. "Right, well I'll leave you girls to have a chat while I check on dinner. Don't be too long."

"Thanks, Liz." The door closed and Kallie turned to Jane. "I can't help noticing that you and Talos seem close and I get the impression Talos wants more?

"Wanting is not enough, Kallie. I need him to love me."

Kallie squeezed her hand. "I couldn't say anything earlier, but I listened at the door when Inspector Gibbs told Jarred and Sam what happened at the prison."

Biting her lip, Jane swallowed hard. Kallie was her best friend and they were closer than most sisters. To never see her again was unimaginable. Yet what choice did she have?

"Ella and I have to go away again. I can't stay here and put your life in jeopardy."

"I'll come with you."

"No, sweetie. What about Sam, and Roy, and your horses?"

"Well then, we'll all stay here. Sam will look after us.

"And how will you feel if a sniper shoots Sam?"

Kallie blinked. "That's not going to happen. I couldn't bear not seeing you."

Flopping back on the bed, Jane stared at the ceiling. "Andrew inferred I should get Talos to hunt down Marzetti's gang and kill them all before they kill me."

"They don't do that sort of thing." Kallie's voice shook.

"No, but Talos said they've been hired to go to Vietnam and break up Marzetti's ring. If they can be positively identified, they'll go to prison, perhaps for life."

"Who is going to identify them? Marzetti won't and Andrew is locked up in jail."

"Andrew's given Inspector Gibbs their code names and the location of their meetings. I guess if they're caught, he will have to formally identify them."

Kallie frowned. "If the team goes to Vietnam, who will guard us?"

"Sam wouldn't leave you alone and I'm to be stuck in another safe house."

"Over my dead body."

Pulling a cushion over her head, Jane groaned. "That's one of the things I'm afraid of."

Kallie hauled Jane up. "I'll think of something, don't I always?"

"That's that other thing I'm afraid about."

"Come on, Ella's asleep and your mum's cooked a roast dinner with custard pudding for dessert. Everything will seem better once we've eaten."

"I guess so."

As they entered the big family room, Ajax barked and bounded to Kallie. Jane laughed. "He's really taken to you, hasn't he?"

"Oh yes, we're good buddies. Ajax even likes Webster. I don't think anyone told him cats and dogs don't get on."

They both gave Ajax a pat and turned to the table where everyone was seated and waiting for them. Jane pushed her hair behind her ears and smoothed her shirt. "Sorry, we were just catching up." Her gaze locked on Talos, her handsome giant and the man she intended to leave behind. Her heart cracked and her appetite vanished.

"This looks delicious, Liz." Kallie slid onto the chair next to Sam.

"It should, I've been peeling vegetables for hours and we had to use the barbecue to cook the meat as there wasn't enough room in the oven."

"Thanks, mum." Sitting on the chair beside Talos, Jane stared at the platter of roast potato, pumpkin and carrot, bowls of steaming peas and cobs of corn, two legs of lamb, and several tureens of gravy. It was a feast fit for a king.

As everyone began talking and passing dishes around, Jane's

stepfather, Ken, tapped a spoon against his glass. "I'd like to say how grateful Liz and I are for what you fellas have done for us. My name's been cleared and you've brought down some very evil people. You saved both Kallie and Jane's lives and helped bring Eloise into the world, which we will be eternally grateful for. Thank you."

Liz smiled at Jane. "And once this court case is over, Ken and I are planning to buy a caravan and we're taking you and Eloise around Australia."

Jane's stomach knotted. *I don't want to leave Talos.*

Talos cleared his throat. "I don't think that's a good idea, Liz. At least not until all Marzetti's partners are in custody. I would prefer Jane and Ella stay here."

Turning to Talos, Jane asked. "Did mum tell you that your youngest sister has had someone knocking on her door late at night and running away?"

He looked at Liz. "No?"

Liz nodded. "Your father left this morning to check on her. He was quite concerned."

"I see." He frowned and rubbed his chin.

Jane placed her hand on his arm. "You should ring and see if everything's okay."

"It could just be kids, but I'll ring Lydia after we've eaten."

Ryan put down his knife and fork. "If there's a problem, I can go. You've got a lot on your plate and I haven't got anything on. Is Lydia still a timid little thing?"

"Timid isn't the word that springs to mind." Talos helped himself to a pile of vegetables. "Still, dad wouldn't go unless he was worried."

Over dinner, Jane noticed Talos's inattention to the conversation and as the others were getting up from the table she nudged him with her knee. "Go check on your sister. You'll never forgive yourself if something happens to her. I'll be fine here."

He grimaced. "If I go, I want you to promise me you won't wander off on your own or go anywhere with Gibbs."

"Gibbs? Why?"

"Marzetti's people found your safe house and I want to know how."

"All right, I promise."

"Good." He placed his hand on her knee and squeezed. A bolt of awareness shot through Jane as his hand moved higher. "I'll be back as soon as I can."

She squeaked. "Okay."

He rose from the table. "Thanks for a delicious dinner, Liz. I'd like to stay and chat, but I need to check on my sister."

"That's quite understandable, James. Maybe we'll see you when you get back?"

"Definitely." He glanced at Jane then strode from the room.

Jane watched him leave with trepidation. *I can't ask him to give up his family for me.*

After tidying the kitchen with Kallie, Jane went upstairs to bathe and feed Ella, then she tucked her into her portable carrier. Jane lost track of time as she gazed at her precious daughter, sleeping soundly, oblivious to her mother's turmoil.

"I love you, sweetie." Jane dropped a soft kiss on Ella's head and tiptoed out of the room, closing the door gently behind her. Kallie was waiting for her in the hall.

"What's really going on between you and Talos?"

Scrubbing her face, Jane sat on the top step. "He wants a relationship with me, but I'm afraid it's for the wrong reasons and I'm terrified he'll eventually break my heart."

Kallie sat down beside her and wrapped an arm around her shoulders. "For what it's worth, I think Talos really likes you. He could barely take his eyes off you today and Sam said Talos is very family orientated."

"That's another thing. If I have to go into long-term witness protection, I can't expect him to give up his family. I don't even know if he'd be prepared to."

"Hey, it might not come to that. How do you feel about him?"

Jane stared into her best friend's eyes. She couldn't lie. "I'm in love with him."

"I thought you might be." Kallie hugged her. "We'll figure this out."

CHAPTER NINE

After a restless night, and a day cooking with her mother, caring for Ella, and raking out stables, Jane climbed the stairs with a heavy heart. She'd spent hours considering Talos's offer, her feelings for him, and their future. But no matter what decision she made, five minutes later she'd change it. Her body ached from physical labour, yet yearned for just one touch from him. Her brain whirled as it battled against her heart to do the right thing and walk away. Jane wanted to kick, and scream, and hit something really hard, particularly Andrew.

As she lay Ella down a beam of headlights tracked across the bedroom wall. Jane ran to the window and craned her neck to see if it was Talos. Sam, Nick, Ryan, and Simon emerged out of the dark and stood under a sensor light on the curve of the drive. A sleek burgundy car pulled up and Jarred Steele climbed out. He spoke to them briefly then all five men headed towards the house, their expressions serious.

"Now what?" Jane picked up her toiletry case and hurried to the bathroom. Dinner was about to be served and Jane smelt of hay, sweat, and horses. No way was she facing Jarred Steele without showering. *Not that I want to impress him, but a girl has her pride.*

Hair shining and wearing a clean pair of jeans and shirt, Jane felt ready to hear whatever Jarred had to say. A shiver of premonition ran down her spine. It wouldn't be good. She opened the bedroom door and jumped at the sight of her mother hovering there, wringing her hands.

"What's happened?"

"I'm sorry, luv, but Jarred Steele has arrived with terrible news. It's rocked us all."

Fear clutched Jane's heart as she stared at her mother's pale face. "Tell me."

"You've been through so much already and this could tip you over the edge. I know how you feel about him."

Talos. Her heart hammering in her chest, Jane tore down the stairs and into the family room. All conversation died as she burst through the doorway. Jane's gaze shot to Kallie sitting on the couch clutching Sam's hand. Ryan, Nick, Simon, and Jarred stood by the fireplace wearing sober expressions. Ken leaned against the kitchen bench looking shell-shocked.

Drawing a shaky breath, Jane focused on Jarred. "Please tell me it's not Talos?"

His steely eyes locked on her. "No, it's not Talos."

"Thank God." Jane sank onto the arm of the couch, the relief turning her legs to jelly. "Mum said you had terrible news."

"I do. Inspector Gibbs rang earlier to inform me that your husband was found dead in his cell this afternoon. I thought I should drive up here and tell you in person."

Jane blinked. "Andrew's dead? How?"

"We won't know until an autopsy has been done, but it's possible his last meal was laced with a lethal dose of poison."

"Poison." Jane endeavored to elicit some sense of compassion for a man who traded in human trafficking and had only married her to get his hands on Kallie's diamond. A man who rejected her when she refused to abort their baby and claimed her pregnant body repulsed him. A man who didn't even enquire about his own daughter's health or apologize for his cruel behavior.

Stiffening with renewed anger and disgust, Jane glowered at Jarred. "I refuse to be a hypocrite and mourn a man I despise. What happens now?"

Jarred placed his cup on the mantle. "Marzetti refused to give up his partner's real names and now you're our only chance to identify them."

"I saw their faces but I don't know their names."

"I am aware of that. Inspector Gibbs has their code names and the dates, locations, and times of the proposed meetings. We will need descriptions from you and then my team will go to Vietnam and liaise with the Serious Crime Unit there. We will endeavor to apprehend the other members and get you to identify them via a video link up. They will be dealt with by the Vietnamese police."

"I see." Jane's stomach twisted and churned as she summed up the courage to ask her next question. "If they're all caught and jailed will I be able to resume my life as I want?"

"It's unlikely. Gibbs is coming to get you in the morning, then after the trial you will be given a new identity and probably moved interstate permanently."

Her mother and Kallie both gasped.

The shock in their eyes was akin to a knife piercing Jane's heart. Digging her fingernails into her palms, she focused on Jarred. "This isn't fair."

"I know and I'm sorry."

"Does Talos know about Andrew?"

"No."

I'll be gone before he gets back. It was hard to breath, her chest hurt as if it were being crushed in a vice. The hope of a future with Talos went up in flames. She blinked back tears and held in a sob, wishing she could throw a tantrum or lash out at someone. If Andrew weren't already dead, she'd punch him in his busted nose. *It's over.*

Tasting blood, she realized she'd bitten her lip. "I think I'll go to my room."

"Luv, what about your dinner?" asked her mother.

"I'm not hungry, and if you don't mind, I'd like to be alone." She turned and trudged from the room, too caught up in her own misery to even try to be sociable.

Upstairs, she spent several hours mulling over her choices. If Talos didn't completely trust Inspector Gibbs then no-way was she going anywhere with him, but she couldn't stay here either. That would put everyone she held dear in danger. *What do I do?*

She eventually eased out of the armchair and stretched her cramped muscles. *Think.* Wandering over to the window she was met with a blanket of darkness. No light, no stars, no moon. It mirrored her uncertain future.

A light knock sounded and Jane turned from the window as the door opened, throwing a shaft of light into the room. Kallie poked her head around the door.

"Hey, how are you feeling?"

Jane shrugged. "Not great."

"I thought you'd like to know that Sam rang Talos and brought him up to date."

"He shouldn't have done that. Talos has enough on his plate without worrying about me." Turning back to the window, Jane stared towards the dark shape of Talos's house. She sighed. "I wish I'd had more time with him, just to say goodbye."

Kallie came to stand beside her. "We can organize that."

"How, he's in Newcastle."

"No, he's not. After Sam spoke to him, Talos decided to come home. He called in but Ken told him you'd gone to bed. He said he'd talk to you first thing in the morning." Kallie crossed the room. "Sweetie, things happen for a reason. If you hadn't married Andrew, you wouldn't have Ella, and you never would have met Talos. Now it's up to you to choose which path to take. You said you're in love with Talos?"

"I am, but it's pointless. We can't have a future together and Jarred's got surveillance cameras everywhere, he'll never let me leave."

"I'm sure I can talk Sam into sneaking you across to Talos's house and I'll watch Ella."

Jane glanced at her precious daughter sleeping soundly in her padded bassinette in the middle of the crib. She bit her lip and turned back to the window and the house in the distance. *This will be the last chance I have to talk to Talos and maybe steal one more kiss.*

"Okay." A thrill of excitement shot through her body. "I'll express some milk in case Ella wakes. Give me ten minutes, no make it twenty."

Kallie grinned. "I'll talk to Sam. He and Simon are on watch tonight. And I'll sleep in here with Ella until you get back." She hugged Jane. "But as your fairy godmother, I must insist you're back before Inspector Gibbs gets here or all hell will break loose."

"I won't be that long." Jane squeezed Kallie tight. "I love you."

"Ditto, sweetie." Kallie returned the squeeze then hurried from the room.

Twenty-five minutes later, Jane tiptoed down the stairs, then past the family room, where she could see Ken watching an action movie. She passed another room where Jarred, Ryan, and Nick were playing a game of pool as they discussed plans for Vietnam.

As Jane eased out the back door, Sam came up the steps. "Give me your hand, we're going by foot and I don't want you falling over."

"Thank you, Sam." Jane slid her hand into his, taking comfort from the fact he was willing to help her at all. A cool breeze caught Jane unawares and she shivered through her thin shirt. Glancing up she noticed a heavy layer of cloud. Thunder rumbled.

They ran across dew-covered grass to a barbwire fence where Sam put his boot on the lower wire and lifted the top one, his muscles bunching as he created enough space for her to climb through without catching her clothes on the barbs. She tried to return the favor but no way could she move the tightly strained wire.

"It's fine." Sam strode to the post and launched himself over with room to spare. He pointed to a white cable running parallel to the middle wire. "That electrifies the fence. Simon's also set up surveillance cameras that are activated by movement. Get Talos to call me before he brings you back and I'll turn them off again."

"Okay." Jane studied Sam covertly as he took her hand again. He wasn't quite as tall as Talos, few men were, but he was just as well built and extremely attractive. Interestingly enough she felt no zing of excitement or racing heart from the touch of his hand. Talos only had to look at her and she melted with desire. His kiss had almost paralyzed her.

As they got closer to Talos's house, Jane heard loud continuous striking and heavy grunts. "What's that?"

"Talos. When he's angry or frustrated, he needs to physically vent."

Jane shivered at the thought of a violent Talos. "What's he doing?"

Sam chuckled. "Chopping firewood. His father, Costa, taught us both to vent our anger by doing something physical, as in exercise or hard labour. It also gives you time to think before doing something stupid and it comes in handy in winter."

"What if there's no axe?"

"Then we beat the shi...stuffing out of a boxing bag or go for a long run. Don't look so worried. Neither of us have ever hit a woman in our lives, but we've wrecked a few sparring bags."

"Why is Talos so angry?"

"I presume it's because Gibbs wants you in protective custody." Sam halted. "You'll find Talos behind the water tank. We're monitoring his boundaries now as well as mine."

"Thank you, Sam." She hesitated. "I'm really glad you and Kallie are getting married."

"So am I." He winked and jogged back into the darkness, barely making a sound.

Jane drew back her shoulders and walked towards the tank. *Maybe Talos cares for me more than I thought. The fact he's angry with Inspector Gibbs is a good sign, isn't it?*

The chopping stopped as she rounded the water tank.

Jane froze and stared in awe as Talos hefted a large log off the ground, the muscles in his naked back and shoulders straining under the enormous weight. He dragged it onto a spiked rack and picked up an axe, raised it high, and swung it vehemently into the timber, his grunt echoing in the still air.

Gaping, Jane followed every movement as he loosened the axe then plowed it into the timber again and again, sending woodchips flying in all directions. When he was half way through the log, he turned and lifted the axe.

Jane's lungs seized. *My God, he's magnificent.* Sweat glistened on his massive chest and arms as he swung the axe hard into the wood. The shadow of bristles on his lower face along with his olive complexion gave him the appearance of a sexy desert sheikh. His trousers sat low on his hips drawing her attention to the bunched muscles spanning his abdomen and the hairline disappearing beneath his waistband. There wasn't an ounce of fat on him, just toned beautiful muscle. *Why would a man like that want me?* She closed her eyes. *This was a terrible idea.*

She realized the chopping had stopped and opened her eyes. Talos stood in front of the demolished log, the axe held across his body, his breathing ragged and his gaze locked on her. She couldn't have moved if her life depended on it. Her feet were glued to the ground.

Talos lowered the axe and blindly reached for the wheelbarrow where he'd thrown his T-shirt. He didn't dare take his eyes off the beautiful woman before him in case she disappeared. She had the look of a deer ready for flight at the slightest provocation.

"Don't move."

Talos reached for his T-shirt then slowly wiped the sweat off each of his arms, his chest and the lower part of his face, conscious her gaze tracked his every move. Not once did he take his eyes off her as lust clawed at his gut. He tossed his shirt across his shoulder.

"Hello, Jane."

She licked her lips. "I needed to see you. To be with you."

There is a God. His lips twitched. "So what are you doing over there?" Talos mentally crossed his fingers and opened his arms wide. "Come here."

"Oh, Talos." She ran across the yard and threw herself at him.

Wrapping his arms around her supple body, he lifted her off the ground and clasped her to his chest. She draped her arms around his shoulders and buried her face against his neck, her warm breath tickling his skin and sending delicious tremors throughout his body. He wanted to bury himself inside her, here and now.

No. He clenched his jaw, reined in his rampant lust, and tried to assemble his scrambled wits. His gaze went to the house where the glow of flames from the fireplace sent shadows flickering across the ceiling of his family room. It looked warm and inviting. *You'll only get one chance to get this right, so don't fuck it up. Make sure she's on the same page.*

"Hey, what's this all about?" Unable to help himself, he stroked her back and kissed her silky head. Her hair smelt of jasmine. He inhaled deeply. It only made matters worse. He was growing harder by the second.

Jane leaned back and met his gaze. "I know I shouldn't be here, but I was afraid I'd never see you again and I couldn't leave without saying goodbye properly."

"Honey, that's not going to happen. You're not going anywhere."

"Last time Inspector Gibbs came for me, it was the middle of the night and he bundled Ella and I into his car. Nobody had any idea where we'd been taken. The thought of never seeing you again..." Her voice cracked. "Talos, I've never felt this way about any other man."

Elation burst over Talos. "God help me, Jane. I've never wanted a woman like I want you." He slowly lowered her to the ground, fearful if he held her close for a second longer, he wouldn't be responsible for his actions.

She placed her small hands on his naked chest. "Then what are we going to do about it?"

All Talos's good intentions went down the drain. "I can think of several things." He slid his hands down either side of her spine, cupped her bottom, and hoisted her up against his erection, crushing her breasts against his chest.

She surprised him by wrapping her legs around his waist and locking her ankles at the base of his spine. Her dilated pupils mirrored the desire racking his body.

I have to get her into the house, but first. Lowering his head he kissed her fiercely and when her lips parted, he delved inside, exploring her mouth with his tongue, demanding everything she had and more. He groaned as lust ricocheted throughout his body. Jane responded by pressing closer. Her kisses were like an elixir to his hardened soul. The sensation of her breasts pressed to his chest had him wanting to tear off her clothes and explore every inch of her.

A moan escaped her soft lips and she wriggled her lower body closer against his erection. Talos had never experienced such an intense craving. No way was Gibbs going to take her away from him.

They broke apart, both breathing heavily.

A soft flush bloomed in Jane's cheeks. "I meant, what are we going to do about Gibbs; not that I'm complaining. I'm glad you came back."

"Wild horses couldn't keep me away and my sister, Lydia, was all for it."

"Your sister knows about me?"

"Yes. Ella's car seat was a giveaway. Lydia wouldn't rest until I told her everything."

"Is Lydia all right? Did you find out who's knocking on her door?"

"No, but I installed a sensor camera and gave the teenagers next-door fifty bucks to keep an eye out. My dad's going to stay there in the meantime, just in case."

A low rumble of thunder sounded in the distance and a cool breeze skimmed over them. Jane shivered. "Here comes the rain."

"Then I'd better get you inside." Talos swung her off his waist and into his arms then strode towards the house. "I'm guessing you left Ella with Kallie?"

"Yes, and Sam brought me over."

"Who else knows you're here?"

"Simon's manning the cameras, so I guess he knows, but that's all."

"How long do we have before you have to feed Ella?"

"She sleeps through now, but I've left a bottle with Kallie just in case."

He mounted the stairs leading up to the decking. "Good, that's suits me perfectly."

"Oh."

Talos felt her shiver. *Slow down buddy, you've got to handle this right.* He reached the decking and crossed it in three strides then balancing her, he managed to kick off his boots.

"When I spoke to Ken earlier, he told me you went to your room without dinner, so how about I make you something to eat, then we can sit by the fire and talk."

"Talk!" Jane's eyes narrowed. "That's the last thing I expected you to say."

Talos couldn't help chuckling. "Once you've eaten, I'd like to kiss you again."

"Um," she blinked rapidly. "I'm not hungry."

"You will be."

CHAPTER TEN

Warmth infused Jane as Talos carried her across the threshold and lowered her to the floor. She dragged her gaze away from his handsome face and scanned the enormous room. A large wooden kitchen with a granite bench took up one end of the room. In the middle stood a solid dining table, eight chairs, and a rustic chandelier overhead. Beyond the dining table on the back wall, a set of stairs led up to the floor above. She glanced to the other end of the room to an open stone fireplace, the logs burning in it encased in flames of red, orange and yellow. A thick rug lay in front surrounded by three lounges.

Talos swung around, closed and locked the sliding window then looked at her. "I built this house. Do you like it?"

"It's lovely." Jane glanced over Talos's shoulder and noticed the wall of glass windows on either side of the sliding door they'd entered through. The house had a warm, inviting ambiance, as if a large family were due home any minute. She repressed the thought. "Mum said you were clever with your hands, but I had no idea."

"Oh, I'm very clever with my hands." His lips twitched as he took her hand. "Come over to the fire, you're shivering." He led her to a thick rug in front of the open fire. "I'd like you and Ella to come and live here with me."

Jane's heart constricted. It was a pipe dream. She couldn't endanger him by staying and she wouldn't take him away from his family and friends. Whatever happened next would be all she would have to remember him by.

He stroked her cheek. "Don't move. I'll be back in a sec."

"Okay." She watched him cross to the windows and pull the heavy curtains closed. He winked and strode to the stairs, mounting them three at a time.

Kicking off her shoes, Jane curled her toes in the thick rug. *We're going to make love.* Her stomach fluttered. *One night of passion is all I can have with Talos to hold in my heart.*

He bounded back down the stairs a couple of minutes later with his arms full. "We might as well be comfortable while we *talk.*" He gave her a wicked grin as he spread out a thick quilt and arranged two pillows.

Jane's heart flipped. *He's a romantic, how lovely.* She focused on his powerfully built chest and shoulders that would leave Hercules feeling inadequate. Raising her gaze, she locked on his cognac eyes. It was easy to imagine him lying here in front of the fire, amongst the rumpled quilt in the aftermath of lovemaking. An olive skinned sheikh in all his naked glory. She licked her lips, stepped closer, and caressed his magnificent chest.

"What did you want to talk about?"

He gave her a lazy smile and placed his hands on her hips. "I want to get to know you. Every beautiful inch of you."

"Arh." Stretching up, she kissed his full lips then flinch as a clap of thunder sounded overhead and the heavens opened, hammering the roof in an incessant drumming.

Talos pulled her against his body and Jane dragged in a breath then slid her palms down his arms, caught his hands, and sank to her bottom, pulling him with her. "I love the rain at night. This is perfect."

"Hmm. It will certainly mask your screams."

She frowned. "My screams?"

"Yes, sweetheart, your screams." He pushed her backwards and fell on her.

Laughing, Jane batted his shoulder. "I don't scream."

"That says a lot. You will with me."

He lowered his head and captured her lips in a kiss that scrambled her wits. For the second time that night, he stole her breath. Talos's huge body pressed her into the quilt intimately. He plundered her mouth, his whiskers tickling her chin and upper lip, his erection pressed hard against her stomach. Jane wound her arms around his neck, wrapped her legs around his waist and wantonly rocked against him.

Talos inwardly groaned. She was like a fantasy come true, delicate to his heavy, soft to his hard, a temptation he couldn't refuse. "Jesus, I've got to get out of these trousers."

She giggled. "That would help."

Grabbing her ankles, Talos pulled her legs from around him and came up on his knees. He stared down at her flushed face. "You first." He flicked the button on her jeans, undid the zipper and dragged them down, taking her silky black panties with them.

Her flush deepened but she didn't stop him as he edged backwards and tugged her jeans and panties off her long, shapely legs. He threw them behind and fastened his eyes on her softly rounded tummy and the thatch of dark curls below. "You're so beautiful." He stood, stripped off his own trousers and jocks, then sank to his knees between her legs.

Her eyes locked on his erect cock and widened. "You're big all over, aren't you?" She swallowed, blinked, and raised her gaze to his.

Grinning, Talos pushed her legs wider. "You could say that."

She chewed her lower lip. "I've never had a one-night stand before."

Talos frowned as unease raced through his body. He'd had plenty of one-night stands. They'd been a way of filling a void without any emotional attachment. Jane was not a one-night stand, at least not from his point of view. He glided his hands over her smooth legs and up her inner thighs as he studied her face. She quivered under his touch.

"Is that what you want, Jane? A one-night stand?"

Her eyes shimmered and she shook her head. "No, my precious giant, but that's all I can have. One night of passion to remember you by for the rest of my life."

Talos drew in a lung full of air. Her endearment and heartfelt words erased his anxiety. Leaning over he brushed her lips with his. "This was never going to be a one-night stand, sweetheart. Now that I've found you, I plan on taking advantage of you every night and every morning for a very, very long time."

She licked her lips. "If this is a dream, I'm going to be very unhappy."

Chuckling, Talos undid her shirt's top button and layered kisses down her slender neck where her pulse beat rapidly then he kissed his way along her shoulder blade. "This is no dream, sweetheart." He undid the next two buttons, pushed her shirt wide, and placed kisses over the black bra to her pebbled nipple.

She arched her back and pressed against his mouth. "Oh, Talos."

He pulled away and undid the last button, peeled her shirt and bra off, then sat back on his ankles to better appreciate her bounty. Lust roared. She was everything he'd dreamed she'd be and more. Leaning down, he kissed her long and hard, then took one breast in his hand and massaged, rolling and tweaking the nipple.

She moaned. "Yes."

Talos turned his attention to her other breast in his mouth, suckling, rolling and licking the nipple with his tongue. Warm sweet fluid filled his mouth. He swallowed. "You're leaking breast milk."

"I'm not surprised. This is very stimulating."

Nudging her knees wider, he rubbed himself against her wet center.

"Talos, I'm going to come."

"No." He pulled away again. "You're one very sensitive lady."

She groaned. "It's been a long time and you have no idea what you do to me." She locked her legs around him. "You're making me desperate."

"Good." Her honesty was another thing Talos found refreshing. He took her mouth again, thoroughly and deeply until they were both gasping for breath, then he nudged her legs apart as he settled between them and worshipped her luscious breasts until she was writhing and moaning under him.

Talos reveled as Jane raked her fingers through his hair, stroked her feet along his calves, and scored her nails over his hot skin, sending electrical pulses shooting through his body. He traced a finger through her wet curls then pushed his finger inside her. She bucked and cried out, digging her nails into his shoulders. Talos inwardly cheered. *Wildcat.*

Edging lower, he kissed her ribs and stomach. A quiver ran over her warm skin. Talos lifted his head and watched her face as he gripped the underside of her knees and lifted them over his shoulders.

Jane's eyelids flew open revealing vibrant green eyes ablaze with passion as her breasts rose and fell rapidly. Sliding his hands under her bottom, Talos lifted her to meet him. She cried out as he thrust his tongue deep inside, licking, sucking, feasting on her flowing juices. Her fingers clamped his hair.

"Talos, oh God, Talos."

He rolled his tongue around her sensitive nub then sucked hard. Her body quivered, she stiffened and screamed, piercingly.

Pleased, Talos lowered her limp legs, wiped his mouth and sat back on his ankles. A soft smile played on her lips, as she lay replete watching him.

She gave a contented sigh. "I've never screamed, ever." Her gaze lowered to his erection and she reached out.

"No." Talos caught her hand. "I'm not finished with *you* yet." He lifted her over his thighs, spreading her knees, then ran his fingers through her wet folds.

She gasped and jerked.

Talos pushed one then two fingers inside her, thrusting back and forth. Her gaze dropped to his erection and he could almost see her mind working. He ran his other hand down her spine, over her smooth backside and pulled her closer. "Don't panic, I'll fit."

She shifted. "It's not that, Talos. I don't want to disappoint you."

"You won't." He took her mouth again as he ran his hands up her sides, under her ribcage and cupped her breasts, massaged, squeezed and stroked. She pressed into his hands and her fingers closed around the tip of him, her thumb sliding back and forth over the head.

She slid her hand up and down his length. Her other hand closed around his balls.

"Do you like that?" she asked in a husky tone.

"I like it a lot." He gripped her backside and lifted her. "But, I like this better." He lowered her gradually, easing inside her. "Oh yeah."

She gripped his shoulders, cried out and arched, her beautiful breasts pushing forward, begging for his immediate attention.

Talos obliged and closed his mouth over her nipple, sucking hard as he eased inside her.

She keened, her fingernails biting into his skin.

He lifted her and did it again and again. Her soft cries were music to his ears. She fitted him like a glove and her breasts were an endless delight. Jane was his perfect mate. Holding her hips, he thrust harder and faster. She clenched around him and climaxed again, her shudders almost bringing on his own climax.

Talos pulled out quickly and lowered Jane to the quilt. He'd heard breast-feeding mothers didn't ovulate as long as they feed their babies regularly, but he shouldn't tempt fate. He reached for his trousers and pulled out the condom he'd grabbed earlier.

Sated and lethargic, Jane lay amongst the pillows and watched Talos rip the small sachet open. He looked more like Hercules than ever, a mountain of a man. As he lowered himself between her legs anticipation built again. Electric frissons shot to every nerve ending in her body.

He pushed her thighs wider and caressed her with his clever fingers. She moaned and bucked. She'd never experienced love making like this. Andrew had always taken rather than given, and most of the time it was all over without her reaching her own orgasm, let alone two. She smiled. *Could be three at this rate.*

Talos feathered kisses across her lips. "You're looking pretty pleased with yourself."

Jane stared into his dark eyes. "No wonder you make women scream." She frowned, not liking the thought of him being with other women.

His lips curved. "You're not jealous are you?"

Jane studied his handsome face as she deliberated. "Yes, I think I am."

He chuckled. "The past is history. You're the only woman I've ever wanted a serious relationship with. You're the only woman who's ever driven me to utter distraction."

Exhilaration radiated throughout Jane. Talos really did want her, but for how long? She wrapped her arms around his broad shoulders, arched up and kissed him, delighting when he took control and deepened the kiss, thrusting his tongue inside her mouth to tangle with her own. His hard body lowered, pressing against her as he nudged her legs apart.

Wantonly, Jane spread her legs wider, locked them round his thighs and rubbed against him. She'd never felt so euphoric and alive. Talos not only desired her, he really did want her. She pulled away, breathing hard.

"I love you, Talos."

A slow, sexy smile spread over his face. "I know." He slid his hands down her sides, gripped her hips, and thrust deep inside her, filling her, stretching her, stealing her breath.

Jane inhaled and clutched his shoulders. A moan escaped as he withdrew slowly, but then he thrust again and again, harder and faster, touching her womb, touching her soul. She rode the wave of sensuality; aware her body had begun to tighten. His unique scent of spice and wood surrounded her. His thrusts grew faster, almost punishing, then without breaking pace he dragged one of her legs higher and rubbed his thumb and fingers over that erogenous spot. She screamed and shattered gloriously for the third time. Talos roared, low and guttural, and followed her over the edge.

Several minutes later, Jane recouped enough energy to open her eyes. She lay in Talos's arms, her head against his shoulder, and her hand on his chest. She wanted to savor and cherish this moment forever, but an unwelcome thought niggled. *Talos didn't say he loved me.* Glancing up she found him watching her with his beautiful dark eyes. She frowned.

"How do you know I love you?"

His traced a finger down her cheek. "It's in your eyes and your actions."

Jane narrowed her eyes. "That could be lust."

He smiled. "Oh, that's there too, but Sam told me how you reacted when you thought something had happened to me and your relief when Jarred told you I was fine."

"That could be because I care about you."

"Maybe, but I've see the way you look at me. You don't even notice the other guys, who are all much better looking than me."

Jane huffed. "No, they're not."

He chuckled. "I rest my case." He eased her out of his arms, removed the condom and hurled it into the fire. "I'm starving, how about I make us steak and onion sandwiches?"

"Okay." Jane studied him as he pulled on his underpants and

jeans. *He hadn't said the words, but his actions spoke loudly, didn't they?* She rolled onto her tummy, rested her chin on her hands, and relished the view of his massive shoulders as he stoked the fire. *How can I be sure he loves me if he doesn't say the words?*

Jane sat up and wrapped the quilt around her. "Do you mind if I have a shower?"

"Not at all." He held out a hand and pulled her up. "The main bathroom is upstairs but it isn't quite finished, so you'll have to use my ensuite."

"Fine."

Not releasing her hand, Talos led her up the stairs and stopped at the first door. "This is my room." He turned the handle and pushed the door wide. "After you."

Jane scooped up the dragging quilt and stepped over the threshold into darkness. Talos moved past her and flicked on a lamp beside the biggest bed she'd ever laid eyes on. "Oh my God, Talos. How on earth did you get that up the stairs?"

He gave her a boyish grin. "I built the frame in pieces then assembled it up here. Getting the mattress upstairs was more difficult. It's so heavy it took four of us to lift it."

Jane's gaze swept over him. "How tall are you?"

"Six-feet-five, but I need space to stretch and once you stick a few pillows on a standard king mattress, my feet hang over the edge. So I had this mattress custom made."

"Hmm." Jane examined the rest of the room. It had to come close to covering the entire floor below. Floor to ceiling windows took up the opposite wall, mirroring the windows downstairs. How lovely it would be to wake up every morning, roll over, and look across green fields to the river. Reality set in. *Another pipe dream I'll never experience.*

Talos strolled over and pulled the curtains closed. "I'm planning on building a balcony out there one day." He walked towards two doors and pointed at one. "That's the walk-in-robe, which I'm still working on, and this is the ensuite."

He opened the door and waved her through. It was enormous. The shower alone could hold two of Talos.

He smiled. "I'll leave you to have your shower while I make us some dinner. Come down when you're ready." He closed the door.

Jane glanced around the well-appointed luxurious bathroom and bit her lip. *I want to stay here. I want to be part of Talos's life. I want to be his wife.* She swallowed, closed her eyes, and whispered to the universe, "I want him to love me forever."

Chapter Eleven

Talos was at his bedroom door when he heard the shower come on. He paused and turned to stare back at the ensuite as images of Jane's beautiful naked curves under the steaming spray filtered through his mind. Gripping the handle, he battled with his own desires. *Jane might be sore and she's probably tired.* He muscles tensed. *I could just offer to wash her back.* Within seconds he was naked and opening the door.

She had her hair twisted up in some sort of knot, her eyes closed and her head forward, allowing the water to rain down on her neck and shoulders. Talos stood in mute fascination as she slowly revolved, dropping her head back to let the steaming water hit her full, rounded breasts. A pang of guilt hit at the blotchy rash on her chin and breasts. *I should have shaved.*

He forgot his guilt as she soaped her arms, breasts, and stomach, then raised each of her knees to soap her legs. Talos sucked in a breath as she swayed under the spray of warm water, rinsing off the soap.

Her hands stilled as her gaze locked with his, then her lips curved alluringly. "Hello."

Talos opened the glass door, stepped in and took the soap. "Let me help you."

She giggled. "If you insist."

"Oh, I do." Talos shifted under the warm spray and rubbed the soap slowly between his hands. He cupped her breasts, gently massaging and weighing each one before moving up over her collarbone and shoulders.

She mewed and stepped closer, sliding her hands up over his chest. "Kiss me, Talos."

Placing the soap back in its dish, Talos slid his hands around Jane's waist and down over her firm backside. "With pleasure." He cupped the globes of her backside and hoisted her up against him, balancing her weight in his hands then he kissed her.

She wrapped her legs around him, kissing him back eagerly, oblivious to the water raining down on her head, soaking her hair. She wriggled in his hands, pressing against his erection.

Talos backed her against the tiles and, taking her weight in one hand, slipped his hand between them, running his fingers along her wet folds.

She broke the kiss and dragged in a breath. "I've never done anything like this."

He re-captured her mouth then thrust his finger inside her. She was hot and wet.

She moaned and rubbed her pebbled nipples against his chest.

Awareness reverberated throughout Talos's mind. He gripped her backside and nudged his erection between her thighs, entering her slowly. Every muscle straining as he held back from taking her too fast.

Jane gasped and rolled her hips, obliterating his control.

Carnal lust exploded. Talos stepped away from the wall and thrust deep. Jane cried out and tightened around him. He lifted her and thrust again as the blood in his veins surged rampantly. He thrust again and again, Jane's soft cries urging him to take all.

She screamed and shattered spectacularly, her nails digging into his shoulders as she convulsed, quivered, and stiffened in his hands.

Talos couldn't hold back and roared as his own orgasm erupted, like lava exploding from the mouth of a volcano.

His strength deserted him and he sank to the floor, taking Jane's limp body with him. Warm water cascaded over them as he held her in his arms, her head resting against his shoulder. Minutes passed and absolute calm engulfed Talos as he stroked Jane's back. He'd never felt so sated, so buoyant, so sure of his future, but they couldn't stay here all night. He kissed Jane's head and raised her chin. Her long lashes fluttered open revealing her stunning green eyes. She smiled drowsily and his heart lurched.

"Finish your shower then come downstairs. I really am going to make those steak sandwiches now, then we really need to talk." He helped her up then opened the glass door, grabbed a towel and wrapped it round his waist. "Don't be long."

Closing the ensuite door behind him, Talos searched out a clean T-shirt and track-pants then grabbed a robe he'd never used and threw it over the bed. As an after-thought he grabbed his toiletry bag from his carryall. *I need to shave before I do any more damage to Jane's delicate skin.* A twinge of guilt hit that he'd taken a woman without protection, the first time ever. *Hell it was worth it though.* He'd never experienced such a connection, such a high.

He was just adding the onion to the sandwiches when Jane came down the stairs. He set the tongs down and watched her descend. His chocolate-colored robe swamped her. She had the sleeves rolled several times and held thick bunches of it in her hands. Her damp hair hung loosely about her shoulders and she resembled a beautiful princess wrapped in a bearskin. *My princess.*

Her gaze locked with his and she smiled. "You shaved."

"Hmm, sorry about the stubble rash."

"That's okay. Can I have a look at the rest of your house?"

"Sure." He strolled over and took her hand then led her to a door on the right of the stairs. "This is my gym." He opened the door, switched on the light and stood back.

Jane stepped past him and came to a standstill as she stared around the state of the art gym. He had a treadmill, rowing machine, bench-press, punching bag and a huge multifunctional type thing. "Wow, no wonder you look like you do."

He laughed. "Being fit was vital in the SAS and it's something I enjoy. Come on, I'll show you the games room." He turned off the light and guided her to a door on the other side of the stairs. "The boys convinced me I needed this. It's a trifle over indulgent, but we've had some good nights in here."

"Really." Jane followed him into the room and gasped. It was the pinnacle in overindulgence. A massive television screen sat on the far wall looking down on an eight-seater curved lounge and low table. Directly in front of her stood a full-size billiard table and another large window with heavy drapes. To her right she sighted a bar, set of drums, and a round table covered in felt. Jane frowned. "What's the table for?"

"Our poker nights."

"And the drums."

"The boys and I have the occasional jam session."

"You guys really do take your leisure time seriously."

He shrugged. "It's a fallout from the SAS. Life was precious and there was always the chance we wouldn't come home."

"How did you all end up working for Jarred?"

"We were part of a special unit in the SAS, so when Jarred decided to start Steel Security, he wanted guys who worked well together, had common interests, and were free to travel anywhere any time."

"Meaning none of you had wives or children."

"Exactly."

"So, why haven't any of you married?"

"In my case, I didn't want to leave a wife or children on their own if I didn't make it back. Secondly, I didn't meet anyone I wanted to be with, until now."

Jane's breath caught in her throat. She stared into his serious face and read the truth in his eyes. Still she hesitated. It was yet to be seen whether they could stay together, whether it was safe, whether he cared enough for her. Better to accept this as one night with the man of her dreams. She took a shaky breath. "Show me the rest of your house."

"With pleasure." Switching off the light, he shut the door and took her hand again. He pointed at a door under the stairs. "That's the wine cellar and I've got a shed outside that doubles as a garage and workshop." He pointed to the right at an L-shaped alcove between the kitchen and the gym. "That hall leads to my study and the front entrance. The laundry is through the door near the fireplace and there's another three bedrooms and a bathroom upstairs, but I'm still working on them."

"You've thought of everything."

He drew her close and kissed her tenderly then turned her towards the fireplace. "Almost. Make yourself comfortable and I'll get the food."

Jane lifted the robe and padded over to the thick rug. Her eyes flicked over the lounges then back to the rug, pillows and glowing fire. She sank onto the rug and propped a pillow behind her back. Tiredness and hunger clawed at her. It had to be close to midnight. She would have to leave soon.

Talos squatted down and handed her a glass of orange juice and a plate with a toasted steak and onion sandwich on it. Her tummy grumbled. "Thank you, I'm starving."

"I said you would be." He grinned roguishly then stood and placed another couple of logs on the fire. "This cold snap is so unusual for January. Back in a sec." He strode to the kitchen and returned seconds later with two sandwiches and a beer then settled beside her.

"You don't have to go with Gibbs. You can refuse and stay here with me."

"I don't want to put you in danger and I'm not brave enough to stand up to the AFP."

"Yes, you are. You thought I was an intruder once and attacked me with an umbrella. You also crawled across a roof while being shot at. You're very brave and that's where my proposition comes in."

"What proposition?"

"We'll tell them we're engaged and that we refuse to be parted."

"We pretend?" Jane's heart sank.

"Yes, but you can't admit that to Kallie or your mother. We've got to make everyone, even the boys think we're serious about each other."

Jane bit into her sandwich. *That won't be hard. I'm in love with you.*

She ate the sandwich and drank her orange juice in silence. His plan might work but it would also put him in danger. The sooner those criminals were identified the better.

Jane leaned against his shoulder and stared into the flames. "Was it scary in the SAS?"

"At times. We trained hard, but there was always the chance something would go wrong and death was never far from our minds."

"And that's the reason none of the others got married either?"

"Nick came close once. He was a chopper pilot in the regular army and engaged to a girl named Ava. They were inseparable, but then Nick joined the SAS and Ava freaked. She gave him an ultimatum and he chose the SAS. Ava cancelled the wedding and took off overseas."

"How sad." Jane bit her lip. "It might not be too late, now that he's out of the SAS."

"It was four years ago and Nick's a very different man now."

Jane frowned. "I know he gives the impression of being an outrageous flirt, but I wonder what would happen if we found Ava and she wasn't married?"

Talos put his arm around Jane and drew her closer. "Don't go there, sweetheart. Nick's a serious player now and has no intention of settling down with any woman."

"What a pity." Jane snuggled against Talos's chest. "Back in Willaroi, Nick took a bullet trying to save my life, so it's the least I can do to find out if Ava is still single."

"I'm sure Ava married long ago."

"Hmm." *I wonder if Simon and all his fancy equipment could track her down?*

That was her last conscious thought until she awoke to a strong, steady beat under her ear. She knew instantly that it was Talos's heartbeat and his arms holding her close. His body was like a furnace and she was so cozy she didn't want to move.

Cracking an eye open she found him watching her. She also discovered the room swathed in morning light. "Talos!" She jerked upright. "It's morning."

His lips twitched. "So it is."

Numerous boots sounded on the steps then someone hammered on the sliding door.

Talos sighed. "That'll be the boys looking for you."

"Oh, God, I didn't mean to fall asleep, I've got to get back." Jane pulled out of his arms and struggled to her feet. "They'll think we've slept together."

"We did." Grinning, he strode to the door, where the hammering continued.

"Wait." Jane bunched up the robe and grabbed her scattered clothes. "Where's my bra?"

He opened the slider. "Morning boys, anyone for coffee?"

Jane groaned and dropped to the rug, using the couch to hide behind. *I'll kill him.*

"Jesus, Talos," came Sam's voice. "I've been trying to reach you for an hour and we just found your fucking phone under a wheelbarrow."

"Sorry, mate, I got sidetracked. What's wrong?"

"Gibbs is here for Jane, and Jarred's on the warpath."

"Where's Jane?" called Simon as he stepped through the doorway. "You were supposed to have her back last night."

"Isn't it obvious," answered Talos. "Jane stayed with me. I've asked her to marry me."

"What?" Nick exclaimed.

Silently cursing, Jane spied her bra under the couch. *Talos is enjoying this.* She grabbed the bra and peeped over the lounge.

All four men's gazes locked on her.

"Hi." She scrambled up, clutching the robe and her clothes. "I'll get dressed.

Talos scowled. "Jane's not going into witness protection. She's staying with me."

Tripping on the robe, Jane dropped her bra. *Shit.*

'What about Vietnam?" Nick stooped to pick it up. His lips twitched as he handed the bra back to her."

Mortified, Jane hurried up the stairs as best she could in the voluminous robe. She ran into Talos's bedroom and dressed quickly, then washed her face and brushed her hair back into some sort of order.

Still highly flustered, Jane descended the stairs to find Talos cooking scrambled eggs, Ryan making toast, Sam brewing coffee, and Nick looking highly amused.

"I have to get back to feed Ella."

Sam pushed a cup of coffee across the bench. "She was still asleep when we left. Eat some breakfast then we'll head back."

Talos heaped a mountain of scrambled eggs onto one plate with a couple of pieces of toast and then a smaller amount onto another piece of toast on the other plate. It was still way too much for her to eat.

He grinned at her. "Now that we don't need to worry about waking anyone, I'll take you back in the CX."

Nodding, Jane took her coffee and eggs to the table. The men followed and began discussing their departure plans for Vietnam. As soon as Nick and Simon finished their coffees, they left. Sam accompanied Jane and Talos to the CX.

Climbing onto the rear seat, Jane took a long, hard look at Talos's beautiful home, locking it away in her memory.

It only took a couple of minutes to reach Sam's house but she used the time to deliberate on her future. If she wanted a normal life, she had to identify Marzetti's partners. To do that she would need to go to Vietnam, which they wouldn't be expecting. *I could wear a disguise and pretend to be a tourist. The alternative is a life in exile without Talos.*

Pain lanced her heart at the thought of never seeing Talos again but she refused to take him from his family and friends. Her only hope was to catch Marzetti's partners then let the Vietnamese courts deal with them, otherwise she'd spend the rest of her life looking over her shoulder. *I have to convince Jarred and Talos to take me with them to Vietnam.*

On opening the car door, Jane heard Ella screaming. She ran up the steps and into the house to find her mother trying to force the teat of a bottle into Ella's mouth. Ella screamed louder, her little face mottled in agitation.

"Oh, sweetie, I'm here."

"And about time too." Her mother glared at her. "Kallie and I haven't been able to calm her. Where have you been?"

Conscious of reproachful glances from her stepfather, Jarred, and Inspector Gibbs, Jane smoothed her tangled hair and took Ella in her arms. "I went to see Talos and we fell asleep."

Liz shook her head and stalked into the kitchen. Ella continued to scream and Kallie gave Jane a reassuring smile.

"She only woke a little while ago."

Sitting in the corner of the lounge, Jane discreetly lifted her shirt and attempted to feed Ella, but she continued to scream, twisting her head away every time Jane tried to attach her. "It's okay, sweetie, I'm here." Ella's distress made Jane want to cry. "Come on, honey."

The couch dipped beside her and Jane lifted her eyes to find Talos beside her. He put an arm around her shoulders then gently stroked Ella's cheek, crooning softly as he sang a lullaby in Greek.

Ella's screams dwindled to sobs then hiccupping breaths as she stared at Talos, then she gave him a teary smile and turned her face to suckle.

Jane dashed a couple of tears away. No wonder she loved Talos.

He could fix anything. Jane gave him her own watery smile. "What were you singing?"

"A bawdy pub song my dad taught me." He chuckled and Ella stopped feeding to gurgle and smile at him.

Jane reattached Ella and lightly slapped his leg. "Don't teach her bawdy songs."

"She likes bawdy songs, don't you little one?" He stroked Ella's head and she stopped feeding again to smile at him. "See."

Jane glanced up to find everyone watching them. Heat flared in her cheeks. She lowered her gaze back to Ella and concentrated on feeding her.

Talos squeezed Jane's knee and stood. "Arh, sorry if we worried you all. I did intend having Jane back last night but we stayed up rather late talking and ended up falling asleep."

Nick cleared his throat. "*Talking,* is that what you call it."

Jane saw Talos send Nick a warning glance before continuing. "Anyway, I've asked Jane to marry me and she's accepted."

A choked splutter sounded from the kitchen and Jane looked across to see her mother wiping tea from her chin.

"You can't get engaged. Andrew only died yesterday. What will people think?"

"I don't give a damn." Jane locked eyes with her mother. "My marriage ended eight and half months ago when Andrew asked me to abort the baby."

Her mother clasped her hand to her chest as her jaw dropped. "You never told me that."

"How could I? You and Ken thought the sun shone out of Andrew's backside."

Her mother paled. "Why didn't you say something?"

"It's not something I like to talk about. Can we just forget it?"

Inspector Gibbs sighed. "I'm sorry, but whether you're engaged or not, I still have to put you into protective custody."

"Not if I refuse to go." Jane tilted her chin and stared the inspector down.

Jarred moved to stand in front of her. "You have to be realistic. My team is heading to Vietnam and I can't leave Talos behind to look after you."

Jane trembled as she looked up into his hard grey eyes. "You won't have to. I've decided to go to Vietnam and find Marzetti's partners before they find me."

Mayhem broke loose as everyone started talking at once. Her mother looked dumbstruck, Kallie horrified and Talos, Jarred, and Sam were shaking their heads.

Her mother hurried across the room. "You can't go and leave Ella, she's too young."

"Ella's coming with me."

The unanimous shouts of, *"no"* only cemented her determination. "I refuse to spend the rest of my life in hiding. I'm going to Vietnam and I *will* identify each of those men so that they can be dealt with properly. You can either take me with you or I'll go on my own." She held her breath, praying they wouldn't call her bluff. If she could convince them she was prepared to take matters into her own hands, they might help her.

Talos squatted in front of her and took her hand in his. "Sweetheart, listen to me. Marzetti will do anything to stop you. Stay here with Sam and Kallie. Let me and the boys find these maggots and deal with them."

Pulling her hand free, Jane straightened her spine. "Vietnam is the last place they'll expect to find me and I have a plan. I'm going."

"No, you're not. I insist you stay here."

"Hear me out. We pretend to be a married couple on holidays with our baby. I will wear a wig and sunglasses at all times. Inspector Gibbs has all the meeting locations and their code names. I know what they look like. We get there early and as soon as I recognize each man, I give a pre-organized signal then disappear."

Talos shook his head, his eyes full of concern.

Gibbs turned to Jarred. "It might just work. Vietnam is the last place they'll expect her to be. It's possible we can apprehend each of Marzetti's partners without alerting the others."

Talos swore and rounded on Inspector Gibbs. "I don't want Jane anywhere near those bastards. She's not coming and that's final."

Inspector Gibbs held up his hand. "Jane won't be using her own name. Under the Witness Protection Act, I can change her name and organize emergency passports."

Talos shook his head. "These people are highly proficient criminals. You are putting Jane and Ella in unnecessary danger."

Jarred rubbed his jaw. "It might work."

Talos turned to Jarred. "You can't be serious, Colonel?"

"I'm very serious. We have an unknown person meeting with each of the partners around Vietnam, who I suspect then reports to some King Pin. No one will look twice at a young couple on holiday with their baby. Having Jane there on the spot will expedite things."

Jarred looked down on Jane. "Do you have a valid passport?"

"Yes." She bit her lip. "But I haven't registered Ella's birth yet. They told me I had sixty days to do it and what with being in witness protection, I didn't get round to it."

Gibbs pursed his lips and frowned. "That might hold things up slightly. Have you got the paperwork here?"

"Yes, but my passport is at my apartment in Sydney."

"No actually, it's here," announced her mother. "Inspector Gibbs asked me to pack up your personal things and keep them safe."

The Inspector rubbed his chin. "We need to go to the nearest post office for photos. Then, I'll take the paperwork to Sydney and check in with my chief. He'll need to approve your trip and authorize a priority birth certificate and passport for the baby."

Elated, Jane turned to Talos. "You'll be there to protect me, day and night. I need to do this for us and to stop the slavery and trafficking of innocent children and women. Once the police have those men we can have a normal life."

His jaw remained clenched, his knuckles white as he stared at her. He looked like he wanted to strangle her. A sliver of fear ran down her spine. She wouldn't like to be on the receiving end of Talos's fury. *Talos would never hurt me.*

He whirled around and stormed out of the room, slamming the back door. Everyone watched through the window as he strode towards a large shed.

Sam shrugged. "He'll come round. In the meantime he's going to chop me a year's supply of firewood." He glanced at Gibbs. "How many people know we're going after Marzetti's partners?"

"Except for me and my chief, no one else in the AFP has been informed."

Jarred stood beside the inspector, his face deadly serious as he looked at Jane. "We will escort you to the post office then I must return to Sydney. There are things to be organized and I want to speak with Gibb's chief. Ryan will return here early Thursday morning and fly you to Sydney for our flight to Vietnam."

Jane swallowed. "Fine." She glanced at the shed where the sound of an axe could be heard smashing into wood. *I'm doing this for us, Talos.*

Chapter Twelve

Jane sat in the shade of the frangipani tree beneath masses of crimson bougainvillea that sprawled across several balconies. Frazzled from lack of sleep and stifling humidity, she leaned back in the wrought-iron chair and let her gaze drift over the hotel's French style courtyard with its peaceful atmosphere.

In the stroller beside her, Ella's eyes were wide, enthralled by the frangipani flowers and leaves fluttering above. She reached out with her tiny fingers for the elusive treasure.

Picking up her iced coffee, Jane took a long cooling drink and glanced up at the second floor gym window, where Talos was working out with Nick and Ryan. *Is he avoiding me?*

It had been three days since he'd strode off to the shed and, true to Sam's prediction, Talos had vented his anger by chopping a trailer load of wood. Once the passport photos were taken, he'd left with Jarred and Inspector Gibbs to meet with the chief of the AFP.

She hadn't seen or spoken to him again until this morning at Sydney Airport where he'd given her passports in the names of Jane and Eloise Talarico. With the rest of the team in close proximity, they hadn't had a chance to talk privately. On the plane, strangers surrounded them so Jane held her tongue, biding her time.

The faint sound of beeping horns interrupted her thoughts. She picked up a menu to fan her face as she scrutinized the hotel's facade. The entire building radiated old-world charm with its ornate ceilings, flower balconies, and ornamental urns. It was also the location for the first meeting tomorrow, which meant she had to remain disguised in a blonde wig that made her head sweat and itch.

Balancing her book on her lap, her attention wandered to a

Vietnamese couple and their two children eating at one of the wrought iron tables. *Will we ever have that freedom?*

Jane perused the area to her left and grinned. Simon sat at a table working on his computer. He wore a grey wig, moustache and spectacles. Two middle-aged western couples sat drinking cocktails and chatting at a table near the bar, and three staff hovered near the doors to the stylish inside restaurant. They'd taken every opportunity to come and coo over Ella.

Across the courtyard, Jarred sat at a table with Elliott Shaw, the man who'd met them at the airport. According to Simon, Elliott owned a company that had offices throughout Vietnam and could provide the team with local knowledge and support if needed.

Tall with fair hair and sky-blue eyes, Elliot was handsome and confident. Upon meeting her, he'd complimented her stunning eyes and smile, then offered to carry her hand luggage.

She smiled at the memory. Talos had bristled, announced she was his wife and that he had it covered, then ushered her ahead of him. His protectiveness had cracked the shell of armor she'd wrapped herself in thanks to Andrew. *If only I could believe it would last.*

An Asian man with a shiny, bald head walked through from the foyer. He sat at a table near the bar and picked up a menu.

Oh my God. A band tightened around Jane's lungs. Perspiration broke out on her forehead and above her lip. Her hand shook as she placed the iced coffee on the table. Raising her book, she frantically tried to signal Simon. He wasn't looking. Neither was Jarred.

Forgetting she was disguised, she glanced up at the gym window and saw Talos looking down. *Thank goodness.* Keeping her book high, she jabbed her thumb towards the man, who was now exchanging pleasantries with a waiter.

To her relief, Talos appeared in the courtyard in less than a minute, casually looked about, then purposefully made his way towards her. Dressed in sweatshirt and shorts, he towered over the hovering staff, emphasising his power and strength. As Jane locked eyes with him, memories of their night together flooded her mind. Her skin prickled and butterflies skittered across her stomach. She reached out with a shaky hand.

"What is it? What's wrong?"

Blinking, Jane dropped her hand and glanced across the courtyard. "That Asian man is one of Marzetti's partners."

"You're sure?" He didn't glance that way.

Not the reaction she'd expected. "Yes. I'm positive."

Pulling out his phone, Talos sat in the chair opposite, blocking her view as he selected a number. A soft humming sounded at the far end of the courtyard.

His gaze on Jane, Talos lowered his voice. "Jarred, the bald guy on his own is one of our targets. What do you want to do?"

Jane watched Talos as he listened then ended the call and sent a text. A ping sounded to Jane's left. Simon checked his phone then stood, closed his laptop, and strolled towards them, stopping at Ella's stroller.

"What a pretty baby," he declared before lowering his voice. "Which one?"

"Thank you," replied Talos. He also lowered his voice. "The bald guy talking to the waiter. Find out which room he's in."

Smiling, Simon raised his voice. "My children are adults now, but when they were young, we had some great family vacations. Enjoy your holiday."

"Thank you." Jane's voice caught as she met Simon's steady gaze. He smiled again then strode across the courtyard, intercepting the waiter who'd just taken the man's order.

Fascinated, Jane watched as Simon spoke to the waiter then borrowed his pen to write something on a card before strolling off towards the hotel's grand foyer. Frowning, Jane leaned across the table. "What was that about?"

"By speaking to the waiter, Simon would have taken the opportunity to look at our target's food order. His room number will be on the docket."

"Good thinking." Easing sideways, Jane spied the man reading his paper. Giddy with relief, she took a deep breath. "He didn't recognize me. What should we do now?"

"I want you back in the suite while we set up surveillance. You may have used your feminine wiles to convince Jarred and Gibbs to bring you along, but I won't have you or Ella unnecessarily exposed to danger."

Flipping her sunglasses down, Jane pushed her glass away and leaned closer. "I thought the meeting was to take place tomorrow?"

"It is, but lucky for us, the guy's got to eat and if he's staying here, we can take him out of the picture early." He picked up her glass and drained it.

Jane clutched his hand. "Talos, we need to talk. I hate that you're still mad at me."

"I'm not mad at you, Jane. It's Gibbs and Jarred I'm mad at." He stood and gripped the stroller handle. "And mad isn't even close to how I feel about you being here. Let's go."

Gritting her teeth, Jane followed in his wake. Talos hadn't touched her since her declaration to come to Vietnam. With a heavy heart, she trailed him into the tiled foyer, past an enormous urn of flowers, and into the narrow lift. Jarred and Elliott Shaw followed her, making it a tight fit.

"Are you positive, he's one of them," asked Jarred. "Gibbs mentioned it was months ago and you didn't spend long in their company."

"Maybe not, but I never forget a face. One of the men was British, one Eastern European by his heavy accent, and the other two were Asian. I'm sure the man in the courtyard is one of them."

"Very well." Jarred pressed the top floor button and turned to Talos. "Once Simon's searched the room and photographed any evidence, we'll make our move."

Rubbing his chin, Jarred looked at Talos. "I want you on hand when we take him down. He'll have minders somewhere close."

"No worries. Who's going to guard Jane?"

"I will for now then…" Jarred glanced at Jane. "Simon will keep you company while he's watching the surveillance stream. The rest of us have to be ready to take down the target the minute he's alone."

Jane frowned at Jarred. "What does that mean?"

"We'll make it appear he suffered a heart attack and died."

An icy chill spread through Jane's body. *Take down the target. Heart attack.* She whirled to face Talos. "You're not going to kill him are you?"

His lips twitched. "We prefer to stay inside the law as much as possible."

Jarred's phone rang as the doors opened, preventing Jane from asking any more questions. She led the way along the wide hall to their suite.

Once inside, Jarred ended his call. "Our target's room is on the floor below. Simon's searching it now and Ryan will alert him if the target leaves the courtyard."

"Good." Talos positioned Ella's stroller beside the bed. "I'm going to take a quick shower." He stepped into the bathroom and closed the door.

Feeling as useful as a flat battery, Jane sank onto the couch and watched Jarred pace back and forth.

He looked at Elliott Shaw. "I need to ring Gibbs. He's meeting with the Serious Crime Unit and needs to be kept informed. Can you have your people on standby?"

"Of course."

As Jarred moved onto the balcony, Elliot made himself comfortable in an armchair and smiled at Jane. "How long have you and Talos been married?"

Jane hesitated, unsure exactly how much Elliott knew of her plight. "Not that long."

He frowned. "I must say, I'm surprised the AFP allowed you to come to Vietnam. What exactly is your involvement?"

"It's a long story, but I'm the only person willing and able to identify the four men that are part of a trafficking ring. I'm sorry, I'm not sure how much I can tell you."

He stood. "I run a software consultancy company with offices here, Danang and Hanoi. We do a lot of charity work with vulnerable and disadvantaged children. I speak Vietnamese and I've been asked to assist Jarred in apprehending the group of predators he's after." He smiled. "Please, let me know if there's anything I can do for you."

"Thank you." She waited until he left the room then opened her shirt and fed Ella. Several minutes later, Simon arrived and set up his monitor on the coffee table. His screen showed a stylish room similar to theirs, an open suitcase, a white towel rumpled on the floor, and a couple of beer cans on the polished mahogany desk. Once Simon was sure everything was working properly, he joined Jarred on the balcony, but their voices remained too low for her to make out what they were saying. She prayed all would work out.

She'd calmed considerably when Talos stepped out of the

bathroom and scattered her wits entirely. Freshly shaven with a towel draped low on his hips, he padded over to a duffle bag she hadn't noticed. Her gaze locked on droplets of water glistening on his shoulders and chest. Desire clawed at her insides along with the need to lick every droplet off his magnificent chest. *Not a good idea, Jane.*

She dragged her attention back to Ella, but the temptation was too much and she raised her eyes again to watch him pull on dark pants and a striped polo shirt that did nothing to hide his powerful thighs and shoulders. Aware she was staring but unable to help it, she followed his every move as he buckled his belt then put on black socks and leather shoes. He straightened and ran his hands through his damp hair, leaving it tousled in an extremely sexy way. She swallowed hard. *Has he any idea how drop-dead gorgeous he is?*

Talos joined Jarred and Simon on the balcony and after a brief conversation, they returned inside.

Simon took up his post in front of the monitor. "The man's name is Huang but don't forget he could be going under the name Lhasa. I've done some research and I think I've found a link between the ring members' code names and their nationalities."

"Oh."

"Lhasa is a city in China, Ripon is a city in England, Kazan is a city in Russia and Rong is Vietnamese for dragon."

"So Lhasa is Huang?"

"I believe so."

Talos nodded. "I'll keep it in mind." He looked across to Jane. "I won't be long."

She swallowed. "Stay safe."

As the door closed behind them, she fought back tears. *Please stay safe.*

Taking the lift to the ground floor, Talos strolled into the stylish a la carte restaurant and spotted their target sitting at the bar. He was attempting to chat up a glamorous Vietnamese woman in a tight black dress and very high heels. Ryan sat at a secluded table across the room, speaking with a pretty waitress.

The woman beside their target picked up her glass, her gaze connecting with Talos's in the mirror behind the bar. The glass halted mid-air. Used to the sexual interest he received from women, he continued his perusal of the room, aware she had swivelled on her stool and was now watching him with interest. He ambled over to a corner table and sat with his back to the window, allowing him an unrestricted view of the restaurant and bar.

A waiter arrived with a menu. After ordering a Tiger beer, Talos sat back to scan the other patrons. Lowered lamps gave the elegant room a cozy, intimate atmosphere, and the furniture had been chosen with comfort in mind. Small family groups, businessmen, and couples occupied tables set with crisp linen cloths and sparkling glasses.

He watched their target attempt to regain his companion's attention. She turned back to the bar, although her focus remained on the mirror behind. There was no doubting the invitation in her eyes.

His phone vibrated. Glancing at the screen first, he raised it to his ear.

"Jarred?"

"I've finished going through the target's briefcase. His passport is in the name of Huang Chen, first name being Chen. He's a Chinese citizen and definitely one of Marzetti's partners. The briefcase is full of photos of young girls, spreadsheets, and bank statements. We're ready to take the bastard down."

"I've got him in sight. What's next?"

"He needs to return to his room *alone.*"

"At the moment he's trying to hit on a glamorous Vietnamese woman."

"Make sure he doesn't leave with her."

"I'm on it." Talos ended the call.

The woman was still watching him. She slid off her stool and wove her way around tables towards him. Talos let his gaze slide down her tightly clad body. There was only one body he wanted to wrap himself up in and she was upstairs under lock and key with Simon.

As the woman approached he smiled. "How you doing?"

She raised an eyebrow. "I think my evening just improved."

"Oh?"

She slid onto the chair opposite and placed her glass on the table. "My name is Lien." Her gaze swept down his chest.

He ignored her provocative smile and thanked the waiter for his beer. The woman was older than he'd first thought; late twenties or early thirties if he had to guess.

"I'm James. Are you a guest here?"

"No, I'm staying at another hotel, but I've always like the atmosphere here."

He leaned back in his chair. "You speak very good English. I take it you've spent a lot if time in an English speaking country?"

"I studied languages at Sydney University."

"So you're not with the guy at the bar?"

She laughed. "No. I like a man who takes care of his body."

Well if that isn't a come on. Ignoring her innuendo, he took another swig of beer. "What do you do for a living?"

"I'm a tour director. Tomorrow I'm taking a group of Germans to Nha Trang." She smiled. "But I'm free tonight, if you'd like some company."

"Sorry, I'm spoken for." He glanced over her shoulder and observed Huang abruptly step away from the bar and collide with a blonde.

Doing a double take, Talos focused on the woman's familiar gaze. Caught like a deer in headlights, she froze momentarily then shrugged Huang's hands off her arms, turned on her heel and darted back towards the door, leaving the man frowning in her wake.

Shit. Talos came to his feet in a rush. "Sorry, I have to run. I hope your tour goes well." Reaching the door, he silently cursed as two Asian men walked in, blocking his exit.

"Excuse me," he murmured, squeezing through. Relief surged as he spotted Jane running up the stairs and Ryan leaving the hotel on the heels of their target.

Talos caught up to Jane as she reached the top of the stairwell.

"Jane, what's happened?"

Her head snapped round then she launched herself at him, slamming her fists into his chest. Eyes sparkling with tears, her lips trembled.

"Why do I fall for men that hurt me?" She hit him again. "You said you wanted a proper relationship with *me.*"

Grabbing her wrists, he pulled her close. "What the hell are you talking about?"

"You were supposed to be watching that man, not flirting with a sexy woman." Wriggling to get free, she kicked his shins with her pointy sandals.

He lifted her off her feet. "That bloody hurt."

"You don't know what hurt is." She tried ramming her elbow into his face.

He reared back. "Listen to me."

"I don't want to hear anything you have to say."

He checked the deserted corridor then threw her over his shoulder and marched to their room. Her puny punches bounced off his back. It was her heartbroken sobs that cut to his core.

Reaching their suite he pressed the buzzer. "Open up, Simon, it's me, Talos."

The door swung wide and Simon stood back, his eyes widening when he saw Jane over Talos's shoulder.

"What's going on?"

"You tell me. How the hell did Jane get out? You were supposed to be guarding her." He strode to the lounge and lowered Jane.

Simon spread his hands wide. "I thought she was in the shower." He glanced at the closed bathroom door where the sound of running water could be heard.

Springing to her feet, Jane placed her hands on her hips and glared at him. "I slipped out while Simon was on the balcony taking a phone call. If I hadn't, I'd be none the wiser."

She could have blown it. Talos took a calming breath. "Why did you leave this room?"

"Because I thought I might be able to identify the rest of Marzetti's partners all in one hit. I was trying to help you, idiot that I am."

"You could have blown the whole operation. I knew it was a mistake bringing you."

She pulled the blonde wig off and hurled it at the wall then marched to the door, wrenched it open, and glared at him. "Get out, both of you."

Clenching his jaw, he looked at Simon. "Ring Jarred, tell him Huang has left the hotel. Ryan is trailing him and may need assistance." Talos strode to Jane, took hold of the door, and closed it. "Nobody is going anywhere."

She glowered. "I want you both to leave."

"Forget it." He grabbed her hand. "I have something to say and you're going to listen."

"I am not." She tried tugging her hand free. "You went off and left me at Sam's and you've barely spoken to me since. You're just like Andrew. You only want me for what you can get out of me."

He hauled her to his chest. "I am nothing like him." He glanced at Simon who was watching with interest as he waited for Jarred to answer.

We need privacy.

He towed her into the bathroom and firmly closed the door. "It's our understanding that Marzetti's partners rarely meet as a group, so there was no need for you to come downstairs. Huang was hitting on that woman and we couldn't allow him to take her back to his room, so when she came over, I kept her talking. There is only one woman I want and that's you."

She stilled and blinked rapidly.

Pushing a dark curl behind her ear, he expelled a breath. "I'd never hurt you."

"I thought you were flirting with her."

"No." Opening the door again, he sent an exasperated look at Simon. "Can you watch Ella for ten minutes? I'm taking Jane with me to Jarred's room."

"Why?"

"So I know exactly where she is. What's happening at the moment?"

"Surveillance is up so we'll know as soon as he returns to his room, but Jarred would prefer to take him down away from the hotel."

Jane frowned at him. "Why can't you just seize Huang and hand him over to the authorities?" She crossed her arms under her breasts.

Determinedly focusing on her eyes, Talos sighed. "We want the other partners to attend their meetings, believing Huang died of a heart attack or an unfortunate accident. They won't risk revealing their identities by trying to collect his briefcase."

Simon grunted. "But if they do, I'll see them."

"That's right," agreed Talos. "If we were to seize him, as you suggest, his partners are likely to go underground. This way, we hand him over to the Serious Crime Unit with the evidence and the other partners are none the wiser."

"Can you trust the police?"

He nodded. "The Australian Police have been working with the Serious Crime Unit here for a considerable time, trying to stamp out trafficking." He grimaced. "Put a different wig on. We need to get downstairs to Jarred's room."

"Okay." She picked up a red wig and headed for the door.

As they passed the lift, Elliot Shaw stepped out. He raised an eyebrow.

"I thought Jane was staying upstairs?"

Talos scowled. "Change of plans."

"Well, you may have to change them again. My people tell me Huang just entered a local brothel. You could set a trap for him on his way back if you're quick."

"Right." Talos sighed. "Do me a favor and return Jane to our room."

She glanced up. "Where are you going?"

"Jarred's room then after Huang."

Shaw smiled at Jane. "I'd be delighted to escort you back to your room and keep you company." He pressed the call button and the lift doors reopened.

Clenching his jaw, Talos strode off without a backward glance. The thought of Shaw spending time with Jane gave him the shits. The guy was a pain in the butt with his Hollywood looks and smooth lines, but Jane's safety came first and both Jarred and Gibbs had vouched for Shaw's integrity.

He clenched his fists. *Bastard.*

CHAPTER THIRTEEN

As Talos strode away, Jane was hit again with the realization he was the only man she truly trusted to protect her, and didn't she have a right to know what was going down.

"I'm sorry, Elliott, I need to go after Talos." She ran along the carpeted hall, joining Talos as he opened a door at the far end.

"Jane!" He reached for her, but she sidestepped him and backed into the room.

"I'm staying with you."

"What's she doing here?" bellowed Jarred in her ear.

She jumped forward, colliding with Talos's hard body.

He closed the door and glowered at Jarred. "I warned you she'd be a loose cannon but you insisted she come, so now you have to deal with the fall out."

A knock sounded and Talos moved her aside to re-open the door.

Elliot stood there. "Sorry, she got away." Closing the door, he ambled in and looked at Jarred. "My people are in position and Huang has entered a brothel."

Jarred's jaw clenched. "I know." He stared at Talos, his eyes shards of flint. "I heard what happened downstairs."

Jane shivered and edged closer to Talos. There was a ruthlessness about Jarred that scared the living day lights out of her. "Sorry, that was my fault."

"You don't need to defend me," muttered Talos. "I shouldn't have left Ryan without backup and it wouldn't have happened if we'd left you with Sam and Kallie." His beautiful eyes had lost all their warmth, leaving her floundering, lost and unsure.

She walked across to the lounge, sitting as Nick stepped out of the bathroom. He glanced up and momentarily froze. "Jesus. Where's the blonde wig?"

"It's in the suite. I was trying to look different."

"Ditch it," he snapped. "Nothing personal, I just don't like redheads."

"Why? Was Ava a redhead?"

His hazel eyes hardened then he turned away.

That wasn't called for. Jane wanted to kick herself. 'Sorry, I didn't mean to upset you."

"Forget it." He strode to the min-bar, grabbed a beer, then stepped onto the balcony, shutting the door firmly behind him.

Guilt flooded her. *Why did I say that?* She moved to follow, but Talos's fingers closed around her arm. He shook his head.

"Don't. Ava's a sore point with him."

Biting her lip, she nodded. "The wig reminded him of her."

"It's not just the red wig. Ava has green eyes as well."

"He's not over her, Talos."

"There's nothing you can do."

Elliott strolled over. "I'll escort Jane back upstairs and keep her company. We're in the way here and it's going to be a long night." He smiled at Jane. "We can order room service."

She caught the irritated glare Talos threw Elliott. *Oh dear, I need to defuse this. I'm causing trouble between everyone.* 'Thank you, Elliott, but I'd like Talos to take me up and Simon's there to keep me company."

He nodded. "Call me if you need anything." He passed her a business card.

"She won't." Talos held out his hand. "Coming?"

Gladly. She gave him her hand, silently rejoicing when his fingers tightened around hers. Glancing up she caught a look of satisfaction on his face. *Men.*

They left the suite, then hurried along the corridor and into the lift. As soon as the doors closed, Talos tugged her into his arms and kissed her deeply. She melted against him as delicious quivers shot to all her nerve endings. She needed more. Stretching on her toes, she slid her hands over his chest and shoulders and pressed closer.

The doors opened and he groaned. "I'll be back soon, but I need my mind on the job, not you. Promise me you'll stay in the suite with Simon?"

"I promise."

He walked her to their door and buzzed. "Get some sleep, you look tired."

"Be careful, Talos. I don't want anything to happen to you."

"It won't." He kissed her again, "Warm the bed for me."

Simon opened the door. "Good, you're back. I'm running out of ideas to entertain Ella."

Talos gently pushed her into the room and closed the door between them.

Her lips trembled. *Come back to me.*

She jumped as Simon placed his hand on her shoulder. "Don't fret, Talos is an expert in his field and knowing you're safe here will be a load off his mind."

"What is his field?"

He hesitated then shrugged. "He's a weapons expert."

"Weapons?"

Simon rubbed his neck. "Let's just say, anything is a weapon in Talos's hands. "It doesn't matter if it's a firearm, knife, frying pan, or pencil. It's a weapon."

"But he hasn't got any of those things. It's just him."

Simon's lip's quirked. "He can turn anything into a weapon, especially his own body. He's a big man, but he moves fast and under the right circumstances, lethally."

"Oh." Her heart pounded as she kicked off her sandals. *These men might as well live on another planet. They're trained soldiers, of course they know how to defend themselves and...kill.* She swallowed.

Has Talos killed...with his bare hands? It was hard to imagine the gentle giant who'd held her in his arms or the exciting man who'd made love to her with such fervent devotion in the role of a hardened soldier. It was hard to imagine any of these men that way. Except. She considered Jarred's flinty stare, Nick's unemotional hazel scowl, and Talos's gaze. A shudder ran down her spine.

It's in their eyes.

Drawing a shaky breath, she wandered over to the stroller where Ella lay, blissfully unaware of the turmoil around her. Jane's angst shifted, as she looked upon her little treasure, sucking her fist, her eyes wide as she stared in wonder at a row of shiny sachets draped across the stroller's hood.

Jane's mouth dropped. "Simon, are they condoms?"

"Yeah, it's all I could find to keep her distracted. I had to use one of your hairpins to put a hole in the corner of each one so I could thread dental floss through." His lips twitched. "It worked, she's really fascinated."

"Oh my God, Talos is teaching her bawdy songs and you're making her mobiles out of condoms." Jane snatched the offending mobile off the stroller and threw it at him.

Ella's bottom lip wobbled, her eyes filled with tears, and she gave a heart broken sob.

"Now look what you've done," accused Simon, laughter in his voice. "She's devastated."

"Oh stop it." She picked Ella up and cuddled her. "Shush, possum. Simon's a naughty boy and you're too young to be playing with condoms." She sat onto the bed and squirmed back against the pillows. "They won't really kill Huang, will they?"

"No, but we need to make it look like he's dead. Huang is in for a rude shock when the boys hand him over to the police. With the evidence we found in the briefcase, he should get a life sentence."

She glanced covertly at Simon as he tapped the keys of his computer. He was the team's telecommunications expert and according to Kallie, he had the skill to hack into any computer system, no matter how well protected. He could find out anything about anyone as long as he had a name. *I wonder?*

"Simon, did you ever meet Nick's fiancée, Ava?"

He cocked his head. "No, why?"

"I was talking to Nick earlier and her name came up. I wondered if we could find out if she's still single, now that he's left the SAS."

He raised an eyebrow. "Nick told you about Ava?"

Sidestepping the question, she pulled off the wig and tossed it on the bed. "It came up because of that wig and I wondered if we could find out if she ever married?"

Simon whistled. "I can't believe he opened up to you. The only time we've heard him talk about Ava is when he's blind drunk."

Avoiding a lie, Jane pursed her lips. "Nick took a bullet for me when I was kidnapped and I owe him big time. Would you please quietly check to see if Ava's still single?"

"I don't know."

Sighing dramatically, she looked at him pleadingly. "He won't ask you himself and surely it couldn't hurt just to check?"

"I suppose not, if that's what he really wants?"

Again she avoided an outright lie. "Thank you. If you find out anything, let me know and I'll pass it on discreetly."

Simon's lips twitched. "Is there anything else you'd like me to do? Perhaps look into Ryan or Jarred's past? Fix a speeding ticket. Deposit a million bucks in your account?"

"You can do that?"

"I could, but I won't."

"Oh." She considered him thoughtfully. There was one thing she'd like to know. "Simon, can you explain why Ella and I have passports under the name Talarico?"

Simon stretched his arms up behind him, his chest expanding, emphasising a quiet power within, yet she felt no stirring or excitement, like she did with Talos.

Simon grimaced. "Talos spoke to the AFP Chief and convinced him it was the best way to keep you and Ella incognito. Apparently it helped that you hadn't registered her birth yet."

Jane frowned. "Why?"

"Because Talos put himself down as her father. It was the simplest way to get your passports and make sure your real surname didn't appear on the plane's manifest. It's no big deal, the AFP would have given you and Ella new names anyway as part of witness protection and they'll change it when you get back to Australia."

"Oh." *What if I don't want to change it?*

He turned back to his monitor. "I'll see what I can find out about Ava. It'll take me a few days."

"I owe you one."

He laughed. "I don't have a broken heart or lost love, so you and Kallie don't need to worry about me. I'm fine just the way I am."

Her interest spiked. "What has Kallie got to do with it?"

Continuing to type, he chuckled. "She has big plans for us fellas and wants us all as *enticed* as Sam. Poor guy."

Knowing Kallie, she meant every word. Jane smiled. "Don't you want to fall in love and have a family of your own one day?"

"Why would I give up my freedom to have a woman nag and whine at me when I want to go out with the boys?"

"Kallie and I aren't like that and there are other women who don't nag and whine, and who wouldn't mind you spending time with your friends."

He held up his hands. "Fine, knock yourselves out. Find us gorgeous, intelligent, woman like you and Kallie, who don't whine." He grinned and went back to typing.

Her cheeks heated at his guileless compliment. He was the quiet one of the team, yet she recognized a hidden strength within—a will of steel, veiled by his calm exterior. She would conscript Kallie and they would find the right woman for each of these men. "Okay, we will."

The buzzer sounded.

Simon leapt up and pulled a gun. "Did you order room service?"

"No." She cuddled Ella closer and eased off the bed. "What should we do?"

"Put the baby in her stroller and stay over there." He walked to the door. "Who is it?"

"Elliott Shaw. Jarred wants me to wait here in case I'm needed."

Simon checked the spyhole then opened the door. "Enter at your own peril."

"Why so?" Elliot strolled in and smiled at Jane.

Shutting the door, Simon indicated to Elliott to sit. "Jane is convinced she can find a bride for each of us guys." Shaking his head, Simon returned to his computer.

Elliott chuckled. "Don't look at fixing me up. I'm already married."

Jane straightened from the stroller. "You are?"

"Yes." He pulled out his wallet and passed her a photo. "That was taken when Mads was eighteen, but it's my favorite shot. Nowadays she's much more chic and stylish."

As he made himself comfortable, Jane studied a young woman with iridescent blue eyes, finely shaped eyebrows, and butterscotch-blonde hair windswept about her face. Her crooked smile hinted at a sense of humour as did the finger she held up. Jane narrowed her eyes. "As a married man, you shouldn't be complimenting woman on their eyes and smile."

"Why not?

"They'll get the wrong idea. As it is, Talos thinks you're flirting with me."

Elliott laughed. "*That's* why he's been giving me the cold shoulder. Well, now you can tell him I have a wife, who also has a lovely smile and beautiful eyes."

Jane studied the woman again. "Why does she look familiar?"

"She's a journalist with some pretty impressive articles under her belt."

"Of course. Madeline Shaw." Jane clasped her hands together. "I read an article she wrote on the oppression of women in India and one on illegal adoption rackets in Asia."

He nodded. "She's in China at the moment, but has an interview lined up in Hanoi next week. I'm sure she'd love to meet you. Human trafficking is right up her alley."

"She's exactly the person we need to bring attention to these monsters."

"Forget it," warned Simon. "Jarred's got a long running aversion to journalists."

"Even beautiful ones like this?" She passed him the photo and sat beside Elliott.

Simon looked the photo a little longer than she thought polite. He raised an eyebrow. "She's gorgeous, but she's still a journalist."

Jane threw up her hands. "An award-winning journalist."

Simon grimaced. "Believe me, it's not wise to cross swords with Jarred."

CHAPTER FOURTEEN

Talos dropped back, allowing the evening crowd to swallow Nick. No easy feat when he also towered over the locals. After a quick glance behind, Talos turned left down a less crowded road and away from the chaos, eateries, and continual beeping of motorcycles and cars. Away from the small shop fronts and eager vendors, hoping to snag a sale from the flow of pedestrians.

Passing a narrow lane, he spotted the van where Jarred and Gibbs waited. He gave a slight nod and turned right. He would have preferred to know Sam had his back, as was their usual modus operandi, but Nick and Ryan were just as qualified and wouldn't let him down.

On either side, neon lights flashed declaring their dubious premises open for business.

Which one, Ryan?

He assessed a bunch of scooters and motorbikes parked on either side, making the lane impossible to enter by vehicle. The proprietors obviously liked to see their customers coming and going. A man looking to get his rocks off could easily find himself boxed in and relieved of his wallet and valuables.

The hairs on the back of his neck bristled as he met the gaze of a huge bouncer, leaning against a wall outside a massage parlour. No prizes for guessing what the bulge under his jacket concealed. A heavily made up transvestite exposing more than Talos cared to see, called out. "You American?"

Talos kept walking.

A girl wearing high, black, shiny boots that reached her thighs stepped in front of him, bringing him to a halt. His gaze dropped to her fake breasts spilling over the top of a dress no bigger than a handkerchief. She couldn't be more than seventeen.

"Hello, mister, you want girl? I give good price."

"No, thanks."

She eyed him up and down. "You want two girls take care of you?"

"Nope."

She pouted. "You like boys?"

"No." He stepped around her.

A man with a shaven head and tatts emerged from the premises on his left. "What you like, Mister? Younger girls? I can get for you."

Disgust welled as Talos clenched his fists, digging his fingernails into his palms. *Think of the mission, you can deal with this piece of shit later. Where the hell is Ryan?*

He kept walking.

The guy called after him. "You want virgin? I give you special price."

Cold fury burned Talos's gut. Unable to take another step, he turned and stared at the man who had just made the biggest mistake of his life. "What?"

"You come in, we make deal."

A poor imitation for a cat yowling came from further along the narrow road. Talos refocused. *Nick. The mission.* "I'm meeting someone, then we'll make a deal. Do you have the girl here?"

"Yes. Who you meet with?"

"Huang Chen. Do you know him?"

"It common name in Vietnam."

"He also goes by another name, Lhasa?"

The man's gaze flicked to the brothel behind Talos. "You friend of Mister Lhasa?"

"Maybe."

"You come see me after you finish with Mister Lhasa. I give you good price."

"Count on it." Striding across the lane, Talos congratulated himself on keeping his temper long enough to find out which brothel Huang was patronizing.

Stepping between the two sharp-eyed bouncers, he entered the brightly lit salon and found several girls lounging on leather couches.

Their demeanor changed from bored to attentive. All except one, who cowered against a wall, eyes red-rimmed, arms crossed over her thin chest. Two heavy-set Chinese men played cards at a table towards the back.

A hard-eyed woman of perhaps fifty approached. "You see girl you like, Mister?"

He browsed the girls then pointed to the one cowering. "Her."

"She not so good. Choose another."

"No. I want her." He kept his eyes on the girl as she shrank further into the corner.

The woman marched over and slapped the girl's face. She cried out, her fear as palpable as the dark bruises covering her upper arms.

Talos clenched his teeth. She looked about twelve.

Shoulders hunched, eyes downcast, she shuffled her feet until she stood in front of him.

Christ. He took one of her tiny hands. It shook badly.

The woman scowled at the girl then focused on him. "Two hundred thousand dong for one hour and no refund."

Twelve fucking dollars, is that all this little girl's worth? He handed over the money and caught the woman's eyes. "A friend is meeting me here. Blue eyes, fair hair, bit shorter than me. Have you seen him?"

"Oh sure, he upstairs."

"I'd like to join him." He passed her another two hundred thousand dong. "What room?"

The woman snatched the money and spoke in rapid Vietnamese. The girl began to cry and tried to drag her hand out of his.

Talos picked her up. He followed the woman up a set of narrow stairs and along a hall reeking of stale smoke. Hanging lanterns cast a muted glow on the greyish walls.

The woman stopped and thumped on a door. "Your friend in here."

After a minute the door cracked open and a bare-chested Ryan glanced out. His eyes met Talos's and he opened the door further. "About fucking time."

Ignoring the woman, Talos carried the trembling girl in, released her, and shut the door. She ran to another girl sitting on the edge of the bed. They clung to each other, their identical, terrified gazes locked on him. *Bloody hell, they're twins.*

Ryan pulled on his shirt. "I couldn't answer the door fully clothed, that hag would've got suspicious." He frowned at the two girls. "After hearing about Shaw's rescue work, I picked that one. She told me she had a sister, but I didn't realize they were twins."

"What's their story?"

"Parents died in a motorbike accident. An uncle brought them here two weeks ago."

Talos fisted his hands. "Their uncle?"

"They've been beaten everyday for refusing to do as they're told." Ryan grimaced. "We have to take them with us, they're only fifteen."

"There's another young girl across the road." Talos pulled out his phone. "I'll get Jarred to ring Shaw. He'll know what to do with them. Is Huang somewhere close?"

"Next room and Nick's watching the back entrance. That's our exit route."

Talos made the call then dropped to his haunches in front of the two sisters. "We're going to take you to a safe place where no one will hurt you. Do you understand?"

They both nodded.

"There's going to be a lot of smoke and noise, but I need you to stay here while we take care of some bad people. Will you do that for me?"

Again they nodded.

Standing, he dug several packets of foam earplugs from his pocket, threw one to Ryan, inserted his own and handed the two girls a packet each. They kept their eyes on him as they put them in their ears.

Satisfied, he drew out three smoke cartridges from his jacket then opened the door and followed Ryan out, closing the door quietly behind them. At the top of the stairwell, Ryan took a cartridge, twisted the lid, and rolled it down several steps. Smoke began billowing downwards.

Talos flicked the fire alarm switch and immediately a high-pitched wail tore through the building. He opened his two cartridges and rolled them along the hall. Within seconds smoke filled the entire area.

Shouting broke out below. Several doors off the hall opened and naked men and girls ran out clutching their clothing, yelling and jostling to get down the stairs.

Ryan stood aside, and then stepped back to guard the stairs.

Talos waited.

Huang's door opened and two partially clad girls ran out, slamming into him in their haste. He allowed them to pass then entered the room and shut the door.

Huang had his pants on and was fumbling to do up the button under his fat gut. His gaze lifted. "Is there a fire?"

"No."

He pulled on his shirt. "I know you. Aren't we staying at the same hotel?"

"Yes."

"What you looking at me like that? Who are you?"

The fire alarm continued to wail.

Talos stepped forward. "I'm the man that's going to beat the shit out of you for ruining so many young lives." He struck swiftly with a sucker punch to the stomach.

Huang gagged and fell forward, face planting in the threadbare carpet. He rolled onto his side, groaning and clutching his fat gut.

"Soft bellied bastard." Talos dragged him up and threw him against the wall, rattling the glass pane alongside. Huang slid to the floor.

"You'll never hurt another girl." Talos reached for him.

"Wait," gasped Huang. "I'll pay whatever you want." He crawled onto his knees.

"I don't want your filthy money, shithead. I want to see you dead."

"No, please. I'll give you anything."

Dragging the creep to his feet, Talos shoved him against the wall again and wedged his forearm against Huang's throat. "I know you're part of a trafficking ring. Tell me your partners' names and your contact or I'll end your miserable life now."

Huang's eyes bulged. "I don't know their real names."

Lifting him higher, Talos increased the pressure. "Not the answer I want."

Huang clawed at his arm. "Why you care? Those girls not important, they nobody."

Talos slammed Huang's head against the wall then heaved him across the room. A chair broke his fall, collapsing with the impact. Huang didn't so much as twitch.

The fire alarm continued to wail.

Talos rolled Huang over. *The piece of shit is still breathing.* He peered out the window onto the lane below. Pimps, bouncers, and prostitutes stood around as bikes were moved to make way for a fire truck.

Twisting the cap off his last canister, Talos dropped it beside the window, waited a couple of seconds then opened the window to let the smoke escape. Several firemen looked up then ran for their ladder.

The alarm continued to scream. Talos scanned the room. He spied a lighter, used ashtray and remnants of white powder on the bedside table. *Perfect, cocaine and sex. Not a good combination for an overweight, middle-aged man.*

He dragged Huang to the door then pulled out the vial of guncotton, emptied it onto the rumpled bedding and lit it with his own lighter. It sizzled then the bedding erupted into flames, their cover story for the fire alarm. *Burn baby burn.*

A crash reverberated in the hall, shaking the door with the impact. Grabbing the empty canister, Talos wrenched the door open. He found Ryan facing off with the two Chinese men from downstairs. One held a switchblade ready to strike at the first opportunity.

Clutching the canister, Talos dragged Huang into the hall and shut the door. He swiveled, found his balance, and lashed out with his size thirteen boot. The snap of bone brought a scream from the man and sent the knife flying. Moving in fast, Talos delivered a hammer fist to his ribs. *Crack.* A palm plant to the jaw. *Thwack.* The man dropped.

Ryan dispensed a kick to his attacker's kidney followed by a knife strike to the back of the head, sending him crumpling to the carpet, out cold alongside his mate.

"Get the girls," yelled Ryan over the wailing siren. He threw two empty canisters at Talos then hoisted one of the men over his shoulders and lumbered downward as Nick bounded up holding another empty canister.

"Back door is clear." Nick heaved the other man across his shoulders.

Talos glanced at the two young girls staring from the half open doorway, their eyes as wide as saucers. They had Ryan's jacket around them. Voices sounded from Huang's room. "Let's go." He waved the twins ahead then bent and lifted Huang onto his shoulders.

Out on the back lane, amongst trash and the stench of urine, two Vietnamese men waited with a gurney. Talos lowered Huang across the gurney alongside his two minders and watched as they were trundled up the narrow lane to where Jarred and Gibbs should now be waiting with the van.

Nick pulled up his hoody. "I'll stay with those guys. Turn on your phone, Simon's trying to reach you." He ran off into the dark.

Talos pulled out his earplugs and turned to Ryan. "Watch the twins. There's something I need to take care of. I'll meet you at the van."

"Shaw's people are here. Let them handle it."

"No. The first sign of anyone official and the other kid will vanish."

He pulled out his phone and selected Simon's contact. "What's the problem, mate?"

"Jane's gone. She took off with Shaw."

Talos's arms became as heavy as lead, and a sharp ache burned in his chest. His brain couldn't make sense of Simon's words. *No, she loves me. She wouldn't go with Shaw.* "You were supposed to be fucking guarding her. How the hell did this happen?"

"Jarred rang Shaw about the young girls you found. He immediately got on his phone and began organizing things. Then while I was in the bathroom, they both disappeared. I've been trying to fucking contact you for the last fifteen minutes."

"Shit." The relief was short-lived. Had Shaw taken her by force or had she gone willingly. "Ring Shaw and tell him to get her back to the hotel now."

"I have. She refuses to come back."

Talos dragged a hand through his hair. "I'll ring her neck when I get hold of her."

Running feet snapped Talos's attention to the right. Sure enough the woman causing him so much grief came hurtling towards them, with no fucking wig.

He glared at her. "You promised me."

She met his angry gaze without the slightest remorse. "I couldn't just sit there and do nothing." She gathered the trembling sisters in her arms. "I'm not as intimidating as you big guys and it's not as if anyone knows I'm here. Do what you have to and I'll wait at the end of the lane. And don't worry, I'll keep out of sight." She hurried the girls away.

Ryan raised an eyebrow. "I'll stay here and make sure no one follows them."

Talos's phone rang. He glanced at the screen then answered. "Jarred?"

"What's keeping you? Let's go."

"There's something I need to do first." He shoved the used smoke canister in his pocket.

"Fuck, Talos. We're operating without authorized approval. Get out of there now."

"I won't be long." He ended the call and ran back into the brothel, past a fireman and out the front entrance. Across the lane he spotted his target standing in the same place, a cigarette dangling from his fingers as he watched the drama. The hard-eyed madam from the brothel stood beside him. *Fuck, mother and son.*

Talos strode over. "Where's the girl?"

The man straightened. "Inside. Where's Mister Lhasa?"

"Dead. He suffered a heart attack. The ambulance men took him out the back way."

The man's eyes widened. "Dead?"

The woman recoiled as if slapped then ran off.

Talos clenched his teeth. "Let's go." Talos followed the man into a hair salon. Several women in short dresses and high heels sprang to their feet. He gestured them away and focused on the man. "I'll pay five hundred American dollars, but I want to see her first."

His eyes sharpened. "Five hundred dollar?"

"Take it or leave it."

"I take it." He led the way up two flights of stairs then crossed the landing to a blue door with several locks. "I keep her in this room so she not escape."

Clenching his jaw, Talos made no comment as the man unlocked the door. The small room was dimly lit with several unmade beds placed haphazardly. Torn blinds covered grilled windows. A bucket stood in the corner, the faint whiff of urine indicating its purpose. Bottles of water and empty food bowls littered the floor. Vietnamese graffiti covered every wall. The room appeared empty then he heard a snivel coming from under a bed.

Keeping one eye on the man, he dropped to his knees and peered underneath. A pair of big brown eyes stared back at him. Talos released his breath. She looked about the same age as the twins, but didn't have their haunted, broken look. He could save her, but she didn't need to witness the violence he was about to dish out. Incensed, he stood and faced the salon's owner. "Let's discuss your payment outside, shall we?"

"Yes, yes."

Talos followed him into hall and closed the door. "Do you have more like her?"

"No, you very lucky."

Talos hit him with a right hook, splitting his lip and sending him crashing into the wall.

The man shook his head then scrambled to his feet, wiping blood from his mouth. "You dead," he shouted, pulling a knife and slashing at Talos.

From below came the sound of pounding feet.

Sidestepping, Talos whipped out the smoke canister and blocked the swinging arm then struck with a hammer fist to the ribs. They cracked and the man doubled over. Talos gripped his wrist, twisted the arm behind, and dislocated his shoulder. The man screamed and fell to his knees. His rescuers thundered up the last stairs. Talos bent and dragged him to his feet.

"This is for all the young girls you've ruined." He threw the monster into the oncoming bouncers, knocking them head over arse back down the stairs.

The owner lay in a heap, screaming. The others picked themselves up and came at Talos. He waited. The first he dispatched with a right hook and heel kick to the bladder, knocking him into next week. The second received a boot to the solar plexus, rendering him out cold before he crashed to the landing below. The third came in swinging. Talos blocked the first blow with the canister then hit him with an uppercut. As the man staggered, Talos turned and struck with a savage kick to the kneecap. It popped and the man bellowed.

The fourth man fled.

Talos leapt down the stairs, landing on one of the owner's legs. It snapped and the man fainted. The last man turned. He came in low, roaring like a mad bull and caught Talos around the torso. He got a couple of punches in before Talos belted him with the canister. As the bouncer fell back, Talos kneed him viciously in the stomach, following through with a hammer punch to the back of the head. The man dropped to the floor. Talos shoved the canister back in his pocket.

Time to go. He bounded up the stairs, over the inert men, opened the door and scooped up the girl as she attempted to crawl back under a bed. She cried and lashed out at his face.

"Shush." He held her to his chest and took the stairs in leaps. None of the men moved. At the entrance, he pushed past a couple of girls, ducked around the fire truck, and jogged up the narrow street and around the corner. Nobody paid any attention. They were too intent on seeing what was happening at the brothel.

As he approached the open van, Jane's voice cried out from the lane backing onto the brothel. "Somebody, please help me. Let go you cow."

Throwing the girl into Nick's arms, Talos sprinted into the darkness, his heart in his mouth. Behind a garbage cart he found Jane blocking the path of the Madam who had hold of both twins and was attempting to drag them away. Relief flooded his body.

The Madam yanked one of the girls hard. "I whip you for this."

Bloody hell. He gripped the woman's arm and shook her, releasing one twin. "I've never hit a woman, but if you don't let go, I'll make you my exception."

"You get your own girls. I pay one hundred dollar for them. They belong to me."

Jane shrieked. "You cow." She sprang forward and punched the woman in the eye.

The madam's head snapped back and she lost her grip on the other twin. Both young girls leapt behind Talos.

Fearing the woman might pull a knife on Jane, he shoved her away, hooked his arm around Jane, and lifted her clear. He placed her beside the wide-eyed twins. "Stay there."

She glared at him. "What are you going to do about her?"

He looked at the woman, sitting on the ground with a hand over her eye. She began yelling abuse at him. "Gibbs can hand her over to the Crime Unit along with Huang, his minders, and any other casualties we've left behind."

Running feet heralded Ryan. He did a quick scan then turned to Talos. "Let's get out of here. I'll take the girls' to Shaw, and Jane back to the hotel."

Talos strode over to the woman and pulled her up. She spat at him and began ranting in Vietnamese. He gripped her elbow and propelled her along the lane in the wake of Ryan, Jane, and the twins. As they reached the van, the other young girl ran to the twins. Their shared hug suggested they knew each other. *Poor little things were probably kept together in that room.*

Talos caught Jane's eye. "Go with Ryan, we'll talk later." He urged the brothel owner into the rear of the van where Huang and his two minders sat gagged and trussed.

Several police cars pulled up across the next street's entrance. Talos ducked into the van and closed the door. It soothed him somewhat to know the police would raid each brothel, release any underage girls, and shut down the premises. On the other hand, Jane's complete disregard for her own welfare rattled him. In these streets, anything could have happened. *I need her safe. I need her secure.* The band around his chest tightened. *I need her in my life.*

CHAPTER FIFTEEN

After a three-hour debriefing with Jarred and Gibbs, Talos was tired and only too glad to get back to his room and Jane. They had two full days in which to get to Nha Trang and plan the next take down. Yawning, he opened the door and slipped in quietly.

Simon looked up from the notepad he was scribbling on and pointed to the couch where Jane lay sleeping. Ella was in her stroller beside Simon.

Talos kept his voice low. "Any visitors?"

"Only the police. They dropped by several hours ago to inform the manager three guests had died as a result of smoke inhalation at a local brothel. They then collected Huang and his two minder's belongings and left. I assume they were from the Serious Crime Unit."

"Yeah, Gibbs did a deal with them. The SCU police will hold each ring member in isolation until we get them all, but we have to hand over any evidence we find and let the Vietnamese police put them on trial in this country."

"So the police are willing to pretend Huang and his two friends are dead for now?"

"Yep."

"What about the agent?"

"Gibbs believes the agent will hear about Huang's demise through the grapevine and won't turn up for the meeting, but if he does, once Huang is late, he won't hang around and neither will we. Catching them all depends on the agent not becoming suspicious."

Closing his laptop, Simon flipped his notebook shut and stood. "I hear you took out a few extra scumbags tonight?"

Talos flicked a glance at Jane. She hadn't woken. "Nothing I couldn't handle. What happened after we left?"

"The police raided both brothels and thanks to your handy work, took in eight unconscious men with multiple broken bones and of course the pissed off Madam. They will also be held in isolation until we have all ring members and the agent." He chuckled. "Witnesses are hailing you, *The Punisher*. I'm impressed."

Talos grimaced. "Sorry, I blasted you earlier. It freaked me out that Shaw took Jane into a situation that could have ended badly."

"Forget it. She's one of those people who care and probably didn't give him a choice."

"Yeah, but he put her at risk." Talos saw Simon out the door then locked it and took a long shower. After donning a pair of boxers he squatted in front of Jane.

"Hey, sleepy head, it's time for bed."

Jane stirred, blinked at him then opened her eyes wide. "You're back!" Her gaze scanned his chest. "Is everything okay?"

"Fine. Huang and his minders are in custody and the three girls have been taken to a rescue facility, where they will get the help they need. Why aren't you in bed?"

"I needed to know you were all right."

He stared into her serious eyes. Elliot Shaw was right. They were stunning and under the light of the bedside lamp, they'd darkened to a warm emerald.

He drew in a deep breath. "What do you think of Elliot Shaw?"

Jane blinked. "I like him, why?"

"I think he's attracted to you."

She smiled. "Is that because he complimented me on my eyes and smile?"

"Elliot bloody Shaw is an opportunist and would say anything to get your attention."

"So you don't agree with him?" One of her shapely eyebrows rose.

"No. I mean, yes. You do have stunning eyes, but I noticed them first."

Jane laughed. "Talos, are you jealous of Elliot?"

"No, I just think you should be wary. He's a smooth operator and he fancies you."

Leaning over, Jane kissed his cheek. "No, he doesn't. He's just being nice, but even so, you don't have anything to worry about because he's—"

"Good." Talos drew her to her feet and turned serious. "You pull another stunt like tonight and I'll personally take you back to Australia and lock you in my wine cellar."

She sighed. "I knew Ella would be safe with Simon and that those young girls would be terrified. I thought my presence might ease their fears." She stroked his face. "And I knew you wouldn't let anything happen to me."

"Christ, I didn't even know you were there." He shook off a sudden chill. "Hearing your voice in that lane took five years off my life."

"I'm sorry. I'm not normally impulsive or brave, and I've never punched anyone before."

He picked up her hand and smoothed the bruised knuckles. "You need to know how to defend yourself properly."

She stroked her fingertips over his chest. "One of the policewomen taught me a few moves while I was in witness protection. I could try them out on you now if you like."

His tired muscles rippled under her touch. *I need to be alert tomorrow.* Reining in his libido, he traced his thumb over her soft lips. "Once we've got Marzetti's partners, I'll take you somewhere nice. We might hire a yacht, cruise around for a couple of days, and you can practice your skills on me all day long."

Eyes twinkling, she gave him a wicked smile. "But how will you occupy me at night?"

His body stirred. "I'm sure something will come up to keep you entertained."

"Hmm, that sounds promising." She stretched up and kissed him. "I'm going to have a shower." She unzipped her skirt and let it fall to the floor then slowly drew off her top.

Unable to look away, he watched her sashay towards the bathroom in a scrap of red lace and matching bra, the soft glow of the lamp accentuating her curves. Again he clamped down on his rising excitement. They both needed sleep if they were to function properly and keep their wits about them.

Turning, she met his gaze. "Do you want to join me?"

Oh God, Yes. He skimmed the swell of her breasts, the soft contour of her hips, and her long shapely legs. *Shit.* Taking a deep breath,

Talos pointed at the bathroom. "Go before you drive me insane. I've had a big night and I haven't slept properly for three days."

She stilled. "Me either, but I will tonight, knowing you're here and I'm one step closer to regaining my freedom."

"Have your shower then you can *sleep* in my arms."

"Deal." She darted into the bathroom.

Yawning, Talos crawled into bed. He was beat and ached where one of the bouncers got in a lucky punch, but all in all he was happy with the way things had gone down. The three girls were safe and a bunch of monsters behind bars. His mind shifted to Jane, imagining her standing under the steaming cascade of water as she lathered her body.

Shit, now I've got a hard on.

He was still wide-awake when she re-entered the room, naked. She shimmied between the sheets and pressed her backside against his groin, which reacted predictably.

"Aren't you supposed to be sleeping?" she whispered.

He grunted and kissed her shoulder. "Yes, but I'm wide awake now." He gritted his teeth as she wriggled again, then to his surprise she chuckled.

"I know a sure way to help you sleep, and I have it on great authority that it works."

Talos laughed and rolled her beneath him. "That was my line."

Spreading her fingers wide across his chest, she smiled. "I know, but it worked. I did sleep well." Her smile faded as she looked into his eyes. "I'm sorry I accused you of flirting with that Asian woman. The last few days have been horrible and I was scared you'd change your mind about us."

"Never. You are the most fascinating and desirable woman I've ever met." He couldn't help smiling as she blushed under his scrutiny. "You're beautiful, Jane. Every damn inch of you and that's something Elliot bloody Shaw will never know."

"Poor Elliott, he hasn't done anything to deserve your contempt and—"

"And he'll keep it that way if he wants to retain his pretty face. You're mine."

"Oh, Talos." She wrapped her arms around his shoulders. "Elliott's not interested in me. He's married to a beautiful woman."

"You're a beautiful woman and no hot blooded male would think twice about making a move on you, whether he's married or not."

"What about your friends?"

He laughed. "Don't think it hasn't cross their minds. The only thing stopping them is their friendship with me and the fact they know I'd break every bone in their bodies."

She raised an eyebrow. "I don't think so."

"I'm serious. You're a very sexy lady."

"Stop trying to sweet talk me and kiss me."

"It's the truth." Lowering his head, Talos lightly brushed his lips across hers, inwardly smiling when she grumbled and dragged him closer.

Determined to go slow and savor each second, he parted her lips and explored her mouth. A shudder ran through his body at the first touch of her pert nipples against his chest. Moving to her neck, he gently sucked, not wanting to bruise her soft as silk skin. She quivered under his lips, a moan escaping as she arched, allowing him better access. His cock throbbed. *Slowly, slowly.*

Shifting to one side, Talos glided his hand over her smooth thigh and hip. "You are everything a man could ever want."

He dragged off his boxers and rubbed himself against her curls.

Mumbling incoherently against his shoulder, she ran her hand down his chest and stomach. He jerked as her fingers closed around his cock, groaning when she slid her palm back and forth. Her other hand closed around his balls.

"I won't last long if you do that."

"I don't care. I like touching you."

"Later." Coming to his knees, he sat back on his ankles and spread her legs wider. "Much better."

She blushed from the tip of her toes to the top of her head, but whether it was from his scrutiny or his stiff cock, he didn't know. He positioned his shoulders between her thighs and blew on her thatch of dark hair.

She squirmed. "Talos, we don't have time for that. I want you inside me."

"Patience, sweetheart. Good things come to those who wait."

"No. You'll make me scream and the guys will hear and come running."

Talos laughed so hard, his eyes watered. "They won't I promise." He cupped her backside and lifted her to meet his mouth then thrust his tongue deep. She was wet and wanton. He licked her juices then went in for the kill, thrusting deep again.

She cried out, quivered and orgasmed around his tongue. "Oh God, Talos."

"I haven't finished yet."

"Stop! I can't take anymore." She tried to push him away. "Talos."

The scent of her nearly sent him over the edge. She was intoxicating. He gripped her tighter and devoured her again.

She screamed and came explosively again, her thighs clamping around his head in a surprisingly strong grip. "Talos, I'm begging. Please, no more."

Releasing her, he wiped his mouth. "Now for your reward." He grabbed a condom off the bedside table, sheathed himself, and gripped her hips, thrusting into her again and again, knocking the breath out of her in harsh puffs.

With heaving breasts and erect nipples, she met each thrust with wild eyes, her fingernails digging into his shoulders so hard, he was sure he'd have claw marks. *Wildcat.*

Pulling out, he flipped her onto her front and dragged her onto her knees, placing her delicious backside right where he wanted it, then he guided his cock back inside her.

She moaned. "You're going to kill me."

He closed one hand over a breast and cupped her wet center with the other. "You can thank me later." He stroked her sex with his fingers, withdrew his cock slowly, and thrust deep, again and again, the raw sensuality of skin against skin nearly blowing his mind. She fitted like a glove, moaning and gasping as she met each thrust with enthusiasm. He was close.

"I'm coming." She shuddered, cried out his name, and tightened around his cock.

Roaring, he reached his own climax, and then collapsed. After a minute, he pulled out, rolled to the side, and traced his fingers over her smooth unblemished back. She didn't move.

Smiling, he continued his exploration across her delectable backside and up the side of her ribs, skimming her breast. A quiver ran through her. "You okay?" he asked, grinning.

"I'm dead; you killed me."

Laughing, he lifted her hair and planted kisses on her neck. "You look pretty hot for a dead woman. How about another shower?"

"I haven't got the energy."

"Leave it to me. I'll take care of you. I'll always take care of you." Rolling off the bed, he strode into the bathroom and turned on the shower. Once he had the temperature right, he went back into the bedroom and scooped her into his arms.

She nuzzled into his neck. "I love you, Talos."

"And I worship you." He carried her into the bathroom and stepped into the shower.

Her eyes sprang open as the warm water hit her. "That's so nice."

Placing her on her feet, he lathered her from head to foot, amused that she didn't lift a finger to help, just leaned against the tiles with a dreamy smile on her lips. Ignoring his hard-on, he rinsed her off, dried her, and carried her back to bed.

She sighed as he drew her into his arms. "That was the most incredible thing anyone has ever done to me. You really do desire me?"

"You better believe it."

"In the morning, I'm going to take care of you, my darling and I've decided I will move in with you when this is all over." She closed her eyes and surrendered to sleep.

He dropped a light kiss on her forehead and smiled. "There was never any doubt about that, sweetheart. You and Ella are mine now." *My precious gems.*

CHAPTER SIXTEEN

Jane lay in a heavenly trance, cocooned within a muscular arm. A large hand cupped her breast, a large body spooned to hers, and a warm breath feathered her neck. *Talos.*

The low hum of traffic intruded on her trance, and she cracked open an eyelid to find pale light creeping in from the edge of the curtain. *No, it can't be morning.*

A lively melody sounded and he rolled away to answer his phone. Disappointed, she rolled onto her back and studied his cognac eyes, proud nose, and strong jaw.

He frowned. "How long have they been there?" Throwing back the covers, he left the bed and strode to the window where he moved the curtain slightly. "I see them."

Jane could happily gaze at his muscled physique for hours. She shifted her attention to his impressive biceps, honed from years of chopping wood, playing drums, and training with the army. Her gaze slid to his firm, naked butt. *Nice.*

His beautiful eyes locked on her. "Is that really necessary?"

"What?" Jane came up on her elbow, embarrassed to be caught staring at his butt.

He held up a hand and spoke to his caller. "We can't leave by the front, they've got a perfect view of the entrance."

"Who?" She slid out of bed and ran to his side, leaning against his warm body as she peeked past the curtain onto the street below. Motorbikes with one, two, and three people on board whizzed past, as did cars and taxis. On the other side of the street sat a shiny black car.

Talos drew her away from the curtain as he continued speaking.

"Ask Shaw to organize a laundry van to pick us up. It can be backed into the lane beside the hotel."

Jane turned to Talos as he ended the call. "What's happening? Who are those men?"

"I've no idea. They could be police, or connected with Huang or his agent, but whoever they are, we're not taking any chances. Get dressed and pack your gear, we're leaving."

"What now?"

"Right now."

"I have to feed Ella."

"There's no time." He strode into the bathroom.

"Shit, my life is turning into Mission Impossible." She picked up her clothes and threw them into her suitcase. *I was looking forward to a little one on one time.* She pulled on underwear, jeans, and a loose top, then shoved the change bag under the stroller and smiled at Ella. "Hello, possum, did you sleep well?"

Ella stopped sucking her fingers and cooed.

The bathroom door opened and Talos came out carrying his toiletry bag. "You bring Ella and I'll get your suitcase. We need to move fast."

"Why?"

He pulled on his clothes. "So we're not taken by surprise."

"I have to use the bathroom." She slid on her sandals, grabbed her own toiletry case, and ran. A quick glance in the mirror confirmed her worst fears. Tangled hair, stubble rash and glowing like a beacon.

"Shit." She took care of business, threw water on her face, finger-combed her hair, brushed her teeth, and strapped on her watch. *My God, it's only five-twenty!*

She emerged to find Talos holding his duffle bag in one hand and Ella tucked up in her sleep carrier in the other.

"Ryan's taken the stroller and Simon's got your suitcase. Let's go."

Running to keep up, Jane followed Talos past the lift and around a corner into another hall that crossed to the rooms on the other side of the hotel. Talos stopped at an exit door where they found Nick casually leaning against the wall.

His lips twitched. "Big night, or is that another wig?"

"Very funny." She tried smoothing her fluffy hair. "It was wet when I fell asleep.

"Hmm, you're obviously very active during the night then."

"Stow it, Nick." Talos opened the exit door and held it wide for her.

Nick laughed, a nice rich sound reminding her she had unfinished business where he and Ava were concerned.

They hurried down the stairs then Talos scanned the courtyard and motioned Jane forward. "Let's go." He strode across the courtyard to a gate in the wall. "Stay with Nick while I check it's safe." He passed the carrier to her and ducked through.

Nick shrugged. "I know this is a pain in the arse, but we can't risk an encounter."

"It's okay. Better safe than sorry." Jane cradled the carrier in her arms, rocking Ella who was beginning to grumble. "Shush, honey, I'll feed you in a minute."

"All clear," called Talos.

She hurried to the back of a white van, where Talos stood with the doors open. Jarred, Simon, and Ryan sat on laundry bags around the walls of the van. Two Vietnamese men sat in the front cab with the engine running.

Talos helped her in, then he and Nick climbed in and shut the doors. No one spoke as the van pulled out into the street and joined the chaotic stream of tooting early morning traffic.

Shuffling her laundry bag into a more comfortable position, Jane leaned against Talos, lifted Ella from the carrier and discreetly began to feed her. "Where are we going?"

Simon looked up from his laptop. "We're on our way to rent a mini van, then we plan to drive three and a half hours to Muong Man, have breakfast, then catch the train to Nha Trang, which should get us to the hotel in time for a late lunch. I just need to book us tickets."

"Can I change Ella and brush my hair before we go?"

Jarred's gaze fixed on her hair then dropped to her chin. "I'll give you ten minutes."

She squirmed, her face so hot she risked internal combustion. "Thanks."

Talos put his arm around her, buffeting her from the wall of the van. "Take care of Ella and I'll get you something to eat." He squeezed her arm. "You look beautiful."

Sure, stubble rash and psycho hair. She looked up and saw open sincerity in his eyes.

Ryan cleared his throat. "Can we trust Shaw?"

"Simon checked him out," replied Jarred. "He's twenty-seven, been married for six years, no children. His father's a High Court Judge, his mother's a psychologist, and his brother's a criminal lawyer. Shaw has a degree in corporate law and along with his business partner, Trang Huynh, runs a successful software consultancy business here in Vietnam. And, he's set up shelters in Ho Chi Min and Hanoi for children rescued from sweatshops and brothels."

"What about Gibbs?" Talos asked. "We know Marzetti had one mole in the AFP but there could be more. Someone told those thugs where Jane was being housed."

Jarred shook his head. "Gibbs has a clean record and some high profile cases under his belt. He's also worked fucking..." He glanced at Jane. "Sorry. He's worked extremely hard on convincing the Vietnamese Crime Squad to work with us."

Nick grunted. "Doesn't mean he's not working for Marzetti. It's a perfect scenario. He gains our trust, is aware of our movements, then when we least expect it, has a couple of hit men take us out."

Shocked, Jane looked at each of their serious faces. "Why go to all that trouble? Inspector Gibbs could have killed me on numerous occasions, but he didn't."

Talos's arm tightened round her. "He wouldn't risk exposure." He glanced at Simon. "Have you found anything on him?"

"I've combed through the file on Gibbs and he's squeaky clean, highly respected, and destined for high places, but there's one thing that bothers me."

"What?" came a chorus of deep voices.

"According to his license, he was born in Australia, yet I can't find any evidence of his birth. Zachary Gibbs does not exit prior to joining the police force."

Jarred's eyes narrowed. "And you didn't think to tell me this before?"

"I only discovered it last night. I was searching for someone else..." His gaze flicked to Nick then Jane, then back to Jarred. "While I was in the Roads and Maritime database, I noted his date of birth then hacked into the Births, Deaths and Marriage database. He isn't there."

Beside Jane, Talos stiffened. "Could his date of birth be wrong?"

Simon shrugged. "I did a deep search on every Zachary Gibbs, using a variety of different spellings, even leaving out the date of birth. And, except for one Zakour Erik Farid Gibbs, born the same day but in Switzerland, I couldn't find a match."

"Could Inspector Gibbs be Zakour and he changed his name?" asked Jane.

"There would have to be a record of it."

"What's your gut feeling?" asked Jarred.

"His mother worked for the Diplomatic Service in Saudi Arabia for many years. It's possible his father is someone very important and she's protecting his identity."

"Why would you think that?" Jane asked.

"Because no father has been recorded on the birth certificate of Zakour Gibbs, yet he had to have been conceived during her stint in Saudi Arabia."

Jane glanced around the van. All five men were contemplating this news. She frowned. "Zakour sounds Middle Eastern."

"Yes." Jarred's gaze locked on her for three heartbeats then he looked at Simon. "Do a deeper check on the mother and any other family. See if that turns anything up."

"Sure."

"Who else were you checking out?" asked Ryan.

Again Simon's gaze flicked to Nick then Jane. "Just doing someone a favor."

Talos turned his head and looked at her, one eyebrow raised, his eyes questioning.

She began fussing with Ella. "I think you've had enough, young lady." She adjusted her shirt then sat Ella up and rubbed her back. "I'd kill for a cup of tea."

Ella's gaze locked on Talos and she began blowing raspberries. He chuckled. "I think that's her way of telling me she likes me."

Smiling, Jane passed Ella into his arms where she immediately snuggled in like a koala. "I think you might be right." Jane yawned and leaned against his shoulder.

The van slowed and pulled into a large warehouse full of cars and mini vans. The Vietnamese man in the front passenger seat jumped out and opened the rear doors.

"You come." He waved them forward.

"I'll take care of the rental," called Jarred climbing out of the van. He hesitated by the door. "Someone grab drinks and snacks to tide us over." He strode to a counter.

Shoving her toiletry case into Ella's change bag, Jane picked up the carrier and scrambled out. She looked around for somewhere to change Ella then fix her own hair.

A pretty Vietnamese woman wearing a soft pastel tunic over blue silk trousers came forward with a tray of liquid filled glasses. "Please, you like honey tea refreshment?"

"Thank you." Jane took a glass and drank the lukewarm brew. It slid down her throat in a delicious swirl of flavors. Mint, honey, and lime juice. "Yum."

"You like."

"Yes, I do."

All five men tentatively accepted a glass of honey tea then downed it in one gulp. Their expressions told her they would have preferred strong hot coffee. She hid her grin and turned to the woman. "Is there somewhere I can change my baby and freshen up?"

"Yes, you come with me please."

Lifting Ella from Talos's arms, Jane followed the woman into a room with a sink, several chairs, a coffee table and a mirror. "Thank you."

"You are welcome."

Jane laid the carrier on the table, changed Ella, then redressed her in fresh clothes. "Now it's mummy's turn." She brushed her wild mess, pulled it up into a high ponytail and applied moisturizer. "From now on, I'll make him shave, unless there's no one around." She packed everything up, put the old nappy in a bin and picked up the carrier. "Let's go, possum."

She came out to find Jarred, Ryan, and Simon deep in conversation beside a large van.

"Where's Talos?"

"Right here, sweetheart."

She whirled around to see him and Nick coming through the main door, each carrying a cardboard container laden with croissants and coffee cups.

Talos's gaze swept over her then he grinned. "You look good enough to eat, but I did enjoy the sexy, just out of bed look."

"Please," called Nick. "There are a few of us not getting any at the moment. Do you have to rub it in?" He handed out coffees and croissants.

Talos laughed. "Sorry, I couldn't help myself." He took the change bag out of her hand and passed it to Simon, then handed her a cup. "They didn't have tea so I got you a half strength latte and croissant."

"Perfect, thank you." She lowered her voice. "I like your sexy, just out of bed look too."

"Hoy," called Nick. "Can you to two lovebirds put a sock in it?"

As Jarred took his coffee and croissant she could have sworn she caught a glimpse of envy in his eyes, before his unreadable expression returned. *What type of woman would interest Jarred? It would have to be someone who doesn't scare easily.*

Talos finished his croissant in two bites and downed his coffee. "Have a croissant. I'll take Ella and put her in the bus."

"Great." Jane handed over the carrier, picked up the delicious looking pastry and bit into it. "On my God, this is incredible. It's so crisp and light, and it's got chocolate inside."

He chuckled. "The Vietnamese are known for their delicate pastries. It's a legacy from when the French colonial rule here. I'll find you a baguette if we have time to stop for breakfast."

"Yum. I could eat these all day, but then I'd never lose weight."

He frowned. "You don't need to lose weight, sweetheart. You've got a great figure."

"I have to agree," called Simon. "I like curves on a woman."

"Yeah, me too," agreed Ryan. "The curvier the better."

Embarrassed, Jane glanced away and straight into Nick's face. He wasn't smiling, just staring at the ground, miles away, his expression bleak.

He's thinking of Ava. I just know it.

"If we want to make that train, we need to move now," called Jarred.

Jane glanced at her watch. *Quarter to Six. We won't have time for another breakfast.* She finished her croissant, gulped down her latte, then climbed into the mini-bus. They had a Vietnamese driver up the front, and seating for twelve in the back. Plenty of space to spread out, which was a good thing as her travelling companions were all big guys.

She slid onto a seat beside Talos who had Ella cradled in his arms. The carrier and change bag were nowhere to be seen. He noticed her looking around.

"They're up with the driver. In case of an accident I thought it safer to hold her in my arms, rather than leave her unrestrained in the carrier."

"Good thinking." She placed her hand on his thigh, leaned against his shoulder and whispered, "I might catch some sleep. I didn't get that much last night."

His free hand covered hers. "Good idea, you won't get much tonight either," he whispered back.

A shiver of excitement raced through her. "In that case, you should get some rest too."

"I'll get some on the train."

Simon heard and turned in his seat. "I've booked two four-seat cabins. That should give you both a chance to catch some sleep. I'll even take the watch."

"I'd appreciate that." Talos squeezed Jane's hand.

CHAPTER SEVENTEEN

Travelling alongside Jane for eight hours had left Talos on tenterhooks. Each brush of her hand or leg tightened his muscles another notch until he felt like a Neanderthal, who hadn't had a woman in months. He inwardly groaned. *I need a run or workout in the gym.*

As their taxi turned into the hotel, Jane gasped.

He smiled at the excitement in her eyes. "You like?"

"Are we really staying here?"

"Yep, and all the suites overlook the ocean.

"You've stayed here before?"

"No, but as the next meeting is in this hotel's coffee shop, we're hoping you spot Kazan before then."

"Which one is Kazan?"

"We assume he's the Russian, as Kazan is the name of a city in Russia."

"That should make it easier to spot him."

"You would think so, but Nha Trang is a favorite holiday destination for Russians."

The driver pulled up in front of an imposing entrance and two porters ran to open their doors. Jane jammed her sunhat on and climbed out, leaving him to follow with Ella. His gaze skimmed gleaming marble floors, a curved staircase, and grand piano. Several groups of people sat about the enormous foyer in fancy armchairs, chatting. Amongst the low babble, he could make out Russian, English, and German.

Jane's eye's sparkled. "I can't wait to see our room and explore Nha Trang."

"I thought you came here on your honeymoon. Is that wrong?"

Her grin faded and he could have kicked himself. *Idiot.*

She shrugged. "I did come to Nha Trang for a couple of days, but Andrew had meetings so I was alone a lot and we didn't go sightseeing."

"Sorry, but it could be important. Where else did you go?"

"We spent a couple of days in Ho Chi Min, Hoi An, and Hanoi then went to Sapa, where we stayed in a villa with incredible views of snow-capped mountains. Andrew said it belonged to an acquaintance."

"Do you remember his name or the address?"

"No, sorry."

"Doesn't matter, keep an eye out for our Russian while I check in." He led the way to the reception counter and handed over their passports. The receptionist took one look at Ella and went to mush, wanting to touch and fuss over her.

Ella in turn, gurgled, cooed and beamed for the smiling young woman.

Eventually Talos was given the keycard then a porter escorted them up to a large airy suite with floor to ceiling views of the ocean beyond.

Jane ran out onto the balcony. "Oh, Talos, come and look."

He tipped the porter and joined her. A cloudless powder-blue sky met the horizon, as did the turquoise ocean. Several islands framed the bay, and golden sand stretched for miles in either direction. Groups of thatched umbrellas dotted the beach, and palm trees lined the grassed buffer between road and sand. Below lay an enormous round pool, surrounded by Roman pillars and white cushioned daybeds. The pool's crystal clear water sparkled like thousands of diamonds across the surface.

"Wow, this is..."

Jane leaned against him. "I know."

He placed Ella in her arms. "How about we go for a swim? I need some exercise."

"Sounds good." She led the way back through to the lounge and into the bedroom. "Oh, look, we can lie in bed and look at the view."

Talos opened his duffle bag and pulled out board shorts. "Once I get you in that bed, I guarantee you won't be looking at the view."

She laughed and wandered into the bathroom. "It's got a nice big shower, which is handy as I owe you an all over body scrub."

His pulse quickened at the thought of her hands and mouth on him. "You'd better hurry before I change my mind about the pool and lunch." He kicked off his runners and socks.

She laughed again, lay Ella in the middle of the bed, and opened her suitcase. "Give me two minutes to change Ella and get my bikini on."

He kept his back to her as he changed, knowing if he watched her, they'd never get to the pool. The bathroom door clicked shut so he figured he was safe to wander over to the bed and entertain Ella.

A couple of minutes later Jane came bustling out wearing a flowery bikini showcasing her curvy body. His mouth went dry. Maybe he didn't need lunch.

"I'm ready," she called brightly.

"So am I." His voice sounded odd even to him.

Her gaze flicked to his eyes. "No, you need to eat."

"We can eat later."

"I might see the Russian." She tied a sarong around her chest and put on a floppy hat. "Will this be okay? I don't want to swim in a wig."

"You're gorgeous. Just keep sunglasses and the hat on and he shouldn't recognize you." Talos squashed his libido. She was right; they could indulge later and until then he would flirt a little. His stomach rumbled making his decision easier. Picking up Ella, he paced to the suite's door and held it open. "After you, sweetheart."

Jane swanned past and blew him a kiss. "Thank you, darling."

His gaze locked on her backside as she sashayed along the hall. *Later.*

They took the lift to the first floor then holding hands, walked out to the pool area.

Glancing at the giant carved pillars surrounding the round pool, Jane couldn't help feeling she'd stepped back in time to the Greek Empire. They stopped by two sun lounges set close together under a white umbrella.

Talos passed Ella over then dragged off his T-Shirt and Jane blatantly admired his chest. *My Greek God.*

His lips twitched. "By the looks of it, I'm not the only one that needs to cool off." He stepped to the edge of the pool and dived in, surfacing on the other side.

"Ha ha, very funny." She kicked off her sandals then sat on a sun lounge, cradling Ella, who began squirming as she impatiently searched for a nipple. "Calm down, sweetie." She untied the sarong, draped the soft silk over Ella's head, then slipped her bikini aside and discreetly fed Ella while surveying the other guests.

A few middle-aged women lay on their sun lounges sunbaking, another older couple lay reading, and several men sat at the bar drinking. No one looked familiar.

Her gaze moved to Talos, swimming back and forth across the pool, his powerful arms plowing through the water.

Several women sat up, their eyes locked on him.

He's mine ladies, eyes off.

She'd lost count of his laps when he finally swam to the edge and stood, his shoulders and chest clearing the water by several feet. "It's refreshing. Why don't you come in and play with me?" He splashed her feet.

"I plan to as soon as Ella's done." She glanced around the pool. All the women had their eyes glued to him. "Do you realize you're the center of attention and I am the envy of every woman here?"

He laughed and heaved his body out of the water. "Mark my words, once you get in that pool, men are going to come out of the woodwork."

She changed Ella to the other breast. "I don't think so."

"Believe it, sweetheart." He grabbed a towel off the other sun lounge and dried his face, chest, and stomach. "I'll order us some lunch." He leaned down and kissed her neck. "Won't be long."

An excited tremor ran through her as she watched him saunter over to the bar, his enormous shoulders glistening in the sun, his board-shorts sitting low on his hips and drawing attention to his broad back and firm butt. Squirming, she dragged her eyes away and glanced around the pool. The women's gazes were still locked on him. "Mine, mine, mine."

Jane adjusted her bikini, burped Ella, then lay her on the bed with a rolled towel on either side. "You have a sleep while mummy goes for a swim."

Talos was talking to the men at the bar so she took off her sunglasses, strolled to the edge of pool and dipped her toes. "Wow, no wonder he looked refreshed." Adjusting her floppy hat, she sat on the tiles and slid into the water, gasping as the cool water covered her heated body. Keeping her eyes on Ella, she treaded water, gradually moving to the middle of the pool. *This is good.*

A splash had her looking over her left shoulder in time to see a large underwater predator about to strike. She screeched, back-pedaled and kicked out to no effect. Caught within his strong hold, she had no alternative but to surrender as he surfaced, dragged her closer, and devoured her mouth.

Jane reveled. *Take that, ladies.* She clung to his big shoulders, wrapped her legs around his waist and rubbed against his erection, purring with pleasure.

Talos broke the kiss. "Damn, I love a wicked woman, but do that again and I'll take you here in the pool." He gripped her hips and launched her backwards through the air.

"No!" Arms flailing, she hit the water several meters away, lost her hat, and sank to the bottom. *Beast, I'll get you for this.* She surfaced, found her hat, and jammed it back on her head.

Talos had already reached the edge and was heaving himself out.

She laughed. "You can run, but you can't hide." She heard his deep chuckle and narrowed her eyes. *Wise guy.*

As she reached the ladder, he slid into the pool beside her with Ella, minus the romper suit. Sheltering her from the sun, he skimmed her tiny feet through the water, laughing at Ella's startled expression. She thrashed her arms and legs about, gurgling with delight.

Jane stared mesmerized as he played with Ella as if she were his own daughter. Tears stung her eyes and she quickly swiped them away.

He looked up and frowned. "Hey, what's wrong?"

"Nothing, I'm just happy you treasure her."

"Both of you." He pulled Jane against his side and kissed her. "My two precious gems."

Closing her eyes, Jane leaned into him. "And you are our gallant giant." She clung to him as he deepened the kiss.

"Hoy, lover boy, your lunch is served."

Jane opened her eyes to find Nick grinning down at them. Jarred stood, pokerfaced beside him as several waiters hovered with laden trays. Simon and Ryan lowered the sun lounges into flat benches.

"About time you fellas turned up," called Talos. He brushed his lips over her ear and whispered. "If that kiss doesn't convince Jarred we're engaged, nothing will."

A chill ran down her spine. *Talos must have seen his friends' arrive.* Was his kiss spontaneous or for Jarred's benefit? She eased away and climbed the ladder, her happy little bubble taking a nosedive to the bottom of the pool.

Nick handed her a towel, but not before his gaze raked over her. "Hot mamma."

Ignoring him, she wrapped the towel tightly around her, slid on her sandals and grabbed another towel, then held it open to take Ella.

Talos laid Ella in the towel in Jane's arms, but she avoided meeting his eyes as she wrapped Ella snuggly and turned away. "I thought you guys didn't want to be seen together?"

Jarred sat on the other lounge and helped himself to a spring roll. "We don't, but since you've been down here for thirty minutes, we figured it was safe." He shuffled along so Nick could sit. "I'd like Jane to eat in the restaurant tonight and if Kazan doesn't show, I want her to visit the sky lounge for a couple of hours. We need to track him down."

"He mightn't even be staying at this hotel." Talos leant over the bed and picked up a baguette bursting with meat, shallots, and carrots. "Who's going to watch Ella?"

"You," stated Jarred. "Gibbs is flying in later tonight and wants to accompany Jane."

"No way." Talos shook his head. "I am not leaving him alone with Jane. She stays with me, day and night."

Jarred expelled a breath. "I've got Simon running deeper background checks on him, but in the meantime, Nick and Ryan will be in the bar. Jane will be completely safe."

"No. It only takes one small capsule to poison a drink and I won't risk it. If you want Jane in the sky lounge then I'm her escort." He glanced at Simon. "Could you do your research in our suite and watch Ella?"

"Yeah, no worries." Simon winked at Jane, his eyes full of

amusement. "I might need to make another mobile to keep her entertained though."

"Don't you dare. If Ella wakes, ring me."

Ryan sat on the lounge nearest her and reached for a meatball. "We don't want too many up there. I'll stay with Simon." He held a plate up to her. "You haven't eaten anything."

"I'm not hungry." Balancing Ella in one arm, she grabbed her sunglasses and sarong. "I'm going back to the suite." Her gaze met Talos's questioning frown. "Stay and eat with your friends. I'll be fine."

"No, I'll come with you." He pulled on his T-Shirt, stepped into his thongs, and picked up the plate of spring rolls. "You fellas can order your own."

Jane felt his gaze on her back all the way to the lift. As the doors closed he gripped her chin gently, forcing her to meet his eyes.

"What's going on? One minute you're all over me like a rash and the next you're running away, and you haven't eaten since this morning, so don't tell me you're not hungry."

"I lost my appetite."

"Why?"

You need to know the truth, no matter how much it hurts. Swallowing, she straightened her shoulders. "I know you desire me, but sometimes I feel like you're putting on a show."

His frown deepened. "I'm not following you?"

"Am I really precious, or did you say that and kiss me because Jarred was watching?"

"Arh." He released her chin and ran his thumb across her bottom lip. "I didn't know the boys were there, which shows how much you distract me. You've become an addiction that I won't give up." He lowered his head and kissed her.

Deep in Jane's soul, a bud blossomed. He hadn't said the words, but it was in his eyes.

He does love me, he just doesn't realize it. Unable to wipe the grin off her face, she rose up on her toes and kissed his cheek. "Shower time."

His lips twitched. There was no mistaking the wicked glint in his eyes. "Then I suggest you eat." He held out the plate. "You're going to need energy."

Cradling Ella in one arm, she took a spring roll. "So are you, my darling."

The lift doors opened and he drew away as two middle-aged women speaking German entered. On seeing Talos, their eyes brightened as if all their Christmases had come at once.

Jane grinned at him. "You didn't press the button, we've gone down to ground level." She bit into the spring roll. "Yum."

"You distracted me, again."

Chuckling, she took another bite as her gaze skimmed the foyer. A man at the tourist desk caught her attention and her skin crawled. She'd barely registered his profile when the doors closed. "Wait." She hit the open button, grabbed Talos by the hand and dragged him forward.

"Quick, it's him!"

Chapter Eighteen

Talos swiftly stepped in front of Jane and guided her behind an ornamental pot, sprouting thick fern fronds. "Where?" he asked, peering through the greenery.

"The large man at the tourist desk."

Pulling out his phone, Talos studied the Russian. He wore a Hawaiian shirt and long baggy shorts, as did his two companions standing on either side. Kazan appeared to be beefy with a sallow complexion, except for the spidery veins zigzagging across his cheeks and nose. *Heavy drinker, 60's, overweight.*

The Russian leaned over the desk and raised his gravely voice. "Don't tell me no. I want to go deep sea fishing tomorrow."

The pretty receptionist edged back from the desk. "I'm sorry, sir. As I explained, they have no more vacancies. I can fit you in the day after."

"That is not good enough. I will hire my own boat if I have to."

"I'll speak to...to my manager." She hurried away.

Talos smiled. "This is too good an opportunity to miss." He passed the phone to Jane, scooped Ella into his arms, and adjusted the towel. "Ring Jarred and tell him we've found Kazan then go back to our suite. I'll be up shortly." He pulled her hat down further.

"What about Ella?"

"She'll be safe, I promise." Unhurriedly he strolled towards the three men. Kazan's two minders watched his approach. Noticing Ella, their stances eased.

Talos nodded. "How you doing? I couldn't help hearing you want to go fishing?"

Kazan turned, his pale blue eyes narrowing, then Ella cooed at

Talos, drawing the Russian's attention. He too relaxed. "That is correct."

"Some friends and I have hired a boat for the day. You're welcome to join our party."

"There are three of us," said the Russian.

Turning, Talos sized up the other two men. Similar in age to him, they both looked fit and had the distinctive bulge of a handgun under their shirts. Bringing them along would make snatching Kazan more difficult, unless they did actually go out to sea.

He turned back to Kazan. "It should be all right. Do you need to hire rods?"

"I have my own equipment and my friends will not be fishing."

Talos feigned surprise. "Then why come? They'll be bored to death."

"They enjoy the sea air. What is the cost?"

"We've already paid for the boat and lunch, but we usually run a wager for the biggest catch of the day. So throw in fifty bucks each and we'll call it even."

Kazan drummed his fingers on the desk. "This is acceptable. What time do we leave?"

"Be out the front of the hotel at seven o'clock. By the way, I'm James...Tanner."

"Aleksey Zhukov." He didn't offer his hand, which suited Talos fine.

"Don't be late." Talos strolled towards the reception lounge and sighted Nick in an armchair reading a paper, his chest heaving as if he'd been running. Veering to the right, Talos stopped by a bookcase stocked with a range of titles in various languages. An ideal location to observe Kazan and his two minders leave the hotel.

"Nasty looking fella," muttered Nick, folding the paper. "What were you discussing?"

"Tomorrow we're going on a fishing expedition and Kazan will be joining us."

Nick smiled. "Really?"

They watched the Russians tramp down the driveway until a small coach drove in and blocked their view. As the excited passengers disembarked, Talos recognized the tour director from the bar of their hotel in Ho Chi Min.

She spotted him through the window, paused, then gave him a wave.

Nick raised an eyebrow. "Who's that?"

"The tour director that was talking to Huang. I can't remember her name, but she mentioned she was bringing a group of German tourists to Nha Trang."

"Hmm. I might have to introduce myself."

Talos laughed. "You never miss an opportunity, do you?"

"Hey, I'm no monk."

The woman escorted her noisy group of Germans into the reception area then briskly walked across the foyer. "Hello." Her gaze flicked to Ella, happily sucking on her fingers. "Beautiful baby."

"Yes, isn't she?"

Her gaze moved to Nick. "You are travelling together?"

Nick gave her one of his, I'm single and interested smiles. "Yes, but unlike my friend here, I'm not saddled with looking after a baby." He held out a hand. "I'm Nick."

"I am Lien."

Raising Ella to his shoulder, Talos softly dropped a kiss on top of her tiny head. "If you'll excuse me, I need to get this precious gem back to her mother. Are you coming, Nick?"

"Give me five minutes."

"No worries." Talos made his way back to the lift and up to level eight. By the time he entered the suite Ella was sound asleep.

Jane came running. "Is everything all right?"

"Fine." He lay Ella in her arms and turned to Jarred who sat at the small dining table with Simon and Ryan. "I've invited Aleksey Zhukov, otherwise known as Kazan, and his two friends to come deep sea fishing with us tomorrow."

Rising slowly, Jarred pinned him with sharp eyes. "How the hell did you manage that?"

"I'll explain when Nick gets here, but I think we're going to need more manpower."

Having laid Ella in her carrier, Jane stepped in front of him and rested both hands on his chest. "You're not really taking them fishing, are you?"

Something in Talos shifted. Her imploring eyes would melt steel. Unable to help himself, he gripped her waist and gently squeezed. "Yes, but they won't be coming back."

Her eyes widened. "What are you going to do with them?"

"Kazan's a heavy drinker and won't knock back free booze, so I figure we hire a boat in *his* name and ply them with alcohol. Once the authorities find the boat full of empty bottles they assume Kazan and his friends got drunk, fell overboard, and drowned."

"But they won't drown, will they?"

"No, we'll transfer them to another boat and rendezvous with Gibbs. He'll have a couple of Serious Crime Unit officers with him." Spying the left over food, Talos released her to wolf down a baguette.

A knock sounded, and after checking the spyhole, Talos opened the door to Nick.

He strolled inside. "Thanks, I'm hooking up with the hot tour guide later." He turned a chair and straddled it. "So, how are we taking Kazan down?"

"We're working on it now," replied Jarred. He turned to Simon. "Access the hotel's booking system and find out what room Kazan's in. I'll need you to search it as soon as he leaves in the morning. Confiscate anything useful, then meet us with another boat." He stood and strolled to the window. "Gibbs has been delayed but once he arrives, I'll get him to organize for Kazan and his bodyguards to be picked up by the Serious Crime Unit."

Talos rubbed his jaw. "What about Jane? I won't risk leaving her on her own."

"Christ." Jarred expelled a deep breath. "Maybe I should get Sam over here. I hate being down a man."

Jane gasped. "No, Sam needs to stay at home and protect Kallie. I'll be fine here."

Jarred shook his head. "Talos is right, until we have the all clear on Gibbs, we can't leave you unguarded." He slapped his thigh hard.

Ella started. Her eyelids flew open and her bottom lip dropped.

Jane scowled at Jarred then turned to Talos. "I'll take Ella into the bedroom. She needs a bath and a feed anyway." Stretching up, she kissed his cheek.

It hardly rated as a passionate kiss but Talos felt another shift in the universe, like a puzzle falling into place, bit by bit. Before he had time to analyze it, she whispered in his ear.

"Fancy joining me for a bubble bath when you're finished?" She chuckled and picked up Ella's carrier.

Images beset him of her naked amongst frothy suds, displaying tantalizing glimpses of smooth thighs and rounded breasts. Clearing his throat, he took the chair recently vacated by Jarred. The boys didn't need to see what was quickly turning into a hell of an erection. "Where were we?"

Simon looked up from his laptop. "I've got Kazan's room. He's on the seventh floor. Once you leave in the morning, I'll recode my keycard and check out his room."

"What about, Jane?" Talos asked, locking eyes with Jarred. "I need her safe."

"Fuck, mate, you're thinking with the wrong organ."

Talos stiffened. "My dick has nothing to do with this."

Jarred choked out a laugh. "I wasn't referring to that organ, mate. You're thinking with your heart instead of your brain."

"My heart?"

"Yes, your heart. I figure you made-up the engagement because you don't trust the AFP, but your preoccupation with her safety is clouding your vision. I need you to focus on the job." He dropped into an armchair, threw back his head and closed his eyes.

Talos glanced at Simon, Nick, and Ryan. Each of them nodded at him. He sighed. These men were his closest friends and confidants. He sighed. "It's more than that. I'm in love with Jane and the thought of something happening to her twists my guts inside out."

Jarred opened his eyes. "I was afraid of that. Okay...there's a tiny beach on Mieu Island. It's secluded but has good amenities. Simon can stay with Jane until we need him. Once we've disposed of Kazan, we'll drop by and pick her up."

Ryan glanced at Simon. "Have you found anything on Gibbs?"

"Indeed I have. Zakour Gibbs came up on the honors roll of a prestigious boy's school in Sydney. I checked out his final year photo and it's our Gibbs all right. And you'll never guess who was in the same year?"

"Who?" they all asked in unison.

"Elliott Shaw."

"Christ," muttered Talos. "It makes sense. They both look like Hollywood pin up boys, and it was Gibbs that vouched for Elliott bloody Shaw."

Jarred stood. "It doesn't mean either of them is dirty. What else did you discover?"

Simon glanced at his notebook. "I ran a deeper search on Gibbs's mother. She lives on a private Island off Fiji and she has a daughter. Safiya-Ameerah, born eight years after Zakour, but there's no father registered on her birth certificate either."

Ryan leaned in further. "Her name sounds Middle Eastern as well?"

Simon nodded. "It is, and in Arabic, Safiya-Ameerah means tranquil princess, but according to the headmistress of the boarding school she attended, Safiya was known as the runaway princess. When I questioned this, the woman clammed up."

"How the hell do you get your information?" asked Nick.

"I had a genius mentor at uni." Simon frowned. "Gibbs is a dark horse though."

"Why?" Talos leaned closer.

"The private schooling explains his manner and confidence, but his salary wouldn't go anywhere near covering the amount of money in his bank account, or the tailored suits he wears, his Alfa Romeo, or his luxury unit over looking Sydney Harbour. He's obtaining funds from somewhere and it's not through his mother."

"Why don't we just ask him when he arrives?" suggested Ryan.

They all looked at Jarred.

He shook his head. "If he's clean, he'll be pissed that we're poking around in his private life. And, if he's dirty, we'll lose our advantage." He tapped his finger against his chin then turned back to Simon. "You said his mother lives on a private island?"

"Yes."

"Find out who owns the island. I have a feeling that will answer most of our questions regarding Gibbs."

"Will do." Simon picked up his pen. "What time does Gibbs arrive tonight?"

"He doesn't. Huang has started talking. It seems Gibbs convinced him that Marzetti squealed on the whole ring, which is exactly what we want them to think. Jane will be of no interest once they turn on each other. Gibbs hopes to be here about ten, tomorrow."

Nick chuckled. "He won't be happy we're taking the Russian down without him."

"Who cares," muttered Talos. "It's preferable to staking out the hotel's coffee shop and exposing Jane."

Through the wall, the sound of running water reached Talos and he wondered how long he'd have to wait before taking Jane up on her invitation. Across the table he met Nick's knowing grin. Choosing to ignore him, Talos drew a folder of hotel stationary over and picked up the pen. "Let's get everything down, so we all know what we're doing tomorrow."

Half an hour later, Talos closed the door on his departing mates and headed for the bedroom. A soft melody played through Jane's iPod and Ella lay sound asleep in her carrier. He kicked off his thongs, disposed of his clothes in record time, and stepped into the bathroom where he came to an abrupt halt.

Looking upon the woman who was turning his world upside down, Talos could do nothing but stare. She'd left the lights off and being an internal bathroom there were no windows. It would have been dark except for the soft flicker of a candle on the vanity. As he'd imagined, she lay amongst a swath of frothy bubbles, her neck against the rim of the spa and her head resting on a folded towel. She'd twisted her hair up in a large clip.

Closing the door silently, he stepped closer and breathed in the scent of vanilla. As his eyes adjusted to the subdued light, he noticed the tops of her knees poking though the bubbles like a naked backside poking through snow. His gaze traveled higher to a vision much better then he'd imagined.

The swells of her breasts lay free of bubbles and gleaming in the soft light. Her eyes were closed, a soft smile on her lush lips. She was everything he wanted in a woman—beautiful without being vain, gentle yet determined, intelligent and sexy. The fact she thought herself in love with him meant little. After the bastard she'd married, anyone offering warmth and protection would gain her admiration.

He frowned. *Hopefully in time she'll fall in love with me for real, and until then I'll do everything I can to make her feel safe.*

Leaning down, he placed a gentle kiss on her lips.

Her eyelids fluttered open. "I was wondering when you'd join me. Have the others left?"

"Yes, it's just you and me."

As he stepped into the spa her gaze travelled slowly down his torso, leaving him tingling with anticipation. "Like anything you see?"

"Oh yes."

Sinking into the cool water, he slid his arms around her and lifted her between his thighs. She immediately leaned back against his chest. "Much better."

He chuckled. "I was trying to concentrate on our plans for tomorrow and all I could think about was you, naked amongst the bubbles." He reached down and slid his hands along her silky thighs. "I had a hard-on imagining what I'd do to you."

She wiggled against his erection. "I was planning to take care of you this time."

"Were you?" He caressed her hips and tummy, deliberately straying lower, sliding his fingers between her folds.

She arched against him, her breasts rising, her legs falling wide. "Yeees."

He nuzzled her neck. "I can stop if you want?" He penetrated her with his finger and stroked in and out.

Her head fell back. "Nooo."

Moving his other hand to her left breast, he cupped her fullness and traced his thumb over her peaked nipple. She arched into his hand.

Withdrawing his fingers from her heat, he circled her nub, while rolling her nipple and layering hot wet kisses over her neck. "You smell divine."

She thrust against his fingers. "Harder, do it harder."

He obliged, increasing the pressure with his thumb, while driving two fingers in and out of her tight sheath. She arched and bucked against his fingers.

He kissed her shoulder. "You're so close, I can feel it."

She wriggled out of his arms, turned and straddled him. "Not without you." Running her hands up his arms, she gripped his shoulders and gyrated against his erection.

Mesmerized, he tracked the glide of a frothy mass of suds down her breast. Watched it hang precariously off her nipple, then drop into the water between their bodies. "I'm not finished with you yet." Bending his head, he laved her nipple with his tongue, drew it into his mouth, and sucked."

She moaned. "I want you inside me."

Needing no further invitation, he lifted her over his straining erection and eased in, inch by inch. "God, you feel good."

She sank lower and rolled her hips. "So do you."

Groaning, he tightened his hold. "I can't get enough of you."

She pushed up and sank down again. "I'll never get enough of you."

God, I hope not. He let her rise then pulled her down to his upward thrust. "I've never felt as alive as I do with you." He thrust again and again.

Her emerald eyes sparkled in the candlelight. "That's how I feel too."

With each thrust her breasts bounced into his chest, sliding over his nipples and shooting fire straight to his groin. She began to tremble, her fingernails dug into his shoulders, and her breathing turned to gasps.

"I...love...you, Talos."

Her muscles tightened around his cock, sending a rush of lust surging through his veins. He could hold back no longer and thrust hard.

She screamed, spasmed, and took him with her over the edge and into euphoria.

Chapter Nineteen

My God, he's magnificent. Jane leaned against the bedhead and fed Ella as Talos worked his way through a series of disciplined martial arts moves. His only item of clothing a pair of silky boxers, which kept drawing her eye to his taut backside, flat stomach, and muscled thighs, not to mention the obvious bulge.

She smiled, recalling the way he'd woken her at the crack of dawn. "It's a good thing you were up early or you'd never get through this routine in time to go fishing."

His lips twitched. "My being *up* early is to be expected when you're lying beside me naked and mussed. You were a tasty morsel I couldn't resist."

"Yes, well, I've never been *tasted* so thoroughly."

He chuckled. "Obviously dinner last night wasn't enough."

"But it was romantic on the balcony with the sun going down over the islands. Maybe our evening stroll on the beach renewed your appetite." She tucked the sheet around her breasts, lifted Ella to her shoulder and rubbed her back. "What sort of Kata are you doing?"

"It's a mixture of Aikido, Krav Maga, Karate and Qi Gong that I've been perfecting over the years. When I finish I usually go for a run."

"I've never heard of Krav Maga. What is it?"

"A hand-to-hand combat system developed in Israel. It involves wrestling, grappling, and striking techniques that are efficient and brutal."

She considered his words as he dug around in his duffle bag. "Simon told me you're a weapons expert and that anything is a weapon in your hands."

He grinned. "I think he's right. You went from purring to

scratching like a tiger." He dipped a shoulder to show her a series of scratches.

"Oh my God, I'm so sorry." Her face heated as she put her hand over her mouth.

"Don't be. It didn't hurt and I like it when you lose your inhibitions." He threw his clothes on the bed and headed for the bathroom. "I've got to move. Breakfast will be here soon and so will the boys, otherwise I'd come back to bed and enjoy your feline prowess a little more." He chuckled and closed the door.

Mortification swept over her as she recalled their lovemaking the afternoon and night before. She'd never been so brazen with Andrew. He'd once rebuked her for talking dirty. *"You're my wife, not a whore."*

If she'd wrapped her legs around *his* neck and thrust her pelvis into *his* mouth or begged *him* to go harder, he'd have asphyxiated.

For a moment Jane wondered about Andrew's mistress. The woman he'd brought into their apartment along with her father and two other ring members. A woman who looked like she belonged on a catwalk yet wanted Jane dead. *I bet she demanded sexual gratification and talked dirty. Andrew was a two-timing, two-faced cad.*

A knock sounded on the suite's outer door.

Laying Ella in the middle of the bed, she grappled amongst the covers for her nightie.

A second knock sounded.

"Argh." Grabbing Talos's shirt, she shrugged it over her head and pulled on a pair of panties. The T-shirt passed as a short dress. She ran to the door, peeped out, and was reassured to see a bored looking waiter with a breakfast trolley. She held the door open for him. "Sorry, I was in the bedroom."

He pushed the trolley across to the dining table. Another waiter she hadn't noticed followed him in, glancing about methodically.

A shiver of apprehension slid over Jane.

The first waiter leaned to one side and looked into the bedroom where Ella could be seen flailing her arms.

Leaving the suite's door open, Jane stepped into the doorway of the bedroom, blocking their view, ready to scream for Talos if need be. "Thank you."

Both waiters bowed their heads slightly and turned for the outer door.

Dismissing her over-active imagination, she made to follow only to stop when the first waiter closed the door. He and his companion turned and Jane's gaze dropped to the long bladed knives they both held.

A blood-curdling scream she didn't know she was capable of left her lips as reality set in. Leaping back, she gripped the door's edge and swung it shut, using her body to hold it, but she wasn't quick enough.

The men pushed against the door. Fear clawed at her belly as she began to slide backwards.

"Talos!"

He slammed naked into the door beside her, forcing it closed with his back.

She'd barely dragged in a breath when he placed his hands around her waist, lifted and tossed her across the bottom of the bed. He roared, yanked the door open and hurtled through.

"No, Talos, they've got knives!"

A loud crash sounded. She scrambled to her feet, sobbing as she stumbled to the dresser, snatched up the phone and searched for Jarred's name.

He answered immediately. "We're on our—"

"Help. Talos is fighting two men with knives."

"Fuck. Go, go, go."

"What?"

"We're on our way." The phone went dead as Talos roared again.

Glued to the carpet, trembling and sobbing, Jane's body turned to ice as she stared at the phone. *They'll be too late.*

Ella began to cry, snapping Jane into action. Dropping the phone she searched for something, anything to use as a weapon. Her gaze fell on a marble lamp by the bed. It was that or nothing. Ripping the cord out of the wall, she picked up the lamp and faced the door. She forced her feet to move, desperately seeking the courage she needed to help Talos, but it was like dragging her body through quicksand.

Heart pounding like tribal drums in her ears, she stepped through the doorway into a scene of chaos. Amongst the remains of the dining table lay a waiter covered in bits of food. He wasn't moving. *Shit, he doesn't look like he's breathing.*

Talos?

Her gaze searched the broken furniture littering the floor and found him standing naked near the window and covered in blood, lots of it as he faced one of the waiters.

Her breathing seized as she noticed the lethal looking gun pointed directly at his chest.

"No!"

The waiter's eyes flicked to her then back to Talos. "Not your lucky day."

"I've been in worse situations," Talos replied, shifting to his left.

Horror punched into Jane as she realized he was putting himself between her and the gunman. Fury rose like a dormant volcano erupting. She screeched like a banshee, rushed forward, and hurled the lamp.

The waiter swung the gun her way.

Talos dived as a loud report reverberated round the room. The lamp shattered mid air sending chunks of marble flying in all directions. Another shot resonated as Talos slammed into the Asian man and the door to the corridor exploded inwards.

Four big bodies hurtled into the room and all hell broke loose. She glimpsed Talos and the waiter on the floor before Jarred lifted her bodily and bore her into the bedroom.

"No, save Talos, he's hurt."

He dropped her on the bed beside Ella, who lay hiccupping, her eyes filled with tears. "Stay," he ordered then charged back out, slamming the door behind him.

"Like hell I will." She ran to the door, swung it open and careened into a wall of muscle.

Jarred swung round and forced her back. "You don't want to see this."

She pushed against his chest. "I need to check on Talos."

"No, you don't." He caught both her hands and again forced her backwards.

She tried to shake him off, kicked out at him and cried. "Please, let me go to him."

He pulled her into his chest and held her tightly. "I'm sorry, Jane, you can't."

"Oh God, no, please don't say that." She sobbed into Jarred's shirt. A vice encased her heart, compressing until it hurt to breathe. *This can't be happening.*

"Talos." She whimpered his name over and over.

"Jane! I'm okay."

Jane stilled, her gaze colliding with the man she loved. "Talos." She twisted away from Jarred and threw herself at Talos. "I saw all that blood and then he fired the gun. I thought…"

"I'm fine, sweetheart." His arms closed around her. "It's just a scratch."

She leaned back, searching bloodied chest and arms for confirmation. A trickle drew her eyes to a deep laceration traversing his chest and one arm. "Scratch? You need stitches."

"Later." He released her, snatched his towel off the floor, and wiped the blood from his chest. Then he grabbed his jocks and board shorts off the bed and pulled them on. "Let's go."

"Ella?"

"Simon's got her." He took her hand and pulled her behind him.

"Who sent those men?"

"I don't know, but I intend to find out." He hustled her out of the bedroom, blocking her view when she attempted to look towards the chaos. Ryan was talking to someone on the phone. She caught a glimpse of Jarred and Nick bent over one of the men.

"Are they dead?"

"No, more's the pity.

Once out in the carpeted hallway, he ran, almost dragging her off her feet.

She glanced behind, surprised to find the hall empty. They ran past the lift.

"Where are we going? Where's Ella?" she asked, her voice sounding unusually high.

"The garage." He opened the emergency exit door and sprinted down the stairs.

Breathing hard, Jane struggled to process what had happened. "Those men were going to kill me. They thought I was on my own with Ella."

"But you're weren't on your own, I was there."

What about next time?

They descended at a speed that scared the living daylights out of her. "Will you call Gibbs to deal with those men?"

"We don't have a lot of choice, but this time he won't know where we are taking you."

"Why weren't there other guests in the hall? They must have heard the commotion?"

"He used a silencer and the walls are solid concrete, plus I don't think there's any other guests down our end."

"Oh."

They raced down the remaining flight of the steps without speaking. On reaching the underground garage, Talos held her to one side, barely raising a sweat as she gasped for oxygen. He opened the door and checked the area. "Let's go."

He ran towards a white van, still holding her hand tightly. "Keep your eyes open."

Her heart thudding loudly, Jane searched the surrounding garage ignoring the painful stitch in her side. *Ella, is she safe?*

The side door of the van slid open and Simon climbed out holding Ella wrapped in her pink baby blanket. Jane almost collapsed with relief as she gathered her precious baby to her chest, climbed into the van, and sank onto the nearest seat.

Simon handed Talos a gun. "The boys are securing the hit men, then bringing our gear down. They'll put a do not disturb sign on the door and ring Gibbs to organize a pick up."

Hit men. She pressed a shaky kiss to Ella's head, her gaze never leaving Talos as he paced back and forth beside the van. "So they're still alive?" she asked, rubbing her cheek against her precious baby's soft hair.

Talos didn't answer as he rubbed his bristly chin. "The only person who knew we were staying here is Gibbs."

Simon's eyes narrowed. "He might have told Shaw. They know each other, remember."

Jane shook her head. "I can't believe either of them would put a hit out on me. Maybe someone recognized me when we went for a walk along the beach last night."

Talos shook his head. "Impossible. It was dark and you were wearing the wig."

She bit her lip. "What if somehow one of the ring members found out we're here."

"No. If that were the case, they'd have cancelled the meetings. It's someone else." He stopped and met her gaze. "How did Rossini know the times and places?"

"I have no idea. He may have been my husband, but Andrew never discussed his business with me. Marzetti must have told him."

"No, Marzetti didn't know he had that information. So how did he get it?"

Jane lifted her shoulders. "Maybe his mistress told him? Her father *is* a ring member."

Talos stared at her. "That makes sense. And as no one knows Rossini spoke to us before being poisoned, there would be no need to change the meetings."

The lift chimed and Talos swung around, sinking into a crouch as he raised the gun level with his face and aimed on the lift.

Jarred, Nick, and Ryan strode out, carrying bags, Jane's suitcase, and Ella's stroller.

"All good?" asked Talos standing. He pushed the gun into the band of his shorts and reached for one of the bags.

"Yeah," replied Jarred. "The SCU have a couple of guys here on the ground and they'll be at the hotel within twenty minutes."

Talos unzipped his bag and pulled out a T-shirt, then tossed the bag into the rear of the van. "We'd better get down to the pier and pick up the boats." He climbed in and sat beside Jane. "Are you okay?"

"Yes." She entwined her fingers with his. "But you need a doctor."

"No I don't."

"Yes, you do."

Jarred slammed into the seat behind. "No, he doesn't. I'll stitch him up."

She gaped at him. "You can't be serious?"

He was.

Twenty minutes later, sitting on the rear seat of a boat by the jetty, Jane nursed Ella and watched appalled as Jarred stitched Talos's chest and upper left arm without anesthetic. She flinched each time the curved needle pierced Talos's skin, but other than a clenched jaw and fists, he gave no other sign of discomfort.

Laying Ella on the seat, Jane shifted closer and spread antiseptic cream over the wounds, then covered them with a non-stick pad she'd found in the first aid kit.

"Thanks, sweetheart." Talos pulled on his T-shirt then glanced at his watch. "We have fifteen minutes to get back to the hotel and pick up Kazan and his two friends.

Jane gasped. "You're not still going through with it? Are you completely mad?"

Talos laughed. "No, not completely." His eyes dropped to her chest. "There's blood all over that shirt. Make sure you change into something else before you reach the island."

Ignoring his request she reached for his hand. "Please don't go."

"It's the only way to make you safe." He kissed her then climbed onto the jetty. "Try and enjoy yourself today. We'll be back before dark."

She bit her bottom lip. "What if you're not?"

He handed her his phone and a wad of money. "If there's a problem, we'll ring you."

Jarred pulled a slip of paper out of his pocket and passed it her. "Once Simon has you settled on the island, he's going to the hotel to search Kazan's room, then he'll stay with you until we need him. If for some reason we're not back by dark, you're to return to the mainland and take a taxi to the address I've given you. The woman there will get you safely to the Australian Embassy in Hanoi."

Jane swallowed down her panic. "Who is she?"

"An old acquaintance of mine."

"What if she doesn't live there anymore?"

Jarred's lips twitched. "She does, I checked last night." He jumped onto the fishing boat they'd hired and looked at Talos. "I'll stay here while you three pick up Kazan."

"All right." Talos turned back to Jane and passed her his phone. "I'll see you later."

Holding back tears, Jane scooped Ella up and watched as Talos strode along the jetty then climb into the van. It pulled away as Simon started the speedboat's engine.

Please be safe, my darling. She closed her eyes for a couple of seconds then carefully stepped over the luggage to the seat beside Simon. "I'm ready."

He pushed the throttle forward. "It'll take us about fifteen minutes to get out to the island and as you've missed breakfast, there's a baguette and orange juice in there for you." He pointed to a paper bag at her feet

"Thanks. Did you have something to eat?"

"Yeah. While Jarred attended to Talos we picked up breakfast, and the supplies for our fishing trip."

"Good." Shivering from the cool breeze and fine spray, she sank lower behind the windshield and rearranged Ella's blanket to keep her warm. Looking up she noticed an island. Huge lettering on a mountain proclaimed it to be Vin Pearl.

From the island and the mainland were a series of steel towers rising from the water. As they passed between she looked up and observed steel cables transporting gondolas back and forth overhead.

"What is Vin Pearl?"

"It's a theme park with rides like we have on the Gold Coast back home."

For several minutes they traversed the ocean in silence then Simon glanced at her. "I checked on Nick's ex-fiancée for you."

She had too much on her mind to worry about Nick's ex-fiancée. She glanced at Simon to find him waiting for her to answer him. He was probably trying to sidetrack her.

"And?"

He smiled. "According to her passport, license, and bank account, Ava's last name is still Mitchell and until three months ago, she lived in England and ran an on-line business."

"What sort of business?"

"It's called Fantasy Pearl Creations. I checked the website and she designs jewelry using pearls from the north-west coast of Australia."

"So where does she live now?"

"Broome, in Western Australia."

"I wonder why she went there? It's on the other side of the country."

"Maybe to be closer to the pearl industry." He grimaced. "I'm just not sure what Nick's going to do when you tell him.

"Hmm."

"I'm still surprised he opened up to you, but don't say anything until this job's finished. We can't afford any more distractions."

Jane cringed. "I can't think about that now, I'm too worried about Talos."

Simon pointed ahead. "That's Mieu Island. It's too early for day trippers yet so I'll tie up to the wharf and you can change while I see if they can accommodate us tonight."

"What if we've been followed?"

He glanced behind then returned his attention to the front of the boat. "I've been keeping an eye out and I haven't detected anyone. Aside from your two visitors this morning, I doubt anyone knows we've even left the hotel."

"If those two men are alive, then why didn't you ask them who they're working for?"

He sighed. "They're professional killers so they won't open up easily, and after the beating Talos gave them, it might be a few hours before they're capable of answering questions." He glanced at her, his expression serious. "I've never seen Talos lose it like that. He would have killed that guy if Nick hadn't pulled him off."

She drew in a shaky breath. "That man was about to shoot me. Then Talos jumped in between us. I thought he'd been shot." Her voice wobbled.

Simon nodded. "The big guy's always had a protective streak, but from the moment he laid eyes on you, he hasn't looked at another woman."

"The first time he laid eyes on me I was eight months pregnant."

"Yeah, go figure."

Jane rocked Ella as she relived the moment her gaze had connected with Talos for the first time. A thunderstorm had been building for several hours and every one had arranged to meet in the pub for Kallie's birthday. As Jane walked in, he'd turned from the bar and their eyes had met and locked. At first she thought she'd been struck by lightning.

"It's hard to believe that was eight weeks ago."

Simon raised an eyebrow at her. "And now you're engaged."

"I'm in love with him, Simon."

He eased off the throttle and looked at her. "Then he's a very lucky man."

CHAPTER TWENTY

Seated in the rear of the van, Talos swallowed the last of his baguette and checked the gun Simon had given him. "Where did this come from?"

Ryan twisted round from the front passenger seat. "Jarred brought it back last night along with the back-packs, handcuffs, and zip lock straps."

"Any more guns?"

"Yeah, a couple of Glocks. I think he got them from a lady friend."

"Why do you say that?"

"Because our leader came back smelling of perfume and looking well and truly fucked."

Nick laughed from the driver's seat. "I came back much the same way, although I'm pretty sure my hot tour guide is some sort of hybrid, alien gymnast. At one point I was afraid she was going to crush my spine between her thighs and her stamina nearly killed me."

"That's saying something." Talos shook his head. "Jane wanted to get out, so I took her and Ella for a walk along the beach."

"Yeah, I saw you," called Nick. "Lien and I were having dinner at a restaurant overlooking the beach."

"There's the Russians," called Ryan pointing ahead. "Keep that gun handy, just in case they're behind your early morning raid."

"No worries." Talos slid the gun into the front pocket of the backpack on the seat beside him and stretched his arm along the backrest. "Park back from the entrance, we don't want anyone from the hotel spotting us."

"Yep." Nick slowed the vehicle and stopped several meters from the Russians, well back from the hotel's driveway. "They certainly look like they're going fishing."

Talos raised an eyebrow. Kazan stood empty handed wearing another loud Hawaiian shirt, long shorts, and a large straw hat. His two friends were dressed similarly and loaded up with rods, tackle boxes, and a large umbrella.

"This should be interesting."

"Jesus Christ, this guy's a real winner." Coughing to cover his laugher, Ryan opened his door and climbed out. "How you doing? I'm Riley."

The two men with Kazan stepped forward, their gazes searching the van as Ryan slid the side door open.

Talos leaned forward. "G'day. Throw your gear in the back. The sea looks nice and calm. Great day to catch a big fish."

"I agree." Kazan climbed into the van and sat by the window in the middle row of seats. His two friends went to the rear of the van with Ryan and loaded their gear then climbed in. One sat in the row of seats behind Kazan near the window. The other sat in front of Kazan, behind Nick. All three turned side on, their gazes moving from Talos to Ryan in the front.

Not taking any chances. Talos relaxed against the rear seat, his hand draped over the backpack. He looked at the man nearest him. "So, where are you fellas from?"

"Moscow," answered Kazan. "My two associates do not speak English."

Yeah right. They understood me when I told them to put their gear in the back.

"So have you been fishing here before or is this your first visit to Nha Trang?"

As Nick pulled out into the traffic, Kazan shrugged his meaty shoulders. "I've been here before but I am not an authority on the best fishing places."

Ryan twisted round. "I spoke to our mate last night and he guaranteed me he knows a spot with a good supply of big fish. I plan on winning the catch of the day."

"Ah yes, the catch of the day." Kazan spoke in Russian to the man nearest Talos, who pulled out his wallet and handed over a wad of money.

"Our contribution, as requested," said Kazan.

"Thanks." Talos shoved the money in the top of his backpack. "With only four out of seven of us fishing, it narrows the odds a bit."

"Seven? Who else is on board?"

"The owner. He's a guy we used to know in the army."

Kazan's eyes narrowed. "I picked you as having a military presence."

If only you knew. Talos laughed. "We're just regular guys."

Nick drove into the parking lot and pulled on the handbrake. "Here we are. That must be his boat at the end of the jetty."

Talos zipped up his backpack and followed Kazan and his two friends out of the van. They congregated at the rear as Ryan placed everything on the ground. Not bothering to lift a finger, Kazan strode along the short jetty leaving his two associates to bring his gear.

Talos exchanged a quick look with Ryan and Nick then threw his backpack over one shoulder and picked up the large cooler. "Wow, how much alcohol did you fellas buy?"

"Fishing is thirsty work," called Nick, tossing a beer to each of the Russians. He picked up the bag of bait and another cooler, then headed for the fishing boat.

Opening the beers, the two Russians set off after Nick as if their lives depended on it.

Ryan closed the rear door and locked the van. "It won't be hard to get those two pissed." He picked up the tackle box and rods Simon had bought from the markets. "I might suggest they sit up the front of the boat with Jarred and the booze. It will give us more room down the back and keep them away from Kazan. Hopefully he'll be too busy fishing to notice Jarred plying his boys with beer and double shots."

"That's the plan." Ryan stepped onto the jetty and led the way to the fishing boat. "What are Nick and Jarred calling themselves?"

"Tom and Jerry. What about you?"

"I'm sticking to James Tanner."

"G'day fellas, it's good to see you again," called a grizzly voice.

Talos looked across the deck and did a double take. Jarred wore a pair of jeans torn off at the knees. He was barefoot and wearing a scruffy shirt that hung out over a belt of green rag. He wore a brown wig that hung around the tops of his shoulders and a thick chain round his neck. "Bloody hell, Jerry, you look like a pirate."

Jarred laughed gruffly. "Good to see you fellas, it's been a long time." He turned to Ryan who had lowered the rods and tackle box to the jetty and had his mouth hanging open.

Aware Kazan was watching, Talos lowered the cooler. "You're looking a bit rough round the edges mate. How's life treating you?"

"Can't complain. I've got a nice little business going with the tourists and I've shacked up with a woman who isn't demanding or fussy."

Ryan jumped onto the deck. "She can't be if she's shacked up with you." He shook Jarred's hand. "I like your place of business."

"Yeah, it's not bad, is it?" Jarred took one end of the cooler and helped Talos lift it onto the deck. "Let's put it in the shade then we'll be off. Grab yourselves a beer. It'll take us a couple of hours to get out where the big fish are biting."

"No worries." Talos opened the lid and pulled out a few cans. He passed one to Ryan and offered another to Kazan.

"Do you have any vodka?"

"Sure." Talos dug through the ice and pulled out a bottle of Stolichnaya. "How's this?"

"Much better." Kazan unscrewed the lid, lifted the bottle to his mouth and took several big gulps then wiped his mouth. "Nobody makes vodka like the Russians."

Behind Kazan's back, Talos noticed Ryan passing the other Russians bottles of vodka and herding them towards the front of the boat.

"So what do you do for a living, Aleksey?"

Kazan took another swig and belched. "I am in the importing business."

In other words drugs and young girls. "You must be doing well?"

"Why do you say that?" His eyes had narrowed.

Talos shrugged. "Anyone with half a brain can see those fellas are your bodyguards. I figured you were either a politician or a millionaire."

Kazan preened. "I do all right. Perhaps you would be interested in working for me?"

"I don't think so."

"You would be a rich man working for me."

"Thanks, but I'm happy being a regular soldier."

Jarred started the motor then called out to Ryan. "Untie the bow-line." He glanced back at Talos. "You want to get the stern-line?"

"Yeah, no worries. What about the spring lines?"

After untying the ropes, Talos returned to his seat beside the Russian. As the boat moved away from the jetty he stretched out his legs. "I've never been to Russia, but I've heard Moscow's a beautiful city."

"Yes, but there are other beautiful cities." He swallowed another mouthful of vodka and looked out to sea.

Talos took a swig of beer. "What's the fishing like in Russia?"

"We are famous for our salmon and trout fishing. If you were to take up my offer, you would accompany me on my fishing holidays."

Talos shrugged. "I'm not a fan of the cold, and Russia's also famous for that."

Over the next several hours Jarred kept the boat well away from other watercraft while the Russians made their way through the vodka and a case of Heineken. Talos found it hard to believe they were still alive let alone standing. Kazan was a little unsteady on his feet but his two compatriots didn't appear to be affected.

Talos joined Jarred in the cabin. "When do you want to do this?"

"I've been waiting to hear from Gibbs. He's at the hospital where the SCU police have been interviewing the two men who paid you a visit this morning. They've both got broken ribs and some internal bleeding. When Gibbs threatened to set you loose on them again, they said they were hired to snatch the woman and baby, but won't say who hired them."

"Fuck." Talos rubbed his chin. "Thank God I wasn't out running."

"I'd like to know how they knew about Jane, and why the meetings haven't been canceled."

"Maybe they have." Talos glanced back towards the bow where Kazan reclined in a deck chair, baiting his hook. "My money is on Gibbs or Shaw. If they're not directly involved, then one of them must have informed someone in the ring."

Jarred stared at him for a moment. "Maybe, but if that were the case then the Russians would be on high alert. I have this gut feeling we've overlooked something vital and it's bugging the shit out of me."

His phone rang. "Speak of the devil." He raised the phone to his ear. "Gibbs, what have you got for me?"

Talos kept an eye on the Russians as Jarred spoke to Gibbs.

"That works. One of my men will pick you up in twenty minutes." Jarred tossed his phone to Talos. "Give Simon the order to pick up Gibbs and two SCU officers. They'll be waiting at the same jetty we left from." He leaned out of the cabin and yelled. "We're stopping here."

Talos caught his eye. "Is Simon safe with Gibbs and those SCU guys?"

"I fucking hope so." Jarred cut the engine. "The second these three let down their guard we make our move. Try not to kill anyone."

"You got it." Talos selected Simon's number.

He answered immediately. "Hey big fella, you missing me already."

"Yeah, like a hole in the head. How's Jane?"

"Insatiable. She can't get enough of me."

Talos smirked. "In your dreams, sunshine."

"I'm serious. She claims I'm far better in bed and that skill eclipses size every time."

Jane's laughter rang out in the background.

It was a lovely sound and Talos smiled. "You're a legend in your own mind, mate. Take that skill of yours and get back to the jetty. Gibbs and two SCU officers are waiting to be picked up."

Simon's voice sobered. "I'll leave straight away. By the way, I've been back to the hotel and searched Kazan's room. He's in human trafficking up to his neck. I've photographed everything in his briefcase and left it for the SCU."

"Good. Did you manage to get accommodation for tonight?"

"No, but they're minding our luggage and they've got a lounge area where Jane can wait if it gets cool. I'll be at the jetty in fifteen minutes then call for your coordinates."

"Okay, watch your back." Talos disconnected, placed the phone on the console, then removed the gun from his backpack, shoving it in the waistband at his lower back. He pulled his T-shirt over the top and stepped out of the cabin. "I'm starving, what's to eat, Jerry?"

Jarred flipped open another cooler and began unpacking plastic containers. "Lobster, crab, prawns, noodles, dumplings, spring rolls, and salad. Grab a plate and take your pick."

Kazan dropped his lure and heaved himself out of the deck chair. "I hope your food is better than the fishing. I have yet to see a decent sized fish."

Jarred shrugged. "It can be like that sometimes, but I guarantee by the end of the day this will be one fishing trip you'll never forget."

"I hope for your sake you are right." Kazan began piling his plate.

Jarred's gaze met Talos's. "I'm rarely wrong."

Once the three Russians were seated and devouring their food, Jarred glanced at Talos and gave a slight nod then stepped behind Kazan's deckchair. "Party's over." He pressed his Glock to the Russian's ear.

Kazan spat out his food and swore.

His bodyguards' heads snapped up. Seeing the gun they threw their plates aside, stood and reached under their Hawaiian shirts.

"I wouldn't," called Talos, bringing his own Glock level with the nearest guy's chest. "Sit back down and raise your arms above your heads."

Both men hesitated, their shock obvious as they took in Nick and Ryan also aiming handguns at them. Slowly they sat.

"Who are you?" demanded Kazan.

Keeping his gun on the Russian, Jarred stepped around him. "Do you know the name, Dominic Marzetti? Or perhaps Andrew Rossini?

Kazan's eyes narrowed. "No."

"Then maybe you know the name, Lhasa? Another member of the trafficking ring you belong to."

Kazan's nostrils flared. "I have no idea what you are talking about."

Jarred smiled. "That's unfortunate, as the Serious Crime Unit here in Vietnam and the Australian Federal Police believe differently. We've got Lhasa and a man by the name of Marzetti in custody. They've given up the rest of the ring members for a lighter sentence."

Kazan glowered. "I have no idea what you talk of."

Jarred's cold stare pieced him. "We're picking Ripon up in Hoi An and Rong up in Hanoi. How do you think we found you, Kazan?"

The Russian shrugged lightly. "You have me mixed up with someone else."

"No, we don't. You have been identified by a person who knows you."

"Who is this person?" The Russian narrowed his eyes. "Tell me their name."

"I'm not at liberty to do that, however, if you want to do yourself a favor, you could tell us the members' real names?"

Kazan's hands clenched on his knees. "This is bullshit." Sweat glistened on his upper lip. "I am Aleksey Zhukov, and I am on a holiday here."

Talos grunted, feigning indifference. "Forget him, boss. We know Lhasa is Chinese and his real name is Huang Chen. We've got Marzetti and we've got the evidence in Kazan's room. In a couple of days we'll have Ripon and Rong."

Jarred nodded. "You're right. Tie them up and we'll hand them over to the SCU."

"Wait!" The Russian held up his right hand. "Ripon is English, Darwin is Australian, and Rong is Vietnamese. We don't know each others real names, only Rong has that information."

"Rong?" Talos narrowed his eyes. "Rong is the boss?"

"Yes."

Jarred moved closer. "Who is the contact you meet with?"

Kazan hesitated. "You don't know?"

"Not yet."

Kazan glanced at his two bodyguards and spoke in Russian.

All three men surged to their feet.

Kazan charged Jarred. His bodyguards launched themselves towards Nick and Talos.

"Fuck." Talos heard another shot as he fired his own gun, hitting his attacker in the shoulder. It didn't slow him down.

The impact of the other man's body took them both over the side of the boat and plunging into the murky depths, kicking and grappling.

Talos released his hold, brought up his knees and kicked his attacker in the chest. Bubbles exploded from the man's mouth as he reached out to regain his grip.

With all the blood in the water, Talos wasn't sticking round. He knocked the man's hands aside and swam for his life. He didn't fancy becoming fodder for the sharks.

With his lungs screaming for oxygen, he broke the surface and found Jarred leaning over the side of the boat. "Swim to the back, there's a safety ladder you can use."

Fearing a sharp set of teeth any second, Talos obeyed and was hauling himself up when a bullet hit the wood several inches from his body. "Fuck." He dived to the deck, rolled, and came up several meters away.

Peering round the cabin he sighted the bodyguard struggling to stay afloat amongst a sea of red as he waved a gun erratically.

"I kill you, fucking pigs." He fired again.

So he does speak English. Talos glanced behind. Kazan lay against the far side of the boat, his hands cuffed behind his back, his ankles strapped together with a zip lock strap. The other bodyguard lay beside him moaning, his hands cuffed and Jarred's rag belt tied around his thigh. It was soaked in blood.

Jarred poked his head out of the cabin. "Let's see what this joker decides to do once I start the engine. He leaned in and pressed the starter."

The engine rumbled to life.

"No," yelled the Russian. "Don't leave me here."

Talos straightened and warily approached the side of the boat. "Drop the gun or we leave you for the sharks."

Tossing the gun, the man began swimming one armed towards the boat.

Once he was close enough, Ryan and Nick leaned down and hauled him aboard then dragged him across the deck and cuffed him.

Talos stared down at Kazan. "Tell me about the attack on a woman this morning?"

"What woman?"

"Just answer the fucking question."

"I know nothing of any attack." Kazan looked at his men.

They both shook their heads.

Not knowing what to believe, Talos turned to Jarred and lowered his voice. "I think it's time we had a talk with Gibbs."

"I agree."

Talos's gut clenched. *Christ, I hope Jane and Ella are safe.*

Chapter Twenty-one

Jane lay on the comfy sun lounge under shade of a white umbrella and looked about with interest. Two jet skiers chased each other across the smooth ocean surface. A speedboat traversed back and forth with a parasail billowing behind, the person dangling in the harness a tiny speck in the sky. Several people frolicked in the shallow water and two children were building a sandcastle at the water's edge. Warmth soaked into her toes and insteps, the only parts of her body exposed to the sun's rays. Across the top of the gentle waves danced thousands of sparkling diamonds.

Laughter drew her attention to the out-door restaurant built several steps above the sand and sheltered from the sun by super large white umbrellas. Her gaze followed the adjoining wide concrete wharf, extending out over the water and around the curve of the island. Large potted palms framed its edges, interspersed with more sun lounges and umbrellas—a lavish welcome to the day-trippers arriving by boat.

Jane finished her crispy noodle salad and wondered again how the fishing trip was panning out. Simon had been gone well over an hour and she hadn't stopped worrying about Talos and his team.

She glanced at the carrier on the next lounge and smiled as Ella opened her eyes.

"Hello, sweetie, did you have a nice nap?"

Ella gurgled and stretched.

"I think that nappy needs changing, then how would you like a walk? I need a bottle of water."

Ella blew a bubble.

"I'll take that as a yes." Jane quickly changed Ella, picked up her wallet and set off for the restaurant, stopping by a bin to dispose of the nappy.

As she climbed the steps a small blue and white ferry motored towards the wharf. *Another group of tourists for lunch by the looks.* Her gaze connected with a slim woman standing stiffly in the bow. For a couple of seconds Jane's mind blanked at the bitterness being directed at her, then recognition struck.

"No."

Terror seared Jane's soul as she pushed away a wave of nausea. Unable to draw breath she stared in disbelief at the woman who wanted Jane eliminated.

Ella squirmed, breaking the spell.

Whirling, Jane dashed among the tables to the back of the restaurant, through a busy kitchen, and out the back door. *I should have kept my wig and sunglasses on. Who told her I was here? What am I going to do?*

Across the yard a couple of middle-aged Vietnamese men wearing ferry uniforms sat around a table eating. Jane hurried past them, skirted a pile of metal crates, and came to an opening in the wall.

Poking her head out, she sneaked a peek to the right and sighted the ferry further along the wharf. The passengers were slowly disembarking and strolling the other way towards the front of the restaurant and beach. *Oh no, my stuff. I can't risk going back for it.*

Tamping down her panic, Jane turned to the left.

She needed a miracle.

At the end of the wharf a young boy was struggling with a large plastic bag as he descended a ladder. Glancing down, Jane found Ella's trusting little eyes watching her. "We need to stay calm, sweetie. Mummy will get us out of here."

Taking a deep breath, Jane hurried along the wharf, risking occasional backward glances for Andrew's mistress.

The boy looked up as she reached the edge, a mixture of surprise and friendliness on his dirty little face. With no time to lose, Jane carefully climbed one handed down the ladder and into his boat.

He began shaking his head and waving his hands. "You no come."

"I'm sorry, but I have to." She ducked below the wharf, and wrinkling her nose, wedged herself between two stinking bags. "I have to get to the mainland. It's an emergency. Please help me. I'll pay you."

The boy, no older than eight or nine stared at her. "This garbage boat."

"I don't care." She lay Ella on her lap, opened her wallet and pulled out one of the notes Talos had handed her. "I'll give you five hundred thousand dong."

His eyes almost popped out of his head. "That too much."

"No, it's not." Thirty dollars was nothing compared to her life. She passed it to him.

His mouth dropped as he stared at the note in his hand, then it disappeared into the pocket of his filthy shorts. "I take you." He scrambled over plastic bags to the back of the boat and pulled a cord. The motor spluttered and coughed then fired to life.

As they chugged away from the wharf, Jane cradled Ella to her chest and sank lower, hiding behind the putrid bags. *What am I going to do once I get to the mainland? I have no change-bag, no luggage, and no way to contact Talos. Shit, I left that address in the bag. Shit, shit, shit.*

Over the next twenty minutes Jane kept looking back, expecting to see a boat bearing down on them, fretting that they'd be followed any second. Relief surged when she realized the little garbage boat wasn't heading towards the main beach but veering off to the left towards a large rusty barge.

The boy brought his boat alongside the barge, tied off the rope and unloaded all the garbage bags. When he climbed back aboard he smiled at her. "Where you want to go?"

Jane stared into his obliging little face. Ella would want a feed soon and a clean nappy and they needed to get to that address Jarred had given her. *If only I had brought the bag with me.* It was too risky to go back but she had to get a message to Talos. *He's going to freak when he can't find me.*

The boy tilted his head on the side. "You okay?"

She shook her head. "Bad people want to hurt me and I've left my bag and phone back on the island. My husband won't know where I am."

He frowned. "Why people want to hurt you?"

"Because I can stop them hurting young girls and my...words will put these bad people behind bars where they can't hurt children anymore."

His eyes widened. "You very brave lady."

"I'm very scared lady."

"I help you." He started the engine and swung the rudder right, directing the small boat away from the barge in a wide arc.

Clutching Ella in one arm, she reached out and grabbed his skinny knee. "No, we can't go back to the island yet, it's too dangerous."

"Is okay, I take you my home." He pointed to a ramshackle cluster of tin shacks floating haphazardly off a small cove. "You be safe there."

"Oh." She expelled a shaky breath. "But how can I get a message to my husband. I have no way of reaching him."

He beamed at her. "I go back and find your bag."

"No! I was the only person on the beach with a baby carrier. They'll be watching my things and I don't want you hurt or followed."

A deep frown appeared between his big brown eyes then he smiled. "I go back for more garbage. You write letter and I slip in your bag for your husband when he come."

"What if the bad people take the letter or grab you?"

"Okay, you write letter and I hide under wharf until your husband come."

Jane rocked Ella as she considered his offer. It wouldn't be hard for the boy to spot Talos but she'd have to be very careful what she wrote in case it got into the wrong hands. *At least that woman doesn't know Talos or that's he's with me, and there's nothing in the bag to identify us.* Her breath hitched. *Oh no! Talos's phone is in the bag and it has photos of us together in the Botanical Gardens.*

"We need to get that bag. Let me think." She chewed her lip as she weighed her options. She didn't want to risk the boy getting hurt, yet if she didn't get that phone and address she would jeopardize the mission and put Talos and his friends' lives at risk.

The boy scowled. "I very quick and very clever. I snatch your bag and leave secret message for your husband."

"Secret message?"

"Yes, that only he understand."

Jane considered the boy, hope welling in her chest. "What's your name?"

"Ming. What your name?"

"Jane. It's nice to meet you, Ming."

"It nice to meet you, Jane. You want me help you?"

I don't have any choice. I have to warn Talos. "Yes, Ming, but only if you promise to be very careful and take no chances."

"I promise." He dug under his bench seat and dragged out grey plastic poncho. "You put on and no one recognize you.

"Good thinking, Ming." She quickly donned the raincoat, covering both her and Ella completely. Now they looked like a father and his son heading home at end of a long day.

Ming directed his small boat amongst the group of dilapidated tin structures floating on an assortment of plastic and metal barrels. Two had completely collapsed and several had serious leans happening. She shivered at the thought of what could happen to these flimsy homes and the occupants during a bad storm.

Except for an old man sitting cross-legged on his porch, the floating village had an eerily abandoned silence. *Perhaps it is.*

The man called out in Vietnamese and Ming answered, his hand pointing at Jane then himself as he spoke. The old man seemed satisfied with the answer and reached out to pat a skinny dog lying beside him.

Jane frowned as Ming brought his boat alongside a tiny shack not much bigger than a garden shed or small bedroom. "How many in your family," she asked, examining the weathered planks that formed a front porch. Would they take her weight? Would there be room inside for them all?

Ming's chest expanded. "This my house."

Does he mean what I think he means? "Where are your parents?"

He shook his head. "No parents."

Jane was aware her mouth hung open, but for the life of her she couldn't hide her reaction. "You have no parents or family?"

"No," he replied simply.

"But, what happened to them?"

"I not know my father. My mother work karaoke bar till she get sick." He shrugged his tiny shoulders. "She make me look for food every day till she not wake up anymore. Then bad man come and lock the door. He tell me go away."

"How old were you?"

He scratched his head. "Seven."

Drawing Ella closer to her chest, Jane tried to hide her shock. "How old are you now?"

He scrunched up his nose and eyes. "Eight."

"But how did you survive on your own? What did you eat? Who looked after you?"

"Bao find me on the street." He looked across the water towards the old man.

Her heart breaking, Jane blinked away tears. "How did you learn to speak English?"

"Bao teach me so I can beg from tourists, but I don't do this anymore. Bao say it safer for me here. I catch fish and work for garbage boat. I very clever." He jumped onto the worn planks and tied the frayed rope to a wobbly rail that also served as a clothesline to several stained t-shirts.

"You come in my home." He held out his hand.

Swallowing her anxiety, Jane tightened her hold on Ella, took his filthy little hand, then stood and with her heart in her mouth, carefully stepped onto the rotting boards.

Ming darted inside the shack and unrolled a mat then pointed to it. "You sit here. I make you cup of tea."

Her gaze wandered round the small area, empty but for a wooden chest, single cupboard and a small portable gas stove. The door was wedged open with a chock and a blanket hung from a peg on the wall. There was no glass in the window frame, although on the floor below stood a square of plywood with hooks on the sides. She glanced back at the frame and spotted metal rings on either side.

Ming noticed her appraisal and grinned. "I make shutter to keep rain out. I told you I very clever."

Jane smiled. "Yes, you did." She shrugged off the poncho, lowered herself to the mat, and lay Ella in her lap.

Ming opened the cupboard, took out a cup, a crockery teapot with a broken spout, a saucepan, a packet of loose tealeaves, and a plastic jerry can. "This safe water, I collect when it rain." He lit the gas stove and squatted on the floor beside it, arranging all his items carefully. "Rats swim to my home and eat my food, so I find..." He frowned and pointed at the cupboard. "I find that. No more rats. I very clever."

"Yes." *You poor little darling.* Jane watched Ming in wonder as he went about making her a cup of tea. One part of her didn't want to be rude by refusing to drink from the chipped cup, while another part of her longed for the liquid on her parched throat.

Ella began squirming, her mouth searching for a feed. Noticing, Ming jumped up, pulled the blanket off the peg and rolled it up.

"You can lean against this while you feed your baby." He placed it between Jane's back and the corrugated tin wall."

"Thank you, Ming."

Discreetly she fed Ella while watching Ming boil the water and make a pot of tea. He then poured her a cup and placed it on the floor beside her and reached over to the chest. He pulled out a worn jumper, pencil, and paper then handed them to her.

"This keep your baby warm then you write secret letter while I make you safe."

"Make me safe?"

"Storm coming."

Jane shivered. Her heart quaked at the thought of being trapped in this flimsy shack while a storm raged around them. *How on earth can I save Ella and Ming if we capsize? Holly crap, how will I get the three of us to land?* Tears filled her eyes as she kissed Ella's soft head. *I should never have put you in danger, my darling. I should have left you with mum and Kallie. I'm such a bad mother.*

Ming touched her shoulder. "You be safe here, it not very bad storm. I find your husband and bring him here." He stuck his chest out. "Yes, I do that." Picking up the plywood he secured it to the window frame. "When the rain comes, you wedge door shut. Okay?" Bending to the cupboard again, he pulled out a box of matches and ceramic orb with patterned holes in the top. "This make you not afraid of dark." He lifted the top half revealing a thick candle. "You like?"

"Yes. You're very thoughtful, Ming." Jane pushed away thoughts of capsizing, wrapped the fishy-smelling jumper around Ella, and stared at the paper. *I wish I knew Morse code.* She tried to remember the code breaking exercise they'd done in year six. Kallie and she had taken it a step further and passed secret messages for the rest of the term. *How did it go?*

She wrote four words then translated it into a coded list, checked it then tore off the four words. *If Talos can't figure it out then Simon surely will.*

"Here you are, Ming. My husband is a big man. He has brown hair and brown eyes and his name is Talos. He looks a bit scary but he won't hurt you." She frowned. "And he has stitches in his chest and arm."

"I find him." Ming folded the message and pushed it into his short's pocket then bent and stroked Ella's head gently with his dirty finger. "I like your baby."

"Thank you, Ming."

"I come back soon." He took the poncho, dragged the chock free, and stepped out of the shack, shutting the door behind him.

Closing her eyes, Jane expelled a breath and prayed Ming would be safe. He was just a small boy on his own. *He needs protection as much as we do. I wonder if Elliott can do something to help him?*

The boat's motor stuttered to life then faded until all that was left was the lapping water against the barrels underneath and the soft pitter patter of rain drops smattering on the tin roof. A clap of thunder boomed in the distance.

Jane cringed.

The old man's dog began to howl.

"I know just how you feel." She glanced down at Ella feeding contently, unaware of the turmoil around her. Jane wiped a smudge off Ella's forehead. "Please let Ming find Talos." She shivered. *Talos can be daunting in normal circumstances. Under pressure he'd be terrifying to a small boy."*

CHAPTER TWENTY-TWO

Talos stood with hands on hips, drenched to the bone, as he surveyed the tiny deserted beach. Darkness was falling and the heavy rain hadn't let up.

He wanted to rip something apart with his bare hands. Strangle those responsible for taking Jane and Ella. Instead he bellowed, "Where the fuck are they?"

"Mate, that won't help." Nick clasped his shoulder. "We'll find them."

"Where? How?" He roared out his frustration at the world, at Rossini, at his own stupidity for not insisting Jane stay in Australia. "I screwed up."

Nick slogged him in his uninjured arm. "Fuck, Talos, get a grip."

Clenching his fists, Talos breathed through his anger. He needed to be in control and thinking clearly. He'd played out every scenario he could think of but kept coming back to one fact.

"She wouldn't leave without her bag and sandals, not unless she didn't have a choice."

"Yet she took your phone?" reasoned Nick.

"Maybe she didn't. Maybe it was stolen from the bag after she disappeared." He pulled Simon's phone out of his pocket and tried ringing his own number again. It rang out.

Ryan appeared over the rocks at the end of the tiny beach. He jumped to the sand and jogged over. "No sign. I've been as far as I can and I doubt she would have gone any further. It's too dangerous."

Talos wiped rivulets of rain off his face. "If she was desperate she would."

"Not without shoes. The jagged rocks would have torn her feet to shreds and she'd need both hands to climb over them."

"Then she's been taken, but why didn't she scream or kick up a fuss?" Talos scanned the empty jetty and restaurant terrace. The tables, chairs and umbrellas had been stacked away and the kitchen locked with the imminent arrival of the storm. All the tourists and staff had left over an hour ago.

Nick looked towards the sea. "Someone could have snatched the baby while Jane was having a swim. She would have had no choice but to go with them."

Talos clenched his fists. "There is no way Jane would leave Ella alone."

"She'd have to if she needed to use the ladies. The cubicles are tiny."

"No. Jane wouldn't take her eyes off Ella. Not for a second."

"Then someone took her by surprise." Nick did his own perusal of the small beach.

Simon emerged from the side of the restaurant and ran down the stone steps, his face grim. "I spoke to the caretaker, who told me there are only honeymoon cabins on this part of the island. I've also spoken to the guests. One couple remembers a western woman with a baby lying on a sun lounge. Probably where we found the change bag and carrier. Another couple said they saw her run into the restaurant's kitchen with the baby, but they didn't see her come out or any time after that."

Nick grimaced. "Why didn't the kitchen staff notice?"

"Probably too busy," muttered Simon. "The place was packed with diners." He looked back towards the wharf. "The caretaker said he was fishing on the next beach all afternoon and no western woman or anyone with a baby passed him."

"Fuck." Talos turned in a slow circle, the rain beating down on his upper body, stinging his recent wounds. *Where are you, sweetheart?* His gaze fell on the counter under the restaurant awning, where he'd put Ella's change bag and carrier. They were gone. He quickly scanned the area. "Did one of you move Jane's stuff?"

They all turned to the counter where a piece of white paper flapped up and down in the breeze, anchored by a fist-sized rock.

Fuck, they're playing with us. A bleakness invaded Talos's body, seeping into his bones like the tentacles of a deadly virus, threatening to suck the life from him. *I'll find you, Jane and then I'll deal with the bastard that took you.*

He drew his gun from the back of his board shorts. "That paper wasn't there five minutes ago."

"Shit." Nick drew his gun too.

"Spread out," muttered Talos going low. "Find the mongrel, he can't be far."

Ryan and Nick drifted into the palm trees edging the sandy beach. Simon took the water's edge, his gun out in front as he worked his way towards the wharf.

Talos ran straight for the steps, his gaze scanning for the slightest movement as sheet after sheet of torrential rain slammed into him. Mounting the steps in one leap, he ran to the restaurant and threw his back against the wall. *Fuck, this could be a trap.*

Simon had disappeared under the wharf. Nick and Ryan were on the far side of the terrace. Other than the swaying coconut palms nothing moved.

Talos reached up and ripped the paper from under the rock. A quick glance had him frowning. *It's a shopping list?*

Further along the wharf a small motor sputtered to life. Talos bounded to his feet, shoved the paper back under the stone and dashed around the side of the restaurant to the wharf where he came to a dead stop.

Other than their own empty speedboat there wasn't another craft to be seen yet he could hear a motor coughing and sputtering.

Shit, it's a runabout. He took off again, his feet pounding the concrete as he sprinted towards the end of the wharf. If the occupants decided to take a shot he'd have no alternative but to dive into the water.

Reaching the end of the wharf, Talos discovered Simon in waist deep water holding onto the side of a runabout as the surge rocked the small boat from side to side.

Turning his attention to the boat's only occupant, Talos found himself looking down on a very wet, very filthy small boy, who held the side of the boat with one hand and the starter pull-cord in the other. His big brown eyes stared up at Talos, widening with fear as his gaze fixed on the gun.

Shoving it into the back of his board shorts, Talos examined the boy and the boat through the heavy downpour, wrinkling his nose at the distinctly rotting smells rising from several black bags.

The boy's gaze moved to Talos's chest then rose to his face. He looked like he wanted to say something but terror held him tongue-tied.

Hunkering down to his haunches, Talos studied the kid's face. "Don't be afraid, we won't hurt you. Have you seen a woman with a tiny baby?"

He shook his head and tried to start the motor again.

"Wait," called Talos. "Was it you who left the list on the shelf?"

The boy stared at him.

"He probably doesn't speak English," offered Simon, reaching for a bag.

"It garbage. I garbage collector." The boy's eyes flicked to Simon examining the bag.

Nick came down on one knee. "Jesus, he's too young to be out in a boat alone."

Narrowing his eyes, Talos watched the boy clench and unclench his fingers as Simon moved several more bags. "I think our little friend has something that doesn't belong to him."

Simon caught the edge of a grey piece of waterproof sheeting.

"No, it's mine," called the boy, pushing Simon's hand away. He yanked the starter-cord and brought the motor spluttering to life.

Lunging out of the water, Simon grabbed the rope and threw it up to Talos. Then he stripped the grey plastic back revealing Ella's change bag and carrier.

"Well, well, well."

Losing his balance, the boy fell into the bottom of the runabout. He scrambled back to his feet and faced Talos. "They mine, I find them."

"No, they're not." Reaching down, Talos lifted the carrier up to Ryan, then grasped the change bag handles and threw it to Nick.

Fisting his hands, the small boy glared at Talos, his fear replaced by rage.

"He probably pilfers anything left here by tourists," said Simon. "Go home, boy, before I tan your backside for stealing."

Again, the boy looked at Talos as if he wanted to say something then he promptly sat and moved the rudder.

Pushing the boat away, Simon swung onto the wooden ladder. "What about the note? Do you think he delivered it?"

Talos wiped the rain out of his eyes again. "Yeah, but it's a shopping list, probably meant for the kitchen staff." Narrowing his eyes as he watched the boy motor away. "But why would it be written in English."

Climbing onto the wharf, Simon raised an eyebrow. "Show me."

With no other lead, Talos retraced his steps to the restaurant counter, grabbed the list and returned to the speedboat. "Here!" Climbing in, he handed Simon the folded list. "You might want to read it out of the rain."

Simon ducked under the canvas awning. "This doesn't make sense."

"Why," called Talos starting the engine.

Simon read out the list. "Milk x 42, Plums x 14, Whole meal flour x 11, Cider x 12, Shallots x17, Honey x11, Grapes x 21, Oranges x 23, Rhubarb x16, Beans x 21, Bacon x 22, Eggs x 23, Apples x15, Beer x 71, Olives x 61, Oysters x 32. Why would you count shallots, grapes, rhubarb, olives and shallots as single items? And the amounts are odd."

"Are you sure it's a shopping list?" asked Nick. "Maybe it's an inventory."

"Hang on a sec." Ducking down, Simon scrounged amongst their duffle bags in the storage cabin. He pulled his own bag forward and searched out a pen and pad then began copying the list furiously.

"What is it?" asked Talos.

"I think it's some sort of code. A very basic one, but give me a sec and keep that kid in sight. If he dropped the list off then he can lead us to the person who wrote it."

It was a long shot but Talos would take that over nothing. He glanced in the direction the boy had gone. The squall had completely swallowed him.

"Hang on." He pushed the throttle forward and brought the powerful boat up out of the water. "Keep your eyes open. I don't want to run over the top of the kid."

Five minutes later Ryan pointed ahead. "There, it's a barge."

Talos pulled back on the throttle. There was no sign of the boy or runabout. A couple of Vietnamese men were climbing off the barge into a long boat.

Simon let out a long whistle. "Fuck, that girl's clever. You gotta marry her, Talos."

"What is it? Tell me."

"It's a code all right. You take the second number of every item and count the same in letters. Milk x 41. You take the second number, which is one and that equates to letter I. Plums x 14. You take the second number which is 4 and equates to the letter M."

"Just tell us the fucking message, Simon," yelled Nick.

"Okay, don't get your jocks in a twist. The message says, 'I'm with garbage boy.'"

Talos smiled. "He's helping her."

"Let's ask those men on the barge if they've seen the boy," said Nick moving to the side of the boat. He cupped his mouth and yelled over the rising wind, "Ahoy there."

The two men looked across, shielding their faces against the rain. Lightning lit the sky.

Talos brought the speedboat closer. "Did you see where the garbage boy went?"

"What he do wrong?" asked one man.

"He didn't do anything wrong. I want to reward him for rescuing my wife and child."

"How he do that? He can't swim."

Nick swore softly. "The kid wasn't wearing a life jacket."

Talos raised his voice. "Have you seen him?"

One of the men pointed to the right. "He live in floating village. Not far."

As Talos increased the power Simon scrambled out of the cabin. "Take it slow, mate. The boy might be helping Jane, but she still could have been taken and held against her will."

"You got it." He let the boat idle along, the thunder masking its powerful motor as the rain and wind slashed at them. Grey shapes formed through the heavy rain.

"As soon as we get Jane and the baby, we should get out of Nha Trang," muttered Nick.

"What about your hot tour guide?" Ryan smirked. "Don't you have a booty call tonight?"

Nick scoffed. "I value my spine too much and I never make repeat performances."

Simon glanced across. "Except for Ava."

Nick's head shot up. "What the fuck?"

"Can it," called Talos. "Look." He pointed at a group of floating shanties, pitching about on the swelling waves. "Surely they're not being held in one of those death traps?"

"Let's find the kid," muttered Ryan.

Talos directed the boat in amongst the creaking shacks, the motor humming softly as he searched for the boy's runabout.

"It looks deserted," murmured Simon.

"There." Nick pointed to a small shack, where the small runabout had been tied.

Pulling out his gun, Talos cut the engine. He let Simon take his place at the wheel and kept his gaze on the dilapidated shanty. No light showed from within. *Not a positive sign.*

Nick and Ryan also drew their guns.

Throwing his legs over the side, Talos waited for the next swell and nimbly landed on the rotting timber of shanty's porch. The boards groaned under his weight. Edging along the corrugated iron wall, Talos strained to hear voices above the rain and lapping waves.

Nothing.

His gaze locked with Nick's standing on the other side of the doorframe. Nick tried the handle then shook his head and mouthed. *Locked.*

Nodding, Talos reached across and knocked twice. A shuffling came from inside then nothing. He knocked again, making sure to stay back against the wall.

Still nothing.

Nick stepped away from the wall and faced the door. He held up three fingers, then two then one and kicked the frail door. It splintered inwards.

A small shape hurtled out, squealing like a stuck pig. It hit Nick mid section and took him through the feeble rail and backwards into the dark swell.

Talos didn't waste time checking on the boy. Nick wouldn't let him drown. Instead he plunged into the shanty, slamming into the rear corrugated iron wall with his sore arm. "Umph." The building tilted dangerously then righted.

He dropped to his knees. "Jane?"

A match flamed to life in the corner. "Talos."

"Jane!" Elation filled him as he stared into her beautiful eyes. Shoving the gun in his shorts, he crossed the hut in two strides. "Christ. I thought I'd lost you." His voice cracked.

"Never." She blew the match out and came into his arms. After a minute, she eased back. "Where's Ming?"

"The boy? Nick has him." He buried his face in her soft hair, drawing in its heavenly fragrance as jubilation poured though his body. "I love you, woman."

Her breath hitched. "Oh, Talos that's…that's." She began sobbing against his shirt.

"Hey." He drew back and lifted her chin, trying to make out her face in the dark. "If I'd known it would upset you this much, I wouldn't have said a word."

She batted him with her hand. "I'm crying happy tears."

Pulling her against his chest again he kissed the top of her head and let out a shuddering breath. Weak with relief, the restriction around his heart and lungs lifted, allowing him to breathe without pain. "I need to kiss you, but first tell me where Ella is? I know she's safe otherwise you'd be wild with hysteria."

She sniffled and eased away. "Give me a minute. I need to light the candle."

Another match flamed then lowered though the darkness to a candle in a bowl, softly illuminating the shack. His gaze dropped to find Ella sound asleep in a small wooden chest.

Jane's eyes were glassy with unshed tears. "The water was seeping through the floorboards and I needed my hands free in case the wrong people followed Ming." She stepped back into his arms. "I knew you'd save us. You always do."

"Sweetheart." He lowered his head and kissed her, long and tenderly. She was balm to his shattered soul.

"Okay you two," called Nick. "Let's get out of this lousy weather."

Talos lifted his head to find Nick standing in the doorway, soaking wet. He had the boy wrapped tightly in a jacket and secured in his arms.

The boy's brown eyes were locked on Jane. "Is he the one you wanted? Not bad man?"

"Yes, Ming, this is the one I wanted. You did brilliantly. You're a brave boy."

"I was scared."

Jane caught Talos's hand. "We have to take Ming with us. He has no family and I thought maybe Elliot could do something to help him."

"Elliott bloody Shaw. That man's got you hoodwinked."

Nick laughed. "I think you're pretty safe, mate. She's only got eyes for you. Come on Ming, you want a ride in a speedboat?

"Okay."

Talos bent and gently lifted Ella out of the chest. He regarded the dismal shack. "Where's the kid's stuff?"

Jane sighed. "Everything he owns is in this little chest." She picked it up.

"All right, let's go. You can tell me what spooked you on the way to the hotel."

"No, we can't go back there." She clutched his arm. "Andrew's mistress is here. She arrived on the island by boat. What if she's behind the attack this morning?"

"Do you know her name or which of the ring members is her father?"

"No, but from her looks I'd say she has one parent who's Asian and one who's Caucasian. Any of them could be her father."

"Great."

"Ming told me you had the change bag. Was your phone still in it?"

"No, I was hoping you had it."

She shook her head. "Jarred's lady friend's address is in it too."

"Come on," shouted Ryan. "We're freezing our arses off out here."

Talos guided Jane to the boat, not trusting the spindly boards under their feet. He sheltered Ella as best he could while Ryan helped Jane into the boat.

She suddenly stopped and called out to an old man standing in the doorway of another shanty. "Bao, we're taking Ming to the authorities. This is not a good place for a child and we have a friend who takes in homeless children and educates them. I will make sure Ming is taken care of properly."

Handing Ella to Jane, Talos studied the old man and his skinny mongrel dog. The man didn't do anything for several seconds then waved them to come closer and disappeared inside his shack.

Starting the motor, Simon looked across at Talos through the downpour. "All sorted?"

Talos held up a hand. "Let's see what the old man wants."

As they motored to the front of the other shanty the old man reappeared with a thin zip lock plastic folder. "This belong to Ming. You see it into right hands."

Talos nodded and took the folder. "Ming won't come to any harm. I give you my word."

The old man nodded then called something out to Ming in Vietnamese.

Ming looked out from the storage cabin and waved. "I talk you later, Bao."

As the boat moved away, Talos pulled out Simon's phone, selected Jarred's number, and put it on loudspeaker. The other three listened as Talos repeated what Jane had told him.

A string of explicit curses came across loud and clear. "All right, get yourselves out to the airport. I'll see what I can do in the way of flights to Danang."

"Arh, Jarred, we've got a homeless kid with us. So you'll need to notify Shaw and we may need to get a private flight to Danang or maybe Shaw could lend us his company helicopter."

"Jesus Christ, is there anything else you'd like?"

"Nah, I'm good." Talos grinned.

"Find another hotel and wait for my call. I'll see what I can do." Jarred ended the call.

"Fuck, I'm cold," complained Ryan, huddling in the front observer seat.

"Me too," muttered Talos, passing Simon's phone back to him.

Nick scoffed. "Says the man with a beautiful woman to keep him warm tonight."

Talos glanced through into the cabin where Jane sat cradling Ella in one arm and Ming in the other. She was smiling at Talos in a way that made his heart skip.

"I do, don't I?"

CHAPTER TWENTY-THREE

Jane glanced around their latest hotel room. They had a king sized bed, two side tables, a bar fridge, coffee table, and settee, which Talos lay on at the moment with Ella cradled in one arm. The room wasn't opulent but any means, but by Ming's reaction you'd swear they were staying in a palace. He'd run around touching and exclaiming over everything, especially their tenth floor view of Nha Trang's rooftops and the ensuite with its spa bath.

Jane pushed the bathroom door wider and chuckled. Ming splashed about in the bubble filled spa, foaming suds covered his head, face, arms, and most of the floor. "You'll be all wrinkly if you stay in there much longer, sweetie. Why don't you come out and have something to eat?"

"I come out soon," he called, throwing a handful of suds in the air.

Talos laughed. "You've been saying that for an hour. Aren't you hungry?"

"Can I come back for swimming before I go home?"

Jane met Talos's gaze, her heart squeezing. "You're not going home, Ming. You're staying with us tonight." She cringed as a whoosh of water hit the bathroom floor.

Ming appeared in the doorway, a large towel wrapped around his body and frothy bubbles covering his head. He stood completely still staring at her. "All the night?"

"Yes, and tomorrow we'd like to take you to a friend who looks after children without parents. He makes sure they have food and clothes and beds."

Ming frowned. "Do he make them go school?"

"Yes, he does. Back in Australia, I'm a teacher and I know that if you go to school and work hard you can have a good life. Ella will go to school when she is five or six."

He looked at Ella, asleep in Talos's arms then stared at the floor. After a moment he lifted his head and solemnly nodded. "Okay. I go there. If I don't like it, I go your school."

"Oh, Ming, it doesn't work that way." Jane swallowed, at a loss to explain. "We live in another country, a long way over the ocean."

"I have a boat."

Talos stood and placed Ella in her carrier on the bed. "Dry yourself and get dressed, buddy. Tomorrow we've got a big day, so you need to eat and get some sleep."

Ming shuffled backwards. "I be ready quick time. You wait there." He closed the door.

Jane smiled at Talos. "He's very shy." She tapped lightly on the bathroom door. "Ming, first thing tomorrow, we're going to buy you new clothes and shoes."

The door flew open. Ming stood there in his dirty clothes, his eyes wide. "New clothes *and* shoes?"

Blinking rapidly, Jane nodded then turned away and dug through her suitcase, searching for a t-shirt that Ming could use for tonight. Anything would be better than his own filthy clothes. Her heart wept for him and his future. *I'd take him in a flash, but the Vietnamese government isn't likely to give a child to a woman with a price on her head. It could be years before the adoption went through.*

"You okay," asked Talos, sliding his arms around her.

She leaned against Talos and glanced across to Ming now standing by the coffee table shoveling noodles into his mouth. "I know we can't take him with us, but is there some way we can sponsor him or make sure he's being looked after properly?"

"We can ask Shaw." He kissed her neck.

A light knock sounded and they both stiffened.

"Stay out of view." Talos strode to his bag and pulled out the gun. "Who is it?"

"Your brothers-in-arms," came a deep male voice.

Shoving the gun in his duffle bag, Talos opened the door.

Nick, Ryan, and Simon strolled in and headed straight for the coffee table laden with plates of spring rolls, soft shell crabs, noodles, and prawns. They'd all showered and changed into jeans and white

T-shirts like Talos. Jane's gaze ran over all four men. Although differing in height, they were all tall, handsome, muscle bound, and on edge. They also made a reasonably sized room appear small.

Little Ming watched warily, his hand hovering over the spring rolls.

"It's okay, sweetie." Jane gave him a reassuring smile. "These men are our friends."

He frowned at Nick. "You not angry I push you in ocean?"

"No, but that information stays strictly between us. I don't want it getting around that a little kid got the better of a big tough guy like me."

Ming smiled. "I very clever kid."

"Hmm." Nick grabbed a large spring roll and sat on the couch. "Jarred rang. He's sent his lady friend to stay with friends in Dalat, but he's concerned that this woman, if she's the person who took your phone, has our names and numbers."

Talos sat on the end of the bed and pulled Jane onto his knee. "She has your numbers, but not your names. I've used Simon's trick."

"What's that?" asked Jane.

"Sam Locke is under Locksmith. Jarred Steele is Tin man. Ryan Dutch is Tulip Supplies. Nick Flanagan is under Irish Pub, and Simon Hawke is under Birdseeds."

"I use that too." Ryan said. "You're down as Greek Restaurant."

"Well that's something," muttered Simon leaning against a wall. "I've locked the phone but you said you had some photos on it."

Talos grimaced. "They're of Jane and I in the Botanical Gardens. I've got my arms around her and there is photo's of Ella and Jane at the hospital."

"That's unfortunate. You'll have to keep a low profile, at least until we get Ripon."

Jane frowned. "Won't the meeting be cancelled now they know I'm here and Kazan is missing?"

"Maybe." Simon shrugged. "But Gibbs wants us to stake out the meeting anyway. The SCU went to a lot of trouble to whisk Kazan away without alerting anyone."

Helping himself to a bowl of noodles, Ryan sat on the floor and stretched out his legs. "Thanks to Kazan's hissy fit in the hotel lobby and the non-return of the fishing boat, the local police put out a missing person alert and searched their rooms."

"Obviously they found the evidence Simon left out?" Talos said.

Ryan nodded. "Nice touch unlocking Kazan's briefcase. The local police called the SCU straight away."

"I'm still concerned about Gibbs," muttered Talos. "And Shaw for that matter."

"Don't worry," called Simon. "Although the SCU are trailing us, they have no idea where we're staying at the moment and I'm using every spare moment to dig deeper. So far Gibbs and Shaw are both clean."

Nick leaned forward and passed Ming a plate of prawns. "Getting back to Rossini's girlfriend. Gibbs reckons she probably doesn't know Rossini is dead. The AFP kept it under raps, so there's a good chance she thinks Rossini brought Jane to Vietnam to kill her."

Jane almost choked. "Why would she think that?"

Silence fell as Jane twisted and locked eyes with Talos. "What don't I know?"

He sent a glare towards Nick then sighed. "The AFP had some information that Gibbs only shared with us today."

A shiver ran down her spine. "What information."

Talos rubbed his forehead. "After we left the prison, Gibbs was sent back to make a deal with Rossini. Total immunity and no jail time if Rossini testified against his father and the other ring members. He agreed, as long as he could make one private phone call to you."

"I never got a phone call."

"No, he rang a number in Hanoi and spoke to a woman; it was recorded by the AFP, although they couldn't trace it. Rossini told the woman he was testifying against his father and giving up the other members of the ring, then he said you would meet with an unfortunate accident and he would bring the baby to her just as they'd planned. The woman appeared delighted with the idea."

Jane gripped his shirt in her fingers. "They were going to take Ella?"

Talos's arms tightened around her. "I didn't know any of this until today or I'd never have allowed you to come to Vietnam."

Ming padded over to Jane. "I protect your baby. Nobody take her away."

Barely aware of Talos rubbing her back or the others exchanging worried glances, Jane stared at her beautiful baby sleeping contently in her carrier beside them. All she could think of were Andrew's last words to her.

"I'm in a relationship with the daughter of one of Marzetti's partners. When she discovered you were pregnant, she wanted you eliminated. I was trying to keep you alive so I told her I wanted the kid. She's been jealous of you since she saw you at our apartment."

'That lying, cheating, hypocrite. He was going give that woman my baby!"

"Shush," soothed Talos. "I'll take you back to Australia on the first available flight."

Jane blinked at Talos. "Why would that woman be happy for Andrew to testify against her own father and the other ring members?"

He frowned. "I don't know. Perhaps she hated her father as much as Rossini hated his."

For a moment Jane considered that. "But if she thinks Andrew is still alive and helping the AFP, she might be hanging around hoping to see him. Maybe she's the one who told him the meeting dates, places, and times. What if she didn't have anything to do with our attack this morning or those men watching our hotel in Ho Chi Min?"

Talos glanced at the others who had all straightened and were listening intently. "It's possible, but even so, I think it would be wiser to go home."

Jane sank against his chest. "It could have been a coincidence that I ran into her today but none the less, we can't go home until we have them all behind bars, otherwise Ella and I will never be safe. We will never be able to lead normal lives." She looked up into his eyes. "And we can't be together. I won't take you away from your family into witness protection."

"There's another couple of reasons we popped by," Nick said.

Jane waited apprehensively.

"Jarred rang Shaw. He's busy at the moment so he can't take the boy."

"Did Elliott say what he wants us to do?" she asked.

"Yeah, bring Ming to Hanoi in five days."

Ming looked at Jane. "You want me go home for five days?"

"No, you'll stay with us until we reach Hanoi. Our friend is going to meet us there."

A smile of delight lit his face. "Okay." He began eating again.

"What's the other thing you need to tell us?" Talos asked.

"After a little persuasion, Shaw has agreed to lend us his company helicopter."

"That's a bonus."

"Yeah, we can't risk using passenger airlines or public trains." Ryan stretched his arms up behind his neck. "Once Shaw heard Nick and I are Blackhawk pilots he agreed."

"So what's next?" asked Jane.

Simon stood. "We fly out at dawn for Danang, which is forty minutes from Hoi An. I've changed our booking and we're now staying at a resort just out of town. I've also arranged for a four-wheel drive to be waiting at Danang."

Jane straightened. "Could Talos and I take Ming to the markets in the morning? He needs clothes and Ella needs nappies."

Standing, Nick shook his head. "Not happening. The markets won't be open that early and you two can't risk being seen."

Ryan shrugged. "The markets are open tonight. We could take the kid shopping now and pick up nappies." He grinned. "And give these two a little time together."

"We could do that." Nick raised an eyebrow towards Jane and Talos.

Jane drew in a breath. "You'll look after Ming carefully? You won't lose him?"

Nick's lips twitched. "Promise. We won't let him out of our sight."

Simon sighed. "Count me out, I've got work to do and the night is getting away." He gave a wave. "I'll see you all bright and early."

Nick ruffled Ming's hair. "Let's go buy you some clothes."

Ming pulled out the five hundred thousand-dong note. "I got this."

Nick whistled. "Where the hell—"

"I gave it to him," interrupted Jane. She walked over and took it out of Ming's fingers. "That's yours for helping me, Ming, but I will look after it until you get back."

Ming's troubled eyes followed her as she went to the wooden chest and slipped it in with his other treasures. Jane picked up her wallet off the bedside table and pulled out another couple of notes and held them out to Nick. "This should be enough for several pairs of shorts, T-shirts, undies, a pair of sandals, and a packet of nappies."

"I've got money." Nick gently pushed her hand aside. "Come on, Ming, let's go."

Ming followed but his eyes stayed locked on her until the door closed between them. Jane sniffed in a shaky breath and glanced up at Talos. "I feel so helpless."

"I know. Come here." He opened his arms and Jane stepped into them, safe and secure against his lovely, solid, dependable chest. His heat and spicy cologne engulfed her, chasing away her anxiety as sensual spears of desire shot through her body.

Easing back, Jane met his dark gaze. "Now that we are alone, I think we should take advantage of that shower."

His lips twitched. "I think that's a very good idea."

Clasping the edge of her shirt, Jane slowly pulled it up over her head and let it drop from her fingers, then she unzipped her shorts and let them slither to the floor.

Talos's gaze swept down over her, heating her with its intensity. Smiling she reached behind, unclipped her bra and eased the straps off her shoulders one at a time. A growl emanated from his throat, his eyes had darkened to almost black. He raised his hand, plucked the bra from her fingers, and tossed it over his shoulder. His gaze devoured her breasts for several seconds then he tore off his shirt and jeans, tossed her over his shoulder and strode into the bathroom.

Jane giggled. "I'm supposed to be seducing you this time."

"You are, sweetheart. I'm just assisting." He lowered her to the floor, taking her panties all the way to her ankles.

Jane stepped out of them and hooked her thumbs in his jocks. "My turn." Sinking to the tiles, she tugged them down his muscled thighs to his ankles. Raising her eyes, she fastened on his erection jutting proudly against his stomach. She licked her lips and leaned forward.

"Wait," he murmured huskily, stepping back. He held out his hand. "Trust me."

Taking his hand, Jane stood and followed him into the large shower recess.

He turned on the faucet, protecting her from its force until he had the temperature right, then stepped aside and rubbed a cake of soap in his hands.

Lovely warm water cascaded over her head and back, easing the tension that had held her in its grip. "I wanted to take care of you this time."

His soapy hands massaged her shoulders from behind. "First let me do this." He kneaded his fingers into her spine then spread his hands over her back, descending down over each globe of her backside, squeezing gently then sliding over her hips, her belly, and up her ribs.

Jane moaned and leaned against his chest, arching her breasts, waiting for his touch.

His hands stilled, a chuckle sounded in her ear, his warm breath tickling her lobe. "Are you trying to tell me something, sweetheart?"

"I need your hands on me, all of me, everywhere."

"So do I."

Warm water rained onto her upturned face as he lavished kisses over her sensitive neck. His hands closed over both breasts, massaging her swollen flesh. He rolled her nipples lightly then pinched. Ecstasy exploded in every cell of her body, drenching her in in desire. She reached behind with both hands and gripped his hips, parting her legs in desperate need.

Another chuckle tickled her ear then he slid one hand down her body and between her thighs, pushing inside her with his fingers, rubbing back and forth over her sensitive skin.

Her body quivered as he thrust his fingers faster. "Oh God, Talos."

"I want your hands all over me too." He nipped her earlobe then lathed it soothingly as he caressed her breasts. He feathered his lips up and down her neck, sending thrilling tingles all the way to her fingers and toes.

"Then I want you to take me in your mouth."

She moaned, the pressure building low in her belly. "I'm so close."

He rubbed his thumb almost aggressively back and forth over her hypersensitive nub.

"Then I'm going to fuck you, here in the shower."

She bucked against his fingers, cried out, and stiffened as her orgasm crashed over her like a colossal wave, building in all in its powerful intensity before careening out smoothly over the soft sand.

As her euphoria ebbed she collapsed against him, light headed and giddy.

Talos kissed her shoulder. "You come apart spectacularly, sweetheart."

"Only with you, apparently." Still breathing hard, she straightened and turned in his arms. "My turn." She reached for the soap, lathered her hands, then dropped the soap in the dish and placed both hands on his chest, careful to avoid his stitches. "I love your body."

He raised an eyebrow. "It's yours to do with whatever you want."

"Hmm, the mind boggles." She slid her hands up over his shoulders and down his massive biceps, brushing her breasts against his chest teasingly.

"I like that. Do it again."

Smiling, she complied with his request, only this time grinding her pelvis against his hard body. He pulled her hips closer with his hands.

"No, no, no." She gently knocked his hands away and lathered hers again. "Rule number one, you can't touch me."

He groaned. "Not fair."

Again she placed her hands on his chest, fanning her fingers wide, then stroked up to his collarbone over his shoulders and down his arms to his hands.

His fingers closed firmly, capturing hers.

"Rule number two, you must obey me."

His lips twitched but he released her. "I'll obey...for now."

"Good man." She again soaped her hands and ran them down his rib cage, over his hard stomach, around his waist, and down over his taut butt. "Nice."

He chuckled and flexed his butt cheeks.

Jane squeezed back then ran her hands up the sides of his torso, under his arms and across his back, again rubbing her breasts against his ribcage.

He swallowed and clenched his jaw but didn't move.

"Hmm." Stepping back, Jane soaped her hands and surveyed him slowly from head to toe, then sank to her knees, running her hands down both legs all the way to his ankles.

"Wait." He leaned out, dragged a towel off the rack and dropped it to the tiles. "I can't have you bruising your pretty knees, plus you may need a bit more height."

Smothering a giggle, she rearranged the towel under her knees then ran her hands up the back of his legs over his butt, around his hips, and captured his erection in her hands. He made a humming sound in his throat, leaned against the wall, and closed his eyes. Jane held his scrotum in one hand and tightened her other hand around his length, stroking back and forth.

"That's so good." His hands reached into her wet hair.

"No. Remember the rules."

He hissed and withdrew his hands.

Stretching, Jane leaned forward and licked a bead of moisture off his tip.

He jerked and opened his eyes. "You're going to kill me."

"I doubt it." She traced her tongue around the head of his penis, tasting him as she continued to stroke back and forth.

He widened his stance and bent his knees, bringing him a little lower. "Again."

Smiling, Jane circled the head with her fingers then ran her tongue down the length of him and back up, squeezing his scrotum gently.

He twitched his fingers by his sides but didn't touch her.

Delighted with her newfound power, Jane leaned in and closed her lips over his head, swirling her tongue around him, sucking and grazing her teeth over the smooth skin.

"Oh yeah." He pushed his thick length further into her mouth.

Jane gagged and pulled away. "Rule three, don't choke your lover."

"Sorry," he whispered playfully.

She leaned in again, taking him further into her mouth and sucking him harder as she moved back and forth. She increased her pace, licking, swirling, tasting, and sucking as the tension in his body tightened. His hips began to follow her, thrusting into her mouth. Closing her fingers around the base of his length she formed a barrier to stop him choking her and matched his thrusts, sucking hard as he withdrew.

"Stop." He pulled away, lifted her to her feet and backed her into the tiled wall away from the spray. "My turn." He raised her hands above her head, caging her with his body.

She gasped. "Rule number four. Do not interrupt your lover when she's about to—"

He lowered his head, captured her lips, and devoured her in a kiss that took her breath then gave it back again. She moaned, melting against his hard body and opened to his probing tongue, taking everything he had to give. *God he can kiss.*

Eventually he eased away and gazed down at her, his eyes dancing wickedly. "Do you remember what else I said I'd do to you, here in the shower?"

Licking her lips, Jane nodded.

"Say it," he whispered.

Heat rose in her face "You said you were going to...to...fuck me."

Keeping his eyes locked with hers, he released her hands, gripped her waist, and lifted her. "Here in the shower."

Jane wrapped her legs around his waist and gripped his broad shoulders. "Yes."

He lifted her slightly and nudged inside her, his hands gripping her thighs as he watched her face. "I've been thinking about doing you all day." He thrust deeper.

"Yes." She locked her ankles and pressed closer. "Faster."

Withdrawing, he thrust again and again, holding her steady as he ploughed into her.

Jane wriggled her hips, grinding her pelvis into each thrust as the tension in her belly tightened. "Harder."

His grip tightened. The muscles in his arms bunched as he thrust deeper, slamming into her body over and over. Then he let go of one thigh and ran his fingers through her folds and over her nub. Jane cried out, her body clenching around him as she came apart, splintering into a thousand pieces like a chandelier dropping from the heavens.

Talos thrust twice more then roared and emptied his seed inside her. For several minutes he held her to him, breathing hard as they both floated back to earth. He let her feet slide to the floor then turned them so the water cascaded over her head, cooling her heated body.

Jane stood inert as Talos lathered her body then he rinsed her off and dried her with one of the fluffy towels. "That was incredible." She stretched up and kissed him. "I love you."

"And I love you." He picked her up and carried her into the bedroom, stripped back the bed covers on one side of the bed and lay her down. "Catch some sleep. We've got an early start tomorrow." He covered her, picked up Ella in her carrier, and placed it beside the bed.

"What about Ming?"

"I'll wait up. He can sleep on the couch."

"Okay, but can you pass me my nightie and then come to bed and cuddle me?"

He smiled. "I can do that."

Stretching out, Jane's gaze followed him. He pulled on boxers then turned the lamp down low and slid between the sheets.

"Happy?"

She smiled. "You forgot my nightie?"

"I prefer you like this." He drew her against his side, encasing her in his arms.

"Talos! I don't want Nick and Ryan to see me naked."

"Neither do I," he murmured, feathering her lips with kisses. "I won't let them through the door. Now go to sleep." He traced his fingers up and down her spine. "Dream about me and the life we're going to have together."

"The life we'll have if we catch Andrew's mistress and the rest of the ring. We will catch them, won't we, Talos?"

"We'll do our best, sweetheart."

Jane closed her eyes and lay her hand over his heart. Its steady beat a reassuring constant. *And if we don't, it is going to tear me apart to leave you, but I will.*

CHAPTER TWENTY-FOUR

Talos stared at the ceiling where a strip of light from the bathroom cast a narrow path. He kept replaying the morning attack in their hotel room, Kazan's take down and subsequent hand over to Gibbs and the crippling fear he'd experienced on arriving at the island to find Jane and Ella gone.

A puff of warmth on his chest brought his thoughts to the present and the woman in his arms. Her dark lashes rested against a flawless creamy complexion. Her rosy lips curved in a gentle half smile. Her cute little nose pressed against his chest where her breath tickled his skin. His own sleeping beauty, safe, secure, and right where she belonged.

A memory stirred and he frowned into the dark. She'd came apart spectacularly in the shower and after he'd told her so, she'd said, "*Only with you, apparently.*"

Talos clenched his jaw. *That idiot Rossini didn't deserve the honour of being her husband and I won't afford him that title, ever.*

He pushed the thought away and concentrated on Rossini's mistress. That woman being in Nha Trang worried the fuck out of him. How did she know where to find Jane? And if the ring members knew the AFP were after them, then why wasn't Kazan on the lookout?

It doesn't make sense.

Closing his eyes, he examined every detail of the team's plans for the next couple of days. They'd stay at a small resort in Hoi An while the team checked out the restaurant where the next meeting was scheduled to take place. Jane would not be left alone for a second. Once she'd identified Ripon, they would whisk her out of the restaurant, set up a tail and at the first opportunity, take him down. Talos's mind eased and he let himself drift.

It seemed he'd barely closed his eyes when a squeak brought him fully alert. Easing Jane out of his arms, Talos threw his legs over the side of the bed and sat, listening intently.

The squeak came again and looking across the room he noticed two tiny fists brandishing the air.

Expelling a relieved breath, Talos turned up the lamp slightly and padded over to the carrier. He stood quietly observing the tiny angel who'd claimed a huge chunk of his heart.

Her fists stilled and her eyes widened as she spotted him, then a gummy smile appeared and she cooed, batting her fists vigorously.

"Okay, okay," he whispered, picking her up. "What are you doing awake?"

Her delight and recognition obvious, she beamed and gurgled at him, her tiny fingers closing around his big thumb.

"Shush, you'll wake your mamma."

A light knock sounded.

Talos glanced at Jane slumbering peacefully, her delectable curves covered by the sheet. He strode to the door before the knocking got any louder. "Who is it?"

"Just me," came Nick's voice.

Talos opened the door then stood aside. "What the hell?"

Nick sidled past with Ming held in one arm, asleep on his shoulder. In the other hand, he carried several stuffed bags and a child's beach towel. Ming had a baby doll and flame-colored dragon clutched in one arm, the other arm hung over Nick's shoulder.

Closing the door, Talos followed them across to the couch and whispered, "You bought him a doll?"

"It's not for him. The kid insisted we buy a doll for Ella. I bought him the cool transformer. It may look like a dragon now but it converts to a robot warrior." Nick dropped the bags and lowered Ming to the couch. "Poor little kid, his eyes nearly popped out of his head when he saw all the toys. I had to buy him something."

"Did you get everything else Jane asked for?"

"Yeah, those markets are massive, but we found a couple of vendors side by side who had everything we needed." Nick glanced at the bed and froze. "Jesus!"

Talos's gaze flew to Jane, curled up, facing the other way, her wavy hair spread over her naked shoulders and back. The sheet had slipped displaying the sexy curve of her waist and hip. Talos reached the bed in two strides and flicked the sheet over her. "You better get out of here before she castrates me for letting you in."

Exhaling, Nick rubbed his forehead and stepped back, banging into the wall, his gaze still locked on Jane.

Talos frowned. "Are you all right, mate?"

"I thought...I thought it was Ava. She used to sleep just like that." He shook his head and turned for the door. "Freaked me out."

"Hey, mate." Talos followed. "Have you thought about contacting her?"

"It wouldn't do any good. She married some other guy within months of leaving me."

"Christ, I'm sorry, mate. I didn't know that."

"Yeah well, shit happens." Nick opened the door and hesitated. "I figured she'd come round if I gave her a little time, but I waited too long. I didn't realize how much I loved Ava until I lost her." He stepped out and shut the door with a resounding click.

Talos stared at the door. *No wonder Nick can't move on, he's still in love with Ava.*

"What are you doing, Talos?"

He gazed at the woman he loved. A sensual goddess with her hair falling in a jumbled mess about her shoulders and her stunning emerald eyes caressing him as she clasped the sheet loosely about her rounded breasts.

Talos smiled. "Our little angel decided it was play time." He glanced down to find the baby's eyes closed. "Little possum is asleep." He placed her in the carrier, tucked the blanket firmly round her, then turned to Ming. The kid still wore his dirty clothes, which Talos determined he'd bin first thing in the morning. Not wanting to wake the little guy, he left the doll and dragon where they were and draped a light blanket over him.

Talos fell onto bed and reached for Jane. He hesitated on noticing the raised eyebrow, shining eyes, and pursed lips. "What's got you so amused?"

"You called Ella our little angel. That's so sweet, Talos."

"Yeah, I'm a sweet guy. Come here and I'll show you just how sweet."

She shimmied down and wrapped her arm around his waist. "As long as it doesn't involve any sexual acts. Ming might wake up."

Groaning, Talos reached for the lamp and killed the light. "I hope they have two bedrooms in the suites at our next hotel, otherwise I won't be a happy camper."

She kissed him and snuggled closer. "Abstinence makes the heart grow fonder."

He chuckled. "Absence not abstinence."

"Same thing."

"The room is in total darkness and as long as you don't scream, I'm sure I can cater to our mutual needs without our little friend ever knowing."

"Goodnight, Talos." She rolled over and splayed out across the bed.

"That's an invitation if ever I had one." He kissed her shoulder and dragged her backside firmly against his erection.

"Talos!"

"Shush, let me work my magic."

❧

Talos woke with a start. He blinked and focused. The room was still in semi darkness but something wasn't right. He lay spooned around Jane, her sweet arse pressed against his morning erection, her breathing nice and even. The hairs on his neck bristled. Someone was standing by the bed.

Fuck, I should have put the gun under the pillow. He tensed. *Why haven't they put a bullet in my head already?* He clenched his fist, bunching the muscles in his arm as he prepared to strike. No way would he go down without a fight.

A warm little hand touched his shoulder then endeavored to shake him. "You wake up."

Stretching his fingers, Talos relaxed and turned to face his assailant. "Hello, buddy. How come you're up so early? The alarm hasn't gone off yet."

"You come put bubbles in water for me."

Talos groaned. "Hey, buddy, can't you wait until we get to Hoi An. We've still got half an hour before we have to be up and I need my beauty sleep."

Ming giggled but shook his head. "I not put on new clothes till I clean."

Crap. "All right, give me a minute."

Ming skipped off to the bathroom and Talos threw back the sheet, sat up, and yawned. *Bloody bubble baths.* He reached for his boxers, pulled them on, then scratched his head. It wasn't much to ask, and he did owe the little guy for rescuing Jane. He checked the phone Jarred had loaned him and found a message from Simon. All was still on schedule so he ambled into the bathroom after Ming.

The boy was hopping from foot to foot, still dressed with a big smile on his face.

"Wait until I get the temperature right then you can get in." Talos turned both taps on and adjusted the temperature, then unscrewed the bubble bath lid and liberally shook blobs of gel under the jet of water. Bubbles began forming immediately.

Ming clapped his hands and ran out of the bathroom.

"Shush," whispered Talos. "Don't wake Jane and Ella."

Ming was back within seconds with the bright beach towel and several items of clothing. "You go now."

"Not yet. I don't want you burning yourself, but you can jump in now if you like."

Ming shook his head. "I wait till you go."

"You are a shy little fella, aren't you? All right, but leave the door open so I can hear you splashing about."

"Okay."

Leaving the bath to fill, Talos opened his toiletry bag and took out his shaving gear. "Might as well do something constructive while we wait."

Ming came and stood under his elbow, staring into the mirror, his eyes following Talos's every move.

"Haven't you ever seen a man shave, buddy?"

"No, do it hurt?"

"No, I'll show you." Talos sprayed some shaving cream on Ming's skinny arm then turned his disposable razor upside down and dragged it through the foam. "Don't ever do this for real though. I'm just showing you what it feels like."

Ming grinned. "It feel nice."

"Hmm, but it's a blood...it's a pain when you have to do it every day." Talos finished shaving, washed his face, patted on a little aftershave, and ran his hands through his hair. "All done. How's that water?"

"Good, you go now."

"Yeah, all right." Talos turned off the water, left the kid to his bubbles and stepped into the bedroom where he found the curtains wide and dawn just breaking.

Back in her nightie, Jane leaned against the headboard feeding Ella. "Good morning."

"Hey, gorgeous, did we wake you?"

"No, Ella started babbling so I decided I might as well get up too."

He strolled over and kissed her sweet lips, then leaned lower and dropped a kiss on Ella's head. "I'll make us coffee, but we'll have to grab breakfast on the way. Jarred wants us out at the military airbase by six-thirty."

"Did he ring?"

"No, I got a text. Nick and Ryan have already left to check out the chopper. Jarred and Simon will travel with us."

"That's good. Ella won't be much longer and it will only take me ten minutes to have a shower and get dressed."

"No worries. Nick got you nappies."

"Yes, I saw. What's with the doll?"

He grinned. "Ming made Nick buy it for Ella."

"Oh, isn't he a sweetie."

Talos made coffee, did his stretching and Kata then called out to Ming. "Come on, buddy, it's time to get out. Jane and I need showers before we fly to Hoi An."

A squeal came from the bathroom, then the sound of water whooshing onto the floor. Talos laughed. "Ming's absolutely rapt in water. When we get to the resort, I'm going to teach him to swim."

"He's never experienced any of the things we take for granted. Wait until he sees the helicopter."

"Yeah. I was thinking we could maybe set up a trust for him."

"That would be wonderful, Talos."

"I ready," called Ming, struggling one handed to pull a yellow T-shirt over his head. He ran to his chest and kneeled in front of it.

Talos observed him as he stuffed the wet beach towel into the chest then reverently lay Ella's doll on top and shut the lid. Then Ming emptied the bags Nick had carried in last night. He picked up a purple and black backpack and shoved in a pair of pajamas with dinosaurs on them, a cap, bright board shorts, and a T-shirt. He zipped the bag up, pulled it onto his shoulders and picked up the dragon, his face alight with happiness.

Talos frowned at the pink and yellow frangipanis all over the kid's shorts. "Surely Nick could have found you something less girly."

Jane laughed. "They're cute and I've seen lots of guys wearing boardies with flowers."

"Yeah, but not pink." Talos muttered.

"The right color pink on a man with olive skin makes him look very sexy."

"No way."

"Yes, way." Jane grinned. "When we get to Hoi An, I'll buy you a pink T-shirt and prove it."

"No, you won't," He said.

"Yes, I will." She lay Ella on the bed, picked up her clothes, and sashayed into the bathroom. "Trust me."

Talos looked at Ming. "Now look what you've done."

Ming grinned. "I like pink."

Talos opened the mini bar and pulled out a couple of bars of chocolate and pineapple juices. "Here, these will have to keep us going until we get some breakfast."

Ming tore open the chocolate bar and devoured it. "I like chocolate. Sometimes cook on island give me chocolate or left over fruits and other food."

"From now on you'll get regular meals and people will look after you properly."

"Okay."

Talos put the clothes he wanted to wear aside and packed his duffle bag, re-checking his gun was on safety before pushing it under everything else. When he turned back to Ming, he found the kid hovering over Ella, making faces and playing with her tiny fingers.

Keeping a discreet eye on them, Talos picked up the phone and rang Jarred. "Hey, boss, we should be ready to go in approximately twenty minutes."

"Good, meet us in the lobby. Simon is picking up some rolls and coffee. He should be back by then and we'll be good to go."

"You got it." Talos hung up, ate his chocolate bar, and polished off the juice.

Ten minutes later Jane came out of the bathroom looking cool and fresh in a mint-green summer dress that came to mid-thigh. Her hair was caught up in a high ponytail and she wore a pair of white sandals. His gaze travelled slowly up her slim legs. "Nice."

She grinned. "Thank you. The bathroom is all yours."

"Great, we've got ten minutes to be down in the lobby." He picked up his stuff and strode into the bathroom.

It took twenty minutes to get to the Danang Airport where Shaw's helicopter had been left at a corporate helipad for them. During the short journey, Jane held Ella in the sling across her chest and rested her hand on Talos's thigh. He held Ming on his lap and kept an eye out for trouble.

Exiting the jeep, Ming clung to his dragon and Talos's hand. Jane stayed close as they approached the chopper, where Ryan and Nick were seated in the cockpit.

"We right to go?" Jarred stuck his head through the open the rear passenger door."

Nick removed his headset and nodded. "Just waiting for clearance."

Talos helped Jane into the chopper then lifted Ming in. As soon as their gear was loaded Talos climbed in beside Jane. Ming immediately climbed onto his lap and stared through to the cockpit, his gaze fixed on the control panel.

Talos pulled the backpack off the little fella's shoulders, then strapped him in and placed a set of headphones on him. As soon as Simon and Jarred were seated, Ryan checked seatbelts and headphones, then Nick went through the start up procedure. Jane held Ella against her chest, covering the baby's outer ear with her hand to reduce the noise impact once the chopper started.

Nick flipped the master switch, checked his gauges, held in the starter button, and adjusted the throttle. After another couple of checks and he gave the thumbs up. The rotor blades began to *whump* overhead.

Having been through this hundreds of times, Talos set his mind to distracting Ming by showing him how to transform the dragon. Who knew what this little boy's future held, but it had to be better than it would have been. And so would Jane's once they had the last members, Ripon, and Rong behind bars.

Chapter Twenty-five

Up in the mountain town of Sapa, a man of mixed race leaned back in his deep leather chair and observed the opulent pool beyond his window. Jade dragons crouched at the four corners, their powerful haunches bunched as if ready to pounce on unsuspecting prey.

Much like myself. He smiled. Life was good to those with power.

Movement drew his gaze to the pool-lounge and his latest conquest—a German backpacker he'd picked up in Hanoi. The girl rolled over, her large breasts jiggling as she settled on her back, allowing the sun's rays to lick her naked body.

Stretching his sore back, Rong silently cursed his ageing muscles and studied the blonde. She was easy on the eye and their arrangement mutually satisfying. He gave her lavish gifts and a roof over her head and she gave him her body as he wished to use it. In-depth conversation was unnecessary although she did speak English if required.

His thoughts turned to business and the only two people he trusted—his child from an ill-fated marriage, and Dominic Marzetti, a man as ruthless and cunning as himself.

It's a set back to have Dom in prison, but it won't be for much longer.

Lillian was another matter. Perhaps he should rein in her power. She had, after all, defied him by marrying Andrew Rossini. What if she defied him again?

It will test her loyalty if she finds out I ordered her lover's death. Andrew was weak and would have cracked under interrogation. Lillian had grown stronger over the years, perhaps too strong. His people had begun deferring to her. *It's time I cut her authority.*

His phone vibrated on the teak desk. The caller I.D. had him smiling.

"Hello, Lillian, I was just thinking about you. What news do you bring your father?"

"Your idiot Russian friend has drowned along with his two bodyguards."

"What?" He shot to his feet, his twinges forgotten. "How did that happen?"

"Kazan hired an old boat without a captain and went out for a day of drunken fishing."

"How is this fucking possible?"

"It's possible because Kazan couldn't wait for a chartered boat the following day and he's a drunk with a volatile temper. I have warned you about him so many times."

"Stop with your speeches and give me details."

"Kazan made a spectacle of himself in the hotel when he couldn't chartered a boat. The reception staff has told police he blew up and threatened to hire his own boat, which apparently he did."

"Go on."

"Kazan went out deep-sea fishing with his two useless bodyguards and when they didn't return by the appointed time, the boat owner informed the police. Local fishermen found the boat, with the ignition switch on but the fuel tank empty. The deck was littered with food, empty beer cans, and vodka bottles. There was no sign of Kazan or his men."

"Do you think it could it be a set up?"

"No. I had Kazan monitored the previous afternoon. There were no police following him. He went to the markets for bait and my man saw him leave the hotel early yesterday morning with his bodyguards and a load of fishing gear."

Even though it grated, he ignored the fact she'd referred to someone in his employ as her man. "This is troubling, especially after Lhasa's ill-timed death. Have you got the briefcase?"

"No, the police have it."

"That is not fucking good enough! What are you doing?" He slammed his fist on the desk and turned to the window. The blonde sat up and frowned towards his open window.

Lillian huffed. "I would have retrieved it, had I known in time.

Don't panic, there won't be anything in the briefcase connecting you to Kazan."

"What you don't fucking understand is that the SCU will now shut down Lhasa and Kazan's operations, which greatly affects my annual income."

"You're right. I am sorry, Papa."

"Argh, let me think." He kicked his chair away and strode around the desk. "We should cancel the next meeting."

"Why? Ripon is not likely to suffer a heart attack and he certainly won't go out on a fishing boat, drunk."

"Are you questioning my authority?"

"No, Papa, never. I am just safeguarding your interests. If Ripon doesn't hand over your share of his profits or his statements, how will we know he's not cheating you?"

"Because, he wouldn't dare. An act of betrayal from anyone in my organization would result in his or *her* immediate death."

"All right, I will be there in two days. I'll get a message to him."

"Leave it. Only my partners and us know of the planned meetings. Send someone to check the resort. If there's any sign of police, I want to know sooner rather than later. And if I have a traitor, I will hunt that person down and kill them personally."

"Yes, Papa."

"What about that obnoxious journalist? When will she be dealt with?"

"I've organized a hit and run, and if that fails she will be taken care of by my man."

"Do not fail me, Lillian. I want that woman to pay."

"She will, Papa. Goodbye."

He hurled his phone at the sofa and rubbed his forehead.

"Is everything okay, Quan?"

Shit. Turning slowly, he observed the naked girl standing in his private study. "I told you never to come in here."

"You were yelling and I was concerned." She shivered. "Sorry, I'll leave."

"Wait." He closed the distance in three strides, rage consuming him, that in less than five minutes, two women had questioned his authority.

Halting several inches away, he sneered. "Perhaps you need a lesson in obedience."

"No, I—"

He lashed out, striking her cheek with his palm and sending her careening to the floor. He grabbed her hair and she screamed, gasping at his hands as he dragged her to her feet.

"Nobody questions me or defies me. Do you understand?" He shoved her hard against the wall and undid his belt. "I will teach you a lesson, you will never forget."

"No, please." She slid down the wall. "I'm sorry."

He paused, studying her as she trembled. His anger dissipated as his gaze slid over her succulent body, more than forty years his junior. Her saving grace was that he'd been speaking in his native language while on the phone; otherwise, he'd have ended her life.

She stared up at him, her imploring eyes reminding him of Lillian's mother when she'd defied him that last time. It was a pity she'd had to die, but taking his child and leaving him had been a betrayal he couldn't excuse.

Rong undid his zipper and let his trousers fall to the floor. "Perhaps you can make it up to me, *Fraulein?*"

❧

Over a thousand kilometers away, Lillian threw her phone on the king-sized bed and stared at it. "Here is your traitor, Papa, but it is I who am coming after you." She dug in her suitcase for her flick-knife and released the seven-inch blade. *Once your empire is destroyed, I shall come after you, Papa.*

She strolled onto the suite's balcony, picked up her glass, and sipped the red wine as she studied Nha Trang's bay of islands. This hotel and room was where she and Andrew had spent their honeymoon. Before he'd been forced to go through with that sham of a marriage.

Lillian's fingers tightened around the stem. Andrew had only agreed to marry Jane Hughes as a way of securing funds, so he and Lillian could escape the clutches of their prospective fathers and start a new life some place far away.

But Andrew had unprotected sex with that cow on their farcical honeymoon. *It wasn't his fault. Who could blame him for getting drunk? It was me he wanted to be with, not that bitch.*

"I will take what should have been mine." Lillian hurled the glass against the wall. Red streaks ran like blood to the tiles below.

"That child is all I have left of Andrew."

Her phone trilled. She strode back into the room and picked it up, speaking in her native Vietnamese tongue. "What?"

"My people can't find them. They didn't come back to the hotel and they haven't turned up at the airport or the train station."

"How hard can it be to find two men travelling with a woman and a baby?"

"They must have had help."

"Did you check that address I found in the bag?"

"Yes. An American woman lives there, but according to her neighbours she's away visiting friends and not expected back for several weeks."

"All right, make your way to Hoi An. That's the next place they'll turn up."

"Anywhere in particular I should look?"

"Try all the five-star resorts and don't snatch the baby until I say."

"Can you give me a better description of the woman? In the photo she is wearing a cap and sunglasses. I can't make out her eye or hair color."

Turning to the desk, Lillian stared at a photo she'd downloaded from her rival's phone. "The woman could be wearing a wig, but her hair is long and dark brown. Her eyes are...green, nothing special." Lillian slammed her blade through the photo, pinning it to the desk.

"And the other man you said is travelling with them?"

Twisting the knife free, she tightened her clasp. "He has light brown hair, hazel eyes, and is around six feet. He's extremely fit and somewhere in his late twenties."

"So when you give the word, I grab the baby and bring it to you. What about the men and the woman?"

Dragging her knife across a photo of the couple with their arms around each other she half snarled. "Forget the two men, you'll never take them by yourself. According to my source, they are trained mercenaries. If the woman and baby are alone, grab them. Otherwise I will deal with her myself." She ran the blade around the woman's face.

"And if I can't find them?

Lillian considered. "If you haven't found them by four o'clock, Tuesday, you are to ring me. I know exactly where they will be at seven that evening, but I may need a scapegoat."

"What sort of scapegoat?"

"Someone who has no inherent value and doesn't know your identity."

"I know someone. As soon as I have news, I'll contact you."

Lillian tossed the phone on the desk and poured another glass of red, then spread out several more photos she'd downloaded before the satellite phone had shutdown.

She stared at the couple holding ice-cream cones and laughing into each other's eyes. It was obvious they meant a lot to each other. A tremor of unease slithered into her thoughts. *What if the baby isn't Andrew's?* She dismissed the thought instantly. One thing Andrew had been adamant about was that the woman had integrity. Even after he'd given her the cold shoulder, she hadn't found comfort with another man. *Yet that big handsome man with the warm eyes is comforting her now.*

The woman was more attractive than she remembered. Lillian thought back to the day they'd all been at Andrew's apartment and the cow had come home from work. She'd looked pale and drawn with her hair in a tight bun and that swollen belly. Nothing special.

Lillian stared at the photos again. At the wavy hair framing the woman's face, the vibrant eyes, and gentle smile as she held her new baby. *Andrew loved me so much he obviously didn't notice her looks.*

Lillian tapped her knife on the woman's face. "What should I do with you?"

The woman evidently cared for this man. Was it because he delivered the baby and rescued her from the safe house? *Witnesses in Ho Chi Min are calling him the Punisher.* "Well maybe it's time *he* was punished."

She stuck the point of her blade into his heart. "Or." She twisted the knife back and forth. "Why should I be the only one to lose the love of my life?" Lillian studied several other photos taken in what looked like a hospital room. They all showed the tiny baby in the arms of the woman Lillian hated. She stroked her fingernail over the baby's face.

"I will have my revenge. One way or another."

CHAPTER TWENTY-SIX

Jane sat on the edge of the pool and dangled her legs in the cool water. Shade from the nearby trees took some of the heat out of the sun, although the humidity was draining her energy. *I miss the ocean breeze of Nha Trang.*

Ming screeched as Talos threw him across the pool. Within seconds his face surfaced, a giant grin from ear to ear. He stroked out awkwardly, the cumbersome life jacket slowing his progress to chase Talos in their game. Ming's high delighted squeals and Talos's deep sexy laughter drew the ladies from the little reception area out to watch.

Jane grinned. *It probably has more to do with Talos's broad shoulders and muscles than Ming's excitement.* She checked Ella was asleep in the carrier on the pavers beside her. A soft flush tinged her face. It would have been cooler in their suite, overlooking the river, but Ming was having so much fun in his board shorts and life jacket that she wouldn't deprive him of this small pleasure for all the world.

Ming caught Talos and squealed again as he was lifted high. "Throw me big far."

"Okay, you ready?" Talos launched Ming several meters through the air, his little arms flapping wildly. Once Talos was sure Ming surfaced safely, he waded through the chest-deep water to Jane and slid his arms around her.

"Come in and cool off. You look hot."

Jane glanced at Ella again. "Soon. I'm waiting for her to wake and we'll both come in."

Talos's arms tightened. "Ella's safe. Ryan and Nick are right behind her on the sun lounges." He lifted her against his chest. "Catch this, Ming."

"No!" Jane did her own impersonation of flying backwards as she sailed through the air and hit the water with a gigantic splash.

She surfaced, pushing her hair off her face to find Ming clapping delightedly.

"Me, me." Ming set off after Talos again.

Jane swam the length of the pool, the refreshing water reviving and cooling her heated skin. At the far end she leaned against the tiled wall, breathed in deeply and let her gaze wander. This resort wasn't as luxurious as their hotel in Nha Trang, but it had character. The restaurant looked over the mirrored surface of the river and paddy fields opposite. Bamboo blinds could be lowered to keep out the sun, but otherwise there were no walls on two sides. Lush green shrubs and coconut palms lined the banks of the river where the occasional fisherman paddled by in his boat.

She looked down the length of the pool and across the manicured lawns and paths, leading to the various units. Their family unit was right by the pool, its French doors on the far side leading onto a private balcony above the riverbank. A tranquil place where she and Talos had sat over the last two evenings after Ming and Ella had fallen asleep.

Footsteps sounded and she glanced up to see Jarred and Simon approaching. By their tight expressions, they didn't bring good news.

"What's wrong?

Jarred's gaze skimmed her bikini then he looked beyond her to Talos, Nick, and Ryan. "We need to talk. Meet me in the restaurant in twenty minutes. I need a shower first." He strode off to his unit.

Talos appeared at her side with Ming in his arms. "What's up, Simon?"

Simon rubbed his chin. "While we were scouting the resort where the next meeting's taking place, several men were escorted off the grounds for masquerading as resort staff. Then we picked up a tail and it was hard to lose him."

Jane glanced at Talos. "They must have been looking for us?"

He looked at Simon. "Maybe they were hoping you'd lead them to Jane and the baby."

Simon shrugged. "Or they're suspicious and keeping an eye on Ripon."

Jane frowned. "Won't it be too dangerous if they're watching Ripon?"

"Is that what's got Jarred rattled?" asked Nick.

"No. Gibbs is on his back, wanting to know our whereabouts and our plans for tonight."

Jane locked eyes with Talos. He was scowling. She touched his arm. "That doesn't mean Gibbs is corrupt. I can leave Ella here with you and wear a disguise."

Ming leaned forward and smoothed her frown away. "I look after Ella for you."

"That's okay, sweetie. I wouldn't leave either of you here on your own."

Talos stood Ming on the pavers and hauled himself out. "We'll change out of these wet clothes and meet you there."

They all nodded and headed towards the restaurant.

Moving to the ladder, Jane pulled herself up and joined Talos. "We have the cover of darkness. That should help."

"I don't like it. It feels like a set up." He took her hand in his. "I won't put you at risk."

"I know." Jane smiled at Ming. "Come on, let's get changed and have an ice cream."

"Yes." Ming ran over to a sun lounge and picked up the dragon and doll.

"He's rather fixated on that doll, don't you think?" murmured Talos.

"He brings it for Ella."

"Are you sure about that?"

Jane watched as Ming stuffed the dragon under one arm and cradle the doll in his other arm, then went to stand beside Ella's carrier.

"I ready."

Jane squeezed Talos's hand. "Maybe he's never seen such a life-like baby doll."

"Hmm, I might get him a fire truck tomorrow." Talos unbuckled the life jacket, took it off Ming, and dropped it in the wicker basket beside the pool towels. "Lead the way, buddy."

Smiling, Jane strolled after them.

Talos entered the restaurant with Jane and the children to find his mates seated at a table overlooking the river. He pulled out a chair for Jane, then placed Ella's carrier on the tiles and took the chair beside Jane. Ming squatted on the tiles beside Ella, licking his ice cream with relish.

Jarred placed his can of beer on the table, moved a dish of nuts aside, and looked at Talos. "I didn't say anything earlier in case things didn't pan out, but Sam and Kallie arrived in Ho Chi Min this afternoon."

"What?" Jane gripped the edge of the table and stared at Jarred. "Why would Sam bring Kallie here?"

His eyebrow shot up. "Apparently Sam didn't have a choice. She did your trick and announced she'd come on her own if he didn't bring her."

"Oh." Jane sank back on the chair, giving Talos a sheepish grin.

"Are they joining us in Hanoi?" Talos put his arm around Jane, glad that he wasn't the only one dealing with a headstrong woman.

"No, they're catching a flight to Danang. They will then drive here, before going on to the resort where the meeting is taking place. I have no intention of informing Gibbs where any of us are staying or that Sam and Kallie are in Vietnam."

Talos withdrew his arm from around Jane and leaned on the table. "So you suspect Gibbs may have a hidden agenda?"

"Somebody does." Jarred exhaled. "Kallie looks...exotic and will draw attention away from Jane, who will be dining with Simon. They will be disguised as an older couple."

"Where will I be?" Talos said.

"With Nick. He will land the chopper on vacant land not far from our target's resort. Once we have Ripon and the agent, Nick will fly us to the airbase, where Gibbs will be waiting with SCU officers."

Narrowing his eyes, Talos focused on Jarred. "Who else will be protecting Jane? And where will Ella be?"

"Sam will be in the restaurant having dinner with Kallie. I'll be there too, which won't draw attention as I've made a point of eating there over the last few days. Ella and Ming will be with Ryan in Sam and Kallie's villa."

Ryan straightened, a look of alarm on his face. "Me? I'm not good with little kids."

"Someone has to guard the baby." Jarred drummed his fingers on the table. "Jane will not be out of our sight." He focused on Talos. "Under cover of darkness, you and Nick will enter the grounds and position yourselves close by, ready for my call."

Talos grimaced. He didn't like being relegated to the sidelines. It was at times like this he wished he wasn't such a big bloke. *At least I'm there.* "All right."

Jarred looked around the table. "This is how it goes down. Talos and Nick take a taxi out to the chopper. Simon and Jane can use the hire car. Ryan will hire a motorbike. I have arranged to meet a lady for dinner at the resort, so I will take a taxi. None of us are to be seen together."

Nick chuckled. "And you know this lady, how exactly?"

"She's a guest at our target's Resort." Jarred glanced at the sky. "We're in for a storm."

Jane turned to Nick. "Will that affect you flying?"

"Probably not, but I'll check with traffic control. They'll have a better idea."

Jarred took several slugs of his beer then looked around the table. "Once Jane identifies Ripon, we will monitor him and the agent. The moment they leave, I will tail the agent and Sam will tail Ripon." Jarred caught Simon's eye. "Leave the keys in the car, in case the agent is staying at another resort."

"And who will be with Jane and Kallie?" Talos crossed his arms, fighting the growing fear that was threatening to well up inside him.

"Simon and Nick will escort them to the villa and wait for word. If they don't hear from us within a reasonable time, they'll get the hell out of there." He handed Simon a piece of paper. "That's the hotline for the Australian Embassy in Hanoi."

Jane frowned. "How are Ming and Ella going to get to the resort?"

"They will arrive with their parents." He glanced to his right. "Speaking of which."

"Kallie!" Jane sprang out of her chair and ran across the restaurant, enveloping her friend in a hug. "I can't believe you're here."

Kallie hugged her tightly. "We couldn't let you guys have all the fun."

After kissing Sam's cheek, Jane turned back to Kallie. "I have so much to tell you."

"So I believe. Where's my beautiful goddaughter?"

A sense of wellbeing filled Talos as he stood and watched Jane lead Kallie to the carrier. Sam followed leisurely. He reached out and shook the other men's hands, then gave Talos a bear hug.

"How ya doing, mate?"

"Not bad." Talos replied. "You're looking happy for a fella who's been hanging out in airports and planes all day."

"I had good company."

Kallie crouched beside the carrier. "My goodness, Ella's grown so much in a week." Picking the baby up, Kallie looked at Ming. "And who is this pretty little girl?"

Lip curving, Talos mouthed. *Boy*. "Ming's coming to Hanoi with us, aren't you, mate?"

Ming nodded, not taking his eyes off Kallie's face.

Talos ruffled Ming's hair. "We need to get rid of that doll, buddy."

Kallie smiled at Ming. "You have lovely eyes." She positioned Ella in one arm and held out her free hand. "I'm Kallie."

Ming lowered the doll and gave her his hand. "I Ming."

Jarred cleared his throat. "Now that we're all here, I'll run through the plan again and then I want you to tell me what can go wrong."

Talos gestured for Kallie to take his seat and brought another two chairs over for himself and Sam. They all took their seats and after the waiter brought more drinks, Jarred went through his plan for Sam and Kallie's benefit.

Sam rubbed his chin. "What if the agent turns up early?"

Jarred steepled his fingers. "Simon and Jane will be in the restaurant an hour prior to the meeting. I shall arrive within half an hour. Nick and Talos will be outside, close by. If the agent doesn't stay, one of us will follow him."

Talos crossed his arms. "Have you considered Rossini's mistress might turn up and recognize Jane?"

Jarred looked to Simon. "Can you make Jane look older and less attractive?"

Raising an eyebrow, Simon shrugged. "I'll try, but I'm not a magician. Even as an older woman, she's going to look attractive."

Jane grinned. "Thank you, Simon, that's very sweet."

"Do your best." Jarred gazed at each of their faces. "If the woman turns up, we nab her as well. I want everyone armed, except of course the ladies."

Talos hid his grin as Kallie looked down her nose at Jarred. "May I remind you, Mister Steele, that Jane and I are country girls and quite capable of handling a rifle."

Jarred's lips thinned. "Fortunately, Miss McNeil, I don't have any spare rifles."

"Getting back to what could go wrong," said Simon. "What if Ripon is suspicious and has extra guards planted about the resort?"

"If he's suspicious then the meeting won't go ahead."

Jane shifted on her chair. "What if any of you are hurt or need help?"

"If you don't hear from us, get out quickly. Simon and Nick will look after you."

"I won't leave without Talos."

Talos met her concerned eyes. "We could be a while. And if things go belly up, I would feel better if I knew you and Ella were on your way to the Australian Embassy."

"And me?" Ming placed his little hand on Talos's leg. "I go Ostalan embossy too."

"If necessary, but tonight I need you to look after Ella while Jane and I are busy."

His eyes solemn, Ming nodded. "I very clever. I take good care of Ella."

"I know you will." Talos winked at Ming. "And tomorrow, I'm going to give you a decent haircut, something like Nick's buzz cut."

"I no like his hair." Ming crunched the rest of his ice-cream cone into his mouth, placed the doll on Jane's lap, and picked up his dragon.

"Let's have a cuppa, Kallie." Jane said. "While these guys sort out the logistics."

Reaching out, Talos caught Jane's hand. "Stay in the restaurant where I can see you."

"Okay."

As they walked away, Kallie leaned into Jane. "You look so happy."

"That's because I'm in love." She met Talos's gaze. "With a wonderful man."

Elation filled Talos. *And I'm in love with a wonderful woman.* He turned back to Jarred. "If Ripon turns up tonight, it's because he or someone else knows Jane is here, and it doesn't take a giant brain to work out why. They will set their own trap."

"Then we'll need to be extra vigilant," answered Jarred. "If necessary, shoot to kill."

Chapter Twenty-seven

Linking his fingers, Talos cupped the back of his neck, stretched and arched his back. His cramped observation post didn't offer the latest in comfort, but at least he was close to Jane if things went sour. It was a stroke of luck that Ripon and the agent were meeting in such a classy restaurant. Numerous glass doors opened onto thick lush gardens on either side allowing the perfect camouflage of his position amongst the elephant leaf shrubs.

Simon and Jane's table was close to an open French door and half way along the restaurant. By seating Jane facing the gardens, her profile was hidden to those behind, whereas patrons on her left or right would only see a side profile. It was the best position in the restaurant if she needed to make a quick exit.

Talos had to admit Simon had done an excellent job disguising her. The grey wig, glasses and extra padding were brilliant. To the casual observer she looked to be an elegant, older woman on holiday with her slightly rotund husband. They both wore audio monitoring bugs disguised as hearing aids. How Simon managed to pull their costumes together in so short a time, he couldn't hazard a guess. The man was a genius.

A waiter approached the table, took their order, and returned with a bottle of wine. "Is that wise?" Talos spoke into his headset.

"Don't panic, big fella. It's only water. Jarred teed it up with the waiter earlier."

Talos studied the other diners. Jarred and his glamorous blonde friend sat several tables away from Jane and Simon by another French door. Sam and Kallie sat towards the middle looking into each other's eyes. She wore a low-backed, red dress and her hair up on top.

Talos grinned. *She will certainly keep the attention off Jane.* "Any sign of Ripon?"

"No," replied Jane. "I don't recognize anyone except Jarred, Sam, and Kallie."

German voices brought Talos's attention to the main entrance where a group of people wearing feathered Venetian masks were waiting to be seated. "What the hell?" Talos's pulse quickened. He wiped his palms down his trousers. "What's with the masks?"

"Shit." Simon muttered. "Tourists in fancy dress. I hope Ripon's not amongst them."

The group made their way to several large tables at the end of the restaurant. A slender woman with glossy black hair appeared to be in charge. It was hard to tell with the mask, but Talos thought it might be Lien, the tour guide. He sent a text to Nick warning him.

Twenty seconds later his phone vibrated. Talos read the message. *I saw her. I'm in the shrubbery on the other side of the restaurant.*

Pocketing the phone, Talos considered each of the German men. They all appeared to be over sixty years of age and with wives, although most of their gazes were locked on Kallie's smooth back. A young Vietnamese man entered the restaurant assisting an older woman. They made their way to the Germans' table and took their seats.

The tension in Talos's shoulders eased as he sank to the ground and checked his watch. *Still half an hour to go.*

After several minutes the waiter appeared with the appetizers.

"This smells wonderful," Jane told the waiter.

Talos's mouth watered at the sight of the piled plates. Ignoring his sudden hunger, he concentrated on the other patrons. He could hear the tour group conversing in German. Kallie's occasional laugh sounded soft and alluring. Dinner music played in the background along with crickets. A droplet of rain hit his forehead. Several more followed.

Great.

Several more couples entered the restaurant as the waiter delivered a steaming platter of food to Jane and Simon. Talos tensed, waiting for some sign from Jane, but after a quick glance at the newcomers she gave a minute shake of her head and murmured, "No."

After another twenty minutes of small talk, Jane suddenly sucked in a breath and brought her hand up over her mouth. "Talos, that's him."

"Where?" Shooting to his feet, Talos brushed an elephant leaf aside and raised his binoculars. Two men had entered the restaurant through a set of French doors at the other end. They both looked to be in their mid-forties, fit, and Caucasian. One carried a black leather satchel. *So Ripon is an Englishman. That means Rong must be Vietnamese.*

The men took their seats and after a brief glance around, picked up their menus.

"Which one is Ripon?" murmured Simon.

"The fair one," Jane said. "I don't know the other man."

Talos kept his gaze on the two men. "Don't look in their direction again. There could be other observers. Just finish your meal and then leave."

"What about Kallie?" Jane asked.

"As soon as you leave, she'll follow on the pretense of using the ladies."

"Okay." Jane ate another mouthful then placed her knife and fork together and looked out towards his position. "Be careful."

"I will."

Simon cleared his throat. "Text the others while I'm paying the bill."

"I'm on it. Don't leave Jane's side."

"I won't."

Keeping his eye on Ripon, Talos waited while Simon and Jane made their way to the cashier. But other than a quick glance as they passed by, Ripon's attention was focused on Kallie. No one else that Talos could see appeared to take any untoward notice of Jane. He sent a group text message to the rest of the team.

A couple of minutes later, Kallie rose from her table and leisurely made her way to the main exit where Nick was waiting out of sight.

Sam called the waiter over and ordered a beer, then went back to eating.

Once Kallie had left the restaurant, Talos edged back a little and waited for Nick to return. The rain was getting heavier and the elephant leaves were of no use at all.

"Pssst, over here," Nick called.

Ducking under the low branches, Talos joined Nick and focused on the restaurant. "Did you notice anyone pay particular attention to the two men or Jane?"

"Nope, a few looked up but then went back to talking or eating. Kallie's the only person that drew attention. Jesus, she looks hot in that little number. I'm surprised Sam didn't knock Jarred's head off for asking Kallie to wear it."

"He wasn't happy, but it worked. No one paid any attention to Jane."

"Yeah." Nick swiped at a drip before it ran down his neck. "Did you notice anyone hanging about outside?"

"No. It makes me wonder if we've got this wrong." Talos frowned.

"In what way?"

"What if Rossini's girlfriend is going through with their original plan and hasn't informed the ring members that Rossini gave the AFP their meeting details?"

"She'd only do that if she's unaware of his death and is hoping to meet up with him."

"She could be out for revenge." Talos wiped the rain out of his eyes. "Suppose she knows Rossini's dead and suspects the ring of killing him?" The thought gnawed at Talos. He shifted, restless. "If that's the case, she won't care who gets caught in the crossfire."

A middle-aged Asian man entered the restaurant and approached Ripon's table.

"Here we go," murmured Nick, straightening. "That must be the agent."

Talos kept the binoculars on the man, following his every moved. The man handed Ripon a note and waited. After reading the note, Ripon glanced around the restaurant then spoke to his companion. He pulled out his phone and appeared to read a message.

Ripon picked up the black satchel and handed it to the Asian man, then waved him away off-handedly."

"What do you make of that?" asked Nick.

"He's a dupe." Talos swung the binoculars over the other diners. Nobody paid any particular attention to Ripon. Talos released his breath as his phone vibrated. "Yeah, boss."

"Change of plans. Send Nick after the folder, you stay with Ripon."

"On it." Talos turned to Nick.

"I heard." Nick ducked under the palms and sprinted off into the dark.

Turning back to the restaurant, Talos observed Jarred stand and escort his guest to the cashier in no particular hurry. After paying they left the restaurant.

Locking his fingers together, Talos observed the restaurant. His gut churned. *Why the messages and quick handover.* He studied Ripon and his companion, now eating. *They don't look bothered. Maybe we're being paranoid and this is normal procedure?*

A message pinged from Nick. *Got the folder. It's genuine.*

Another message pinged from Simon. *All good here. Ladies safe.*

Leaning back against a rutted trunk, Talos exhaled. With Jane safe he could concentrate on the job. A few more couples entered the restaurant and were quickly seated. Ripon and his companions' main courses arrived. The young Asian man who'd assisted the elderly German lady to the table got up and left the restaurant. Soft music drifted through the French doors as a waiter approached Sam's table with a mouth-watering dessert.

At least someone's enjoying himself. The humidity was stifling and then the rain got heavier. Talos pulled his collar up. He was wet, sticky, and uncomfortable.

Another half hour passed before Ripon and his companion stood and left the restaurant. Darting from under the foliage, Talos made his way to the path leading from the restaurant, where he waited in the shadows of the building.

An English accent heralded Ripon's approach. "I shall contact Rong first thing in the morning. With the demise of Lhasa and Kazan, I feel their operations should be divided between us."

"Will he accept that?" asked his companion.

"I don't see he has any choice. He may head up our syndicate, but we are equal partners." Both men passed Talos's position, holding umbrellas over their heads. They continued along the wide path.

Another twenty seconds and Sam came striding along the path. Talos stepped out from the shrubbery and fell into step beside him. It was still very humid, but the rain had almost stopped. Too late for his leather jacket and shoes, they were soaked. "So far so good."

"Yeah, Jarred sent me a message. Nick had no trouble with the agent. They've got him and the folder at the car. The man is fairly shitting himself apparently."

Talos checked their immediate surroundings. "That's not the behavior of an operative from this caliber of people."

"No, I think we're all having similar thoughts."

Sliding his hand inside the jacket, Talos closed his fingers over the Glock. "Best be ready for anything."

Sam drew his handgun. "You smell a rat too?"

"Yeah. Ripon's turning off. That must be his villa."

"Let's get off the path in case he looks back."

They swerved onto an adjoining path then crossed the lawn, coming around the back of the villa Ripon had entered. Lights came on inside and out the back. Both Talos and Sam ducked for cover behind shrubs.

Stepping onto the covered patio, Ripon lit up a cigar, its pungent aroma filling the air. The other man joined him with three wine glasses and a bottle of red wine.

Leaning closer, Sam whispered. "It looks like they're expecting company."

"Message Jarred. I think he should be here."

"I'm on it."

Ten seconds later Sam's phone vibrated. "Jarred is on his way."

"I think this is the real meeting." Talos frowned, his apprehension growing. "But why pass genuine documents to a dummy agent." He raised his binoculars and did a sweep of the surrounding area. "I can't see the sense in it."

Sam shifted away from a dripping palm. "I guess we'll find out soon enough."

As they waited for Jarred, Talos continued to scan the area, watching for any sign of movement. He also worried that Jane was safe and checked his watch several times.

"Anything new?" Jarred crept in under the palms beside Talos. Ryan was with him.

"Not yet, but they're waiting on someone." Talos passed Jarred the binoculars. "They've brought out a bottle and three glasses."

Two gunshots pieced the air and all four men hit the ground.

"Holly fuck, is everyone all right?" Jarred asked.

"I'm good." Talos lifted his head and checked on the others.

Everyone nodded but stayed low. They all turned to the patio, where Ripon and his companion now lay crumpled on the patio.

"Fuck. They were the ones being set up," murmured Ryan.

A chill ran through Talos. "We need to get to the villa."

"You two go," Jarred ordered. "Ryan, you come with me. I want to check inside."

Talos leapt over small shrubs and garden ornaments. He hit the pathway and took off, his feet pounding into the soft earth as fast as his legs would carry him, dread filling his heart and each step. *Fuck. Ripon's not the only one who's been set up.*

ॐ

Jane laid Ella in the carrier on the couch beside Ming, then she finger-combed her hair, glad to be rid of the grey wig. "This is one very luxurious villa, Kallie. It must be costing Jarred a fortune."

"I'd imagine so, this is a six-star resort." Kallie padded over to the couch and stared down at Ming, curled up in his dinosaur pajamas. "He's so sweet. What will happen to him?"

"Once we've put the ring behind bars, I'd like to try and adopt Ming, if Talos agrees." Jane dimmed the table-lamp and tucked the pink bunny rug around Ella. "I've heard it's a long and expensive process."

A rapid knocking sounded on the villa's door.

Simon ducked out of the kitchen. "Stay there." He pulled a handgun from inside his jacket and strode across the living room. "Who is it?"

"Hotel security, sir. We have had a bomb threat and are evacuating all guests to the beach."

Simon edged the door open. "I need to see some I.D."

Kallie ran past Jane and pulled the curtain aside. "I can see people and staff running towards the beach."

Simon turned. "Stay away from the window, Kallie. We should wait here for—"

Crack!

"Simon!" Jane recoiled at the gun's impact with Simon's skull. His eyes rolled back in his head and then he dropped soundlessly, blood trickling down the side of his face.

Kallie screamed and scrambled around the couch, clutching at Jane's hand.

Frozen, Jane broke out in a cold sweat, her heart in her throat as she stared at the Asian man standing over Simon, pointing a gun at her. "Wha...what do you want?"

The man's gaze drilled her. "I will kill your friends if you don't bring the baby and come with me immediately."

"You have to be joking." Shaking violently, Jane stepped in front of Kallie and the children. "This resort is crawling with federal agents. The moment they see me leave with you, they are going to react. You will never get away alive."

Ming began crying. "I scared."

"It's okay, Ming." Kallie's voice wobbled. "The bad man is leaving."

"Not without the baby." He waved the gun.

"I will not let you take my baby." Jane dragged Kallie back behind her as she tried to step forward. "No, stay behind me."

The man sneered. "I have been all over the resort. There are no agents, just the three men with you and this woman."

Clenching her fists, Jane stared him down. "How did you find us?"

"Your disguise was good, but not good enough to fool my employer. Old women don't have smooth skin and your eyes gave you away."

My eyes. Oh shit. Jane swallowed. "You were at the table with the Germans?" Her heart constricted. "That woman with the long dark hair, she's behind this, isn't she?" *Oh my god. Why didn't I see it earlier?* She was my husband's mistress, wasn't she?"

"No, she was his wife." The man leapt towards her, swinging his arm. His fist hit her hard in the cheek, sending her careening into Kallie and onto the floor.

"No!" Jane tried to scramble to her feet.

He kicked her shoulder, knocking her down on top of Kallie again. Then he fired a shot, missing them by inches.

Ming cowered on the floor against the couch, crying loudly as he huddled over his doll.

The man grabbed the carrier and ran out through the open door.

"No!" Her heart tearing in two, Jane gripped her shoulder and clambered to her feet, sobbing as she chased after him. "Please, don't take my baby."

A group of resort staff stopped and stared at her after she screamed at them to get out of her way. Jane pushed through them, ignoring the burning stitch in her side. "Please, somebody stop that man. He's got my baby."

"Jane!" Talos roared from somewhere behind her but she didn't stop. *I can't lose Ella.* A sob tore from her throat.

The man zigzagged around several people and shot off across the grass towards the resort's main hub, Ella's carrier swinging from his hand.

Clutching her side, Jane tried to pant through the pain as she followed him. Suddenly her feet shot from under her and she crashed to the ground, jarring her knee. "No!" Struggling to her feet, she hobbled round the side of the building to the resort's car park.

Where is he?

She heard gears grinding then a small white car reversed out from between two other vehicles and for a couple of seconds the driver's face was lit up by an overhead lamp.

"Stop!" With her heart in her mouth, Jane threw herself at the passenger door, grasping its handle. The car kangarooed forward and the door swung open. Fighting to hang on, Jane looked up, straight into the barrel of a gun. *Shit.*

"Let go, Jane!" Talos bellowed. He sounded so close.

The car jerked again. Jane swung wide and the Asian man fired the gun at her. The bullet hit the door she was hanging onto. "Talos! Help me!" She lost her grip and fell.

CHAPTER TWENTY-EIGHT

Christ, don't shoot her. Talos ran in front of the car, planted his feet wide, raised the Glock, held his breath, and fired. The windscreen shattered and the driver fell sideways.

Talos dived clear, rolled, and came up on his feet again as the car mounted a garden bed and smashed into a coconut palm. "Jane!"

"I'm okay." She crawled to her knees, sobbing."

Nick came running across the car park. "What the fuck, Talos?"

"That bastard took Ella." Still breathing heavily, Talos lifted Jane her to her feet. "I got you, sweetheart."

"Ella?" Jane sobbed."

"I know. Kallie told me. Stay here." Talos ran to car, and ignoring the unconscious driver, searched the interior. There was no carrier in sight. *Fuck.* He leaned across and released the boot, praying Ella hadn't been hurt with the impact.

"Where is she?" Jane had the rear door open, her gaze locked with his. "Oh, God."

Ella wasn't in the boot.

Jane stared at him, her eyes wild. "She has to be there. He took her."

Talos rubbed his forehead. "Jesus. Did you lose sight of him?"

"Only for a few seconds when he left the villa, and when I fell, but I saw him running with the carrier. She's got to be here."

"He must have passed her to someone before he reached his car." Talos turned to Nick. "Did you see him?"

"Yeah, I saw him run to the car but he didn't have a baby carrier."

"Oh God." Jane collapsed against him and wept.

He cleared his throat. "Nick, find the others, we have to keep looking."

His phone vibrated. "What?"

"We've got Ella and she's fine." Sam said. "Meet us at the back car park."

"Thank God." Talos gripped Jane's shoulders and held her away. "It's okay, sweetheart, Sam's got Ella."

She gripped his shirt, her fingernails biting into his skin. "How? Is she all right?"

"She's fine. But we've got to get out of here. They'll meet us at the other entrance."

Nick opened the rear door of their hire car. "Get in. We don't want to be seen and I've got the bogus agent trussed up in the back."

Jane stared at him; her eyes glistening with unshed tears. "You're sure Ella's okay?"

"Yes, Sam assures me she's fine."

Wiping her eyes and nose, Jane looked towards the crashed car. "What about him?"

Talos urged her into their hired vehicle. "He'll live. The cops can deal with him."

Nick climbed in the front and started the car. "I'm only guessing here, but I think Rossini's girlfriend is going through with their plan to give up the ring members and in the process, kidnap the baby." He put the car in gear and drove around the main complex.

Jane hiccupped. "She was in the restaurant with those German people."

"What?" Talos and Nick chorused.

"She was there, disguised in a mask."

"But that was Lien, the tour guide," Nick said.

"Fuck." Talos slammed the seat. "It makes perfect sense. She was at the hotel in Ho Chi Min talking to Huang at the bar. Then she was in Nha Trang, staying at the same hotel as Kazan. I'm surprised Jane didn't recognize her."

Jane sniffed. "She had her back to me in the bar and I had my back to her in the restaurant, plus she had a full mask on, and I was looking for a man."

Nick drove into the rear car park, turned off the engine and twisted in his seat. "So Lien uses the tour group as a cover. Christ." He rubbed his forehead. "I was having dinner with her in a restaurant overlooking the beach when you and Jane strolled past."

Sitting straighter, Jane clutched Talos's arm. "That's how she knew I was here. And then the next morning those men came to the suite. She must have sent them and when that failed, she went island hopping in an attempt to find me."

Exhaling, Talos scrubbed his face. "Or she was taking the Germans on a daytrip and just happened across you."

Nick pointed. "Here come the others."

"Ella." Jane scrambled out and limped to Kallie, who laid the baby in Jane's arms.

The vice crushing his heart eased as Talos observed Jane press her lips to the baby's head, tears streaming down her face.

Jarred opened the front door and helped Simon onto the seat. "He took a nasty whack to the head and needs stitches."

Sam met Talos's eyes as he lowered Ming onto the back seat. "You'll never believe where we found the baby."

"Tell them later," called Jarred. "We need to move before the local cops arrive. We'll meet you at the chopper." He sprinted across to where Ryan was revving a motorbike.

Talos stood aside while Sam climbed into the back with their captive, then slid onto the middle seat beside Jane. Kallie had Ming on her lap.

Nick started the engine. "We're lucky it's dark and the resort is so far from Hoi An, otherwise the police would have been her within minutes." He put the vehicle into drive; chucked a tight U-turn, then hit the accelerator.

"What happened to the bastard that hit me?" Simon half turned in his seat.

"Talos put a bullet in his shoulder," answered Nick.

Talos shrugged. "I thought he had the baby and when Jane caught up to him, he tried to shoot her." Lifting Jane's dress, Talos hissed at the deep scratches on her knees.

Jane sniffed. "He threatened to shoot Simon and Kallie if I didn't take Ella and go with him. When I refused he punched me in the face and then kicked me in the shoulder."

Bastard. I should have killed him. Talos lifted Jane's hair away from her face and scowled at the ugly bruise forming. "I want to know everything that happened."

She leaned her head against his shoulder. "I saw him with the

Germans in the restaurant. Lien must have recognized me." Jane eyes filled with tears. "She wasn't Andrew's mistress. She was his wife."

"Pardon?" Talos frowned.

"I may not have been legally married to Andrew."

Talos shook his head. "That bastard didn't deserve to be married to you." Anger coiled within him like a death-adder ready to strike. He wanted to bash the shit out of these trafficking mongrels.

Nick pulled up alongside the chopper. "What's the plan?"

"Let's check with Jarred."

Ryan rode up, stopped by Nick's open window and Jarred dismounted. "Photograph the evidence then I'll take it and the courier to Gibbs. He's probably already heard about the shooting and added two and two together."

"Who do you want with you?" Talos asked, helping Jane out of the car.

"Ryan and Nick. You stay with the ladies at our resort and Sam can take Simon to the hospital and get him checked out. Once I've spoken to Gibbs, I'll decide on our next move and how much to tell him."

Talos met Jarred's gaze. "Was there anything in Ripon's villa?"

"Not really, although his real name is Robert Quinn and he lives in London."

Jane frowned. "I still don't understand what happened to Ella?"

Kallie pointed at Ming. "That clever kid took Ella out of the carrier and replaced her with the doll, then he huddled against the lounge protecting Ella and pretending to cry."

"Ming!" Jane wrapped one arm around the little boy and hugged him. "You are so brave."

"You find doll?"

Talos frowned. "Ming, I thought the doll was for Ella?

"She too little."

"Buddy, boys don't play with dolls."

Jane drew in a deep breath and locked eyes with Talos. "But girls do, don't they, Ming?" Tears glistened in her eyes.

Lost, Talos looked from Jane to Ming. "What am I missing here?"

"Oh my God," Kallie exclaimed. "I knew Ming was too pretty to be a boy."

"Too pretty?" Talos studied Ming's bent head. "You're kidding me, right?"

Going down on his knees beside the car, Talos lifted Ming's chin. "Ming?"

"I a girl, but my friend Mao say I safer a boy."

Nick jumped out of the car. "Why didn't you tell us?"

"I not know you good or bad."

Clearing his throat, Talos leaned in and pulled Ming into his arms. "I'll buy you a hundred dolls if that's what you want."

Ming giggled. "I can only carry one doll with my dragon."

Nick shook his head. "It was bad enough thinking he was a boy collecting garbage without a life jacket. This is doing my head in." He strode off to the chopper.

"Right." Jarred locked gazes with Talos. He appeared to be as stunned as everyone else. "Get moving before someone notices us gathered here in the dark."

"Let us know what happens with Gibbs." Talos followed Jarred to the back of the car. "Exactly how hard a hit did Simon take?"

"Fairly hard. He needs a few stitches and should have an x-ray." Jarred opened the rear of the door of their vehicle and dragged the handcuffed man. "Let's go."

The man grabbed at Jarred's shirt. "I paid to make pick up, that's all."

"Tell it to the police." Jarred pushed him into the rear of the helicopter then turned back to Talos. "Do you want me to speak to Gibbs about the little girl? He might know someone who can do something for her."

"Yeah, see if we can sponsor her or maybe...take her back with us."

"Are you sure you want the extra responsibility?"

Talos shrugged. "The poor little thing has no family. She rescued Jane from the island and probably saved Ella's life tonight. We have to do whatever we can for her."

"All right, leave it with me, and for God's sake keep a low profile." He climbed into the back of the chopper with the courier.

"I'll ride the motorbike," offered Sam. "Once we're back at the resort, I'll get Simon to the hospital while you pack up. I'd say we'll be making a quick exit once the others get back."

As Nick and Ryan went through their start up procedure, Talos loaded everyone into the car and drove off the empty block. He was impatient to get back to their resort so he could take care of Jane's injuries and then he needed to hold her in his arms. Just hold her.

It was almost midnight when Talos's phone rang. He rolled away from where Jane lay sleeping with Ella tucked in beside her. "Jarred?"

"What's the diagnosis on Simon?"

"They did an x-ray and stitched him up. He'll have a headache for a few days but otherwise he's fine. What's happening your end?"

"The fella we brought in *was* a dupe. The SCU have picked up the injured man and the other two bodies. They've also put out an arrest warrant for the tour guide, although she's using a phony name, so that makes things harder."

"Do we know which one of the ring members is her father?" Talos padded past Ming, asleep on the couch and slipped out onto the balcony.

"Yes, as it happens. Once Kazan heard about the hit on Ripon, he started talking. I think his running scared. He and Huang both insist Rong is the boss of the outfit and he is the girl's father. She apparently is the agent that they all meet up with, but neither of them know her or Rong's real names."

"So there's no need for the final meeting, if she's his daughter?"

"You would think so, but Gibbs wants us to go to Hanoi anyway. If that woman is setting up the ring members, then there's a chance Rong is next on her list."

"Her own father," Talos breathed deeply. "She must really hate him. What about Gibbs? Do you trust him?"

"I don't trust anyone other than you men, but the SCU are very keen to nail these guys, and Gibbs does appear committed."

"All right," muttered Talos. "How do we get to Hanoi without detection?"

"Gibbs has organized for us to be flown there in a military plane. He wants us out of here and ready to go in an hour. There's an escort vehicle on its way to you now."

"An hour." Talos glanced back into the bedroom, his gaze resting on his precious family. "What about accommodation once we get to Hanoi?"

"I've called in a favor. We'll be staying in a Foreign Dignitary residence in Ba Dinh. It's in the political district, a couple of minutes from the old quarter of Hanoi and the house is surrounded by walls."

"I hope that's enough. Okay, we're on our way." Talos ended the call, stepped back inside, and gently shook Jane. "Wake up, sweetheart, it's time to go."

Drowsy with sleep, Jane stretched. "What time is it?"

"Just after midnight." He kissed her then bent over the couch and scooped Ming into his arms. "I'll wake the others while you get organized." He turned towards the door.

"Wait." Jane turned the lamp on and picked up Ming's backpack from the side of the bed. "Take this." She hooked it over his hand. "I'll be ready to leave in five minutes."

❧❧

As Talos brought the car to a stop behind their escort vehicle, Jarred strode from the military base hangar beside them. Nick and Ryan followed him. Glancing into the hangar, Talos observed Gibbs pacing back and forth, his face like thunder.

Talos opened his door. "What's wrong with Gibbs?"

Jarred gave an off-hand shrug. "He's pissed that we kept him out of the loop, and he's threatening to send us home unless I give him my word it won't happen again."

"What did you say?"

"I told him to arrange the fucking flights."

Chuckling, Talos climbed out of the car and opened the rear door. "And is he?"

"No, but he's working himself up to having a stroke. It turns out there's been reports floating around for years regarding this mysterious Rong person. He's been linked to drug smuggling, prostitution rackets, illegal adoptions, human trafficking, and several murders. Yet no one has been able to find out his real identity or his whereabouts."

Scowling, Sam joined them. "So what you're saying is, this is the closest they've ever come to catching him?"

"Yes, and Gibbs now believes it may have been Rong who ordered the death of Rossini, which has pissed off the daughter and that's why she's out for revenge."

"I had a similar thought," Talos said.

Scrambling out of the car, Jane grabbed Talos's arm. "I think I know how we can find Rong and his daughter, but it will depend whether Simon is up to it."

Jarred focused on Jane. "How?"

"According to that man who tried to take Ella, I was never legally married to Andrew. He may have already been married to the woman I thought was his mistress and as such there would have to be a record of their marriage."

Simon leaned out his window. "I can probably access the records, but my vision is a bit blurry and I will need someone who can read Vietnamese."

"Elliot Shaw can help you," announced Gibbs stepping around Jarred.

"Fuck," muttered Sam, coming round the front of the car. "Don't you know it's rude to eavesdrop?"

"I don't give a shit," Gibbs said. "We have maybe twenty-four hours before tonight's shootings go public. I know you don't trust me, but I am not your enemy. If Jane and Kallie want to live normal lives, we need to work together."

Talos gripped Jane's hand. "Then let's work together, and if you betray us, I will hunt you down and kill you myself."

CHAPTER TWENTY-NINE

Jane wandered about the prestigious home, examining original artworks and expensive figurines. Gibbs and Simon had gone off to meet Elliot Shaw and a Government official. Kallie and Sam were out shopping with Ming for a new doll and some dresses. Nick and Ryan were in the basement gym and Talos had gone running with Jarred.

They'd all arrived at the Foreign Diplomat residence in the early hours of the morning and although exhausted, Jane had been unable to sleep. It didn't matter that the building had a state of the art security system or that she was surrounded by highly trained ex-SAS soldiers. She felt wired and on edge as if something big were about to happen.

The front gate buzzer sounded.

That's scary. She picked up Ella and padded over to the security screen, which showed a striking blonde in sunglasses standing on the footpath. Jane pressed the intercom. "Hello, can I help you?"

The woman raised her sunglasses. "Oh, hi, I'm Madeline Shaw. My husband asked me to drop by and deliver some paperwork to Jarred Steele."

Releasing the button, Jane bit her lip. *Oh my God.*

The blonde reached out and buzzed again. "Hello, are you still there?"

Jane pressed the button. "Sorry. Jarred's busy at the moment, can I help you?"

"No, I've been instructed to hand them to him personally and I'm in a bit of a hurry."

Jane glanced at her watch. *Jarred should be back any minute.* She pressed the release lock. "Come on round the side to the pool area. Jarred won't be long."

"Sure, thanks."

Jane padded out to the patio and lay Ella on the sun lounge. *This is too good an opportunity to miss. Madeline Shaw can bring the world's attention to human trafficking, if I can convince her to write the story.*

High heels clicked on the path and Madeline Shaw appeared carrying a folder. She wore a stylishly cut navy jacket and matching skirt reaching just above her knees. A soft pink blouse, sheer stockings, and strappy heels added a flattering touch of femininity.

Jane's gaze fell on the woman's impeccable makeup and her butterscotch-blonde hair woven into an intricate braid. A slim bag hung from her shoulder and she smiled as she stepped onto the terrace. Madeline Shaw was an extremely beautiful woman.

"Hello, I'm Jane."

"Hi, Jane, I'm Madeline." She shook Jane's hand then glanced around expectantly.

"Jarred should be back any minute." Jane pointed to the outdoor setting. "Please have a seat while you wait?"

Madeline glanced at her watch and Jane's gaze fell on the folder in Madeline's hand. "Is that what you need to give Jarred?"

"Yes." She placed the folder on her lap. "I've never meet Mr. Steele, but my husband needs these papers signed as soon as possible."

"If you're in a hurry I can give Jarred the folder."

"No, Elliott gave me strict instructions to hand it to Jarred Steele personally."

Ella gurgled.

Leaning over, Jane picked her up then sat on the other chair.

Madeline's gaze locked on Ella. "Oh my goodness." Madeline's whole demeanor changed. The sophisticated woman fell away as she edged closer. A soft smile formed on her lips. "She's tiny."

Turning Ella around, Jane smiled. "Yes, she was a month premature, but she's now eight weeks old. Do you have children?"

Madeline's smile faltered. "No, but I hope to one day, if I'm lucky. What's her name?"

"Eloise Kalista, but we call her Ella."

"That's lovely." Madeline captured one of Ella's tiny hands with her fingers then her eyes lifted to meet Jane's. "I have a job interview this morning, that's why I'm in a bit of a hurry but if you have time, I would love to come back later and speak with you."

"I'd like that too. What's the job?"

"It's with a London publication. They actually flew here to interview me. All I have to do is turn up and the job's mine."

"Will your husband go to London with you?"

"No, he's based here." She looked down and played with her skirt. "Our jobs keep us apart for long periods so it won't be any different."

Jane frowned. "Would you like a cup of tea or a coffee, Madeline?"

"I'd love to but..." She looked at her watch again. "Maybe just a glass of water."

"I'll get it." Jane stood and adjusted Ella.

Madeline's gaze stayed riveted on Ella. "You're very lucky."

Jane smiled. "Would you like to hold her while I make the tea?"

"Oh, yes." Madeline laid the folder and her keys on the table and carefully gathered Ella within the cradle of her arms. "She's like you around the eyes. Hello, little one. Uh-oh! I just felt a rather strong vibration."

"I'll get a nappy. Could you lay Ella on the sun lounge for me? I'd hate you to go to your interview with a stained suit."

Jane hurried inside and grabbed what she needed. As she returned to the terrace heavy feet pounded on the side path. *They're back.*

Covered in sweat, Jarred was the first to explode round the side of the bungalow, his expression ferocious and riveted on Madeline, who stood leaning over Ella.

He roared.

Madeline swung around, shrieked, then fumbled inside her bag.

"Jarred, No!" Jane dropped the change bag and ran forward.

Too late.

Jarred ran at Madeline dropping his shoulder. He hit her like a front row forward, lifting her off her feet and propelling her backward, straight into the pool. A titanic wave of water washed over the edges and they both disappeared below the surface.

Holding her hand to her mouth, Jane stared in disbelief. *Jarred, what have you done?*

Talos appeared round the corner breathing heavily. He grabbed

Jane by the shoulders. "Why is the gate open? What's happened? Are you all right?"

Jane nodded. "I'm fine, but Jarred's in trouble." She pointed to the pool as Jarred surfaced with a bedraggled Madeline Shaw, coughing and spluttering. Her open shoulder bag floated nearby along with a lipstick and pen.

"Big trouble."

Jane gaze flew back to the pool as Madeline swung a punch and screeched. Jarred caught her wrist, spun her round and locked her within his arms, then he dragged her towards the steps.

Ryan and Nick burst onto the terrace, guns in hands. They came to a grinding halt when they saw Jarred in the pool with Madeline.

"Take your hands off me, you moron." She clawed at Jarred's arm and screamed. "Are you mad? What the hell do you think you're doing?"

Reaching the steps, Jarred released his hold and hoisted her higher, sending one of her high-heels plonking back into the water, where it sank to the bottom.

Jane cringed. *Those shoes look expensive.*

"Put me down or I'll have you arrested for...for...assault, you imbecile." Madeline got an arm loose and elbowed Jarred hard in the chest.

"Shut up." Jarred stepped out of the pool holding her off the ground. He glared at Talos. "She was about to snatch the baby."

Talos swung to face Jane. "Did you let her in?"

"Yes. Her name is Madeline Shaw and she came here to give Jarred some papers he needs to sign. She was putting Ella down after having a cuddle, not abducting her."

"You opened the gate to a complete stranger?"

"Don't give me that look. I know a good person when I meet them."

Talos's hands fisted as he stared at her. "Oh, yeah. So how come you ended up married to such a bastard?" He stiffened. "I'm sorry, I didn't mean that."

Jane bit her lip as pain lanced her heart. "That wasn't called for." She turned back to the pool. "Jarred, please release Madeline. She hasn't done anything wrong."

Madeline spluttered. "You mean this moron is Jarred Steele?" Madeline got a hand free again and brushed her fringe out of the way. Black smudges ran above and below her eyes, her skirt and jacket clung to her body like a second skin, and her hair was sticking out all over the place. She looked a wreck.

Jane placed her hands on her hips. "Let her go, Jarred, she has a job interview."

The woman huffed. "As if I can turn up for an interview like this."

Lowering her, Jarred spun Madeline to face him, grabbed her upper arms, and leveled an intimidating stare on her. She blinked but didn't move.

Talos crossed his arms. "I'm impressed. Most people cower under that glare."

Narrowing his eyes, Jarred focused on the woman. "I was expecting Elliott Shaw, not a woman. I need proof you're who you say you are."

"Proof!" Madeline pulled out of Jarred's arms, hobbled lopsided in her remaining high-heel to the table, picked up a blue folder, hobbled back, and thrust it at him.

"I am Elliott's wife, you twit, and those are the papers you required so urgently that I had to rearrange my whole morning. And now, thanks to your overactive imagination, I look like a drowned rat." She whacked him in the shoulder.

"I apologize. I thought you were about to take the baby, and you did reach for a gun."

"I reached for my mace, you idiot. And why in God's name would I want to take a baby?" She sent a scathing look across the terrace. "What's so bloody funny?"

Glancing across the terrace, Jane saw Nick and Ryan shaking with silent laughter. She turned back to Jarred who looked dumbfounded. She bet nobody had ever called him a moron, idiot, or a twit to his face before.

Bending down, Jane picked up a pair of sunglasses and handed them to Madeline. "I'm really sorry. There's been a big mistake." She bent to pick up a set of keys and the statue behind her exploded. Right where her head had been a second before.

"Ryan, grab the baby." Talos bellowed before lifting Jane off her feet. A bullet whistled past her head as he launched them both into the pool. The chilly water took her breath away but then time slowed. Her mind registered Talos's body plastered to her, his arms wrapped tightly around her. *Ella.*

They hit the bottom and Jane glanced up as the surface broke. Jarred and Madeline descended toward them. *Shit, she's really going to be upset now.* Talos dragged Jane out of the way, avoiding a tangled heap. She noticed a phone, purse and high heel shoe on the floor of the pool. *Really upset.*

I have to get to Ella. Jane let go and began clawing her way to the surface. Talos beat her to the surface and dragged her to the edge.

"Stay down, someone's shooting at you."

"Ella!" Jane gasped for air. "I have to check on her."

"Wait."

Jarred surfaced in front of them and hauled Madeline to the edge. He looked at Talos. "Did you see where the shooter is positioned?"

"He has to be on the lane wall somewhere."

A boom thundered, lower in the garden, and Jane began struggling. "Ella."

Ryan poked his head out from behind the now headless statue of a woman carrying an urn. "Ella's safe. I took her inside. That's Nick shooting at the gunman. Stay down."

Jane trembled. "How did they find us?"

Talos held her firmly against his chest. "You have my word, sweetheart. I'll do whatever it takes to stop these vermin. Whatever it takes."

"What are you people involved in?" Madeline pushed away from Jarred.

A motorbike powered up on the other side of the wall then took off. Ryan stepped from behind the statue and signaled Talos and Jarred. "You can come out now, it's clear." He strode to the edge and hoisted Madeline up and out.

Free of both shoes, she glared at Ryan then ran toward the side gate.

Nick stepped in front of her and wagged his finger. "Oh no, you don't. No one's going anywhere just yet."

"Get out of my way."

"Sorry, honey. You're not leaving until the boss says you can."

Jarred hoisted himself out of the pool and grabbed Madeline's elbow. "Everyone inside." He strode into the house, dragging a dripping and cursing Madeline along beside him.

Jane held on to Talos's hand and waded to the steps. After a quick glance at the high wall he scooped her up and strode inside, setting her down in the kitchen. The instant her feet touched the tiles, Jane ran to where Ella lay in her carrier on the floor. She lifted her out and held her in her arms, rocking. "I've got you, honey. Mummy's got you."

Glancing across the kitchen, she saw Talos run a shaking hand through his hair before glowering at Jarred. "That was too fucking close." His gaze settled on Jane and he stepped forward, enclosing her and Ella in his arms. "Are you both all right?"

"Yes." Jane rested her head against his chest. "We are now."

"Will somebody tell me what the hell is going on here? That man was shooting real bullets at us."

Jane lifted her head to see Madeline stalked over and poked Jarred with a manicured nail. "You have just ruined the most important interview of my life."

Jarred raised an eyebrow. "I'm sure if you ring and explain—"

"How? The number is in my phone at the bottom of *your* damn pool."

"Calm down. Once you dry off, you can ring and explain you were delayed. If they want you badly enough, they will reschedule."

"Reschedule!" Placing her hands on her hips she fumed. "They're flying back to London this morning." She grabbed a pen and scribbled on a notepad beside the phone. "You blew my interview, you fix it." She thrust the note at Jarred. "That's their hotel and suite. I'm leaving this mad house."

Jarred's hand shot out like a missile and captured her wrist. "You're going nowhere until I'm satisfied you're not in league with that shooter."

"What?"

Jane pulled away from Talos, who was looking very amused. She touched Madeline's arm. "Come with me, Madeline. I'll show you where you can have a shower and I'll find you something to wear. Then, we'll explain. I think we owe you that much."

Madeline glared at Jarred a moment longer. "Very well, but if there's anything illegal going on, I'm informing the police." She yanked her wrist free of Jarred and followed Jane out of the kitchen and up the stairs.

Having no idea which room had been allocated to who, Jane opened the first door she came to. "Have a shower and I'll bring you some dry clothes, then we can go downstairs and I'll tell you why we're in Vietnam."

"As long as I don't have to deal with that man, I'll be happy."

Jane pursed her lips, her arms tightening around Ella. "Jarred was just trying to protect me and Ella. I'm in witness protection and that shooter was after me."

Madeline's eyes widened. "After you?"

"Yes, he works for a ring of human traffickers."

"How did you get involved with traffickers?"

"It's a long story but those men downstairs are all ex-SAS soldiers who are trying to save my life. I came to Vietnam with Jarred and his team to identify a trafficking ring before they succeed in killing me. And, there's one left to find before I'll be safe."

If it were only that simple. Jane swallowed her fear and gently pushed Madeline through the doorway. "Have a shower, then I'll explain everything."

Jane closed the door and opened several others before finding her suitcase on a luggage stand. She lay Ella between two pillows on the huge bed, grabbed some capris pants, a light top, and fresh underwear, and headed into the bathroom for a very quick shower.

In record time, she was showered, dressed, and after checking on her sleeping baby, Jane stepped out into the thickly carpeted hall, just as female scream rang out.

A male voice swore loudly and glass shattered.

"Madeline! Shit, Jarred." Jane ran along the hall.

Heavy footsteps thundered up the stairs behind her and Jane heard Talos bellow her name, but she didn't stop. She burst into the bedroom where she'd left Madeline and found it empty. *Where is she?*

A muffled squawk and another male oath sounded from the bathroom.

Jane had almost reached the door when she was roughly lifted off her feet and thrown onto the large bed.

"Stay there," Talos yelled. He moved toward the bathroom with a deadly looking gun in his hand.

"No, Talos, it's..." Rolling off the edge of the bed, Jane darted after him just as he threw the door wide.

"Struth."

Grabbing Talos's waist, Jane peered around him. *Uh oh.*

Jarred stood with his back to them wearing only his jocks. Jane's gaze travelled up his muscled legs, firm butt, tapered waist, and broad back. He swung around and Jane gasped. Madeline was locked against his chest by one of his arms, well off the floor. She clutched a towel in front of her, the upper swells of breasts and her long legs exposed.

Jarred's other hand was clamped over Madeline's mouth. The smudged mascara and eye shadow had disappeared but she looked wild-eyed and furious as she wriggled frantically. Her unbraided hair hung about her shoulders and a strong scent of cologne filled the air.

Stepping clear of bits of broken glass, Jarred lowered Madeline and released her.

She backed against a wall and scowled. "What is wrong with you?"

"I didn't know you were in *my* bathroom."

"You shouldn't have grabbed me. I was naked."

"You were screaming like a banshee." His gaze fell on Jane. "Why did you put this bloody woman in *my* bathroom?"

"Sorry." Jane lifted her hands. "I didn't know it was yours."

Madeline shook her head. "You are the most infuriating, obnoxious, and unthinking man I've ever met in my entire life."

"You are..." He inhaled deeply. "You shouldn't be here." He brushed past Jane and Talos, picked up his duffle bag, and strode from the room.

"Watch the glass." Talos pulled the door closed and raised an eyebrow at Jane. "I suspect that's Jarred's expensive cologne all over the floor. Another reason he's not happy."

Jane rolled her eyes and gently tapped on the door. "Madeline, I've got clothes for you."

CHAPTER THIRTY

Wearing dry clothes, Talos leaned against the island bench and observed Jarred as he stalked back and forth across the large kitchen, like a tiger in heat. "When I heard that scream, my first thought was the shooter had gained access to the house. Fuck. I was sure he'd kill Jane before I got up there."

Jarred swung to face him. "There are only three outsiders who know where we are. My contact in the Australian Embassy is above reproach. That leaves Gibbs and Shaw."

"Shaw would hardly risk his wife's life and she was almost hit by one of those bullets."

The front gate buzzed.

Turning to the security monitor, Jarred raised an eyebrow. "This should be interesting. It's Shaw." He pressed the unlock button for the gate.

Fifteen seconds later, Elliot Shaw burst across the patio and leapt through the open doorway. "Where's Maddy? Is she all right?"

"Your wife is fighting fit and presently in my bathroom," snapped Jarred. "Where's Gibbs? My instructions were that you both return here immediately."

"He and Simon are on their way. Did you identify the gunman?"

Jarred's eyes narrowed. "We were hoping you might enlighten us as to his identity."

"I have no idea who it could be."

"Why the fuck did you send your wife to deliver those papers? Surely you realize the less people who know about us, the better."

Shaw shrugged. "You wanted to fast track Ming's identity papers and Jane wanted to meet my wife. I decided to kill two birds with one stone. I certainly didn't tell anyone else."

"How well do you know Gibbs?" Talos asked.

"We went to school together. He's a fitness fanatic, stands up for what he believes, and has a very low tolerance for racists and bigots."

Pulling out a chair, Jarred sat. "Could Gibbs be on the take?"

"No way. He's as straight as an arrow and his father's as rich as Croesus."

"You know his father?" Talos asked.

"Yes, why?"

"Who is he?" Jared asked.

"That's not for me to say. If you want to know anything else, ask Zac." Shaw frowned. "What did you mean by, my wife is *fighting fit?*"

Jarred cleared his throat. "I thought she was abducting the baby and about to pull a gun on me, so I tackled her. She's pissed off about missing her interview and the fact that I won't let her leave this house, among other things."

"Thank God you didn't." Shaw pulled out a chair and sat opposite Jarred. "They might have taken another shot at her."

Talos met Jarred's gaze then looked at Shaw. "Why would you assume your wife was the shooter's target?"

"Because she's ruffled some very dangerous feathers lately."

"How?" Jarred leaned across the table, his grey eyes fastened on Shaw's face.

"She wrote several hard hitting articles, exposing an illegal adoption racket, sweatshops that use children as slave labour, and an in depth editorial about the ill-treatment and repression of women in India."

"Your wife is a journalist?" Jarred pushed back from the table, the loathing on his face almost comical. "She's a scare monger more interested in a good story than the truth?" He almost spat the words out.

Noticing Jane and Madeline in the doorway, Talos signaled Jarred.

Madeline Shaw placed her hands on her hips and glared. "I am a professional journalist, Mister Steele. I do my research and I write the truth, no matter who I offend."

"Mads!" Elliot jumped up, strode across the room and hugged his wife.

She patted her husband's back while continuing to glare at Jarred. Talos frowned as the tension in the room rose to ignition point.

Jarred's face blackened. "Shaw, I advise you to take your wife on a long holiday or go back to Australia. This is not a safe place for her and getting more perilous by the second."

"Perhaps she could lay low with your team for a few days?" Shaw's lips twitched. "That is if you can keep from killing each other?"

"Elliott!" Madeline glowered at her husband. "If you expect me to stay in this house with that...that menace, you've got another thing coming. I'm getting my wet clothes." She stalked out of the room.

Jane rolled her eyes at Talos and ran after Shaw's wife. "Wait, Madeline. We could make good use of this opportunity."

Something is off here. Can't the fool see his wife and Jarred rub each other up the wrong way? Talos glanced at Shaw to see him grinning. "What's so funny?"

"I haven't seen Mads so fired up in years." His smile faded. "I really do fear for her life. Last week a man pulled a knife and tried to abduct her. This morning she was jogging when a car mounted the footpath and almost hit her."

"Could be a coincidence," Talos said.

"That's what Mads believes, but I'm convinced someone wants to get rid of her."

Jarred leaned back in his chair. "You'll have to come up with another solution. I will not put my team or the witnesses we're protecting in any more danger than they already are. And a journalist is the last person I want under my roof."

The gate buzzer sounded again.

Talos wandered over to the security monitor and observed Simon and Gibbs on the screen. He switched the release button, checked that no one followed them through the gate then released the lock on the front door. "Simon and Gibbs are back."

"Good," replied Jarred. "Let's see what Gibbs has to say for himself."

The moment Simon and Gibbs stepped into the kitchen, Talos knew by the excitement in their eyes that something big had happened.

Tossing a folder onto the table, Simon pulled out a chair and sat. "First of all, did you get the shooter?"

"No," muttered Talos, running his hands through his hair. "The bastard took off on a motorbike. How did you go?"

"We sorted out Ming's identity thanks to the documents the old man gave us. Ming's mother died several years ago and there is no record of a father or any other relatives." Simon glanced at Elliott. "Thanks for your help with that."

"You're welcome." Shaw turned to Jarred. "I spoke to a contact of mine in Child Welfare regarding the adoption of Ming. He gave me several documents that need filling out and signing, which are what Maddy was delivering."

Jarred nodded and focused on Simon. "What else did you discover?"

Simon opened the folder. "Andrew Rossini married Nguyen Chi Lillian, otherwise known as Lien almost two years ago here in Vietnam."

Clenching his fists, Talos exhaled. "So Jane's wedding *was* a sham?"

"Exactly."

Jarred leaned his chin on his interlocked fingers. "May we presume you've traced this woman's parents?"

"Yes," answered Gibbs, rubbing his hands together. "Her English mother died fifteen years ago when she lost control of her car. Lillian's father is Nguyen Chi Quan, a prominent businessman who has semi retired to his home in Sapa, which is high in the mountains."

"Sapa?" Talos straightened. "Jane told me Rossini took her to a private villa in Sapa during the honeymoon. Nguyen Chi Quan has to be Rong."

"Do you have the address?" Jarred asked.

"Yes." Gibbs flipped open a small notepad. "We also have Lillian's address here in Hanoi. I can ask the SCU to pick both of them up."

Rubbing his chin, Jarred stared at Gibbs. "Before we go any further, I need to ask you several questions."

"Let me guess," offered Gibbs. "You want to know how I can afford to own a top of the range Alfa Romeo and a water front apartment on Sydney Harbour? I could ask you the same question."

"I collected a huge inheritance and earn big money protecting important people. You on the other hand, are on a Federal Police Inspector's wage, which isn't enough to cover the repayments, let alone own one of the most expensive Alfa Romeos on the market and penthouses on the Harbour."

Gibbs shrugged. "Fair enough. They were gifts from my father."

"And your father is?"

"A wealthy man, who shall remain anonymous and who likes to bestow his only son with certain luxuries."

"Very well, I'll find out his identity myself." Jarred drummed his fingers on the table. "Did you advise anyone that we were staying here?"

"No, nor did I give anyone the safe house address where Jane was staying in Sydney."

"Then how did they find her?" Jarred stood and stepped over to the coffee machine.

"I suspect a tracking device was attached to my car, either while it was parked in the garage under my apartment block or at my local shops. As for today, I have no idea."

Simon shifted from foot to foot. "Do we let the SCU pick up Rong and his daughter, or do we take care of them ourselves?"

Jarred placed two cups under the coffee machine before looking at each of their faces. "I'd rather not inform the SCU yet. If Nguyen Chi Quan is a prominent businessman then the police will be reluctant to move without strong evidence and I don't want him to escape."

Pulling out the only spare chair, Gibbs sat. "If you were to capture Nguyen Chi Quan and prove beyond doubt that he's Rong, you will be heroes. But, if you're wrong, I wouldn't like to be in your shoes. I believe he has a lot of powerful friends."

"So do I," Jarred replied coldly. "My team will set up surveillance on both Rong and his daughter. We'll stay here, as it's more secure than a hotel. Simon can set up our command base and man the security cameras."

"What about the next scheduled meeting?" Gibbs said. "It's a couple of days away and by then Rong will know Ripon is dead. He'll guess the other two were taken out as well. If I were him, I wouldn't come anywhere near Hanoi."

Jarred removed the filled cups and put them on the table, then placed another two cups under the spouts. "Rong will most certainly cancel the meeting and lie low, but he'll want to know who betrayed him and who is taking his people out. He may well have his daughter go to Sapa or meet with her elsewhere, and we need to be ready."

The front gate buzzer sounded again and Talos checked the monitor. "It's Sam and Kallie with Ming."

Elliot frowned. "Who?"

"Sam's another member of my team and Kallie's his fiancée." Jarred passed two more coffees across. "From now on whatever we discuss or plan will go no further than this room." He regarded Gibbs. "The success of our mission depends on total secrecy from the outside world. You can't inform your chief in Australia or the Special Crime Unit here in Vietnam."

Jarred turned to Elliott. "And you can't say a single word to your wife. The last thing we need is a journalist sticking her nose into our business."

"Too late, Mister Steele." Madeline Shaw padded barefooted across the kitchen. "Jane has told me the whole story. This man Rong has come up in my investigations on several occasions. He is one nasty man and I want him caught. So, I'm in, hook, line and sinker." She handed him a cup. "I like my coffee with milk and one sugar, please."

She looked across the table, her eyes widening when she saw Gibbs. "Zac, what are you doing in Vietnam?" She ran around the table and hugged him.

"I'm well, Madeline, and you?"

"I was fine until a moron crash tackled me into the pool and then…" She blushed. "Invaded my privacy."

Talos fought not to laugh at the look of incredulity on Gibbs and Shaw's faces. Jarred also appeared lost for words. Not many people managed to get the better of him. *Odd that she didn't mention her nudity.*

Jarred drew in a deep breath, placed the cup Madeline had handed him and another under the spouts and shrugged. "I told you I thought you were pulling a gun on me and I had no idea you were in *my bathroom.* But, now that you are privy to our mission, Mrs. Shaw, I insist you stay under this roof as our guest."

"No." Madeline stalked over to her husband. "I will be leaving with Elliott."

Shaw rubbed his chin. "I would prefer you stayed under Jarred's protection. I think you were followed here today and that shooter was after you."

"What?" She glared at her husband. "There is no one after me and I can't stay here with that man. He's...he's..."

"In charge," said Jarred. "A journalist is the last person I want under my roof, however, I will not allow you to risk this operation." He glanced at Talos. "Lock us down, Captain."

"Yes, Colonel." Glad to have something to do, Talos pulled a lever beside the security box and steel shutters descended on all exterior windows and doors. It also eased his mind that the shooter might have been after Madeline Shaw. They would have to move locations, but it might have been worse. He expelled his breath.

The kitchen door swung open and Jane ran in. "What's happening?"

Jarred kept his eyes on Madeline Shaw. "We're taking precautions."

Madeline's eyes flashed daggers at Jarred. "I assure you, Mister Steele, I know when to keep my mouth shut." She rounded on her husband. "Elliott, let's go."

Shaw raised his hands. "Sorry, Mads, I want you here with these men to protect you."

"Argh."

Jane glanced at Talos. "If that man *was* after Madeline, can we assume Rong doesn't know the rest of us are here?"

Talos shook his head. "We never assume anything, sweetheart. We hope for the best and plan for the worst, but we do have some new info that I'll tell you about later."

She nodded and turned to Madeline. "Come on, I'll introduce you to Kallie and Ming."

They both left the kitchen as Sam strolled in.

"Who's the stunning blonde who looks like she wants to strangle someone, and why are we in lockdown?"

Talos grinned. "The blonde is Madeline Shaw and this is her husband, Elliott." He turned to Shaw. "This is Sam Locke the final member of my team."

Sam shook hands with Shaw. "I've heard you've been assisting the boys, but I don't understand why your wife is here?"

Jarred snorted and placed another two coffees on the table and sat. "She's a journalist who now knows about our operation and who may well be on someone's hit list."

Sam glanced back at Shaw. "Hit list? Why?"

"For printing the truth. An hour ago a man took a shot at her by *your* pool."

"Here?" Sam swung toward Jarred. "Can we be sure he was after Elliott's wife?"

"It's possible. Fortunately the man wasn't a sniper." Jarred squared his shoulders. "Otherwise both Mrs. Shaw and Jane would now be dead. I have invited the damned woman to stay with us and she's not exactly thrilled about it."

Sam raised an eyebrow. "That, I could tell. You must be losing your touch, boss."

Talos grinned. "How'd you do with Ming?"

"She's a sweet kid. We bought her another doll and a stack of essentials. No wonder women have so much stuff. They start young. Ming couldn't wait to get back to show Jane."

Jarred tapped the table. "We need to work out our strategy and I'd rather we did it while the ladies are occupied. From now on they stay inside this building, while we handle things."

"Good. I couldn't agree more." Talos picked up a pad and pen from the bench and sat alongside Jarred. "How do you want to do this?"

Jarred looked at Sam. "Nick and Ryan are in the study which is now our command post. Can you call them in?"

"No worries." Sam strode out of the kitchen and returned a couple of minutes later with the other two men.

For the next hour all eight men worked together, planning the best way to get access to Rong and his daughter's homes so they could set up surveillance and listening devices. They were just finishing up when Ryan spoke.

"There's something I need to mention."

"Go on," said Jarred.

"You asked me to contact the people Madeline Shaw was to be interviewed by."

"And?"

"They don't exist. No one by those names is presently staying in that suite or at that hotel. So I rang their publication in London. And, although they've heard of Madeline Shaw and have great respect for her, they did not send anyone here to interview her."

Both Elliott and Jarred leaned back in their seats.

Ryan glanced at Shaw. "I think it was a set up to get your wife out in the open."

"I knew it." Elliott shook his head. "Madeline said, if it hadn't been for a fire hydrant, the car would have crushed her against a brick wall." He drew in a deep breath and faced Jarred. "I know you and Mads got off on the wrong foot, but I would appreciate you and your team keeping her safe until I can get her on a flight back to Australia."

"It appears I have no choice," muttered Jarred.

Gibbs's phone shrilled. "Excuse me, it's my chief." He stood and walked across to the kitchen bench. "Gibbs speaking."

Talos observed his teammates. They were all watching Gibbs, and waiting. The other man finished the call and turned to them. "I've got bad news."

"What?" Talos sensed the tension in the room rise.

"Yesterday, Marzetti was being transferred to a maximum-security prison in the Blue Mountains when unknown snipers shot out the transport vehicle's tires. It careered off the road into bush, injuring the guards and several prisoners. The police arrived to discover Marzetti missing."

Simon frowned. "I thought all prisoner transport vehicles were fitted with live CCTV feeds, GPS tracking, and back to base alarms?"

"They are," said Gibbs. "The assailants set up their ambush on a stretch of road thirty minutes from the nearest police station. They wore balaclavas, blew the emergency exit off the transport vehicle, and got Marzetti away before any other vehicles arrived on the scene. It was a well executed hijacking."

Talos narrowed his eyes. "If it was yesterday, why are we only hearing about it now?"

"Bureaucracy. Alerts were issued to all domestic and international airports, but because of the sensitivity of this case, the AFP was hoping to recapture Marzetti before word got out. It was never announced that he'd been caught in the first place."

"So now he's on the run." Sam met Talos's gaze. "I'll ring Fergie and Ken to stay alert in case Marzetti comes looking for Kallie and Jane at the farm. Thank God the girls are here with us." He pulled out his phone and left the kitchen.

Talos slowly came to his feet and stared at Gibbs. "Marzetti's original plan was to escape on a freighter bound for Asia. The AFP should check every tanker headed to Asia."

"Not a chance," said Gibbs. "Do you have any idea how many freighters leave Australia's east coast each day? It would be like looking for a needle in a haystack."

Talos rolled his shoulders and neck, relieving the tightness. "Let's hope the police catch Marzetti by the time we return home. In the meantime, we need to get after Rong and his daughter. I'm going upstairs to tell Jane that guy was right, her marriage wasn't legal and that Marzetti's on the loose."

Jarred stood. "Once you've spoken to Jane, I want you, Sam, and Nick to grab your gear. The sooner we set up surveillance on Rong the better."

"I agree," said Talos. "Does Sapa have an airport?"

"No. The train takes eight hours to Lao Cai and then it's another fifty minutes by car, or we can drive the whole way, in which case it will take nine hours." He looked at Shaw. "Can we borrow your helicopter and fly up there ourselves?"

"Sure. It'll take two hours and there's a couple of places to land, but who will help guard the ladies?'

"Simon and Ryan will be back shortly and I'll leave you a gun."

"I'd like to come with you," said Gibbs. "No one can get inside this place and the shooter won't be back, not now that he knows there are armed men here."

"All right." Jarred turned to Elliott. "You'll be on your own for an hour or so. Simon and Nick need to set up surveillance and listening devices in Lien's apartment, then they'll come straight back here."

Simon passed a piece of paper to Shaw. "Here's my number. We won't be long."

Talos followed the boys out of the kitchen then ran up the stairs. On the landing he met Sam. "Grab your gear. Jarred wants us to go with him to Sapa, and he's allowing Gibbs to come with us. I still don't know if I trust that guy."

"Obviously Jarred doesn't either." Sam rubbed his chin. "Otherwise he would have left Gibbs here to guard Jane."

Talos exhaled. "We need to watch each other's back."

"Don't we always." Sam gave him a friendly punch. "Come on, big fella. Let's get this over with so we can take our ladies home."

Talos glanced into a lounge area where Jane, Kallie, and Madeline were deep in conversation. "Yeah, I'm looking forward to that." A sense of unease filled him.

CHAPTER THIRTY-ONE

A lone figure stood by the cliff edge and brooded. A chilling breeze cut through his silk shirt like shards of glass, clawing at his skin and adding to his irritation. Who had betrayed him? He'd initially accepted Lhasa had died in the brothel fire. The man had been overweight and over sexed, but why hadn't his body been released? Kazan's disappearance was another mystery. *No one crosses me. No one.*

It grated on him to have sent the blonde backpacker on her way, but it wouldn't do to have her in the house with his brother due to arrive at any minute.

His phone chimed. "You have news for me?"

The thin hollow voice of his English assassin replied, "Ripon passed his briefcase to a third party under your daughter's eye. The man was then ambushed and dragged away by a tall white man."

"Go on."

"Ripon left the restaurant, but he was followed back to his accommodation by another two men. Big guys, I'm guessing ex-military and most likely Australian or English. They hunkered down to observe Ripon and were joined by a third white man."

"What did you do?"

"I followed your instructions. Ripon is dead."

"Good. Did you take care of that other business?"

"Not yet. Your daughter had someone try to run down the journalist with a car. He failed. Then the man followed her to a home in the Ba Dinh district, where he again botched the job."

"Fucking incompetence. I should have sent you in the first place. Do you have anything else to report?"

"Yes. The men who were following Ripon are in the same house as the journalist and they're armed. I witnessed five military types enter the premises along with another man, an Asian child, and a woman your brother knows. Then steel shutters came down over the doors and windows."

"What woman?"

"The beautiful one who thought Dominic was her grandfather."

"Kalista McNeil. Now *that* is interesting. Did you by any chance see Andrew Rossini's wife and baby?'

"No, but the man with Kalista McNeil was carrying a box of nappies."

"I see. Stay where you are and keep me informed. If the opportunity arises, shoot Jane Rossini. She is the one who can identify me. I'll worry about the journalist another day."

"Boss. You don't think Dominic has betrayed you, do you?"

"We will know soon enough. Bring me Kalista McNeil. Alive."

"Wait. Seven men are leaving the house. They have duffel bags and are taking two vehicles. Do you want me to follow them?"

"Seven men? No. I will organize a diversion and contact Lien to assist you. I want you to bring me all three women and the baby, alive. We may need them yet. I will call you back."

The man slid the phone into his shirt pocket. "Who betrayed me?"

As the shutters descended, Jane leaned against the solid front door and sighed. "Please God, don't let anything bad happen to them. This Rong person scares the life out of me."

Kallie hugged her. "They know what they're doing, Jane. Come on. Let's have a cup of tea and something to eat. We can fill Madeline in while we wait for news."

Madeline Shaw descended the stairs with Ella cradled in her arms. "I've been hearing stories about the man known as Rong for several years. They say his mother was a Vietnamese prostitute and his father was an Australian expat on the run from police. I also heard that Rong killed his father and mother in cold blood."

Jane shivered. "He sounds just like Marzetti."

"He might be worse." Kallie bit her lip. "Tea."

They all trooped into the kitchen where Elliott was pacing back and forth, speaking to someone in Vietnamese. He hung up and grimaced.

"I've arranged for the helicopter to be refueled and clearance given for takeoff. There's bad weather expected in Sapa, so they need to get moving."

"Thanks, Elliot." Jane opened the fridge and pulled out several sealed containers. "We should eat something."

Over lunch, Jane and Kallie told Elliott and Madeline the whole story behind the Kalista Diamond and how Dominic Marzetti had come to Willaroi Downs. Madeline scribbled notes the whole time, in between asking questions. Jane would have smiled if it weren't so serious.

As they cleared away the empty plates from lunch, piercing sirens sounded, growing louder and louder until they seemed to be outside the house. Jane raced up the stairs behind Kallie to a lounge area that overlooked the street. Although the shutters were down, they could see the street below through tiny slits. Police vehicles and motorcycles were parked all over the road chaotically. Police officers crowded round each of the home's security gates, yelling and pointing.

"What's going on?" Jane turned to Elliott, who had followed her and now stood watching the commotion below.

"Could be a bomb threat. We have a lot of visiting dignitaries at the moment."

The security gate buzzer peeled and continued to peel.

Elliott strode to the door. "I'll see what's going on. Stay here."

Jane followed Elliott to the kitchen and watched him as he argued with the police via the intercom in Vietnamese. After several minutes he hit the gate release and switched the lever to open the shutters.

"I have to let them in. The whole street is being evacuated."

A cold chill ran through Jane as she stared at him. "You shouldn't have opened the shutters. What if the sniper is out there, waiting for a chance to take Madeline out?"

Heavy hammering sounded on the front door, and Elliott held up his hands. "We don't have a choice. According to the police, multiple bombs have been planted along this street and they're due to go off in twenty minutes."

Bombs.

Her heart matched the hammering on the front door. "I think we should ring Simon and Nick, so they can get back here."

Elliott ran a hand over his chin. "I'll speak to the police. You get the others and bring whatever you need. We won't be allowed back until they've cleared all the homes."

Jane ran back up the stairs to where Kallie and Madeline were peering round the edge of the curtains. The shutters were now up and it was chaos in the street below.

"We have to go. Several bombs are set to go off."

"Bombs!" Madeline and Kallie both stared at her.

Jane pulled the baby sling over her shoulders and took Ella from Madeline. "Yes. Where's Ming? Kallie can you grab the nappy bag?"

"I've got it." Ming stood in the doorway with her backpack on. She had the change-bag in one hand and her doll in the other.

"Good girl, let's go."

They raced down the stairs, descending to the foyer as police swarmed in past Elliott. The police rushed them out of the house towards a van. Jane breathed a sigh of relief. There were so many police around them, that there was no way a sniper could hit Madeline.

"Wait." Kallie yelled. "We need to ring Simon and Ryan before we go anywhere. Otherwise they'll get back here and freak out. And we should ring Sam and Talos so they know what's happening."

"There isn't time." Elliott strode back across the street and took her arm. "You can call them when we're somewhere safe."

A boom like thunder sounded and the ground under Jane's feet shook. Screaming and yelling echoed up and down the street as panic set in.

"Hurry," called a policeman. "Get in the van."

Jane followed Madeline and Ming into the van and turned to see Elliott helping Kallie up off the road. The policeman slammed the sliding side door shut.

"No, wait. There are two more to come."

He didn't react. "Maybe he can't hear me for the noise." Another booming clap sounded as the policeman jumped into the front of the van with the driver. Jane grabbed the steel grill dividing them and banged on the thick glass. "Wait. You can't leave yet."

He either couldn't hear or was ignoring her.

"Don't worry," called Madeline. "I saw your other friends running up the road. They'll get Kallie and Elliott out of here."

"Who, Simon and Ryan?"

"Yes. And once we get to the police station, it'll be sorted out."

Jane glanced at the two policemen in the front. *Something's not right.*

The driver worked his way round the obstructing police vehicles and a set of barricades. Once they were clear he turned on the siren and picked up speed. Jane glanced at Madeline to see her frowning.

"This isn't normal is it?"

Madeline shrugged. "I wouldn't have thought so. But maybe they're with the SCU and know how important you are."

"Then why are we heading out of the city?" Jane whispered.

"I don't know. Let's hope the others are following us."

Jane stared back through the rear-tinted window. Heavy traffic flowed in both directions across the four-lane motorway. "I don't think they had time." She cuddled Ella close, dread filling her heart and soul as she watched Hanoi disappear in the distance.

Madeline's eyes locked with hers. "This isn't good." She began looking on the floor and behind seats. "We need a weapon."

There wasn't anything.

The van sped along the freeway and over a major bridge. After another ten minutes, they turned off onto a smaller road and then through a gate to an airfield. Several helicopters sat near a big hangar. Jane reached for Madeline's hand. "We could try to take them by surprise?"

Madeline shook her head. "Let me handle it. They're not interested in you."

"No!"

The van stopped beside a blue and white helicopter and both policemen jumped out of the front and ran around the van. As the door slid open, Jane was not surprised to see them both pointing handguns at her and Madeline. *Shit.*

Madeline pushed Ming behind her. "What the hell is this?"

The two policemen moved aside to allow a third person to step between them. Jane's heart plummeted. *Lien.*

"Get out and don't try anything stupid. I would love a reason to shoot you in the head." Lien's eyes flicked down to the baby sling and then over Madeline, holding Ming. "You're the journalist. I would kill you now, but my father wishes to deal with you himself."

Madeline glared back. "And your father would be the man known as Rong, right?"

"That's his code name. His real name is Nguyen Chi Quan."

One of the policemen shot a swift glance at Lien. "No names."

Lien shrugged her shoulders. "They won't live long enough to do anything, so what does it matter? Bring them." She climbed into the front passenger seat of the helicopter and pulled the door shut.

The man nearest waved his gun. "Move."

Jane slid out carefully, so as not to wake Ella. Ming followed, clinging to Jane's hand.

As Madeline climbed out, she faced the two men. "Take me, but leave Jane and the children. They are of no use to you and they know nothing."

He stared at her coldly. "My orders are to bring all of you."

Jane closed her eyes and shivered. *Oh, Talos, I'm so sorry.*

Clasping Ella tightly and guiding Ming, Jane followed Madeline into the helicopter. Ming scampered onto Madeline's knee and shrank against the far door as she watched the men warily.

One of the men threw the nappy bag on the floor and climbed in beside Jane. The other sprang into the pilot's seat and began the startup process. Jane's hands trembled, her heart raced and her stomach churned. She was clammy and nauseous. *We're fucked.*

As they rose into the grey sky, Ming poked Jane in the arm then pointed out the window. Leaning across, Jane saw a silver four-wheel drive skid to a halt beside the police van. Simon and Ryan jumped out, waving their arms wildly.

They can't help us now. We're on our own. Jane attempted to smile at Ming, ignoring the little girl's fingernails digging into her arm. She didn't bother asking where they were being taken. She doubted they'd answer, and the whooping of the helicopter blades made it impossible to hear anyway. Instead she held her hands on either side of Ella's little head in an attempt to block out the noise. Amazingly, Ella hadn't woken. Jane glanced at the sun. They were flying north-west, in the same direction as Sapa. It wasn't much to cling to, but if they were being taken to Rong, and if Talos made it there ahead of them, and if Simon could get a message to Talos, then they might have a slim chance of making it out alive.

That was a lot of *ifs*.

❧

Talos climbed out of Shaw's helicopter and stretched. As he reached in for his duffel bag the phone vibrated in his jacket pocket. He put the phone on speaker. "What's up, Simon?"

"Jane and Elliott's wife have been snatched."

"What?" The phone shook in his hand as Talos locked eyes with Jarred. "Fucking hell, how is that possible?" He broke out in a sweat. "I should have stayed there."

Jarred took the phone from his shaking hands. "Tell us, exactly what happened?"

"There was a bomb threat and a couple of minor explosions. The street was evacuated and men disguised as police officers directed Jane and Madeline into a van and then took off."

"What about Kallie?" yelled Sam.

"No, she stopped to ring me and got left behind with Shaw. He's taken her to his place."

Sam exhaled and then met Talos's gaze. "We'll find her."

Gibbs frowned. "Could they be SCU police?"

"Unlikely," replied Simon. "We tailed them to a small heliport half an hour out of Hanoi, but they took off before we could stop them."

Barely able to breathe, Talos leaned against the chopper. "What direction did they fly?"

"North-west. My guess is they're heading to Sapa. I checked the chopper registration and it's owned by Nguyen Chi Quan, or as we suspect, Rong."

Dropping his head between his knees, Talos fought for calm. *I have to think like a soldier.* The frantic despair suffocating Talos eased. He began to breathe deeply, drawing on his years of training.

"Fuck." Jarred rubbed a hand over his jaw. "Get a chopper and follow them. I don't care if you have to steal it, just get one."

"Already done. There was a scenic flight hangar at the heliport. Ryan borrowed one of their choppers. With a bit of luck, we'll have it back before they open in the morning. We're in the air and about twenty minutes behind Rong's chopper."

Nick climbed out of the cockpit. "Let's hope you're right and they're coming here."

"Yeah. I'll text you when we arrive."

Jarred handed the phone back to Talos. "We need to be in position before Rong's chopper arrives."

Gibbs pulled out his own phone. "I'll call the SCU. We're going to need backup."

"No!" Jarred took the phone from Gibbs. "I don't want a cock up. We do this my way and when it's over you can call anyone you like." He pocketed the phone. "Let's go."

Talos hailed the first taxi he saw and directed the driver to the street they needed. He intended to do a drive by first then double back by foot. Nick stayed with the chopper in case they needed a quick getaway.

Within twenty minutes they were all armed with semi automatic rifles and concealed around the perimeter of the palatial home. On top of a stone wall and camouflaged by thick foliage, Talos trained his scope on the pretentious pool area. At each corner stood an enormous dragon, and if he wasn't mistaken, they were made of jade or marble. *This man is seriously wealthy and showy.* Disgust ate at Talos as his gaze skimmed the massive home and grounds, bought on the proceeds of human trafficking, slave labour, and drugs.

He reined in his anger and concentrated. Two armed men were patrolling on this side of the house. They crossed paths; spoke briefly, then strolled off in opposite directions. A third armed man stood by a set of French doors smoking. "I've got three bogies on my side of the house."

"Two on my side," came Sam's voice.

"One at the gate," said Gibbs.

Talos focused the scope down his side of the house towards a clump of shrubs at the back of the property. "What have you got, boss?"

"No access from the rear. It's a sheer cliff. We'll have to go in from the sides and front. Now we wait. Don't take anyone out until I give the word. We want that helicopter to land."

Talos waited until the patrolling guards were out of sight then he pushed aside the heavy foliage, and dropped from the stone wall. He flattened himself to the grass.

Nothing stirred.

After another couple of minutes he slithered to what looked like the gardener's shed. A guard stood smoking several meters away.

If they hurt Jane, I'll kill every single one of them with my bare hands. Talos slipped inside the shed and took up a stance by the grime-covered window. He had a good view of the pool area, helipad, and French doors leading into the side of the house.

The next forty minutes crawled by for Talos as he monitored each guard's position, and prayed that Jane was on her way. The thought of her being taken somewhere else or being thrown out of the chopper had him dry retching. Something that had never happened to him before, no matter how serious a situation.

Jarred, Sam, and Gibbs continually reported any movement in their sector. All up Talos accounted for six armed men outside the house. If Rong was in residence, he had to assume there were more men inside.

"Incoming blue and white helicopter." Sam sounded wired.

"Thank God." Talos pinched his nose, taking a minute to get his emotions under control. He'd never considered failure an option and he wasn't going to start now.

"If you get a chance and it's safe, take out a few of the patrolling guards," Jarred ordered. "Otherwise wait for my word."

Talos slipped out of the shed and around the side. He spotted another guard looking board as he picked his nose. *I wonder if he likes cats?* Talos drew back and covered the side of his mouth. "Meow."

The guard twisted to look over his shoulder and Talos jerked back. "Meow."

Footsteps approached eagerly and Talos raised the butt of his rifle. *I'd heard the Vietnamese like to eat cats, but this is one guy who is going to be very disappointed.*

The guard came rushing round the side of the shed, his eyes widening in shock at Talos stepped forward and then rammed the rifle butt into his face. The guard dropped soundlessly to the ground.

Talos dragged the man into the shed, secured his hands behind his back with a zip lock strap, and then hog-tied the man's feet to his hands. He glanced around for something to use as a gag and his gaze fell on several deflated pushbike tubes. *That'll do.*

"One down on my side," came Sam's voice.

"One on mine." Talos replied, knotting the tube.

"Gate's taken care of," said Gibbs. "I'm working my way towards the house now."

Dropping to the ground again, Talos crawled to the back of the pool house. He could see a guard striding towards the helipad and one still on guard by the French doors. Raising the scope, Talos sighted another guard taking a leak in the rear garden. An arm suddenly wrapped around the guard's neck from behind and he disappeared between two shrubs. A couple of loud thuds sounded through the com-set.

"Another one down," called Jarred. "Don't take out any more until I give the word."

Talos noted the guard by the French doors had disappeared inside, so he slid out of the pool house, dropped to his belly, and crawled closer to the house, taking cover behind an elaborate concrete fountain. "I'm in position."

The blue and white chopper came in low over the house, hovered for a moment then sank to the helipad. Talos held his breath and raised the telescopic lens. A man in police uniform climbed out of the rear and then dragged Jane out by one arm. She stumbled slightly then recovered and shrugged him off. In her other arm she held Ella in the baby sling. The man pushed Jane forward.

Talos clenched his jaw. *Mongrel. I'm going to hurt you bad.*

Madeline Shaw scrambled out with Ming in her arms and shouted, "There's no need to be so rough, you fucking moron."

Talos heard Jarred chuckle softly. "At least she only called me a moron."

The pilot, also in police uniform climbed out and waved at the guard striding towards the chopper. Then a woman came around the front of the chopper.

Lien.

Talos held still, his finger balanced lightly on the trigger as he concentrated on calming his breathing. To take the kill shot he needed to stay perfectly still, empty his lungs, and then pull back on the trigger. Easy in practice but a nightmare when the woman and baby he loved were so close.

"I can't get a clear shot," said Sam. "I'm moving closer."

"Me too," came Gibbs.

No one else emerged from the chopper. Talos kept his scope trained on the group now moving towards the house. Jane looked about as if she expected to see someone she knew. *I'm here, sweetheart.*

CHAPTER THIRTY-TWO

Jane cradled Ella in one arm and held onto Ming's hand as they were urged towards a massive pale-yellow home. Everywhere she looked there were men with rifles. High rendered walls surrounded the property. She kept glancing across the gardens, but there was no sign of Talos or his team. From the air she'd noticed the home was perched on the edge of a cliff. The only way in was through the front gate. Her heart sank.

Lien shoved her. "Keep walking. You can't escape so there's no point in trying."

They entered a wide foyer and were directed into a room on the right. The hairs on the back of Jane's neck bristled as she stared at the man sitting on a white sofa. His cold eyes raked over her as they'd done months ago in her apartment, and she remembered the peculiarity of an Asian man having such blue eyes. Jane swallowed the lump in her throat and drew Ella closer.

Madeline halted beside her and glared at him. "Nguyen Chi Quan, I presume, otherwise known as Rong, which I believe means dragon in Vietnamese?"

He uncrossed his legs and stood, his gaze slowly roving over Madeline and then Ming. The satisfaction in his eyes scared Jane. *What does he intend to do with us?*

"You are very well informed, Mrs. Shaw. Welcome to my home." He placed his hands behind his back and strolled around their small group slowly.

A chill ran down Jane's spine and her knees shook violently. *Where are you, Talos?* Her thoughts jumped about wildly in her head as Rong continued to stroll around them. *Talos is an SAS solder. He will save us, but what if he needs more time.* In the movies the heroine always managed to stall for time. *This isn't the movies.* Jane inhaled a shaky breath.

"Why have you brought us here?"

Rong met her gaze. "You are the only person who can identify me and your friend here has been causing me a lot of grief."

Madeline's chin rose. "Are you going to kill us?"

He half smiled. "Eventually."

Jane shivered. "What about the children. They're innocent. Let them go, please."

"Innocent?" His gaze dropped to Ming. "This one shall bring big money. There is always someone willing to pay for innocence."

"You bastard." Jane shoved Ming behind her. "I won't let you harm a hair on her head. I will fight to my last breath before I let a scumbag like you near her or my baby."

He sneered. "I don't want your baby. She belongs to someone else."

Lien smiled. "Thank you, Papa."

Rong frowned. "What for. I'm not giving her to you."

A man ambled in from the foyer. He had an amused smile on his face as he observed Jane. "I believe you have brought me my granddaughter."

Bile rose in Jane's throat as recognition hit. The beard was gone and a nasty jagged scar ran along his chin and cheek. It looked like a very old injury, but the same cold blue eyes stared at her. Something he had in common with Rong.

"Dominic Marzetti.'

"Yes, Jane. I must thank you for making this so much easier."

"I heard you escaped from the prison transport van, but how did you get out of Australia?"

"It's not hard when you know how. A small plane to the Northern Territory, then a private jet to Laos, and a helicopter here. I've done it numerous times. Now, the child, please."

Jane shook her head and stepped back. "I'm not letting you evil people near my baby."

Lien marched over to Dominic. "The baby belongs to me. It's my right to have her."

Marzetti raised an eyebrow. "Why on earth would you think you have more right to her than me? I am her grandfather."

"No, you're not." Lien clenched her fists. "Andrew wasn't your biological son. He swapped places with your real son when they were sixteen and living in foster care."

Dominic's eyes narrowed. "You lie."

"No, I don't. Your real son didn't want anything to do with the biological parents who deserted him at birth. So when Donna Rossini showed up wishing to reclaim him, the real Andrew Rossini talked another foster boy called Alex into swapping places. It was a decision Alex regretted very quickly, but he couldn't back out. You would have killed him. So Alex became Andrew."

Jane edged further back. *Thank God Ella doesn't have Marzetti's blood. Poor Andrew. No wonder he was cold and distant. He hated what he'd become and couldn't get out.* With all eyes focused on Lien, Jane stole another shaky step backwards, taking Ming with her. Madeline followed.

Rong strode up to Lien and slapped her hard across the face, knocking her to the floor. "You knew this and you never told me."

"I loved him." Lien sat on the floor cradling her face.

Jane shot a glance at Madeline and indicated the open doors behind them, leading into the foyer.

Rong spun around and looked directly at Jane. "Who told your friends about the ring members and our meetings?"

Shit, this isn't good. Where are you, Talos?

Rong snatched a rifle off one of the guards and aimed it at Madeline. "Tell me or she dies now."

"Andrew did a deal with the AFP. He told them everything in return for a lighter sentence."

Rong lowered the rifle, his shoulders sagging. "So I was betrayed by one of the two people closest to me." He looked down at Lien then across to Dominic. "But which of you was it? My daughter or my brother?"

Jane stared at Marzetti. "Do you mean to say, you're brothers?"

He had tensed and the veins in his neck stood out against his pasty skin as he focused on Rong. "I would never betray you. Did I not agree with you to have Andrew silenced? I put my brother ahead of the man I believed to be my son."

Jane glanced at Lien.

The Asian women's eyes blazed. She stood and balled her fists.

"I'm the one who told Andrew about the meetings. He was my husband and supposed to be part of the inner circle. How dare you make a decision to eliminate him."

Rong stared at his daughter coldly. "I rule this empire. I make the decisions and *you* abide by them. You should never have defied me and married him in the first place." Rong paced to his desk and spun back. "Why didn't you tell me the truth when Lhasa and Kazan disappeared?"

Jane shivered as Lien looked nervously between her father and Marzetti. "I didn't think it was connected."

"Liar." Rong raised the rifle.

"Wait, Quan." Marzetti held up a hand. "We need to know exactly what Andrew told the AFP. Perhaps Lien can redeem herself."

They're going to kill Lien. Jane's bottom brushed against a mahogany sideboard. *And then they'll kill Madeline and I. God knows what will happen to Ming and Ella. We have to make a run for it.*

Marzetti turned and looked at Jane, his eyes narrowing. "Where are Kallie McNeal and Sam Locke?"

"Back in Australia."

"Don't lie to me, Jane, or I'll hurt your friend. She will keep my men amused for several hours and then I will slit her throat. I know Kallie is in Vietnam. Who else is here with you?"

Jane glanced at the two Asian guards. One held a rifle tightly in his hands, the other stood stiffly by the window. Another white man lounged against the desk, holding a handgun. Jane bit her lip. *I might as well tell the truth, they probably know it anyway.*

"Kallie was with Madeline and I when we were abducted. She got left behind. There is a team of SAS guys in Vietnam searching for each of your ring members." She flicked a glance at Rong. "How can you two be brothers?"

"We are half-brothers," replied Marzetti. "We share the same father."

Rong lashed out and sent a Chinese vase flying across the room. It hit the tiled floor exploding into hundreds of pieces. "I had Ripon eliminated because I thought *he* was our betrayer." He focused on Lien again. "But it was *you* all along, wasn't it?"

She didn't answer.

"Let me guess. You and your husband were planning to take over my empire?"

"No, we just wanted to get away from you! It was bad enough that you murdered my mother, but I will never forgive you for ordering my husband's death."

Jane shivered. The air in the room was tense and heavy as if a storm were about to break inside and out.

Rong waved the rifle at Lien. "Ah, now I see. So when you found out I ordered Andrew's death, you decided to destroy my partners and my empire?"

"And you." Lien sneered. "It's only a matter of time before the police close in."

Rong looked at Marzetti. "I think we should dispose of them all and disappear."

"So do I." Marzetti pulled out a handgun.

The other three men in the room stood alert and waiting.

Jane trembled as she edged Ming completely behind her. "You won't get away with this. The police know your identity and that you have us here."

Rong ignored her. "It's a pity to destroy such beauty." He raised the rifle. "But you were always going to die, eventually."

A sporadic burst of gunfire filled the room, shattering several windows. Madeline crashed into Jane, knocking her to the floor. Jane managed to twist and land on her side, shielding Ella from the impact. Ming had rolled under the mahogany dresser.

Jane crawled to her knees, the smell of exploded firecrackers invading her nostrils and throat, causing her to cough. Tears streamed down her face from her stinging eyes. Her ears were ringing. Time seemed to slow as she took in the chaotic scene. Rong had been hit several times in the chest and lay sprawled against the white sofa, which was now splattered in a crimson spray. The three guards had crashed face first into the tiles, surrounded by pools of blood. Parts of their skulls were missing exposing a pinkish, beige matter soaked in blood. Jane's gaze followed a streak of blood down the far wall, where Marzetti sat inert, a bullet hole between his two vacant blue eyes.

Lien lay curled in a ball, screaming into a phone.

Ella began to bawl.

Loud yelling sounded outside and more rapid gunfire. From the rear of the house came running feet and Vietnamese voices, heading their way.

"Go, go, go." Madeline dragged Jane up by the arm. "Come on, Jane. Move. We need to find a place to hide."

"Wait." Jane reached down and pulled Ming out from under the sideboard. "Run, Ming. Run for your life."

Ming took off up a staircase, her backpack swinging from side to side. Jane chased her and could hear Madeline close behind. Their rescuers could only be Talos and the team, but would they make it in time? Jane gasped for breath. She had to hide her little posse. Talos would do the rest.

Ming tore down a carpeted hall and into a room at the end. Jane raced after her with Ella screaming her lungs out. Heavy footsteps thudded on the stairs. A bullet whizzed past her head and into the architrave, shattering the wood. Jane ran on, crouching lower over her distraught baby.

"Don't shoot," screamed Lien. "You might hit the baby."

Shit, doesn't that woman ever give up? Jane swung into the bedroom and as soon as Madeline crossed the threshold, slammed the solid door shut and turned the key. "Quick, see if we can get out a window."

Madeline unlocked a set of French doors onto a small balcony overlooking snow-capped mountains.

Jane ran forward. "Shit." She reared back and gaped at the sheer drop below them. Her stomach rolled and nausea rose. Taking small breaths, she stared down at the jagged cliff face, dropping away to the green valley below. Out in the distance, terraced rice fields tiered down the mountainsides, descending into a wide valley. "Holy crap."

"What we do now?" Ming looked at Jane earnestly, as if she had all the answers.

"Keep your head," Madeline cried. She pulled a plaited rope from around the nearest curtain. "There's enough room under this balcony for us to hide. We just have to get down there. Then we can figure out our next move."

Sweat broke out on Jane's lip and forehead. Her palms became clammy and her stomach rolled again. "I'm not good with heights."

Someone shoulder charged the door. It shook, but held.

Jane glanced at Madeline. "But I'm not good at dying either. Let's do this. I'll lower you down and then Ming and Ella."

"No, I'll lower you and Ella down first and then Ming."

"But—"

"Open the door," screamed Lien. "I want that baby."

Jane gripped Madeline's arm. "You go first. I'll try and delay Lien. If anything happens to me, promise, you'll get Ella and Ming to Talos?"

Bullets sprayed into the other side of the heavy door. Madeline closed the French doors. "I don't have any children, Jane, and these two need their mother. You're going first." She looped another plaited rope tie through the first and threaded it around the railings. "Hang on to each end in case you fall, and try to swing towards the house as you drop. I won't let go of my end."

"Thank you, Maddie." Jane adjusted Ella in the sling and climbed over the railing. *Don't look down.* She looped the rope-tie around her wrists and gripped the metal bar then lowered her knees to the concrete capping. Ignoring Ella's little sobs, Jane held on to the metal, and eased her knees off the capping and dropped, her hands taking all her weight.

Don't look down. Slowly, she slid her hands down the metal railings, wincing when a sharp edge sliced into her right palm.

"Good, now grip the rope tightly and as you drop, swing in and let go." Madeline instructed. "You can do it."

Jane took a breath, gripped the rope and let go. She dropped no more than a couple of feet, but it felt like a thousand. A terrifying fear engulfed her as she swung to and fro, out over the cliff face and back towards the house.

"Come on, Jane. You have to let go." Madeline ordered sternly. "Otherwise, Ming and I can't get down."

"Okay." Jane wriggled her wrists out of the loops until just her fingers held the rope. "One, two, three..." She let go and landed on soft damp earth. "I'm down." The relief that filled her almost had her crying, but that would have to wait. "Send Ming down."

Ming scampered over the railing so fast, Jane nearly had heart failure. "Slowly, Ming."

She stood to the side of the balcony and watched as Madeline looped the rope tie through Ming's backpack straps and around her little waist then lowered her into Jane's arms.

"I've got her. Now it's your turn, Maddie."

Jane watched in awe as Madeline climbed over the railing, slid down and neatly landed beside her. "What are you, an acrobat?"

"Don't tell anyone, but I used to do a little pole dancing."

"You're kidding?" Jane gaped at her.

"Not that sort of pole dancing. It was an exercise class." She took Ming's hand and keeping close to the house, led the way along the narrow strip of ground.

Jane said a prayer of thanks. Madeline Shaw was full of surprises.

"Shit." Madeline had stopped at a concrete wall. "Dead end."

They turned around as the French doors on the balcony crashed open, several panes smashing on impact with the outer wall. Lien and a guard burst onto the balcony. "There." Lien pointed at them. "Get me that baby."

Madeline grabbed Jane's arm. "We have to go down the cliff face."

"What!"

"I can see a way down to a ledge. We don't have a choice."

Jane looked back to see the guard climbing awkwardly over the rail, his rifle slung over a shoulder. "Okay, but you take Ella."

"All right." Madeline lifted the sling off Jane's shoulders and onto her own. Then she looped the plaited rope that was still tied to Ming over her wrist. "Follow me."

Jane envied Madeline and Ming's coordination, agility, and fearlessness. They were mountain goats, descending quickly and easily. She, on the other hand, had her heart in her mouth, her head pounding, her whole body shaking, and sweating as if she had a raging fever. It was all she could do to keep the nausea under control and cling to the rough rock as she felt for foot and hand holds. She heard gunshots from above, then a scream of frustration.

Jane looked back up to see Lien scowling as she stood beside the guard on the cliff-face. It was much higher than she'd thought. Maybe they did have a chance. Large raindrops pitted Jane's face. *Oh no.*

"Shoot them," yelled Lien.

Jane ducked as bullets ricocheted off the cliff and bits of rock pinged her like hail stones. Another shot rang out and the guard's body came toppling over the edge and plummeted into the abyss below.

Talos. Jane searched the balconies and cliff-top but couldn't see anyone other than Lien, who had dropped over the edge and was climbing down the cliff-face.

"Come on, Jane. You haven't got far to go." Madeline called.

Sinking her teeth into her lip, Jane blocked out Lien and the gorge below as she steadily descended. Then raindrops turned into a downpour making the rocks slippery. "Fuck, I don't need this."

Madeline's steadying hands guided her down to a wide ledge. Ming was tucked in a crevice out of the rain, with Ella cradled in her skinny little arms.

Madeline hugged Jane. "Good, girl. You made it."

"But what do we do now?" Jane glanced up to where Lien was still working her way down. "We can't go up and we can't go down. With the rain, it's too dangerous."

The whooping of helicopter blades resonated from the other side of the house.

"If your friends are as good as they're supposed to be, they'll get us off this ledge. In the meantime we just have to deal with her." Madeline's gaze rose. "That bitch has a knife between her teeth, but she hasn't got a gun. We need something to defend ourselves."

"Maybe she'll be shot before she gets to us?"

"Whichever of your friends shot the guard was positioned on the concrete wall but he didn't have the angle to shoot Lien and he's gone. They can't shoot from above as they might hit us." She inhaled. "I'm sorry, we're on our own until that helicopter gets here."

Jane nodded. "I'm not going down without a fight." She untangled the plaited rope from Ming's backpack and swung it like a lasso. "You take the backpack and use it as a shield."

"Good thinking, but keep your back to the rock. This rain is getting heavier and the wind is picking up. We don't want to get blown off this ledge."

"I think the wind and rain is the least of our worries." Jane tensed as Lien nimbly landed on her feet further along the ledge.

"Give me the baby and I'll let you live."

"Go to hell." Jane moved in front of Ming and Ella's hiding place, the rope gripped tightly in her hands. "You have two choices, Lien. Give yourself up to the police or join your friend below."

Lien took the knife from between her teeth and laughed. "I am trained in the martial art of Vovinam. You are no match for me."

Madeline stepped away from the rock wall and faced Lien. "Ever heard of sheer determination?" She lunged at Lien, thrusting the backpack out in front of her.

Lien jumped back, found her balance then launched a kick into the backpack, knocking Madeline hard against the rock face.

Fear like talons clawed at Jane's insides. The little bit of self-defense her minders had taught her wouldn't save them. Surprise was her only hope. She sprang forward and swung the rope. It caught Lien unaware and knocked the knife out of her hand.

Lien instantly spun on her heel and came back with a savage roundhouse kick, catching Jane in the hip and sending her crashing on top of Madeline.

Elliott's black helicopter whooshed out over the top of the house and descended to hover off the cliff-face. Jane didn't know how they could help, but Nick was at the controls, fighting to keep the helicopter steady against the increasing wind. Talos and Gibbs occupied the front and back seats nearest her and held rifles aimed towards the cliff.

Madeline sprang to her feet and hurled the backpack. Lien ducked and Madeline struck out with a forward kick, followed by a palm strike to Lien's chin.

Lien staggered slightly then screeched and came straight back with two fast chopping moves before spinning in a half circle and ramming her elbow into Madeline's stomach.

Jane gasped as Madeline collapsed on the ledge, winded. Then Lien launched a savage kick and sent Madeline sprawling towards the edge.

Crying out, Jane reached for Madeline, but Lien blocked her with a sweeping kick that knocked Jane's feet from under her. She landed hard, jarring her whole body as Madeline toppled off the ledge. "*Nooo!*"

Screaming like a banshee, Jane scrambled to her feet and ran at Lien, whipping at her with the plaited curtain tie.

Lien spun and launched out with a heel kick. She connected with Jane's thigh and knocked her off her feet. Jane screamed as she slid over the edge, her arms flailing wildly. She heard the whooping of the helicopter and then Talos roar her name as if in agony. *This wasn't supposed to happen. Ella! Talos please save her!*

Jane fell a couple of meters then vicious pain shot through her shoulder and wrist as her arm was almost wrenched out of its socket. She was struggling to cope with the pain and comprehend what had happened when her gaze fell on the curtain-tie, wrapped around her wrist. The other end had hooked on a jagged rock above her, leaving her dangling thousands of feet above the ground."

"Hang on, Jane." Talos yelled. "Don't move. I'm coming."

Fighting her rising hysteria, Jane risked a look down, searching for a foothold. Her eyes fell on Madeline, splayed limply on a narrow ledge several meters below. *Maddy.*

"What does it take to get rid of you two?"

Jane looked up to see Lien leaning over the ledge with the knife in her hand. The other woman sneered. "A pity I can't reach that cord, but you can't hang on forever."

Jane gasped, trying to hang on with her free hand and ignore the excruciating pain tearing through her shoulder. "Please, Lien, don't take my baby."

Lien stood. "She's my baby now."

Two shots rang out and Lien collapsed to her knees, staring at the hovering helicopter in absolute shock. Jane risked a glance behind and almost choked as a sob rose in her throat. Talos stood on the undercarriage frame, balanced against the open door. He wore a crude looking rope harness around his body and held a rifle in his hands. The helicopter was rocking wildly.

Hope bloomed in Jane's chest as she clung to the tieback. It was cutting the circulation in her wrist and she didn't know how much longer she could hang on, but Talos would save Ella and Ming.

And that was all that mattered.

Jane glanced up at Lien. "You're going to jail for the rest of your life.'

"Never." Lien struggled to her feet, clutching her shoulder. Blood ran down her arm and thigh. "If I can't have Andrew's baby than neither will you."

"No." Jane sobbed, her gaze flying to Talos.

The helicopter was being battered by the wind. He had the rifle up but it was an impossible task. He might hit Ella or Ming.

Oh, God, Ming. Jane screamed. "Ming! Run."

Ming screamed. "You no hurt Ella."

Lien came staggering backwards to the edge of the ledge and Jane's heart lurched as she saw Ming, head bent forward like a footballer in a scrum, pushing against Lien. "No, Ming."

Lien lost her footing and snatched at Ming as she fell.

Jane watched in horror as Lien hit a jutting rock, bounced sideways and silently fell to her fate. Ming had managed to grasp the ledge but couldn't hold on. She began to slide down the rock face, her little fingers grappling for grip. Jane let go of the curtain-tie with her good hand and caught Ming as she fell. The added weight sent waves of agonizing pain into Jane's shoulder and wrist. Faintness and nausea threatened to overwhelm her as she clung to Ming.

"Wrap your arms around my neck, Ming, in case I faint."

"Hang on, Jane," Talos roared. "I'm coming."

Jane glanced up and prayed as he repelled down a rope towards her and Ming. She winced as his body slammed into the rock wall on her left, then seconds later his back hit the wall on her right.

"I'm almost there." He called out.

So close, yet so far.

Blackness closed in as strong arms came around her and lifted her. The searing pain in her shoulder eased. *Talos.*

CHAPTER THIRTY-THREE

"Gotcha." Talos held Jane and Ming tightly to his chest as the chopper rose. The next bit was tricky. At any second, a sudden gust of wind could slam them back into the cliff, but Nick knew his stuff. He was one of the best chopper pilots in the business. They soared away from the cliff and up over the house.

Jane stirred in his arms and stiffened. "No, we have to go back for Ella and Maddy. Talos, she's in a crevice but she'll freeze to death."

"It's all right. I'll rappel down the cliff. We'll get them."

Nick hovered over the garden. At least the wind wasn't buffeting them on this side of the house. As soon as Talos's feet touched the ground, he lowered Jane, then Ming, and released the harness clips. "Run to Sam, Ming. It's safe now."

Ming tore across the grass and into Sam's arms. Talos released a breath as he watched Sam carry Ming towards the pool house out of the rain. "Come on, sweetheart, let's get you out of this weather." He pulled the harness off and scooped Jane into his arms.

Jane clung to him. "I don't want to go inside. I want Ella."

"All right." Talos strode to the back of the house where Jarred and Sam had smashed open a steel gate. He lowered Jane to the ground. "Give me your hand and watch where you step, the ground is slippery."

She clutched one arm to her chest like a wounded bird and held out her other hand. "I didn't think you'd make it in time."

He grimaced. "It was touch and go." He led Jane along the narrow path to where Jarred had anchored several ropes to the balcony above. The cold wind whistled through Talos's shirt, reminding him a tiny eight-week-old baby was lying in a crevice. Each second counted.

At least she's out of the direct rain and wind. But what if she manages to roll out of there. Shit.

He frowned at Jarred. "What's taking so long? We need to get down there."

"Hold your horses. It's fucking dangerous and I'm not risking any lives."

Nick came running along the narrow path, holding the crude harness Talos had worn earlier. "Here you go, mate. You'll need this to support you while you rescue Madeline."

Jarred confiscated it. "I'll do the rescue. It's my fault she's down there in the first place." Jarred climbed into the harness and flexed the rope hanging from the balcony. He glanced over the edge of the cliff. "I'm going to need help to get her back up."

"It has to be by chopper." Nick studied the sky. "The wind has dropped. If you go down and secure her, I'll drop a line from the chopper and fly you both out. It's the quickest way."

Talos tested the other rope. "I'll get Ella."

A little voice called him from above. Talos looked up to the balcony to see Ming waving a towel and pillowcase at him. "Ella might be cold."

"You're an angel, Ming." Talos caught them and tucked both items inside his jacket.

"I'll ride shot-gun with Nick." Sam handed Talos and Jarred a pair of gardener's gloves and strode off with Nick.

"Let's do this." Jarred dropped off the edge of the cliff.

Jane squeezed Talos's arm. "Be careful. I don't want to lose either of you."

He kissed her. "I'll bring Ella back safely." He pulled on his gloves, took the rope, and followed Jarred over the edge. The rocks were slippery, making it hard to get a good grip with the soles of his boots. He covered the twenty-meter drop as quickly as he could and landed on the ledge without incident. Jarred had almost reached Madeline Shaw.

Ella lay sobbing in the soaking sling, inside the crevice. *I'm here, sweetie.*

Talos undid the sling and his jacket, then wrapped the dry towel around her shivering little body and slid her into the pillowcase. He tucked her against his chest, zipped his jacket, and tied the wet sling around his waist to keep her from sliding down.

Peering over the ledge, he called down to Jarred. "Is she alive?"

Jarred glanced up. "Yes and starting to come round."

Talos watched as Jarred crouched beside Madeline and waited for Nick to get the chopper into position. Once Sam had dropped the line, Jarred secured the harness, released the other rope and scooped Madeline into his arms. They swung away from the cliff and up into the air without mishap. It was a perfect extraction under extremely dangerous conditions.

Talos gripped his rope and smiled as he began the slow climb back up. Marzetti, Rong, Lien, and Ripon were dead. There were no witnesses who could identify Jane. Lhasa and Kazan would spend the rest of their lives in prison believing their partners had betrayed them. Jane was safe and the future glowed with possibilities.

Jarred, Sam, and Gibbs were waiting with Jane as he pulled himself onto the cliff top. Once they were around the side of the house, Talos unzipped his jacket and passed a now sleeping Ella to Jane. "We need to get her into a warm bath and then wrapped in something warm. She should be checked out by a doctor as soon as we get back to Hanoi."

Jane bit her lip. "Thank you." She ducked her head and kissed Ella's head then leaned against Talos. "You'll have to do it, my arm is too sore."

Talos wrapped his arms around her and nodded at Gibbs. "Thanks for your help."

Gibbs gave a slight lift of his shoulders. "With Marzetti dead, you now only have my word that I wasn't on his payroll."

"Then I guess your word is going to have to be good enough. With all the gun-fire, I'm surprised the place hasn't been swamped by police." Talos kept his arm around Jane as he guided her off the narrow path and around the side of the house.

Gibbs led the way. "There's not a lot of local police up here. But you're right; people have reported gunshots. I rang the SCU and they're on their way. The local police have been instructed to stay outside the property and guard the gates."

Sam fell into step with Jarred and Gibbs. "We need to get back to Australia before the shit hits the fan."

Gibbs shook his head. "It's not a good idea for the six of you and the three ladies to return to Australia at the same time. Word will get out, and a group of ex-SAS soldiers arriving in Sydney will stand out like a sore thumb. I have a suggestion."

"Go on." Talos said.

"You all fly back to Hanoi. I'll arrange for a private jet to fly you to Fiji, where you'll be transferred to a chopper then flown to a private island. I suggest *you* stay at least a week, but the longer you stay the better. I predict the Australian airports will be monitored."

"I'm presuming the jet and island belong to your father?" Jarred said.

"Yes. He's in Europe with my mother. Don't waste your time probing, the staff is very loyal."

Jane smiled at Gibbs. "Thank you, Zac, but Kallie and Sam are getting married shortly and we need to go home for the wedding."

Sam chuckled. "I think I can persuade Kallie to change our wedding plans slightly. And for now, it might be wise to keep Madeline Shaw with us."

Jarred huffed. "The woman is a bloody journalist. Of course we're keeping her."

A helicopter swooped in over the house and Sam looked up. "That'll be Ryan and Simon. Let's load up and get out of here."

"I need to get Ella warm and dressed first." Talos guided Jane in through the French doors and along a hall to the large kitchen. Once he'd taken care of Ella, he wanted to have a closer look at Jane's arm.

❦

An hour later with her arm strapped to her chest, a bandage around her hand and wrist, and several sticking plasters on the deeper of her cuts, Jane was ready to leave. She ached all over, but at least nothing was broken. She'd fainted when Talos popped her dislocated shoulder back in, but now there was no need to stop by a hospital. Amazingly, Ella didn't show any signs of hypothermia and after a warm bath and feed had fallen asleep. As Talos guided them towards Elliott's chopper, Jane noticed Nick slouched against the pilot's door. Ming and Madeline were strapped in the back.

"Are you okay, Maddy?"

The other woman gave Jane a faint smile. "I will be." She closed her eyes.

Talos kissed Jane. "I need a quick word with Gibbs about Ming. I'll be back in a sec." He jogged over to the other chopper.

Jane smiled at Nick. "Thank you for coming to my rescue again. At least this time you didn't get shot."

He chuckled. "I've always been a sucker for green eyes."

Jane hesitated. "Nick, there's something I need to tell you."

"Oh." He grinned. "Let me guess. It's me you're in love with, not the big fella?"

"No. I'm definitely in love with Talos."

He chuckled. "Okay, so what do you need to tell me?"

"Ava never got married and she's living in Broome, designing jewelry."

The cheeky grin faded away. "Her father is a minister and he told me she got married in England. He wouldn't lie."

"Well, he did. Simon checked every continent. Ava never married and she arrived back in Australia about three months ago. Her company's called Fantasy Pearl Creations. I checked the website. She's in high demand and her creations are magnificent."

Nick shifted away from the door and straightened. "People change, Jane. I'm not the same person I was back then, and it was Ava who walked out on me."

"People also make mistakes, Nick. I believe you're still in love with her. What if she's still in love with you?"

"It's ancient history. She's got her life and I've got mine. End of story."

"But you obviously can't move on. So what have you got to lose?"

"I'll think about it." He climbed into the cockpit and closed the door.

At least he didn't swear at me and tell me to mind my own business. Jane cuddled Ella to her chest with her good arm and strolled towards Talos. She heard his deep sexy laugh then he gave Sam a friendly thump and jogged back to her.

He had a smile as big as Christmas. Jane walked straight into his arms. "Thank you for making us safe. For giving me my life back, and for loving me."

"It's not hard, sweetheart." He lowered his head and kissed her. "Jarred's spoken to Elliott and asked him to organize for a doctor to look at you and pediatrician to check Ella out as soon as we get back to Hanoi, then we'll head for Fiji."

"Good. What's with the huge smile?"

"Sam's decided to marry Kallie on the island as soon as he can get a license, which will be approximately four weeks from now."

"That's so romantic."

He smiled. "I was wondering if while we're all on the island, you would marry me?"

When she just stared dumbly at him, he clutched her good hand. "I love you, Jane. You and Ella are my world. My precious gems. Gibbs is certain that the Vietnamese Government will more than likely fast track Ming's adoption. We can be a family, if you'll have me?"

Jane burst into tears. "Yes, to everything. I love you, my darling."

"Excellent." Talos kissed her again then put his arm around her gently. "Your chopper awaits, sweetheart. Come fly with me."

"Anywhere, anytime."

Epilogue

Jane glanced across the soothing ocean, absorbing the cooling breeze ruffling the hem of her gown. Wispy, white organza curtains billowed around her where they'd escaped from the sashes binding them to the gazebo. She could have been a Grecian goddess, surrounded by tall ceramic urns overflowing with crimson bougainvillea. Peach-colored rose petals scattered about her silver sandals, as the gentle breeze lifted them. The housekeeper had told Jane the island was nicknamed Eden. It was very fitting, and a perfect place to celebrate a Valentine's day wedding or two.

A deep chuckle resonated behind her. "Daydreaming, Mrs. Talarico?"

Jane sank against Talos's chest and put her hands over his as they came round her waist. "I feel like I've woken from a nightmare and fallen into a wonderful dream. I'm scared I'll wake up and discover none of this is real."

"It's not a dream, sweetheart. This is reality. You, me, this island, it's all real." He kissed her cheek. "Although, earlier when you were walking across the lawn to become my wife, I couldn't help but think I was the one dreaming. You were a vision of perfection, and I'm so glad you married me. Happy Valentine's day."

Jane squeezed his hands. "I saw the love in your eyes and nearly cried. It was a good thing Ming threw her basket of rose-petals at you or I would have ruined my makeup." She tilted her head back and kissed him. "Happy Valentine's day, my darling."

Talos turned them so they were facing the gardens and the most important people in their lives. Not a huge number. Talos's father sat with Ken and Fergie around a wrought iron table, deep in conversation.

Jane shifted her gaze to the patio where several Fijian men were strumming their guitars and singing a soft melody. A Maid placed an array of tropical drinks on the table where Talos's two older sisters sat with her mother.

Jane smiled. "Mum looks over the moon, doesn't she?"

"Why wouldn't she? She's got her three month old granddaughter in her arms, has just witnessed her beautiful daughter marry a fantastic guy, has gained a second little granddaughter, and she's holidaying on a tropical island. Life doesn't get much better."

Glancing towards the pool, Jane observed Talos's younger sister Lydia sitting with Zac Gibbs, listening intently to whatever he was saying. Roy and Bunny swung gently on a garden lounge listening to the singers. Ming was racing round, squealing with delight as Simon and two of Talos's nieces chased her across the manicured lawn.

"Thank you for agreeing to adopt Ming." Jane leaned back and raised her eyes to his. "I dreaded sending her back to Vietnam."

"Me too. That's another thing we have to thank Gibbs for. Besides providing us with this safe haven, he was the main force behind us getting Ming so quickly."

Jane nodded and breathed in the fresh ocean breeze. Across the lawn under a Frangipani tree, Kallie and Sam stood with their arms around each other. Sam raised a hand and saluted.

Jane waved back. "Mr. and Mrs. Locke look very happy with themselves."

"Hmm, but what's going on over there?"

Jane's gaze followed the direction of Talos's finger. Jarred and Madeline were by the edge of the garden, facing each other, their postures stiff. "Oh no."

"What?"

"Those two worry me. When they're together, sparks fly. Yet it's as if they're magnetically drawn to each other against their will."

"Jarred's not the type of man to cut another man's grass. And I got the feeling Madeline and Elliott Shaw are pretty close."

"Yes, but they lead separate lives and she wants children, whereas Elliott doesn't. I think they care deeply about each other, but I'm not sure they're in love anymore."

They watched as Madeline turned and stalked away. Jarred's hand snaked out and dragged her back. She stumbled and fell against him.

For several seconds, neither moved as they stared at each other.

"I see what you mean." Talos murmured.

Boom.

Jane flinched as the ground shook under her sandals and a rocket shot into the air from the beach below, exploding into thousands of blue shooting stars. "Fireworks."

"I think that was an accident. Ryan's got them set up to go off when it's dark."

Jane glanced back to Jarred and Madeline. He was now striding towards the pool area. Madeline stood facing the ocean, the hem of her violet dress fluttering about her ankles.

Jane inhaled. *What is their problem?* She ruffled her own flowing skirts and touched her halo of flowers. "We should join the other bride and groom."

As they strolled hand in hand across the lawn, Jane appraised Kallie's stunning wedding dress. They'd both opted for ivory, full-length gowns. Kallie had chosen a lace design, whereas Jane's was strapless and beaded with tiny pearls. Both were delicate and feminine.

Kallie beamed at them. "This has been such a wonderful day. It's a pity Nick couldn't be here."

"Nick doesn't do weddings." Sam frowned. "But for the life of me, I don't know why he's gone to Broome?"

Jane gasped. "Broome? Ava's in Broome?"

"Is she really?" Sam raised an eyebrow.

"Sorry about that. Ryan jogged over, a wide grin on his face. "I was helping one of the security guards lay the firework fuses and we got a bit carried away."

Ming raced past, her halo of flowers in one hand, feet bare and pink ribbons streaming behind. She twirled and danced away from Simon's outstretched hands. He laughed, waved her off and strolled over. "No wonder Ming survived so long on her own. The kid's like a tornado on steroids. I'm safer sticking to my computer skills."

Talos looked over his shoulder. "Speaking of which, have you discovered the owner of this island?'

"Possibly. I traced the private jet and helicopter to a company owned by a multi-billionaire. He's Middle Eastern and his name is Sheik Tariq Zakour Farid. I think our friend Gibbs comes from a very wealthy family."

"That explains his coloring." Jane glanced at Talos. "What I don't get is why he's working for the AFP?"

"Perhaps he likes to feel he's making a difference." Talos shrugged. "Look at Jarred. He needn't work a day in his life, yet he joined the army and then the SAS."

Sam scratched his jaw. "It's the only thing that makes sense." His phone vibrated. "G'day, Nick. I hear you're in Broome?" Sam listened then frowned. "Yeah, hang on a minute." He waved at Jarred. "Hey, Boss, Nick needs to speak to you. It's urgent."

Jarred clapped Roy on the shoulder and jogged across the lawn. He took the phone and listened intently for several minutes then he turned to Simon. "I need you to do a background search on Damon Pearce? He's a rich guy with interests in Broome's pearl and tourism industry."

Talos moved aside to allow Madeline to squeeze between him and Simon. She looked directly at Jarred. "Damon Pearce is a self-centered playboy from Melbourne. He's full of his own importance, and I've heard he's heavy handed in getting what he wants."

Jarred slowly placed the phone against his ear. "Did you hear that, Nick?" He listened then told Nick he'd be in touch and ended the call. "Enjoy the rest of your night, folks. Tomorrow we're leaving the ladies here and flying to Broome."

Jane felt Talos stiffen beside her. "I'd prefer to take Jane and the kids home first."

"They can travel back with the rest of the group at the end of the week. I need you and Simon with me." Jarred waved Gibbs over then glanced at Madeline. "Can you give me any more information on Pearce?"

Her chin rose. "Certainly, but it would be better if I came with you. As a journalist, I can request to interview him on his entrepreneurial skills or his outstanding success. That is sure to fly his kite."

"Why?" Jarred's eyes narrowed.

"Because he loves women, has a fondness for talking about himself, and I met him six months ago at a fund raiser in Melbourne. He stalked me most of the night, knowing I was married and not the least interested in him."

"Then I don't want you anywhere near him."

Sauntering across the grass, Gibbs glanced round the circle. "This looks serious?"

"It is." Jarred turned to Ryan. "I want you and Sam to fly back to Sydney tomorrow. Collect the Black-Hawke and meet us in Broome."

"Broome?"

"Yes, we have a new mission, and this one is personal. I'll explain inside the house."

Jane squeezed Talos's hand. "Perhaps Madeline *should* go with you. Her insight could be very helpful and if anyone can dig up the truth, she can."

Before Talos could answer her, Jarred nodded. "I agree." He looked at Madeline. "You may accompany us, but you'll do exactly as I say. At no point will you go near Pearce without my approval. This is not about checkbook journalism."

Her eyes flashed. "I am not a child, Jarred. Nor am I a checkbook journalist, and for your information, I can take care of myself."

"It's not negotiable, Madeline. If you don't accept my terms, I'll leave you behind."

"Fine. I agree."

Jane's curiosity was set to explode. "Jarred, did Nick say anything about Ava?"

"He's found her but..." Jarred's lips thinned. "He got more than he bargained for."

"Any more news from Vietnam?" Talos asked, looking at Gibbs.

"Yes. The SCU searched the house in Sapa. They found enough evidence to shut down all the Ring's operations. Unfortunately there are still too many human traffickers destroying people's lives."

Jarred expelled his breath. "Gibbs, if you can spare me twenty minutes, I'd like to discuss Nick's situation with you and my team?"

"No problem." Gibbs strode away with Simon, Jarred, and Ryan.

"Wait. Why are you interested in Damon Pearce?" Madeline bunched up her violet skirts and ran after them.

"Two down, four to go," said Kallie, smiling at Jane.

"What does that mean?"

Kallie chuckled. "Six weeks ago I told the guys that they'd all be enticed into love, just like Sam and me. Talos has been enticed by you. So, two down, four to go."

Talos drew Jane into his arms and dropped a tender kiss on her soft lips. "I'm not complaining. Six weeks ago I thought you were beyond my reach and now you're my wife. I'm one of the luckiest men alive."

"And I'm another." Sam kissed Kallie. "We'd better join the others."

They left their wives and strolled towards the back of the sprawling villa. As they reached the patio, Talos grimaced and lowered his voice. "Nick wouldn't ask for our help unless something was seriously wrong."

Sam met his gaze. "And Jarred wouldn't commit us, the Black-Hawk, and a journalist that riles him unless he agreed. Whatever's going on in Broome is serious.

Talos glanced back at Jane and Kallie who were talking animatedly as they walked towards the gazebo arm in arm. "What's the odds those two will quit with the matchmaking."

Sam laughed. "Nil to zero."

"I thought so." Talos clapped his best friend on the shoulder. "Let's go see what our next mission entails."

Note to Readers

I hope you enjoyed Talos and Jane's story. Book Three of the Steele Ops Series is *Jewel of the Kimberley*, set in Broome, Western Australia. The Kimberley region is famous for its rugged gorges, spectacular waterfalls, pristine beaches, and magnificent pearls.

Blurb:

Nick Flanagan had two passions in life—his fiancée, Ava, and flying Black Hawks. Then he passed the stringent recruitment process to become a commando in the elite Special Air Service Regiment. It was a dream come true, but it cost him Ava.

Now working as part of an independent special ops team, Nick is faced with an opportunity to win Ava back. First though, he must contend with a millionaire rival who is a dangerous adversary, and involved in diamond smuggling.

Ava Mitchell was engaged to marry the most wonderful man in the world...then everything went pear-shaped. He joined a dangerous branch of the army without consulting her. In anger she gave him an ultimatum—it backfired, and she left. Nine months later, she learned he'd died in a training accident.

Ava now operates a jewelry design business centered round Broome's pearl industry. She is also about to risk her heart again when the unimaginable happens—Nick walks back into her life. Can she trust him, or does he have an ulterior motive that will destroy her life all over again?

ABOUT THE AUTHOR

Erin Moira O'Hara grew up in the Blue Mountains of Australia, with a garden backing onto native bushland, hidden caves and fabulous lookouts. Weekends were spent exploring, climbing trees and creating secret bases. Her love of reading began with visits to the local library, where she became absorbed in a world of intrigue, fantasy and action-packed adventures. The moment Erin read her first romance; she recognised the importance of finding the right man to share her life. She now lives with him close to the largest saltwater lake in Australia. Their home overlooks bushland and is surrounded by an abundance of bird life and an ever-growing garden.

Erin's writing encompasses everything she loves—intrigue, suspense, passion and romance.

If you would like to know more, please visit:
http://www.erinmoiraohara.com